A SHOT AT LOVE

A SHOT AT LOVE

TB MARKINSON

CHAPTER ONE

THE SMALL RED VAUXHALL CORSA RENTAL sputtered along the narrow and curvy country lane, winding its way through rolling green pastures. How were they still so green this time of year? The leaves, or what was left of them, were vibrant red, orange, and gold.

Josie Adams's phone, attached to her personal vent clip she always traveled with, a necessity for the *always on the move* woman, rang. Her mum's number appeared. Josie sighed but didn't answer. Not just because she had to crank the wheel for another hairpin turn while downshifting, but she still wasn't ready to talk. Not on the phone. Josie needed to speak to her mum face-to-face. After a hug. That had been her first priority after the October surprise that ended her life as she knew it. And, there were still a handful of days left in the month. She yanked on the wheel again, muttering a string of curse words under her breath.

If Josie hadn't been driving, she might have been able to enjoy the scenery and experience whatever kumbaya feelings people experienced when reconnecting with nature as a way of dealing with the disappointment that was called her life. *No.* Josie wrapped her fingers tighter around the steering wheel, her knuckles turning a sickening bloodless hue. Disappointment wasn't strong enough. Utter devastation. Complete ruination. Shaking her head, Josie was infuriated with herself for not having the right words to describe the feeling, which given the situation was a sick sort of irony. The last thing Nora had said to Josie was, "You're supposed to be a whiz when it comes to writing speeches. You failed me and the country."

Screw the beautiful scenery. It wasn't going to save Josie from her dark thoughts, growing exponentially darker with each passing second. Besides, she was grateful to be behind the wheel. Josie was a terrible passenger for two reasons. First, she liked to be in control. Second, and perhaps more importantly at the moment, Josie suffered from motion sickness, and on these types of roads, she'd be hanging her head out the window to combat the need to puke.

After yet another sharp bend in the road, Josie had to quickly swerve back onto the other side of the street to avoid getting creamed by a sleek BMW heading in the other direction, the horn blaring, the driver shaking a fist.

Josie sensed all the sheep in the field turning their puffy heads to condemn her lack of driving skills. She downshifted and punched the gas to give the vehicle more power to crest a hill.

"Britain ruled the world for centuries but never mastered driving on the right-hand side of the road," Josie mumbled to herself as she eased the car back into the middle of the lane since the two-way street was more suitable for one. Each time she had to move to the left, she feared destroying the paint job by scratching it either on a rock wall or overhanging shrubs.

She'd checked out of the London hotel early after

getting a fitful night of sleep. Her last-minute flight from Boston the previous day had been delayed four hours and then circled Gatwick Airport for another forty-five minutes before landing midday, instead of at eight in the morning. After getting through immigration and making her way to the city, Josie had done her best to stay awake until seven at night to help jump-start her system to adjust to Greenwich mean time, but she'd only lasted until five in the evening before crawling into bed and covering herself with the bedspread to have a good old-fashioned cry that didn't make her feel better.

The surrounding fields were dotted with white, which Josie assumed were sheep. Did they always stay exposed to the elements, or did the creatures have some type of enclosure for nasty days? Her mum had been born and raised in the area, so Josie thought she should know this answer, but if she did, the knowledge was buried deep inside or completely forgotten. At least there wasn't snow in the fields, unlike Pennsylvania, the last place she'd been on the presidential campaign trail. As Josie's eyes scanned the scenery, a momentary peacefulness she hadn't felt in months started to nibble at the tension. "Jesus!" She swerved out of the way of an expensive-looking car she couldn't name, let alone dream of affording. "What are all these rich Cotswolds bastards doing on the road so early on a Monday morning?" Didn't they know Josie's life had crashed and burned, and the possibility of her taking out the next asswipe in a fancy car, just out of spite, was high? Josie had never been the violent type, but...

Since Josie was alone in the car, no one responded to her outburst. Probably for the best. Americans weren't high on the respectability list worldwide once again, especially not one who was grumbling while driving in the middle of the road, acting like a typical American who wanted things to go her way.

It was probably time to stop for breakfast. Josie needed to eat on a regular basis, or she was a nightmare to be around, according to everyone who had attempted to live with her. The list included two exes and numerous coworkers who had bunked with her in hotels all over America on numerous campaign trails.

Her destination this bright October morning was Upper Chewford, one of the quaint villages in the Cotswolds. The Cotswolds, in South Central England, covered roughly seven hundred square miles and was the second largest protected area in the country. Given the laid-back vibe of the landscape outside the car windows, Josie didn't want to return in a rip-shit mood. Not after such a long absence.

She steered the car through a picturesque village tucked into a valley. The name of this particular place escaped her, but no matter. Josie was doing her best to embrace not knowing everything about every village, town, city, and state to pepper a political speech to make the locals feel like they mattered. She couldn't see how anything would matter ever again.

A charming tea shop on the corner caught her eye, and she parked in a spot that'd just been freed up when a Mercedes pulled out with a vengeance and roared to life, fleeing the peacefulness of the main street in its tracks. It seemed everyone was heading in the opposite direction. The story of Josie's life, really.

* * *

SITTING at a table in the corner, nursing a second cup of tea, Josie stared at her phone, determined not to check the news. The whole point of dashing to Britain after being scapegoated was to escape all campaign news. What was the point of following what would inevitably become one of the worst electoral routs of all time?

If only Nora had read the words how Josie intended. She'd been clear. Say the words like an unrepentant male who'd been caught in a scandal. Not show weakness by groveling and asking for Americans to forgive her. Josie had penned the words without an ounce of remorse.

Nora had panicked in front of the cameras and gone off script. Josie could still picture the exact moment Nora had turned away from the teleprompter to speak from the heart. She'd done it many times before, but this was the one moment that Nora needed to do what she'd been told. The second before Nora opened her mouth to speak the words, "I'm so sorry I let you down," Josie knew it would go south. It wasn't solely the words. It was the way they were spoken. The shame etched into Nora's expression. Her quivering bottom lip. The shakiness of her voice. Everyone in the room knew right then and there it was all over. Nora Ackerman would never become president of the United States.

Afterward, Nora pinned the blame on Josie.

The speech Josie had written was brilliant.

Wasn't it? Josie sipped her tea.

She'd poured her heart and soul into the words after her candidate had been caught flaunting her goodies by a reporter who had been embedded into the campaign to catch the billionaire Nora in everyday actions to humanize her to average American voters. The reporter had earned the trust of everyone on Nora's staff, even Josie.

Josie had forgotten the one rule about reporters: they are never your friend. They adhered to the desire to hold all candidates accountable, regardless of party or common sense. The reporter in question torpedoed Nora's campaign over something so minor compared to other scandals simply because the reporter could, for her own personal gain. If Nora had been a man, it wouldn't have become such a big deal, which was why Josie had instructed Nora to talk like a man. Unabashed. Push back. To speak with righteousness on Nora's side. Be a fucking man! Josie shook a fist in the air, remembering that second before Nora tossed everything away. If only Josie could have nipped Nora's instinct with a firm shake of the head or something.

Josie's phone sat on the tabletop as if mocking her for being a scaredy-cat for not looking.

But Josie didn't want to give in. She wanted to stay strong. Her role in the campaign was over. She pressed a finger onto the table as if to reinforce that into her brain. Josie was no longer a part of the campaign. The last thing she needed was to check how bad it was going. Before Josie had boarded the plane, it looked more than bleak for Nora. Was it worse now? Part of Josie wished it was if it made people realize Josie wasn't the reason for Nora's debacle. Nora was responsible for it all.

She scooped the phone into her hand, pressed her finger to unlock the screen, and logged onto *The New York Times* app only to be met with the headline "Dead on Arrival." *The Washington Post*'s headline screamed Nora shouldn't have ever been a candidate: "America Deserves Leaders, Not Fame-Seeking Harpies."

That seemed somewhat harsh. All presidential candidates, no matter their background, were egomaniacs. That was the very nature of the office. No rational person would look at their reflection in the mirror and think, "I should be president of the United States."

What rational person, though, tried to help a person

reach the highest office in America? This was Josie's third and last attempt.

"What's going to become of me now?" She stared at the dregs of tea at the bottom of her cup, trying to see her future but only glimpsing the remnants of what might have been. She'd missed her shot at the ultimate posting for a speechwriter, and it stung more than she'd cared to admit.

CHAPTER TWO

A STOOPED WOMAN ANSWERED THE DOOR, HER wrinkled face not giving Harriet much insight into the woman's inner thoughts.

"Mrs. Cavell?" Harriet asked, unsure if she should have spoken louder.

"Yes." The woman's voice was mostly clear, just a wisp of old lady to it.

"I'm Harriet Powell. We spoke on the phone last week." Harriet chewed on a fleshy part of her inner cheek. "Do you remember?"

"Of course. I'm old, not stupid."

Harriet smiled awkwardly.

"You wanted to interview me. Why I don't know." The frail woman waved a hand in the air.

Harriet was mesmerized by the woman's sharp blue eyes.

Mrs. Cavell motioned for Harriet to step inside the cottage. "You live in Upper Chewford, two villages over?"

"Yes, that's right."

The woman looked Harriet up and down. "You're not

from there." It wasn't a question. She gestured for Harriet to take a seat in the living room.

Harriet sat in an amethyst tartan wingback chair. "I recently moved to the area."

"Are you one of those looking for a simpler life?"

"Not sure about simpler, at least it's not turning out that way." Harriet dragged her hand through her hair.

The woman lowered herself carefully onto the sofa. "Nothing in life ever does turn out the way you want it."

Harriet nodded. "True."

"From our conversation, I gathered you're taking over the paper from Regis."

"Yes. He's my uncle."

"I never liked him."

Neither did Harriet, but she opted not to smear her uncle, who had given her the opportunity to turn around a fledgling local paper and to move into his cottage, which he hardly ever stayed in, when Harriet's life in London went tits up.

"Would you like a cup of tea?" The woman seemed remiss she hadn't offered earlier. "Everyone says I make the best."

"I'd love a cup. Can I help?" Harriet started to rise.

Mrs. Cavell waved for Harriet to sit. "I can manage. You can snoop or whatever you people do when unsupervised."

Harriet laughed. "I'm not that type of journalist."

Alone in the room, Harriet went over the notes she'd jotted down. Last week, she'd interviewed Mrs. Cavell's cousin, who at the age of sixteen had joined the armed citizen militia called the Home Guard during the final year of World War II.

Mrs. Cavell returned with a teapot and cups on a tray. She poured two cups. "Jerry told me he talked your ear off."

"That he did." Harriet accepted the tea. "Thank you."

"I've never understood why Jerry or anyone enjoys talking about the war as if they were the good old days." Mrs. Cavell retook her seat, a cup and saucer on her lap.

Harriet wasn't sure how to broach the start of the interview after that comment.

As if Mrs. Cavell sensed this, she launched into it. "I was in Coventry with my mum. She had a job at one of the factories. It was an industrial city, which made it a target for the Germans to bomb. After the air raids in 1940, Mum wanted to send me away, but I didn't want to leave her side. As it turned out, I survived. She didn't. The final raid occurred in 1942. Not many died during it, but..." Her voice trailed off in a forced *c'est la vie* way.

Harriet sipped the tea, agreeing it was one of the best but didn't feel it was the right time to compliment Mrs. Cavell.

Mrs. Cavell set her tea on a side table. "My father died in North Africa during the Second Battle of El Alamein. I believe that was"—she closed her eyes—"in October of 1942. The air raid was in August that year."

"How old were you?" Harriet asked in the softest tone she could.

"Eight." Mrs. Cavell briefly looked away. "It was so long ago, and yet, it feels like yesterday."

Harriet bobbed her head in understanding. She'd conducted many interviews over the years, and she instinctively knew when to stay silent, to let the subject set the tone and pace during emotional parts.

"Mum always said I'd be a heartbreaker because of my blue eyes and dimple." Mrs. Cavell placed a hand on her right cheek.

"Were you?"

The woman laughed quietly. "I may have broken one or

two hearts in my day." She rose and pulled a framed photo off the black Steinway piano in the corner, making the room seem so much smaller and cramped but homier in an odd way. "This was taken when I was seventeen."

Harriet stared at the younger version of the strong-willed woman, her shoulders back, a seductive smile, and an expression that claimed she could take anything that came her way.

Mrs. Cavell sat on the piano bench. "Mum was so proud of my dimple. Back in '36, a woman in New York invented a dimple machine. Mum never tried it herself, but she probably would have if given the opportunity. The contraption had knobs that pressed into the cheeks." Mrs. Cavell jabbed two fingers into her cheeks. "It's odd to think people covet dimples when they're actually a deformity." She laughed, seeming lost in a memory. "But you came here to hear how I survived losing my parents in the war."

"Yes, if you feel up to talking about it."

"It was all so long ago," she repeated.

Harriet wasn't sure if this meant Mrs. Cavell wanted to speak about it or not.

Mrs. Cavell sighed. "I have no idea why it matters to people today. The world is so different now."

"Yes and no. People love to read origin stories, especially if someone overcame great obstacles to succeed, like you. You became a concert pianist who's played all over the world."

"I was lucky. After Mum died, Jerry's family took me in. They had a piano, and after Thomas, Jerry's dad, heard me play once, he hunted high and low for a teacher. This was during the war." She laughed, suddenly looking much younger, but it faded quickly. "I do believe playing piano saved me. It gave me something to focus on for hours at a time. I think Thomas knew that deep down, which was why he paid for all the lessons. He lost an arm in the war. Everyone lost something or someone."

A silence overtook the room.

"Do you still play?" Harriet asked.

"I do. Would you like to hear something?" There was a sparkle in her eyes.

"It'd be an honor."

* * *

AFTER THE INTERVIEW CONCLUDED, Mrs. Cavell asked, "Why don't you have a podcast?"

Harriet closed her notebook. "Do you listen to them?"

"Oh, yes. My grandson got me hooked on them. My eyes aren't what they used to be, and it's so much easier to listen."

"What's your favorite?"

"*Fortunately… with Fi and Jane.*"

"I haven't listened to that one."

"You should. They seem down to earth. Like women I could be friends with. That's what I like about podcasts. It's easier to trust people when you hear their voices. You have a lovely voice. I'd listen to you."

"Is that right?" Harriet took in a deep breath and slowly released it. "I'm not sure I have the personality for it."

Mrs. Cavell stared deeply into Harriet's eyes. "You never know what you can handle until you have to."

"That's very wise advice."

"I'm at the age where everyone thinks whatever I say is wise. It comes with the white hair and wrinkles." Her grin conveyed a secret reservoir of knowledge.

"I may look into podcasting, then."

"If you do, I'd love to be one of your first interviews."

"You have my word."

"I'll hold you to it. I may be old, but I don't forget promises."

Harriet believed her.

They said their goodbyes, and Mrs. Cavell shut the door.

Harriet climbed into her car, but before she inserted the key, she took out her iPhone and downloaded an episode of *Fortunately... with Fi and Jane*. She hit play.

CHAPTER THREE

A FEW HOURS AFTER JOSIE SATIATED HER appetite and took a walk in the countryside to kill time and center her chi, a new obsession as of this morning now that she could think of things like that, Josie had decided she couldn't delay anymore. It was time to reach her destination. Her family had no idea she was even in the UK since Josie had hopped the first flight she could catch to flee America.

Josie abandoned the rental in the parking spot behind the church she'd attended occasionally during her childhood, the yellow stone spire piercing the deep-blue sky. Inhaling the crisp air, Josie stretched her arms overhead, bending to the right and then left.

Now, according to her iPhone, it was several ticks past ten in the morning, and Josie stood next to the Ale River, a little waterway that carved its way through the center of Upper Chewford, bringing a smile to her lips. On her right were butter-colored houses constructed with the distinctive Cotswold stone. Each one with a unique garden, making it clear the neighbors were competing with everyone else by adding what they considered that special touch to garner more attention and, in all probability, an increase in photos posted on social media. Josie preferred the lot with a wooden doghouse that had a white, curly-haired dog snoozing inside with his head resting on his front paws. She peered in to see if the dog was real. One of the ears twitched.

Josie scanned the green fields to the left of the river. Why would anyone want to leave this place? All the maniac drivers she'd passed didn't know how good they had it here. Only sociopaths would dash toward the craziness of city life. However, Josie had never actually lived here, and her visits had been few and far between since becoming an adult two decades ago.

Now, as Josie stood in her mum's village, she was unable to banish the thought that she had failed. Maybe coming here was a mistake. What did Josie think she'd find in the Cotswolds?

Her eyes landed on The Golden Fleece, Josie's ultimate destination. The pub was mere steps from the river. All she had to do was cross the river and then announce to her mum... something. *Come on, Josie. Words are your thing.* Spin this disaster into something other than a catastrophe.

Her eyes fell to the water once again. Did it really classify as a river? It was only thigh-deep and about thirty feet wide. It had several stone footbridges crossing it, but Josie determined, if need be, she could ford the river without too much trouble. She chastised herself once again. Why did it matter if Ale could actually be classified as a full-fledged flowing watercourse or not? *Stop being so American! And stop stalling the inevitable.*

Josie's gaze took in everything again. This place was the definition of charming. It was as if Josie had stepped into a painting depicting the perfect old-fashioned English countryside village that'd stopped in time when everyone and everything moved at a reasonable speed. Before the destructive twenty-four-hour news cycles, the internet, social media. All the components that'd recently brought everything crashing down in Josie's life, forcing her to retreat from the career she'd painstakingly built since high school when she first volunteered for a political campaign for the not-so-famous Upper Chewford to lick her wounds and decide what was in store for her next phase. Yes, that was the right track. A new beginning. Because there was no going back to speechwriting. Not after everyone in the business basically witnessed her firing, when Nora had reamed her in front of a reporter's camera. The same off-air reporter who had filmed Nora, instigating everyone's downfall. Josie shut her eyes, not wanting to give everything too much thought, fearful she'd break out into full-on panic mode.

"Now or never, Josie," she said as a way to bully her nerve.

Making her way across one of the footbridges, Josie headed for the entrance of the pub. Although she wasn't particularly tall, a hair under five feet, six inches, Josie still ducked her head when walking through the door. It was much darker inside, even with sunlight streaming through the nine-paned windows. Josie released the handle of her rolling luggage, her gaze taking in the stone floor, yellow stone outer wall, wooden tables, and two cozy wingback chairs by the fireplace. As she edged farther into the pub, the warmth of the fire enveloped Josie, and she made a mental tick in the *cheer up Josie* column. How could anyone feel depressed in a charming English pub?

A chubby bulldog wobbled up to her, acting like a creature who knew no one could resist giving his head a scratch.

Josie had always wanted a dog, but she traveled so much for work she couldn't even keep a cactus alive. She hunched down. "Well, hello there. Who might you be?"

The dog, his face adorably wrinkled and his lower teeth jutting out, leaned into her legs, making snuffling noises.

A man behind the bar said, "That's Winston, love."

Josie gave Winston's head one last pet before straightening to appraise the man, who was one year younger, almost to the day, than Josie. His ginger hair was cut short. He had an affable face with quizzical green eyes.

"You don't recognize me, do you?" she asked.

The man blinked, enhancing his thick, long lashes. "Can't say that I do. Have you been here before?"

"To the pub? Not that I remember, but I do remember the village. It's been years, though. I'm pretty sure you weren't in Upper Chewford the last time I visited, so I have no idea when we interacted last." Feeling mischievous, Josie asked, "How's Mum?"

He tilted his head. "Do I know your mum?"

"I should hope so since you're her brother, not to mention the co-owner of this pub."

Her uncle Clive stared, gobsmacked. His six-two frame hunched down some to peer into her face. "Josie?"

Josie nodded, smiling at her mum's much younger half brother.

He came out from behind the bar, took five massive steps, and pulled Josie into a bear hug, his way of greeting most people if Josie remembered correctly, but Josie needed this particular hug more than she cared to admit. As if he sensed this, Clive pulled Josie even closer, healing another tiny morsel of her soul.

"How have you been, Uncle Clive?" It was nearly impossible not to sound sarcastic when saying *uncle*, considering Josie was older.

They separated, but he kept a hand on each of her shoulders. "Couldn't be better. Let me take a look at you. Your hair is long now."

Josie ran a hand over her head. "Too long. I barely have any curl left."

"What's it been? Eight years?"

"Going on twelve if my math is correct, but I've always been better with words, not numbers." Until recently. Maybe Josie should switch to numbers. Surely, they were easier to manage than emotions.

"Don't trouble yourself, Clive. I'll set up for the day while you doddle about." Josie's plump mum waltzed through the walkway that connected the two rooms of the pub and stopped in her tracks. "Josie!" With brimming eyes and a wide smile, she rushed toward her daughter. Wrapping Josie into her arms, her mother said, "I've been trying to call you."

Josie melted into her mum's embrace, feeling like a ten-year-old child being consoled after falling off a bike, scraping both knees and elbows. "I've needed this hug since... it happened."

Eugenie held her daughter tighter. "It's going to be okay, darling. Clive! Get some tea, you lazy prat. I think a family talk is in order."

"Right. Tea. I can do that." Clive nodded as if encouraging himself he was indeed capable of the task.

Josie's mum rolled her eyes. "It's amazing he's co-owner. The man is about as useful as a three-legged horse at the race track."

"Why'd you go into business with him, then?" Josie swallowed her laughter. Maybe she got her mum's business sense and that was why she stood in the pub without a job.

"He's my brother." Her mum shrugged. "Can't imagine working with anyone I can't wallop without risk of being sued. Besides, visitors find him charming for some reason."

"Don't ever go into my profession. Even family members are out for blood."

Her mum gazed into Josie's green eyes. "I'm surprised to see you, considering the election is in a few days." Although Eugenie said she was surprised, her expression conveyed she really wasn't.

"Yes, but it's essentially over. Besides, my role is... done. No need to hang about to see the final nail in the coffin." Josie made a hammering motion with her hand to punctuate the finality of everything.

"There'll be another campaign soon." Her mum slanted her head in her motherly way and made a soothing hum sound, all the while squeezing Josie's shoulder.

"Not for me. Not only is the campaign done, but so is my career. And life. It's all over." Josie waved, indicating her mum should take her pick of all the items that had shriveled up, leaving Josie a shell of herself.

"I see," her mum said in the way that implied she needed a second or two to craft the right response, but she settled on, "Where is Clive with that tea?" She wrung her hands together.

That seemed like the perfect thing coming from her mother, who'd been born and raised in this tiny village. She'd married Josie's father, an American who had visited the village one summer in the eighties, wooing Eugenie and leaving a piece of himself behind that wasn't realized until many weeks later. Josie's father had rushed back to Upper Chewford and asked Eugenie to marry him. They did two weeks later and, considering they barely knew each other aside from a short-lived summer fling, had a happy marriage for nearly thirty years until her father suddenly passed away after a massive heart attack. Days after his funeral, her mum had ditched Boston and returned to her roots, seeking the comfort of village life. Much like Josie now.

The three of them sat around one of the tables in the pub, which Josie suspected was so Clive and her mum could keep an eye on the action. Only one lone gentleman entered, asking for a coffee, which her mum prepped. The guy took a seat in the dark corner, occupying himself on his phone.

Retaking her seat, her mum poured three cups of tea. "Tell me about Nora, love. I thought she was leading in the polls and would be a shoo-in as the Democratic candidate. Until…" Her mum cleared her throat.

"Her double-digit lead went up in smoke overnight." Josie added three lumps of sugar into her cup, rethought it, and added one more. "Not even the silver-tongued Nora could conquer Stripper-Gate."

Clive's eyes boggled. "You worked for a stripper? Here I thought American politics were boring."

Josie wasn't too surprised Clive hadn't heard the news, although she couldn't escape the coverage during her brief time in London. The Golden Fleece didn't have a television blaring like the corporate owned pubs in bigger cities. "I wanted this time around to be boring."

"Did she really strip?" her mum asked, slightly flabbergasted, but she did her best to tamp down the judgment flaring in her chocolate-brown eyes.

"No. Well, yes… er, at least when she was younger." Josie made an exasperated sound, and continued, "That's how she paid her way through college and law school. This was pre-social media days, so it never surfaced." Josie stifled a yawn. Just thinking about the past thirty-six hours made her body want to shut down.

"I'm not following. If it never surfaced back then, how

did it end Nora's campaign?" Her mum took one of the shortbread cookies Clive had set out.

"She enjoyed reliving the good old days—and the rest is *herstory*." Josie stirred her tea well past the time needed, but she couldn't seem to stop.

"This must be hitting you hard. Four days ago, when we Skyped, you were absolutely convinced you'd be writing speeches for the next president of the United States."

"I know. I really thought I'd caught the winning wave this time." Josie pantomimed this with her hand. "Once she was caught on camera stripping, everything crumbled faster than a sandcastle being hit by a tsunami." Josie shook her head, running a hand through her red hair as she forced the limp curls into a ponytail. "She's the only pol I've ever respected. I mean, truly respected." Josie flicked a tear away, remembering Nora saying Josie had failed her and the country. Not wanting to remember Nora that way, Josie continued. "The way she could connect to people from all walks of life all the while getting into the weeds of policy. She had plans and wasn't afraid to talk about them. It only proves a woman will never reach the highest office. No matter what, the opposition will dig through her past to find something to tarnish her."

"Why did she start stripping again? At her age?" Her mum's voice was dubious at best, and her shocked expression was priceless. Josie, though, had seen that look on so many lately she wanted to scream.

"She wasn't doing it professionally." Josie shifted on the wooden chair, causing it to creak. "It was something she did for her husband on special occasions. Apparently, that was how they met, and it became their thing. Once the video went viral—" Josie's rapid hand motion implied sayonara. "It's not a good look for any woman running for office, but at sixty-five—"

"Sixty-five?" Clive's pinched face reminded Josie of all the jokes on the TV shows about grannies in the nude.

Josie's anguished sigh expressed more than a response would.

"What's wrong with a mature woman taking off her clothes?" Josie's mum demanded.

"Nothing as long as the lights are off," Clive quipped.

She whacked her brother's arm. "Nora's a good-looking woman."

Josie conceded with a nod. "I had no idea she was a day over forty when I first met her."

Clive pulled out his phone. "What's her name again?"

"Please tell me you aren't looking for the stripping footage," Josie groaned.

"I hadn't considered that. Is it available still?" He looked hopeful.

"Yes, but I forbid you from viewing it."

"Forbid me." Clive laughed. "I know you're older, but I'm still your uncle. You don't have the power to stop me."

"*I* do." Josie's mum came to the rescue. "Can't you see how torn up my daughter, your niece, is?" She thwacked his head with the tea towel she had on her shoulder.

Clive shook off the assault and gazed from Eugenie to Josie, a look of defeat creeping into the corners of his green eyes. Josie was willing to bet, by the end of the day, Clive would view it many times over. Because why not? It seemed everyone else on the planet had before taking to social media to tear apart a woman who only wanted to bring back happier days, if that was possible. Too bad it had involved taking off all her clothes and swinging her boobs with cupcake nipple pasties and teal tassels, garnering another moniker: Tasty Nora.

"I'm shit out of luck," Josie announced.

Her mum tutted but didn't correct her daughter's

language. Instead, she shouted, "Clive! Don't feed Winnie any more shortbread. The poor bugger won't be able to walk by the end of the year if everyone keeps feeding him."

Winston snorted his contempt for the comment.

Clive gave the dog a look that implied, *What can you do?* "He's not fat. He's fluffy."

"He's a bulldog. He barely has any hair to speak of." Her mum turned her attention back to Josie. "What's your plan now?"

Josie blew out a breath. "I need a break. I've been living on the road for years, it seems, with Nora's senate run, and then this one. I do know one thing for certain, I'm officially done with politics. If I never write another rousing speech, it'll be too soon. Good people can't win anymore. The public and reporters won't let it happen. All they care about is tearing people apart as if no one should have a past."

"I'm not sure that's true. Maybe you just need to find a candidate who doesn't have such a colorful sex life," Clive said, looking as if he was doing his best to seem helpful.

Josie leaned back in her seat to stretch the muscles in her lower back, but the action didn't accomplish much.

Clive was back on his phone, but his sister swiped it from his hands before he could get past the home screen. "Hey, I need to check my email."

"No, you don't." Eugenie waggled a finger in his face. "I know you better than you do. Josie came home for us to prop her back up. The least you can do is support her one wish and not check out Naked Nora."

"Her stage name was Pussy Pride," Josie confessed in a tone that suggested she knew exactly how bad that sounded for a presidential candidate.

Her mum's arched eyebrow said it all, but she added, "Oh, dear. No wonder it ended her career. She should come to us. This is the perfect place to hide while the dust settles. That is if she could avoid getting caught by a picture-happy tourist. I swear. They're worse than rats in the New York subway."

"You have a high opinion of seventy percent of our patrons," Clive joked.

"I love tourists with a mighty thirst and bigger wallets. I just wish there weren't so many Americans in the bunch."

Josie cleared her throat.

"I don't mean you, dear. You're a good one." Her mum patted Josie's hand.

"Oh, thanks. That eases the blow that everyone hates Americans. And this was the trend even before…" Josie waved a useless hand. "No. I'm done with politics. That means no more chatter about it. My life up until this point is over. I'm hitting the reboot button." Josie pressed her finger onto the tabletop. "Day one of my new life."

"How exciting!" Her mum wiggled in her chair, pressing eager palms together. "What's on the agenda for the first day of your life?"

"Uh, a nap. The drive here was a bit stressful."

"Did you drive all the way from London on your own?"

"Yes."

"It's only a few hours away. Why was it so stressful?" Clive asked.

"You people drive on the wrong side of the road."

"No, we don't." He crossed his arms, which had unruly red hairs poking out from the cuffs of his plaid shirt.

"Literally, Americans drive on the right side of the road. Do I need to say more?" Josie flicked her hands in the air.

"Just so you know, this is why so many don't like Americans. Your incessant need for everything to be just like it is back in the States while traveling and experiencing the

world. Next, you'll be saying, *Why don't you speak American?*"
Her mum laughed.

"Please. Every time you visited me in the States, you brought special tea bags from England because the Yorkshire Gold available in the US isn't quite the same as what you get here."

Her mum tutted but didn't mount a defense.

"I didn't bring any of my creature comforts from the US. The only thing I want to change is the side of the road you drive on." Josie mimed holding onto a steering wheel. "The entire way here, I kept chanting in my head, *I'm driving on the wrong side of the road.*"

"Poor you." Clive smothered her hand with his. "We'll fix up one of the rooms upstairs so you can rest. Then, we'll plot out your new life."

"Yes. That's the plan. Nap and then world domination." Her mum nodded, taking to the idea. "You know, this might be the time to consider settling down with someone. There's got to be a woman who—"

Josie snorted and motioned for her mum to stop right there. "I'm at my lowest. This most definitely isn't the time to think of that. I need to get my shit together. That's my focus."

Clive attempted to get his phone back, but Eugenie swatted his hand away. "No naked chicks for you."

"You're such a mean lady." He stuck out his lower lip.

Josie yawned, her mind and body shutting down. "Trust me, Clive. Naked ladies only cause mayhem."

"Oh, he's aware of that," her mum said with an ominous tone.

Clive rolled his eyes. "Why am I the only feminist in this family?"

"Ogling a stripper doesn't make you a feminist," her mum countered in the tone that made it clear the subject had been officially closed. "And for you, my darling daughter, I'll brainstorm what your first step should be. I leave you alone in the US and look how that turned out."

Josie was too tired to tell her mum not to put too much thought into what steps Josie should make. If her mum had it her way, Josie would move permanently to the village and date every available lesbian. The idea made Josie's blood turn into icy sludge. Long ago, Josie had learned she'd never find the one who'd accept her independence and stubborn streak. The last thing Josie needed was disappointment in the dating department. From her experience, women were ungrateful, soul-sucking creatures who stole Josie's youth and left a dried-out husk. No, relationships were dead to Josie. Along with her career. Fuck, what did she have?

CHAPTER FOUR

HARRIET PLACED A PINT OF COTSWOLD IPA IN front of her cousin and settled into a wood chair, sipping a gin and tonic, which was woefully short on gin. Harriet could only blame herself since she'd asked for a single instead of a double. Her much younger cousin could be difficult to contain even on her best days, meaning Harriet needed her wits about her.

Camilla sampled the beer, not voicing an opinion either way on the beverage, which Harriet took as a silent victory. Cam had opinions on just about everything under the sun, but oddly, when left to her own devices, Camilla had a habit of ordering cheap beers even though she had a well-paying finance job in Canary Wharf. Harriet believed life was too short to waste on drinks like Stella or Fosters.

"I don't know how you survive here." Camilla's eyes panned the interior of The Golden Fleece, not seeming to appreciate the traditional feel of the establishment, one of Harriet's favorite aspects of this place in Upper Chewford instead of the one closer to her cottage.

"Considering the village is located at the end of the

Earth, we're barely hanging on by our fingertips." Harriet acted this out, trying not to laugh at Cam, who took two heartbeats longer than necessary to realize Harriet was teasing about Camilla's snobbish ways.

"I'm serious, Harry. There's no theater in this village. Nor a cinema. Not one art museum." Camilla counted them off with upraised fingers, showcasing her manicured nails, which was odd given she hated paying for high-end beer but never balked about self-care on this level. "These were the things that got your blood pumping. You were constantly attending events. Going out. Now, I picture you sitting in this sad pub, night after night. Do they even serve food?"

"Yes, they do." Harriet glanced about, clocking the original stone floor and walls, fresh flowers in vases on every table, a roaring fire to combat the rather chilly night, and a few pairs of leather wingbacks throughout, but sadly they had already been claimed by the time Harriet and Cam arrived. "The pub closest to me tries too hard to be trendy and doesn't pay homage to the history pubs had played in society over the centuries. This, on the other hand, is one of the nicest I've been in. Much better than my London local that smelled faintly of urine and was populated by even smellier old men griping about the football results."

"But, it's not your scene." Camilla's face puckered.

"How do you know? I like it here. There's even a pub dog." Harriet pointed to Winston on his bed, snoozing in front of the fireplace. "It's quiet. That was my goal when moving here. To slow down. Enjoy the little things in life. See what I've been missing hustling about in a soul-crushing environment like London."

"Soul-crushing." Camilla sneered.

Harriet ignored Cam's interjection. "You're forgetting,

one of the reasons I was constantly going out was because it was literally my job to review the events I attended."

Harriet had always wanted to be a journalist along the lines of Studs Terkel. He had collected reminiscences of over one hundred people involved in World War II in the Pulitzer prize winning book *The Good War*. She'd always been drawn to stories with heart, much like Mrs. Cavell's life, but until taking over her uncle's paper, Harriet had always ended up with frivolous postings. How many times did the musical *Cats* need to be reviewed?

"Slow down! How much slower can you go?" Camilla crossed her right leg over her left. "Can you even remember the last time you've been shagged?"

Harriet laughed. "Is that the definition of living life to the fullest? Sex?"

"It's an important part, yes." Camilla's eyes scouted the interior again. "I imagine it's harder for your type around here."

"Pray tell. What exactly is my type?" Harriet took a fortifying sip of her drink, ruing her decision to go light on the gin.

"The shy middle-aged lesbian who up and left London after getting divorced and sacked within six months of each other. I mean, you're even menopausal."

"You love to mention that every chance you get." Harriet leaned back in her seat, needing more space from Camilla. "Sugarcoating has never been your forte, has it?"

"I don't see the point to it. The truth is the truth no matter how you coat it." Camilla hefted one shoulder.

"Who says the corporate types are heartless?" Harriet stopped her eyes from rolling, not wanting to waste the effort.

"Since when is being honest, heartless? Do I need to mention that you literally live on Never Street?"

"It's Nevern, not Never," Harriet corrected in her *I'm older than you* voice to inform Camilla to back off or else.

"Same thing." Camilla opted to ignore Harriet's tone, or had she not picked up on it? "The N at the end doesn't change the situation. I feel it's my duty, as your cousin, to point all this out so you'll realize how much damage you're doing."

Harriet eyed Winston on his bed, wishing she could trade places with the bulldog. "Circling back, there's honesty, and there's rip the scab right off."

"Is that what I did? Are you not over Alice?" Camilla moved her index finger up and down in the air, her other hand still clutching the pint glass. "Is that the vibe I'm picking up on? Brokenhearted?"

"Brokenhearted, no. I haven't given her much thought. On the precipice of another career going tits up. That's a whole other story."

Camilla uncrossed her legs and then recrossed her left over her right. "It's not like you'll starve, right? You still have your inheritance from your parents, and Regis won't kick you out of the cottage."

Harriet groaned. "All the same, I'd rather not stumble from one failure to another."

"If that's your goal, maybe you shouldn't have taken over the paper. The entire business is dying an excruciatingly slow death. News flash, Miss Publisher, no one likes the news anymore. It's way too depressing." Camilla let her upper body go limp to make it absolutely clear she found Harriet's career choice boring. "Why after getting sacked from a much larger operation in London, did you take on a paper in a much smaller region? It's like you're a glutton for punishment. Smarten up. Newspapers will never make you happy. You gave it a go. Maybe it's time to think of a new direction. You aren't getting any younger."

Harriet had heard Mrs. Cavell's words about not knowing what you can handle until you tried, although it was too soon to bring up the podcast idea to Camilla. Harriet didn't like to quit, which she knew was a flaw, but she also believed in putting one's head down and plucking away. Finally, she said, "Easy for you to say. They're my passion. They have been ever since I saw *Citizen Kane*."

"*Citizen Kane!*" Camilla shrilled, bouncing back to life. "How that movie is ranked as *the best* movie of all time baffles me." She made quote marks in the air with her left hand. "It's so tedious, and then you find out it was about a sled. Talk about the biggest letdown of all time. Who cares about a sled named Rosebud? Such a con and a waste of two hours of my life I'll never get back. Can I sue?"

"Who? Orson Welles? He's been dead thirty-something years." Harriet's body relaxed some knowing Camilla's antics would keep her mind off the paper, the podcast, and everything in between.

Camilla's lips curled. "Making the world's worst movie probably did him in."

Harriet shook her head, knowing it was useless to point out the movie had come out decades before Welles's death. Nor did she see much point in bringing up how many times she'd watched the movie. It was fitting for Camilla to overlook Harriet's connection to the film and to zero in on how the movie affected only Cam. Camilla wouldn't understand, and Harriet was simply too tired to hash it out.

The pub door opened, letting in a rush of cold air. Camilla shivered, pulling her jacket onto her shoulders. "I still can't believe you moved to the Cotswolds. It's much colder here, and I bet you'll get more snow this winter."

"I wanted to be alone," Harriet said with hopes the sentiment would sink into Cam's thick skull. Her cousin was a whiz when it came to crunching numbers but wasn't excellent at picking up on social cues, even if Harriet used that against Camilla at times.

"That's right. I remember you saying that when you first told me, and I said you were bonkers. Well, mission accomplished. This is the loneliest place in Britain."

"Is that right?" Harriet didn't mention the significant number of tourists who flocked to the region every year.

Camilla gazed at her cousin. "Very much so. You seem beyond lonely."

The assessment cut to the bone, because while Harriet found the idea of living alone charming, the actuality of it was terrifying. Adding the failure of *The Cotswolds Chronicles* only made everything so much worse. Harriet was lonely, and she was facing the crushing failure of everything on her own. Everyone in her immediate family had carved out their own successful niche. Harriet's brother was a brilliant playwright. Her father had been a painter and her mum an Oxford professor before her parents died in a car accident.

"It's a good thing I came to visit. I'll perk you up." Camilla's exuberance reminded Harriet of a puppy wanting to cheer up the world all the while being adored.

Harriet laughed despite herself. While Camilla was self-absorbed, she was the only relative who came to visit. Harriet's brother hadn't even bothered to text happy birthday, and not for the first time.

"Your gift has been ordered, so keep an eye out for it." Camilla beamed.

"Can't wait." Harriet could. Last year, Camilla had given her a copy of *Tipping the Velvet*, a book Harriet had read when it came out twenty years ago, and to add insult, Harriet had given her cousin a signed copy after interviewing Sarah Waters at her old newspaper job. The copy Camilla had given Harriet came from a charity shop with the two quid price written in pencil on the inside page.

What would this year's gift be? A scratched Indigo Girls CD? Apparently, Cam's knowledge of lesbian clichés ended circa 1998. Had she never seen an episode of *Orange is the New Black*?

"Well, hello, Harry. Who might this be?" Clive asked.

"Allow me to introduce my cousin Camilla." Harriet waved as if Camilla were royalty, but it seemed neither Clive nor Camilla picked up on the attempted sarcasm. No one ever seemed to get Harriet's jokes.

Clive took a step back, with a forefinger pressed to his lips. "I'm not seeing much of a resemblance."

Camilla smiled. "For years, I've been telling Harry that I'm adopted. It's the only explanation."

"Yet, I was there when you were born and the entire time your mum, my aunt, was pregnant with you." Harriet flourished her drink before taking another tug.

"Mix-up at the hospital, perhaps," Camilla said matter-of-factly. "Have a seat." Camilla waved for Clive to pull up one of the nearby chairs.

Clive obeyed. "This seems to be the week for family visits. My niece arrived this morning. She has red hair like me." He leaned closer to Camilla and whispered, "But she has her mum's bossy tendencies."

Harriet had to smile, knowing Eugenie was always lecturing Clive. "Is she here? Your niece?" She scanned the pub, looking for a young woman, her eyes landing on someone roughly eighteen years old but without the red hair.

He shook his head. "She's resting upstairs. The poor thing has had a few bad days. We weren't expecting her at all." There was some silence, and Clive added, "Loved the *missing ginger* ads this week."

Harriet fortified herself with a deep breath. "I'm sure you did." This was a source of contention with Eugenie, and Harriet was convinced the publican wanted to throttle Harriet.

"What's this?" Camilla perked up in her seat.

"Oh, nothing." Clive exaggerated a wink at Harriet.

"It's Harry's birthday," Camilla said, much to Harriet's surprise. Usually Camilla highjacked conversations to focus on herself, leading Harriet to think Camilla couldn't come up with anything else to say. "I drove all the way here to help her celebrate. Otherwise, she'd be drinking alone, and what kind of cousin would I be to let that happen?"

Ah, that was more like Camilla.

Clive nodded. "Family is the cornerstone of society. I own this pub with my sister."

"That's wonderful!" Camilla turned to Harriet. "If you left the newspaper biz, we could start a business together."

"What are you envisioning?" Harriet asked.

"Oh, I don't know. But we should consider a business that actually turns a profit."

Go ahead, Camilla. Twist the screw a bit more.

If Harriet started a podcast, what should she call it? *Life Stories*? Or something more along the lines to make listeners envision a quilt, each square telling a person's story and the compilation adding to oral history, like Studs Terkel? Was Camilla right? And Mrs. Cavell?

"There are a lot of opportunities in the area. The tourists can't get enough of what the Cotswolds has to offer." Clive ogled Camilla's ample bosom, and Harriet was sure he was attempting to speak in code, but the obviousness of Clive's intentions made it difficult for Harriet to believe it would work on anyone.

However, Camilla gobbled up Clive's attention, motioning for him to scoot his chair closer. "That's good for you. Happy tourists are good for business, I imagine."

"I'm all about making people happy. Especially my new

favorite clientele, like Harry here. Speaking of Harry, to celebrate your birthday, can I buy you two a drink of your choice?" Clive rose to his feet.

"One drink to share?" Camilla batted her eyelashes, looking foolish.

Clive grinned at the joke. "Of course not. A drink each."

"I'd love to taste your whisky." Camilla gave Clive a come-hither look.

He cleared his throat and then asked, "Harry?"

"Uh, I'm a bit knackered." Harriet yawned.

"Come on. One birthday drink," Camilla encouraged. "Don't be a party pooper."

"A gin and tonic, then," Harriet acquiesced.

"Coming right up." Clive strode behind the bar.

"I'm pretty sure he wants to shag you tonight," Harriet warned.

"I'm banking on it. Unlike you, I'm not living like a nun after my divorce."

"No one would ever accuse you of that."

"I'm the opposite of you. When down, I seek the company of those who can cheer me up." Camilla eyed Clive behind the bar. "He's just the type to help me recover from Neil."

"Who's Neil?"

"The guy I broke things off with yesterday."

"You've only been divorced for three months, and you were already seeing someone seriously enough to have to end it?"

Camilla shrugged. "I'm not getting any younger."

Another not-so-veiled dig at Harriet's age.

"Here you go, ladies." Clive set down their drinks, including a pint for himself. "Harry, how old are you today?"

"Forty-five." Camilla added, her fingers splayed on her low-cut shirt. "I'm ten years younger."

"I'm only two years older than you." Clive moved even closer to Camilla, resting his arm on the back of her chair.

"Has anyone ever mentioned you look like the ginger version of George Clooney?" Camilla practically purred.

Harriet nearly choked on her drink, causing her nose to burn.

"Is that right?" Clive rubbed his chin as if he thought this feature and his jawline were where the resemblance resided. "I think you're the first to mention the similarity."

"I speak the truth. Turn your head so I can see your profile." Camilla nudged his chin with a delicate finger. "Yes. Most definitely. You're the ginger George. That's what I'm going to call you."

Clive sat up straighter in his seat, seeming to suck in his gut.

Harriet yawned again. "I think it's time I call it a night."

Both looked in her direction, not saying a word to encourage her to stay.

"You do look tired," Camilla said.

"I made a birthday pledge to be kind to myself." Harriet picked up on Camilla's conflicted expression, which was odd, and quickly added, "No need for you to leave, though. Enjoy your… whisky."

"Are you sure?" Camilla latched onto the tumbler as if giving it up would rip a hole in her heart.

"I am. Do you know how to find your way home?"

"No worries about that. I'll take good care of her. I promise." Clive placed two strong hands over his heart.

Harriet was sure he would, but not in the way the words implied.

Harriet said goodbye and exited the pub. A slap of cold wind whipped across her face. She tightened her jacket around her and placed a bobble hat onto her head. A swirl of unease danced inside her stomach, but Harriet had long given up lecturing Camilla about anything, including who she shagged. Two acrimonious divorces wouldn't change her cousin. Camilla worked hard, and she played even harder.

Harriet walked across the stone footbridge and then ambled along the pavement, following the flow of the river to the old stone and now defunct mill, where she turned right onto Nevern Place, remembering Cam calling it *Never*. The nearly full moon shone overhead, and Harriet paused to study it, failing to see a face. Fitting. Even the man on the moon dodged Harriet on her birthday.

CHAPTER FIVE

ON THE SECOND NIGHT AFTER JOSIE'S RETURN, she sat at the bar, leafing through the latest weekly edition of *The Cotswolds Chronicles*, which had been printed two days prior and had seen much wear and tear.

She looked up to her mum, who was pulling a pint for a ruddy-faced man on Josie's left. "Who's Mrs. Frost?" Josie asked.

"Beatrice?" Her mum scooted the pint toward the man who paid with exact change, stacking the pound coins on the counter.

An attractive, older woman on Josie's right, chuckled quietly to herself. Josie didn't know why Beatrice Frost warranted a snicker, but perhaps the woman was thinking of something else.

Josie shrugged. "It just says *Mrs. Frost is missing her ginger, making the nights cold and lonely*." Josie glanced up. "That's kinda weird. I've never known cats to be super snuggly. Not on their owner's terms, at least. I do hope she finds her cat. Dogs are more faithful."

"Not in this case," her mum said.

The blonde woman laughed into her shoulder again.

Her mum, who had started pouring another ale, nudged the tap back up, even though she was only halfway done. "Where's Clive?"

"Dunno." Josie turned the page, her eyes back on the newsprint, staring at a profile of a ninety-nine-year-old woman who'd lived in the same village her entire life. Josie was drawn to a photo of the woman in a nursing uniform standing next to a World War II ambulance.

"Beatrice Frost!" Her mum harrumphed, topping off a pint of Doom Bar for the older gentleman on Josie's right. "Here you go, William."

His thanks was garbled, as if he'd never mastered the art of carrying out a conversation, but there was something in his manner, hopeful perhaps, that snared Josie's attention. The stooped-over gentleman looked to be in his mid-seventies. He wore a gray Harris Tweed jacket, canary-yellow vest, scarlet tie, striped blue and white shirt, and threadbare wool trousers. The man ambled to a chair by the fireplace. Winston raised his head briefly from his bed as a way of saying, "What food do you have?" Once the dog figured out no food was in the offering, he settled back down.

The woman who'd chuckled earlier ordered a gin and tonic.

"I'll bring it over to you, Helen."

The woman said thanks and deposited herself at a table in the front.

Josie's mum leaned over the bar and whispered, "She's like you."

"Beatrice?"

"What? No. Helen. She's gay and not dating anyone."

Josie casually glanced over her shoulder. "That surprises me. She's stunning."

"She does the monthly pub quiz. You love random facts."

"Is that a fact?"

Her mum rolled her eyes. "Go ask her out."

"How old fashioned, aside from the *girl asking a girl out* part." Josie pinched the bridge of her nose. "Do you have back issues of the paper? Do they all have stories like this?" She tapped the photo of the World War II nurse. "This is the type of journalism I respect. Not hit pieces."

"I'm sure I can find some," her mum said with little enthusiasm. "Back to Helen. Do you want me to set you up?" Her mum's eyes widened with hope.

"Mum. We've talked about this. I'm not looking for a relationship."

Her mum made a grunting sound, waved to Olivia, one of the kitchen staff, and instructed her to deliver the drink to Helen.

A few more customers ordered drinks, the noise inside the pub rising, the aroma of fish and chips permeating the air.

Josie's eyes fell back to the paper. "Oh, this is interesting. There's another *missing ginger* ad. Is Upper Chewford a black hole for ginger pussies? You should have warned me." Josie laughed at her own joke, fluffing her red locks like a Hollywood starlet.

"You have nothing to fear. Your uncle, on the other hand, he's asking for it." Her mum's eyes sought out her brother.

Josie regarded her mum to judge if she was serious or not. "What'd Clive do? Does he not understand the meaning of cat burglar? I can explain to him it doesn't actually involve stealing cats from old ladies. That's just mean."

William was back at the bar, pointing with a shaky finger. "Crisps."

"We have lightly salted or salt and vinegar. Unfortunately, we're fresh out of your favorite: cheese and onion."

"The first," he said, seeming put out having to answer a simple question.

"Check you out, William. Got a hot date?" Clive sidled up to the older man and gave him an *attaboy* look.

A slight blush tinged William's pasty-white cheeks, but he took his bag of crisps back to his seat by the fire. William's rheumy eyes were glued to the pub entrance, but Josie couldn't tell if the man was waiting for someone or just staring in an old person way.

Clive whispered behind his hand to Josie, "His tie is the color of a hooker's bedspread."

Josie chuckled silently and whispered back, "Do hookers use their own beds when turning tricks?"

"How would I know?" Clive put a hand to his chest, making him look guilty as hell.

Eugenie took the paper from Josie, rolled it up, leaned over the bar and swatted Clive with it three times in quick succession.

He rubbed his arm. "What was that for?"

"You agreed!" She walloped him again, this time on the head.

"To be beaten by my own sister?" He stepped back from Eugenie.

"To stop sleeping around. At least not with every widow and divorcee within our village."

"For the record, I never agreed. You demanded I stop, and I didn't say anything. Meaning there was no agreement set in stone." Clive planted his feet in preparation for another assault.

"Your silence was you agreeing!" she whispered in an angry tone.

"It was me ignoring you," he whispered back.

"There are three pubs in this village. You can't sleep with every woman without threatening our business."

The door opened, and a gush of cold air whooshed in. Josie glanced over her shoulder and spied a white-haired woman, who gave a tentative head tilt to William before making her way to the bar. Removing her jacket, Josie spied a royal blue pleated wool skirt, with matching knit cardigan, a polka-dot blouse, blue-tinted tights, and chunky black shoes that brought to mind the queen.

"Good evening, Agnes. What can I get you?" Josie's mum offered a welcoming smile, disguising the fire still in the corners of her eyes.

"Gin and tonic, please."

"Single or double?"

"Make it a double, or what's the point?" Agnes tittered in the way old ladies did when making a joke they'd probably said a zillion times over the decades.

Josie eyed her mum while she added the gin over three measly ice cubes, woefully short on ice from what Josie would expect in an American establishment. Her mum twisted the cap of a tiny tonic bottle and placed it next to the glass. Agnes handed over a ten-pound note, and Josie's mum gave Agnes the change. Agnes settled on the opposite side of the pub within view of William. Josie had to wonder if Agnes was the reason behind William's flashy tie. The thought made Josie smile, even if the image of two people in their dotage having sex wasn't the most pleasing thought. That was taking the thought of bumping uglies to a whole new level.

"I hope when I'm that age, I'm still drinking gin and tonics," Josie said.

"A great life ambition, darling daughter." Her mother's grin muted her sarcasm. "If you'd settle down, perhaps you wouldn't be drinking them alone."

"Is Agnes an old maid?" Josie asked in a soft tone.

"Widow," her mum mouthed.

Josie was about to comment that her mum's theory was flawed, but the door opened again, revealing a woman in her mid-fifties. "Yoo-hoo, Clive!" She flicked her fingers in a girlish way, making her appear more like a lovestruck teen, not a middle-aged woman hoping for whoopee.

"Beatrice." Clive seemed to psych himself up before rounding the bar and whisking the woman to the back of the pub.

Was this Mrs. Frost of the *missing ginger* ad? She didn't seem too bent out of shape about her cat.

Josie's mum looked like she wanted to shove bamboo shoots under her brother's fingernails.

Within five minutes, another woman in her fifties breezed in, dressed to the nines and wearing enough perfume to asphyxiate an elephant. "Oh, Clive!"

Clive forced a grin, keeping his cool under Beatrice's glare at the competition.

Josie's mum groaned.

"Margaret," Clive said, making his way to the second woman—so far. "A white wine?"

"You know me so well." The woman made eyes at Clive.

The sexual vibe from Margaret made Josie squirm on the barstool as she tucked her head down to avoid witnessing more. How did Clive handle it? Surely, he wasn't taken by the overt desperation, although he was a single man. On the other hand, just yesterday morning he'd made a comment that older women should only be naked when it was dark. Which really didn't negate the possibility Clive was sleeping with either woman.

Clive measured the wine, appearing to purposefully ignore his sister's glaring and snorting. "Let's get you settled over here." Clive steered Margaret through the arch leading to the other side of the pub and away from Beatrice. Josie wondered if Clive had mapped out the different parts of the pub before he and Mum purchased this one. He was putting the nooks and crannies to good use.

"How does he keep so cool?" Josie whispered to her mum.

"Because he's a man."

"Who has the energy for two women?"

"Two? Try twenty."

"There's no way it's twenty."

"If it isn't, it's not far off the mark, given the evidence. This village is filled with horny middle-aged women, and Clive thinks he's the modern-day Marquis de Sade."

"You know he was a sadist, meaning he derived sexual pleasure via violence. That's how the term originated."

Her mum's purplish-red face was proof enough she was in no mood to debate whether or not that was the correct historical reference regarding her brother.

Josie steered the conversation back to Clive. "How do you know this?"

Her mum tapped one of the *missing ginger* ads.

"I'm sorry, what's the connection between missing cats and Uncle Clive?" Josie bit down on a hangnail, deep in contemplation. "Something tells me I'm missing the obvious. Is this an example of British and American miscommunication?"

Her mum leaned over the bar. "Clive is the missing ginger."

Josie's eyes sought out her uncle, who was now

engaging Agnes in chitchat, surprised he was talking to the oldest woman in the pub, not either of the recent arrivals who clearly desired Clive's undivided attention. "But he's not missing. He's right there." She pointed at him as if needing to reassure herself.

Her mum yanked Josie's hand down. "I know! Your uncle is a womanizer."

Josie blinked as if the impact of the words sank into her brain. "Wait. Are you telling me these ads are placed by women who want Clive in their beds?"

"Yes. This is their way of staking claim on his time."

"Oh, wow. This is…" Josie made a *mind blown* motion with her hand. "And here I thought village life would be simple. Not brimming over with sex scandals involving my own family. This is what I ran away from." Josie sat ramrod straight on the stool, remembering Helen's laughter. "Wait. Does everyone know the true meaning behind these ads?"

"It's become quite the village joke."

"I don't understand. If everyone is in on the joke, how does Clive hold it all together? In my experience, women don't like to know there's competition for… attention." Josie said the last word in a hushed tone.

"That's exactly my point. Clive is such a man. He has no idea the danger that's brewing under the surface. Both of our livelihoods depend on this pub."

Another woman entered the pub, clearly on the hunt for Clive.

Josie scratched her head. "From what I've seen tonight, they all seem pretty content with things as is. Like it's all good fun."

"For now, yes. But the frequency of the ads has spiked. Not to mention the desire every night to outdress the other women in the village. It's only a matter of time until it all boils over. Clive doesn't seem to understand he's sitting on top of a volcano that's about to wipe us out. I keep thinking of Pompeii."

"That seems a bit dire." Josie's eyes panned the pub, taking in Beatrice as she shamelessly rested her arms on the tabletop in a way to push up her bountiful bosom to nearly spilling out over the top of her shirt. For a woman her age, she still had game. Josie tried to remember the last woman she'd been with, but once she counted back one year, she gave up, disgusted by her lack of sexual activity. While she'd sworn off relationships, she didn't want to live like a nun, either. What Josie needed was a fuck buddy. Or did Brits say shag buddy? Bed buddies? That sounded too much like bedbugs.

Noticing her mum watching her, Josie asked, "How long has it been going on?"

Her mum hefted a shoulder. "Who knows? I think Celia started it last month when she took out a full-page ad with a cartoon drawing of a ginger tomcat, but it may have started sooner. I don't always have time to read the paper. After that one, though, they exploded. Your uncle thinks it's funny, not to mention he's giddy from the huge ego boost."

"And so many in the States think gays are the shameless whores." Josie's mind kept flitting back to the fact that Clive barely spoke to the women seeking his attention. Right then and there, he was conversing with a table of tourists, his back to Beatrice and her spilling cleavage. Even Josie was enjoying the view. Was Clive playing hard to get? "It's been a long time since I was in demand, and I don't think I'd ever reached the point where every available woman in a ten-mile radius wanted me."

"It's not just available women."

"Come again?" Josie leaned onto the bar. "Is Clive playing both sides?"

"What?" Her mum seemed to realize what Josie was implying. "No. Not that. Two married ladies have placed ads. That I know of. That's the part that really worries me. An angry husband wanting blood."

"Any of these married? Mrs. Frost?" Josie whispered, her eyes sweeping the pub once again.

Her mum shook her head. "Widow."

Was Chewford the place where widows went to die?

William was back for another pint.

"Doesn't Agnes look lovely tonight?" Her mum asked while pulling the tap.

He gave a slight nod, a blush creeping into his cheeks.

Josie casually glanced over her shoulder to witness Agnes's interest piqued, although she avoided looking in William's direction for long, burying her head behind a battered copy of *Jane Eyre*. Were all village pubs in the Cotswolds like this? Was it just Upper Chewford? Or was The Golden Fleece a hotbed of sex? Josie wiggled on her barstool.

Her mum, taking note, asked, "You aren't getting a cold, are you? Should we add more wood to the fire?"

"Nope. I think someone just walked over my grave."

"What?" Josie's mother handed off William's pint.

"Oh, nothing. I'm going to step outside for a minute."

Her mum put up a *stop right there* hand and then made her way around the bar. "Arms up?"

"What?"

"Just do as I say." She motioned for Josie to assume the position.

Josie raised her arms, and her mum proceeded to pat her down, discovering a pack of smokes in the pocket of the L.L.Bean fleece vest.

"I thought so."

"How did those get in there?" Josie endeavored to

sound astonished, like she'd never seen a pack of cigarettes in her life.

"You probably put them there."

"Oh no. I quit smoking five years ago and swore to you I'd never touch another cigarette again."

Her mum steadied a motherly gaze on Josie. The one that made Josie feel like she was a mere child caught with her hand in the proverbial cookie jar.

"Okay. I admit it. Since losing my job, I started up again." Josie's gaze dropped to the stone floor.

"How could you? Your father smoked a pack a day, and he didn't make it past sixty. I forbid you to die young. My heart can't take it."

Josie sucked in a repentant breath. While her father hadn't died from lung cancer, his habit had contributed to his heart attack. "I'm sorry, Mum. Keep the pack."

"I plan to, and I'm tossing your room before I go to bed."

"The black bag. You'll find two more packs."

Josie's mum struck her arm. "What am I going to do with the two of you?"

Clive approached them. "Why's Josie in trouble?"

Her mum held up the green pack of Mayfair menthols.

"Oh. I'll take care of those if you want me to. And I don't even like menthols. Too girly." He made it seem like he was doing both women a huge favor.

"But you'll smoke them anyway?" Her mum didn't sound impressed by his so-called sacrifice. Quite the opposite.

"If I must, I must. You can't just throw out cigarettes. Think of all the poor kids who don't have any." Clive did his best to sound sincere.

"Out of my sight. Both of you." Her mum made *be gone* motions with her hands.

Josie looped her arm through Clive's. "Let's take in the full moon."

Winston waddled out with them, snorting with each step.

"On a scale of one to ten, how mad is your mother with me?" Clive blew into his hands before shoving them into his pockets.

"Thirteen."

He nodded. "She doesn't understand."

"What?"

For a brief moment, Clive looked vulnerable, but it morphed into arrogance. "She's not like us, Josie. Women —they're addicting. Like your cigarettes."

"You know that's a bit degrading, right? Comparing women to cigarettes. I'm saying this as your niece and as a woman."

"Yes, but you also like women, so you know what it's like." He kicked at a broken piece of flagstone, avoiding Josie's glare.

"Not sure I do. Not in this regard. I haven't juggled two women since my college days, and even in my twenties, it nearly killed me. How do you manage?"

He shrugged, staring off into the distance. "It's not hard, really. The difficult part is deciding who gets the pleasure of my company each night."

Josie's stomach lurched at the thought. "Seriously, Clive. Mum's right. You're asking for trouble."

"Hey, it's not my fault I came out this way." He jutted his chin as if claiming he was some type of Adonis. "The other night, a woman called me the ginger George Clooney."

"How are we related?"

"My dad is also your mum's father, but we have

different mothers," he explained as if Josie were completely unaware of the family tree.

Josie stared at Clive wondering if he really was unjaded, a difficult concept for Josie to understand. For as long as she could remember, she was always trying to stay three steps ahead of any type of verbal jab. If Clive was so innocent, what about the ginger ads? Maybe he *was* the Ginger George and had acting in his blood.

There were some fireworks off in the distance.

"It's not even November, but Chewies are antsy for bonfire night." He stomped his feet in what seemed like an effort to stave off the cold.

Josie briefly closed her eyes to conjure the poem her mum used to recite. "'Remember, remember! The fifth of November…'" She motioned it continued, but that was all she could call forth. Her eyes stared at the brilliant white moon hanging above, its reflection dancing on the river's surface. "The sky here is so different from what I'm used to. Crisp."

Clive looked up. "I don't know how you survived so long in America. I tried London but only lasted a year or so. I can't imagine living anywhere else."

A lone figure standing on the footbridge caught Josie's attention. The person stared at the night sky in quiet contemplation, as if searching for an answer to life's riddle. Slowly, the person turned their head, causing a ripple of excitement to swell in Josie's chest.

"Who's that?" Josie asked Clive.

He squinted. "Harry, I think."

"Oh," Josie said, disappointed that it was a guy. It was probably for the best, though. The last thing Josie needed right then and there was a complication. Her entire life at present was brimming with them. What Josie needed was to be alone to focus on rebooting her life. She was fine with momentarily hitting the pause button, but not for long. Josie had always been eager to get to the next stage: bigger, better, and more prestigious than before. Another reason why the end of the presidential campaign had been such a crushing blow. Josie had been on the pinnacle of the ultimate success, only to have everything swiped away with one ill-timed video.

But there was something about the individual on the bridge. As if Josie had known the person all her life. Which was a bizarre thing to think, especially when she factored in it was a man. Josie had never found any man all that interesting. She also wasn't the fanciful type and didn't believe in the whole soul mate concept. Only fools bought into that. Desperate ones at that.

CHAPTER SIX

HARRIET'S GAZE FELL FROM THE STARS, AND A figure standing next to Clive outside of the pub entrance caught her attention, making Harriet's heart skip a beat for some inexplicable reason. The light overhead the pair highlighted the woman's red hair. Next to Clive, she looked tiny, but Harriet had heard more than one villager refer to Clive as the Ginger Giant. Was this Eugenie's daughter Harriet had heard mentioned just yesterday? The one who returned from America without so much as an advance notice? From the gossip Harriet had heard in the coffee shop earlier in the day, the person in question had been a speechwriter, or spin doctor, for the American candidate who had all but conceded the election even before millions of Americans cast their votes.

Even from this distance, Harriet could appreciate the woman's beauty. The way she held her head up high, her shoulders back. The confidence. How very American of her. Admittedly, Harriet had always been attracted to strong women, although Harriet had sworn never again after a short-lived fling with an American woman. While the two had spoken the same language, Harriet soon learned they were never on the same page. Simple miscommunications had led to epic meltdowns. True, the passionate make-up sex had almost made it worthwhile, but even that plus soon entered the negative column. Hot sex could only go so far.

The two seemed to lock eyes, a sizzle coursing through Harriet, but she chalked it up to a breeze. Never mind that the air was frigid and the feeling Harriet felt was anything but. Thinking otherwise was confusing, because Harriet wasn't the type to believe in a moment. The notion was utterly absurd.

It reached the stage when Harriet knew she had to proceed off the bridge or it would become awkward. Or more so, since Clive's cocked head and expression slowly edged into confusion, at least that was what Harriet imagined. Clive was a simple man, sweet, but not a lot of depth to him.

Why did the thought of ending the stare down with a woman she'd never met disappoint her? It must be the full moon making the sensible Harriet think crazy thoughts.

As if in tune with Harriet's gawkiness, Clive formed a megaphone around his mouth and shouted, "Harry! You coming or going?"

A blush seemed to creep up all the way from Harriet's toes to the tippy top of her head, and she imagined steam spouting out of her like a kettle well past the boiling point. She continued her trek to the entrance of The Golden Fleece, trying to conjure up words to explain her action, or inaction, on the bridge.

Clive's beaming smile eased the transition. "Harry, allow me to introduce my lovely niece, Josie."

They seemed to be the same age, but Harriet recalled hearing that Eugenie and her brother were half siblings.

"I've heard all about her." Harriet stuck out her hand for Josie to shake, relieved she didn't get overly tongue-tied, a typical curse when around strangers.

"I hope you haven't heard about me via trashy ads in the Cotswolds rag." Josie shook Harriet's hand.

Clive guffawed.

Harriet tried to mask a cringe.

"Harry actually takes part in the ads," Clive said as if the true meaning behind them were a badge of honor.

Josie turned to Clive. Then Harriet. And then back to Clive. "Oh, I didn't…"

"It's not what you think." Clive waved Josie off whatever track her mind was on, and given the context, Harriet didn't even want to contemplate it too deeply. "Harry's the publisher of the local red top."

Josie jacked up an eyebrow at Clive, her cheeks tinging red. Was it from anger or embarrassment from referring to Harriet's paper as a sensational rag?

Clive pressed on. "I don't know if Americans use that as slang for a tabloid newspaper."

"I've heard it before. I didn't know you were responsible for *The Cotswolds Chronicles*." Josie's cutting tone didn't give Harriet a warm, fuzzy feeling. Somehow, though, the sizzle Harriet experienced on the bridge deepened. Josie was simply the most beautiful woman Harriet had ever laid her eyes on.

"Guilty as charged, although only the ads are scandalous. The rest consists of local stories, but the ads help keep the paper afloat." Harriet wanted to kick herself after clarifying the point since the hardening expression on Josie's face made it crystal clear she was unhappy about the *missing ginger* ads. Not that Harriet could blame her. They were about Josie's uncle.

Another whip of wind kicked up.

Clive rubbed his hands together. "Let's go back inside, ladies. Before my privates freeze off, killing off Harry's lucrative ad business." He started to laugh, but it cut out with another gust of wind.

"Charming, Clive." Josie wheeled about without another word, stepping inside the pub.

Clive raised a brow at Harriet in the way that conveyed *whoops*, but from his stiff posture he wasn't ashamed, something Harriet was never able to comprehend about the gregarious publican.

Inside, Eugenie flicked her fingers in a bossy way for Harriet to come straight to her station at the bar. Harriet suppressed an *oh shit* sigh. Just last week, Eugenie had made it clear she wanted Harriet to put a stop to the ads. And the week before. Basically, almost from the beginning, Eugenie had expressed her displeasure.

Sure enough, after Eugenie poured two pints for a couple of blokes, she started in with, "Please, Harry. No more *missing ginger* ads."

Harriet took a seat at the bar. "I can't turn away paying customers. What would you say if I asked you not to serve all the drunks in town?"

"We wouldn't have any patrons," Eugenie stated without irony.

"Exactly." Harriet nodded to emphasize the point.

"But, Harry, the ads are going to destroy Clive. He's too stupid to realize he's playing with fire."

Harriet couldn't disagree. "He's not placing the ads, though."

"They're about him!"

Harriet sucked in a deep breath and decided the only course was to change the topic. "Is it nice having Josie back home? I just met her outside." Not that Harriet had made a great impression. Had she wanted to? Surely, most wanted to impress the likes of Josie, Harriet even more so since Eugenie was none too pleased with Harriet. Maybe going through Josie would be the way to win over Eugenie.

Josie returned from wherever she'd stormed to and took the seat next to Harriet, a copy of the newspaper on the bar in front of her.

Eugenie shook a finger at Harriet. "You're trying to steer the conversation away from the ads."

"Very much so." Harriet bobbed her head to prove her nervousness.

"Mum, it's not Harry's fault. It's the *nature of her business*." Josie sounded like she meant it, and Harriet had to wonder how Josie's mood had softened so quickly. Or maybe Harriet had misread her earlier.

On second thought, after replaying the comment in her head, Harriet zeroed in on how Josie had said *nature of her business*. There had been a trace of condemnation in the pronunciation.

Harriet's journalistic mind kicked in. Did it have something to do with Josie's sudden appearance in Upper Chewford? Or did Josie subscribe to the theory that all newspaper people were rabble-rousers? A stereotype Harriet had been battling from the first day on the job. Granted, the *missing ginger* ads didn't do much to counter this belief. But Harriet needed to pay her bills like billions of others on the planet. How many had pure jobs that didn't have a negative impact on anyone? It wasn't like her company poured toxins into the village's water supply.

"I know most right now think the ads are funny..." Eugenie didn't complete the thought.

Josie swept up the latest copy and read, *"Missing ginger. Mrs. Jones yearns to once again stroke her ginger all night long. If found, please send the naughty boy to 23 Nevern Place."*

Harriet pinched her eyes shut and steadied her breathing.

The sweetest laughter tickled Harriet's ears. She opened her eyes to see Eugenie glaring at Josie, who it turned out was the source of the merriment.

"I'm sorry, Mum, but it's kinda funny. Maybe I should advertise my copywriting services to jazz up the ads. I mean, this example proves how just the right pinch of subtlety would have a bigger impact. Sometimes, it's best to play coy. If a woman placed this ad to lure me back, I would never visit her bed again."

Did that mean Josie was gay?

"Is that right?" Eugenie asked, a hardness in her tone.

"Not at all. These need someone like me, and I am out of a job." Josie shrugged.

"Because of Naked Nora! Do you really think getting into the middle of the ginger ads controversy would be the right course of action?" Eugenie's steely-eyed stare intimidated Harriet.

Josie seemed to take it in stride.

Eugenie stepped away to the end of the bar to take William's order.

"Is Josie short for anything?" Harriet asked, unable to come up with another conversation starter.

"Nope. Not unless you count it being short for Josie."

That made zero sense, and Harriet tried to suss out if Josie was intentionally tricking her before responding, "Yes. I mean no... uh, Josie is a lovely name." Harriet felt her cheeks turn to *fry an egg* temperature.

Josie's forehead crinkled, and her emerald eyes sparkled. "Harry? Is that short for anything?"

"Discombobulated."

"Wh-what?" Josie cleared her throat. "How does that work?"

"That was supposed to be a joke."

Josie narrowed her eyes, as if thinking Harriet was trying to make Josie look like an idiot. They'd known each other under thirty minutes, and so far, they were proving conversation was a fine art neither had fully mastered. Ironic given Harriet was a journalist and Josie a speechwriter.

Harriet suppressed a smile. "Harriet Powell, but everyone calls me Harry."

"Did you mean you or me?" Josie crossed her arms, but there was an endearing smile in place, allowing Harriet to see an adorable dimple in Josie's left cheek.

"I'm sorry. Are you referring to my name?" Harriet's mind raced to recall a fact she'd recently heard about dimples. It was on the tip of her tongue.

"No. The joke. Were you saying I'm discombobulated or you are?"

Harriet placed both hands on her chest in a guilty fashion. "Me. Most definitely. I'm not known for being smooth."

"Are you trying to be smooth?" Josie uncrossed her arms, her smile becoming wider.

Harriet wasn't sure, but she thought Josie's long lashes fluttered for a nanosecond. "I... I'm not sure. Sometimes I have no idea if I'm coming or going." Just like Clive had said earlier.

"But you run the paper?" Josie asked in a way that suggested she wasn't buying Harriet's statement.

"Yes." Harriet delivered another mental swift kick to the arse. "I took it over from my uncle."

"Ergo, shouldn't you be informed?" Josie's smile was becoming bewitching, and Harriet knew she was in trouble. Redheads were nothing but trouble. An American redhead doubly so. She needed to put up a wall to stop the charming ginger from making Harriet think things that would only cause trouble. Harriet's sole focus right now was surviving.

"You'd think so, but…" Harriet juggled her palms in the air, unsure what she was trying to convey.

"And the paper is struggling enough to accept the ginger ads. From the look on your face outside and your squirming when Mum badgered you, I'm gathering you're not particularly fond of them."

"True. The troubles with the paper just reinforce the whole *I'm an idiot* thing. Clearly." Harriet flicked a hand in the air.

Josie didn't seem fazed by this confession. "Do you write articles or run everything?"

"It's a one-woman show, meaning I do everything, even when it comes to crafting the crosswords. My passion—"

"Puzzles are your passion?" Josie interjected.

Unaccustomed to being cut off, Harriet replied, "No. Well, in a way, yes. I mean, as a writer, I like words and how they can be used in many different ways. But stories about ordinary folk are my true passion. Every single person has a history that plays a role in the grand scheme of things." Harriet intertwined her fingers. "All of us have something in common, even if we think we don't. The crosswords…" Harriet waved. "I find them relaxing."

"That's because you know all the answers. What else do you cheat at?" Josie bumped her knee into Harriet's.

Harriet couldn't decide if Josie was being friendly merely because she was American or if there was something else involved. Was it wrong to suppose Josie was gay from her ginger-ad comment? It wasn't like Harriet could come out and ask, "Your comment earlier, was that hypothetical, or did you mean as a lesbian, you wouldn't sleep with a woman who placed an ad like that?" It would make things simpler if she could. Harriet laughed nervously. "I fear the impression you have of me is going from bad to worse. With the ginger ads and now your assumption I cheat."

"I'm sorry." Josie seemed at a loss for words before she confessed, "It's just in my old job, I spent way too much time hating media types. It's not personal."

Harriet nodded. "I know the drill. You were in politics until fairly recently, if the village grapevine can be believed."

"I was. Not anymore." Josie's gaze momentarily looked away.

"May I ask in what capacity?" Harriet was testing the accuracy of the Chewford grapevine. Also, she failed to think of something else to say. What was next? Commenting on the weather?

"You can. Doesn't mean I'll answer." Josie's playfulness was back.

Harriet mimed waving a white flag. "I promise I'm off the clock. Not looking for dirt."

"Oh, I doubt you'd find much dirt about me. For many years, I'd been too busy writing speeches for a woman I thought would become the next president of the US. Now, she's about to have the worst showing since Alf Landon's defeat."

"Who?"

"Exactly! He ran against Franklin Roosevelt in 1936. FDR received ninety-eight percent of the electoral vote." Josie shook her head. "Nora's showing might be even worse, meaning a scumbag will sit in the oval office, proving that my profession is just as bad as yours." Josie's cheeks turned fire-engine red. "I didn't mean to include you in that. It seems I can only sound brilliant when putting words into someone else's mouth. And now, I've implied I think I'm brilliant." Josie bonked her head with a palm.

"Do you know what one of Tony Blair's closest advisors was called?"

Josie flinched some about the sudden change of subject, or so Harriet thought. "Can't say I know it off the top of my head."

"Sultan of Spin."

Josie laughed.

"Have you ever been called something like that?"

Josie's laughter subsided. "I take it you don't hold political types in high esteem."

"What? I didn't mean it to sound bad." How had Harriet meant it? "I was just referring to your job. Having to spin things for your candidate. Distorting people's perceptions."

"Distorting!" Josie rested her chin on her hand. "I don't know how to take that, and considering I was fired for being unable to wipe the image of my candidate stripping for her husband… I guess that means I don't merit such a clever but evil nickname like Sultan of Spin."

"I'm so sorry. I didn't mean to bring up your firing."

"Is this tit for tat? Since you know I'm not fond of media types and the desire to showcase salaciousness, even with advertising." Josie's expression softened a little, and there was a feistiness in her eyes that Harriet admired.

"I didn't intend for it to come across that way. Maybe we should both get a crowbar to dislodge our feet from our mouths."

"Sounds painful." Josie laughed, showcasing that dimple again.

Harriet motioned to Josie's cheek. "You have a dimple. Did you know only twenty percent of the population does? I learned that fact after interviewing a woman in Gatbury just the other day. People love them, but in reality, they're a defect caused by shortened muscles."

Josie slanted her head, started to speak, but then snapped her mouth shut, clearly unable to come up with a response.

Harriet rushed to say, "Not that you're defective. Just your—no... people love dimples. Many who don't have them, want them. There was a woman who developed a contraption that was intended to create dimples by press-ing... knobs or something into a person's cheeks." Harriet squeezed the sides of her cheeks, wishing she hadn't rambled, but how else could she repair the damage? Calling Josie defective when she was anything but.

"Did you always want a dimple?"

Harriet had this uncontrollable desire to place a finger on Josie's dimple, but Harriet sensed this wouldn't be the right thing to do or admit at the moment, so instead she opted for, "I wouldn't get surgery or anything." Why, oh why had Harriet blundered into this dimple morass? It wasn't like Harriet was always this moronic when around a beautiful woman, but there was something different about Josie. What Harriet couldn't figure out yet was why she was acting about as suave as a monkey grunting and scratching his armpit at a wedding. Harriet puffed out her cheeks, realizing much too late she shouldn't have drawn any attention to her dimple-less cheeks.

"My mum always said my dimple would get me into trouble, but she never told me the truth: I'm defective." The glimmer in Josie's eyes let Harriet off the hook some.

"Really, I didn't mean it that way. Maybe I shouldn't say this, but I feel like I should clear the air. I was trying to compliment you." Bloody hell, it was going from dreadful to insanely horrible.

"I'll give you the benefit of the doubt. And now that

we've reached this truce, perhaps it would be best for me to say good night and get some rest. I'm trying to catch up from always being on the go the past decade."

Disappointed Josie was saying good night so soon, but not surprised the woman wanted to escape, Harriet tried to mend some of the damage. "Americans and their drive for success. It astounds me the energy you all have."

"Until we collapse, that is." Josie yawned, covering her open mouth with a palm. "Goodness, I'm fading fast."

Harriet couldn't help thinking how beautiful Josie looked with her guard completely let down. "Perhaps next time we can chat about something other than ginger ads, dimples, Alf Landon, Sultan of Spin, or politics in general." Because Harriet couldn't handle these topics without looking like an arse.

"Gosh, are there other things in life to talk about?" Josie asked with mock-sincerity, or so Harriet thought. "Until next time, Harry the Local Scandalmonger."

"Good night, the Sultana of Seduction." Harriet couldn't believe the words left her mouth.

"Now there's a nickname I can get used to." Josie grinned ear to ear.

CHAPTER SEVEN

JOSIE STAGGERED INTO THE PUB KITCHEN, WHERE her mum sat at a table in the corner, nursing a cup of tea. None of the staff had arrived yet, much to Josie's relief. She craved quiet this early in the day, and she hadn't adapted to living above the pub quite yet over the past couple of weeks.

"Morning," Josie grumbled.

Her mum tutted. "You were never a morning person."

"Nothing good ever happens in the morning." Josie stretched her arms overhead.

"Not true. I've been sitting here enjoying the birdsong."

"Birds are obnoxious morning creatures that should be shot." Josie made a gun with her fingers and pretended to shoot imaginary birds from the sky. "Are there even birds out and about in November? They should hibernate."

"How can anyone hate birds?"

"They wake people." Josie's scrunched face screamed, "Duh!"

Her mum shook her head, grimacing. "The kettle is

warm if you want tea. I suggest three cups to improve your mood. Perhaps thirty."

Josie rubbed the sleep from her eyes with the backs of her hands. "I'm sorry. I'm grumpier than normal. I have too much free time on my hands, and it's only a reminder of getting canned."

Her mum nodded sympathetically but stayed mute.

"Need a refresher?" Josie hoisted the silver kettle to indicate she was referring to tea water, not the plight of her life.

"I've already had three cups."

"How long have you been up?"

"An hour or so. When you get to my age, it's hard to sleep in."

Josie poured herself a cup, adding an English breakfast tea bag and a splash of whole milk. "Every time someone mentions something about being old, it makes me want to die young."

"I am not old!" Her mum's nostrils flared.

"Absolutely not. Gray hair is a sign of youth."

"That comes from having a child at such a young age. You weren't easy to raise, I'll have you know." Eugenie waggled her finger at Josie. The smile on her mum's face ensured Josie knew she wasn't serious.

"I know, I know." Josie hiked a not-so-repentant hand in the air, in a playful manner. "It was so rude of me to ask to be born when you were only nineteen. I take full responsibility."

Clive entered the kitchen, looking haggard.

"Speaking of trouble, there's my no-good brother." Again, there was a smile on her mum's face, but the tone was harsher, causing Josie to cringe some.

"You wound me, Hells Bells." He grinned, nodding to

Josie who'd elevated the kettle as a way of asking if he needed a cup.

"Hells Bells?" Josie questioned as she poured a cup for her uncle, placing a Darjeeling bag, Clive's go-to, into the water.

Clive took a seat at the table. "From what I've heard, before your mum married your saintly father"—Clive made some type of religious symbol with his hands that didn't resemble anything Josie had ever seen before—"she had quite the reputation in the village. Our cousin, who was a huge AC/DC fan at the time, nicknamed her that, and it stuck."

"It did not!" her mother protested, her face turning redder.

"Jonathan has told me every boy was madly in love with you," he added to buttress the nickname.

Josie set a cup down for Clive and then leaned against the counter, holding her cup with both hands. "Is that right? She was just telling me how having me turned her hair prematurely gray, because"—Josie halfheartedly covered her mouth and whispered—"she's not old enough for gray hairs. Maybe it had nothing to do with me at all and more to do with your philandering days in your prime."

Her mum snorted.

Clive laughed. "She's always quick to blame others for everything."

"I am not!" Josie's mum shook her head. "Nice try, Romeo. Framing me as the footloose and fancy-free member of the family. You're the nightmare in this family."

"Nightmare, am I?" Clive winked at Josie, showing he clearly didn't take offense to Eugenie's words or antics.

"Weren't you wearing that shirt yesterday?" Josie jiggled a finger in the air. "Who was the lucky lady last night? Beatrice? Margaret? Celia? Another one I haven't had the pleasure of meeting yet over the fortnight? Isn't that how you Brits say two weeks?"

"We Brits?" Her mum sniffed in that way of hers when she thought Josie was being ridiculous. "You're half British."

Clive placed a finger to his lips. "A gentleman never says." He yawned. "I'm heading to my place to take a catnap." Unlike Josie's mum, who lived above the pub, Clive had a place less than five minutes away.

"Exhausted by all the women missing you?" Josie asked. "Wait a minute. You haven't been home at all? Your hair looks like you just got out of the shower. The women in this village are understanding. From my experience, my one-night stands wanted me out of their place pronto."

"No. I realized... er, remembered I'm out of tea and stopped by here to grab a cup to take home." Clive shuffled on his feet.

"Some real-world experience you garnered in the States," her mum grumbled.

Josie hitched a shoulder.

Clive yawned.

"Make it a short nap. I don't want to set up all on my own three days in a row." Her mum hollered after him.

Clive made a grunting sound that could either mean, *stop nagging* or *I see your point*, on his way out of the kitchen, tea mug in his hand.

"He makes me so mad!" Her mum fumed, not able to hide her *glass half empty* personality that had always driven Josie's father crazy.

"You can't be that worried. From what I've seen, the pub does a rip-roaring business."

"It's only a matter of time for Clive's house of cards to come tumbling down. You mark my words."

"Maybe not. Everyone involved is old enough to know what they're getting into."

"Yes. When matters of the heart are involved, every single person on the planet always acts rationally." Eugenie's sarcastic tone could cut glass.

"Do you think any of them are actually in love with Clive?" Josie sipped her drink.

"I have no idea. It's hard for me to fathom what any of them see in the man."

Josie nodded in agreement. She didn't want to think about any of her family members' or friends' private lives. And, hearing Clive mention her mum's nickname reminded Josie, yet again, everyone had a past. Should people like Nora be punished for not being the Virgin Mary? It seemed women were held to a much higher standard when it came to that.

Her mum continued, "Besides, he's a bad role model for you."

Josie placed a hand on her chest. "For me? What do you mean? I'm not exactly a kid anymore. We had the birds and the bees conversation eons ago. Of course, you neglected to give me the birds and birds portion." Josie laughed.

"Yet you've managed that part all on your own."

"Just barely. Maybe it would have helped if you had told me about dating women."

"That's my point." Her mum nodded in emphasis.

"You're concerned I don't know the ins and outs of lesbian relationships. Wait a minute. Do you think you know more about them? Are you trying to tell me something now that you think I'm old enough?" Josie joked.

"You can be such a smart-ass when you want to be."

"I got it from both parents." Josie refilled her mug.

"Moving on to what I actually wanted to talk about,

you'll always be my daughter who needs guidance. And, in my humble opinion, it's time for you to settle down."

"Weren't you just saying popping out a kid at an early age gave you gray hair? I'm rather fond of my red locks." Josie ran a hand over her unruly mess, her natural state before hopping into the shower.

"Who's talking about having children? I'm suggesting you find yourself a nice lady. Get married. Find a cottage in the village. Adopt two cats." She waved, implying it was as simple as that.

Josie chuckled, ignoring the comment about the village, not wanting to burst her mum's bubble. While Josie didn't have a clue about what her next steps would be, she knew she had no intention of residing permanently in Upper Chewford. This wasn't exactly the place to set roots to conquer the world. "That's how you envision the perfect lesbian marriage? Two cats?"

"The cats are optional. Get rabbits or potbelly pigs for all I care, but I want to see you happy."

"I'd rather have the cats and not the lady. And, I'm not even a cat lover."

Her mother inhaled sharply as if needing extra moments before blowing her stack.

"Don't start, Mum. I've only been here two weeks."

"It's closer to three. That's another thing. How long do you plan on staying?"

Josie faked a coughing fit, not wanting to delve into a topic she knew would lead into an argument.

"In that case, it's time you stop wallowing and get back to work."

Josie closed her eyes and groaned. "I don't want to write speeches anymore. That part of me is dead." Not by her choosing, which made it an even more difficult pill to swallow.

"You still have dramatic flair, though."

"I'm a woman. It's in our DNA." Josie boosted a hand in the air matched with raising her shoulders, insinuating it couldn't be helped.

"I wasn't going to tell you to go back to politics. I never liked that life for you. All the traveling. The stress. And for what? Every time, it crushed your heart. Politics isn't for good people, and you, my darling daughter, have a heart of gold."

And Josie missed all of it. Even the stress.

"You might be slightly biased." Josie held a finger and thumb an inch apart. Sighing, she said, "The thought of finding a new career is beyond me at the moment. I really don't know what the next stage of my life will entail, but it's going to be epic." She flashed her most confident smile.

"How very American of you. I'm not suggesting you figure your life out right here and now. What I'm proposing is much simpler. You should start working in the pub."

"You want me to pull pints?"

"Why not? Is it not good enough for the fancy-schmancy speechwriter?"

Josie showed a palm. "I didn't mean it that way, I promise. I just hadn't considered the possibility. That's all."

"It'll do you some good. Give you a chance to interact with some of the people here." Her mum sipped her coffee. "You know, Natalie Hill plays for your team. I'm friends with her aunt Yolanda."

"And what team is that?" Josie teased.

"The *girls who like girls* team."

"I don't know what you're talking about."

"Maybe we should have had the birds and the birds lecture after all."

"Oh, you mean she's gay. Why don't you fix her up with Helen?" Josie pantomimed a light bulb going off over her head. "By Jove, that's what I'll do. Become Upper Chewford's matchmaker à la *Hello, Dolly!*"

"Given your track record with women, I don't think that's a good fit for you."

"You're only proving I shouldn't be in a relationship."

"Or you should let me pick the woman for you." Her mum's expression perked up.

"Yeah, that sounds like the best idea ever." Josie's gaze flicked upward. "I wouldn't let you select a goldfish for me."

"Why are you so difficult?" Her mum's exasperation was getting dangerously close to her breaking point, which only egged Josie on as if she were a surly teenager once again.

"I don't know, Hells Bells. Why don't you tell me?"

"I'm going to kill your uncle."

"For busting you?" Josie quirked her brow.

"For turning my own daughter against me by spreading malicious lies." Her mum hugged her chest.

"Oh, that's not possible. A girl couldn't ask for a better mum."

"Flattery will get you everywhere." Her mum's posture dramatically softened.

"I know." Josie yawned again. "I think you're right."

"About you settling down? Shall I get you either Helen's or Natalie's number? No, wait, leave it with me."

Josie wouldn't turn down Harry's number, but she couldn't picture Harry going on a date for some reason. She seemed way too serious, and more than likely, only weird facts, like dimples being a defect, got the woman excited.

"Hard no. Fun fact, not all lesbians are attracted to any available lesbian. It's a difficult concept for most people to understand."

"You haven't even given either of them a chance!"

"Another fun fact, I'm not looking for any type of relationship, given my life has imploded." Her mum started to speak, but Josie motioned for Eugenie to zip it. "What I was going to say is I think you're right about me working in the pub. It may be just the thing I need. Give me something to do that isn't too taxing on the brain."

"You have such a high opinion of my business."

"I didn't mean it that way. After I return from my visit with my friend in London, I'll get back behind the bar."

"Who's this friend again?" Her mum sounded hopeful.

"He's a guy I went to college with."

Her mum's smile fell. "Does he have a lesbian in the family?"

"Not that I remember. Should I ask for you? Maybe one of his great-aunts or someone might be interested in a sexy lady in her late fifties. My team is always looking for recruits, no matter the age. I'm one conversion away from receiving an all-expense-paid trip to Maui."

Her mum groaned and shook a fist at Josie. "Why do I even bother?"

"It's a mystery for both of us. For as long as I can remember, I've been telling you I don't like being micromanaged, yet you keep trying."

"You need it now more than ever!"

"And you think you're up for the task. You can't control your brother, the ginger sex machine." Josie mimicked a middle-aged white man who thought he had impressive dance moves, singing *bow-chick-a-wow-wow*, while flapping her arms about.

Her mum did her best not to laugh.

Josie downed the rest of her lukewarm tea and then rinsed her cup. "I'm going to go for a run now that I'm waking up some."

"You didn't get that gene from me."

"Which one?"

"The exercise gene."

"It's the American part of me. The incessant need to stay busy." Josie went to her bedroom to change into running pants and a long-sleeve shirt.

* * *

AFTER FOURTEEN THOUSAND STEPS, according to her Fitbit, Josie slowed to a walk. A figure up ahead on the path caught her eye. Without thinking, Josie quickened her pace, calling out, "Hey!"

Harry turned around, the confusion on her face easing into a smile. "Hey back."

"Sorry about that. I keep forgetting I'm in polite British society."

"I don't think Americans are the only ones who shout *hey* at strangers." Harry's pupils enlarged, causing a frisson of excitement in Josie.

"Are you a stranger, though? I mean, we've chatted at the pub on several occasions, traded barbs in what I hope was a playful way, and heck, I even know your nickname. That should edge us past the stranger category." Josie made a motion with her hand, suggesting they'd blown past one category, landing into another.

"Heck," Harry parroted and laughed. "I do love your Americanness. But, back to the matter at hand, to which level have we entered?"

"Good question. Possibly friends. Or at least friendly."

"Are you starting or ending? Given..." Harry, looking slightly uncomfortable, circled a finger in the air. "I'm guessing you're ending."

"At being friends? That might be the shortest-lived

friendship on the planet." Josie whistled and jabbed an elbow into Harry's side.

Harry laughed again. "I meant with your run?"

"I figured that was what you meant, but couldn't resist. I just finished. Are you heading back?"

"I am, although I'm more of a walker who stops to smell the flowers."

"Nothing wrong with that. Care for some company."

"Absolutely."

They started back toward the village center, walking side by side in silence.

Josie racked her brain for a conversation starter, but could only come up with, "I'm assuming from your accent, you didn't grow up in Upper Chewford."

Harry shook her head. "Correct. London."

"What made you leave the city?" Josie pushed, wondering if Harry was always super shy or indifferent to Josie's feminine wiles. Not that Josie was interested, but would it be wrong to have a fuck buddy while Josie picked up the pieces of her life? Harry's short, razor-cut honey-gold hair, with a sweep of bangs to one side was sexy as hell. Then there were her piercing blue eyes behind the trendy black-framed glasses. Intelligent women were hot as hell.

"Honestly, I needed a fresh start. I'd lost my job and partner."

"Oh, I'm sorry to hear about that." Josie placed a hand on Harry's shoulder. "My dad died eight years ago. Mum still hasn't recovered."

"Oh, I didn't mean to suggest my ex-wife died. She left me."

Harry had an ex-wife. That shocked the hell out of Josie. Harry had fallen in love and gotten married? It was so hard for Josie to wrap her brain around the idea. "That's rough. Why'd she leave?" Josie stopped herself from joking Harry had probably called her wife defective or something. "I'm sorry. It's none of my business."

"It's okay." Harry turned her head away from Josie and spoke in a quiet voice. "I still haven't quite figured everything out."

Josie sensed Harry was the type who needed to do a full postmortem on all relationships, and perhaps she needed someone to talk to. "She didn't give you a reason?" There was a possibility Josie was overly curious as well. If there was hope of them being fuck buddies, didn't Josie need to know more?

"She did. You know, the usual *we've grown apart* line you say to save someone's feelings." Harry's eyes stayed glued on the ground as if she needed to remind herself to put one foot forward, then the other.

"It does happen, though." At least Josie had been told it did, since her job was the only thing Josie had fully committed herself to. Josie eyed Harry's stiffening posture. "But you don't believe that?"

"Not sure. It was weird since we never had an argument. And then—"

Josie bounced on the balls of her feet and made an *aha* gesture. "Maybe that's the key. You have to care in order to fight." Had Harry married a cold fish? Was that the type she was attracted to? Bad news for Josie if that were the case.

Harry stopped in her tracks. "Are you saying I didn't care about her? Or vice versa?"

Josie suppressed a sigh. "I'm sorry. It's not my place to play therapist. I'm just being the typical American, butting in and speaking before thinking."

"It's kinda refreshing. We've only spoken on a handful of occasions, and we've already had more frank conversations than Alice and I ever had." Harry's face paled. "I didn't mean to imply—"

"Don't worry. I didn't think that." Josie motioned to a fallen branch so Harry wouldn't trip over it. "If it makes you feel better, I've crashed and burned in the relationship department on several occasions. At least you got married. I haven't been close. Mum was just riding my ass earlier about it being time for me to settle down. I don't think she believes me when I say I'm done with relationships." Josie slapped her hands together in a finito manner, wondering why she made a point of saying the words and then pounding the point home to Harry of all people.

"For good?"

"Let's just say for the moment, although I don't think I'll ever find the kind of relationship my parents had, and anything less wouldn't be worthwhile." At least that was truthful. "Not one of my exes truly got me, and I'm not interested in settling with a warm body just to have one, you know?" Josie chewed on her lip, letting that thought settle in. Was that what had stopped her all this time, and she was just figuring it out?

"My parents had a terrible relationship. Before they died, they couldn't be in the same room without major fireworks."

"That sounds awful."

"It's been harder on my brother. He's already been divorced three times, and he's only two years older than I am."

Josie guessed Harry was in her early forties. "That's too bad. Any kids?"

"No, thank goodness."

"I always wanted a brother." Josie kicked a stone off the footpath.

"Do you have a sister?"

"Nope. I'm the typical only child—self-centered and spoiled if you believe most I've dated." Josie laughed.

"I have a hard time believing that."

"Give me time. I tend to disappoint women. It's my magical power." Josie made a wand motion with her hand, looking silly, but not truly caring. It was nice to be her goofball self around Harry instead of trying to be the person she thought she should be.

"Again, I don't believe that."

Josie nudged her shoulder into Harry's. "Women. Can you ever make one happy?"

"You're asking the wrong person. I'm thinking of adopting a dog."

"Mum thinks lesbians should have two cats."

"Have you always called her Mum?"

Josie gave Harry a questioning look.

"I mean, you grew up in the US. I'm surprised you don't call her Mom."

"Oh, that." Josie nodded, trying not to smile over Harry's fact-collecting ways, which Josie couldn't help think was charming. "I've called her Mum for as long as I can remember. She probably encouraged it as a way to always keep a connection to here. Mum was always ensuring I appreciated my Britishness as well as American-ness. I slip from American and British words without giving it much thought, much to the annoyance of many. Sometimes it gets me into trouble because I forget not everyone is multilingual." Josie laughed over the word choice, and Harry seemed to nod in understanding. "Once in college, I told a woman I liked her jumper, meaning sweater as you know. I touched her arm while speaking, and she thought I said I wanted to jump her. I'm pretty sure she was homophobic and wanted to twist any words I said to feed whatever thoughts were going through her head. But it was awkward. So very awkward."

"That sounds terrible."

"It was in the moment. Now it's kinda funny."

"These are the types of stories I like hearing. Not that I relish other people's embarrassing moments."

Josie smiled at Harry. "I knew what you meant. The woman wasn't even my type, so she had nothing to worry about."

"Do tell. What's your type?"

"And take the fun out of you figuring that out on your own?"

There was a curious glint in Harry's eyes, but the rest of her seemed to be reserved. "The other day after we talked, I did a little digging about the different variations of *mom*. In *Little Women*, the March sisters called their mother *marmee*. The author, Louisa May Alcott, grew up in Massachusetts, and more than likely she dropped her Rs, making it sound more like *mommy*."

"I never knew that. I'll have to tuck that away." Josie motioned locking the fact inside her head, touched Harry had looked into it after hearing Josie say *mum*. It was odd but the type of peculiarity Josie found intriguing since she too was curious about the origination of words. Although Josie struggled to banish the thought no one could be as genuine as Harry, media types were not to be completely trusted. While Harry didn't give any clue she was playing a game, Josie had been burned very recently by a journalist she had trusted.

"Do you want cats?"

It took Josie a second to comprehend Harry had circled back to the original conversation about lesbians and cats. "Never took to cats. Maybe I haven't found the right one." Josie scratched the back of her neck. "Do you like cats?"

"If I wanted a creature to ignore me twenty-three hours a day, I'd find a girlfriend."

Josie chortled. "You may have a worse opinion of women than I do."

"I wouldn't say that. It's just I've never had much luck in the love department."

"You know what they say about luck."

Harry turned her head to Josie. "What's that?"

"I'd tell you, but it's better if you find out on your own."

"Well, if that isn't a cliffhanger, I don't know what is."

CHAPTER EIGHT

LATER THAT DAY, HARRIET SAT AT HER DESK IN her office, aka the guest bedroom, tapping a mechanical pencil against her forehead. Every time she let her mind wander, Harriet saw Josie's captivating green eyes and thought about the way Josie's laughter had filled Harriet's ears with goodness. Harriet let out a puff of air. "She's a spin doctor. Don't forget that," she said aloud as if she needed to hear the words, not just think them.

On the other hand, Josie would probably have insight about setting up a podcast. Harriet knew one thing about the possibility of podcasting: she needed help. If she had any desire to turn the business around, she'd have to leave her digital dinosaur ways in the past and step out into the unknown. The idea of her interviews reaching a broader audience was more than intriguing. Each person's story was a stich in human history and deserved to be known.

First, though, she needed to finish crafting a crossword for an upcoming edition of *The Chronicles*.

Her cousin rang on Skype.

Before Camilla could say anything, Harriet asked, "What's a five-letter word for cute?"

"Why not just say cute?"

"Because I can't supply the word *cute* and have it also be the answer," Harriet explained, not for the first time, to her cousin, who enjoyed telling Harriet she'd never attempted to solve a crossword in her life. How were they even related?

"What are you—oh, you're working on next week's crossword puzzle. Now, I'm following." Camilla switched gears. "Are you coming to London soon?"

"I haven't considered a trip there. Is there a reason I should?"

"For someone who used to hobnob with who's who, you're remarkably ambivalent about life these days."

"I'm not sure that's true." Harriet used the pencil to scratch an itch in between her shoulder blades, doing her best not to think about a certain someone's green eyes.

"What about Christmas? Surely you'll be here then."

"It hasn't really pinged my radar yet. Are you planning a brunch or something?"

"No. Why do you ask?" Camilla snapped her fingers. "Oh, I know. Saucy. Or sassy. How about the saucy minx?"

Harriet swept some blonde hair out of her eyes. "What in the world are you talking about?"

"A five-letter word for cute. Isn't that what you asked?"

"Right. Can't use saucy minx, though. I only have five spaces." Harriet tapped the pencil against her forehead again. "Sassy would work." She filled in the letters. "Now I need a clue about being unlucky."

"Unlucky how?" Camilla leaned closer to the camera, making her head comically large.

"Just unlucky, I guess." Harriet had been thinking of Josie's comment ever since they parted this morning.

"I need more. Do you mean unlucky in life? Love? Getting struck by lightning? Hit by a bus? The list is endless."

"Love is too obvious," Harriet said, not addressing the other types Cam listed.

"Right. You want to drive crossword lovers insane. I've never understood the appeal. I'd rather bang my head against the wall."

"Words were never your thing," Harriet said absently, her mind still puzzling out a clue.

"They get me in trouble. Just the other night—"

"That would work for nine down." Harriet penciled in the word *bard*.

"What would?"

"Bard for wordsmith."

"That has nothing to do with unlucky." Cam pitched her hands in the air, but only the tips of the fingers were visible on the screen.

"I know, but when I said words, it spurred this clue. The crossword muse works in mysterious ways, but I never question her. It's better to go with it."

"Are you even listening to me?" Camilla crossed her arms.

"No. Was I supposed to?" Harriet bantered. "It would be helpful if you gave me a signal for the important bits I should pay attention to. Some of us actually have work to do."

"I'm starting to figure out why you're alone. Women don't like being ignored."

"If that's the case, why do you keep calling me?" Harriet sipped from the glass bottle of her daily juice consisting of apple, carrot, lemon, ginger, and turmeric. She banished the guilt of purchasing the juice instead of buying all the ingredients and making it herself. If her business didn't pick up soon, she'd have to forego this luxury and a few others. Another reason to enlist Josie's help in setting up a podcast. Harriet's juice habit.

"You're family. The blood flowing in our veins gives me permission to annoy the shit out of you."

"Mission accomplished." Harriet jabbed the air with her pencil.

Camilla's smile proved she took the comment as a compliment.

"What's a three-letter word for emerald?"

"Is that a trick question?" Camilla's face twisted up in confusion.

"Not overly tricky. It's on the tip of my tongue." Harriet tugged on her bottom lip, moving it side to side.

"Gem."

"You're brilliant!" Harriet filled in the letters. "Okay, I think I can make thirteen down bewitching. What's a clue for that?"

"Magical?" Camilla said unsure as if she once again thought Harriet was attempting to make her look foolish.

"That would work, but I was hoping for something more like captivating."

"Why not use captivating. Or how about cute or ravishing?"

"There's already a cute clue, remember." Ravishing conjured the wrong thought for Josie. She was stunning, but ravishing had too many ugly connotations to it. Harriet couldn't associate Josie with anything negative. Not for the first time, Harriet rued her faux pas of stating Josie's dimple was a defect. It was adorable. Everything about Josie was adorable. Even her brash Americanness. How was that possible?

"Right." Camilla laughed. "If I didn't know better, I'd think you were trying to craft a love poem of sorts via your crossword puzzle. Dropping nuggets for a special some-one." Camilla acted this out with one hand.

Harriet bristled. "Don't be absurd. This puzzle is no different than all the others I've crafted."

"Harry…" Camilla left the rest unsaid in the way she did when she thought herself overly clever.

Damn. Becoming defensive was always Harriet's dead giveaway, but she opted to brush it aside. "Camilla…?"

"You're impossible. I may just have to come up there to scope things out myself."

"I'm impossible?" Harriet chuckled. "If you believe for one second that I think you're coming here for my benefit, you're delusional." Harriet glanced down at the lower third of the empty crossword puzzle. "What's a clue for delusional?"

"Harriet."

"Too obvious," Harriet parried.

"Is my room available this weekend?"

Harriet looked into the camera on her laptop. "Your room? When did it become *your* room?"

"I'm the only one who visits." Camilla shrugged that it only made sense.

Harriet conceded with a nod. "True. And, your first visit was only two weeks ago. Two visits in a year—that'll be a hard record for anyone in the family to break."

"Please. It's not like your brother will ever visit."

"You're probably right. We're not exactly close."

"You two are too similar to be close. We're nothing alike. That's why we get along."

Harriet laughed, knowing this was partly true. Most in the family didn't bother much with either Harriet, the lesbian, or Camilla, the loudmouth, and this fact made them closer as a way of survival. "If you say so, but I'm well aware you're only interested in coming so you can shag Clive again."

"Is that how you talk to your adoring cousin?" Camilla pressed her palms together and made eyes at Harriet.

"Truthfully? Yes." Harriet punctuated it with a firm nod.

"You wound me."

Harriet slanted her head. "I sincerely doubt that, and you know it's our thing."

"I'll be there Friday night. Let's have dinner at the pub."

"Just so you know, you might have to take a number. Clive's in high demand. The *missing ginger* ads have spiked this week."

"The man needs to be tamed." Her voice made Harriet think Cam had her sights on doing just that.

"Are you saying you're the one who'll accomplish that?" Harriet wasn't convinced a man like Clive could be tamed. Was that a family trait? *Whoa. Where did that thought come from?* Josie didn't give off the philandering vibe at all, but should Harriet be cautious considering the ginger ads? Now there were two checks against Josie: being a spin doctor and philanderer.

"Not a chance in hell, but I'll enjoy the ride until he is. Learn from me—all's fair in the shagging biz."

"You're the role model for the twenty-first-century woman. No morals whatsoever."

"You're grumpier than usual. Why?" Camilla seemed genuinely concerned.

While Harriet appreciated Camilla's rare sincerity, she wasn't in the mood to have a heart-to-heart. "I'm not."

"I think you are, and it's probably because no one has been down south to visit Miss Fanny in God knows how long."

"I don't even know where to start with that."

"I'm aware. This Friday, I'll help you get laid." Camilla bounced around on the screen like a child on Christmas morning.

Harriet made a gun with her right hand and pretended to blow her brains out.

"You know we're on a video call. I can see you."

"Oh, right." Harry pointed her finger gun at Cam's image, making an accompanying *pow* sound.

"What do you have against sex?" Camilla asked, appearing flummoxed.

"Nothing at all. It's the complications that arise from it that I object to."

"You can be such a girl sometimes."

"I know. Have been since the doctor slapped my bum and shouted, 'It's a girl.'"

"You know that's not how it works, right? You were a girl before the slap on the ass."

"Wow! I had no idea!"

"I really hope by the time I get there on Friday, this"— Camilla circled an index finger in the air—"has passed."

"What?"

"Your grumpiness. If you won't find someone to shag, at least buy a vibrator or something. You need a release. And soon. For all of our sakes." Camilla ended the chat.

Harriet scratched the back of her head with the pencil. "She's insane. I'm not grumpy." She spoke to the plaster gnome, which had an orange shirt and red hat, on her desk. Did Josie speak to inanimate objects? Did thinking a question like that place Harriet in *lost her mind* territory?

Her eyes fell back to her work at hand. "Oh, enchanting. That'll work for bewitching."

CHAPTER NINE

THE DAY AFTER JOSIE RETURNED FROM LONDON, she sat in a small but trendy café in the village square. The owners had a thing for classic films, considering the walls were slathered with Charlie Chaplin, Cary Grant, Shirley Temple, and Greta Garbo prints. She'd just completed a run but hadn't been back to the pub yet. The previous night, her mum had talked nonstop, trying to convince Josie to call Natalie, one of the *Eugenie approved* dykes in the area. Her mum acted as if Josie should snatch Natalie up or Josie would forever rue missing out on this woman like she was a golden ticket to the chocolate factory.

Josie had to wonder why her mum never mentioned Harry as a possible candidate. True, she published the ginger ads, but was that the sole reason for her mum's aversion. Josie smiled. The fact that her mum didn't approve of Harry ticked her up the list of dating prospects. That was if Josie was looking to date someone, which she wasn't. A fling yes. Relationship—full stop. They'd only caused her problems in the past. Besides, there was no altering the fact Harry was a journalist. Josie chanted in her head, *Reporters are not my friend*.

Josie looked over the menu again, her stomach grumbling to refocus on the immediate need. The service, unfortunately, was on the slow side. She'd managed to order a tea but hadn't been able to make eye contact with the waitress since to order her meal. To pass the time, Josie snagged a copy of Harry's paper and attempted to solve the crossword. She found a pen tucked into the crack of the bench cushion as if solving this puzzle had been ordained by the universe to keep her from dying of boredom.

A herd of tourists piled into the café, taking up the remaining tables. Josie hoped they were on the way out of the village, wanting a relaxing work night as it'd be her first night tending bar.

Bard! Josie filled in the spaces.

The door opened again, and Harry edged into the café. Looking but not finding a spot to sit, she started to exit.

"Harry!" Josie shouted before her brain kicked in and she remembered her chant from moments earlier: *reporters are not my friend*.

Harry glanced over her shoulder, smiling when she located Josie.

Josie beckoned with a friendly wave. "Join me, please." Again, her mouth and brain were on different wavelengths.

"It's packed in here." Harry took a seat on the other side of the table.

"I should warn you I've been trying to flag down the waitress for a good ten minutes, so I hope you aren't starving."

Harry put a finger in the air, and the waitress stopped, smiling.

"Coffee, please. Josie, are you ready to order food?"

"I am. The full English breakfast, please."

The woman looked to Harry, who ordered the same.

After the woman left, Josie said, "You're like a lucky charm."

Harry's shy smile was adorable, and it filled Josie with happiness, making her grin back at Harry much like a schoolgirl with her first crush.

"Oh, do you know a five-letter word for cute?" Josie blurted.

"Now who's the cheater?" Harry playfully crossed her arms.

"What?" Josie shook the pen at Harry. "Oh, right. You know all the answers."

"Only when it comes to my crosswords in the paper. The rest of the time, I feel like I'm out to sea."

"I'm not sure about that. You seem like you have your shit together. I mean, I'm sitting in a café in my running clothes and can't even manage to order breakfast without your assistance."

"I wish your assessment was correct. Any chance you can let your mother know there won't be any *missing ginger* ads in next week's edition? I have a feeling she doesn't like me much."

As a businesswoman, Josie was certain her mother would understand on some level the reason why Harry published the ads. Was there another reason for Eugenie's aversion to Harry? "What does that mean?" Josie hadn't meant to say that aloud.

Harry, not privy to Josie's inner thoughts luckily, looked confused. "In what way?"

Josie thought quickly. "Are... are the women in this village done with Clive?"

"Oh, no. Plenty wanted to place their usual ads, but I've shut them out." Harry acted out slamming a door closed.

Josie felt her eyes widen. "Can you afford to turn down

the business?" Why did Josie care, considering the ads were about her uncle and her mum was worried they'd destroy the pub's business?

Harry shifted in her seat. "Time will tell."

"Is your decision solely because of my mum? If you want, I can talk to her." It seemed odd that Harry was making this decision now. Had something happened while Josie was in London? Was there another reason?

"I never felt great about accepting them. Well, truth be told, at first, I didn't even know they were about Clive. After I learned, it made me feel too Rupert Murdoch-y. *The Cotswolds Chronicles* won't ever be like *The Guardian*, nor do I want it to be like *The Daily Mail*. The ads were pushing me in that direction."

"You've listed the extremes between credible and trash." Josie toggled her palms in the air. "It seems the middle ground has been swallowed whole."

Harry's snort made Josie think Harry struggled with this dichotomy, making her newspaper endeavor even more of an uphill battle than Josie realized. She had to admire the woman sitting across from her, even if Josie thought Harry's desire to unite people from all spectrums somewhat naïve.

But her mind flickered to a book she'd read in college about World War II. What was the name of the book or the journalist who compiled the oral histories? They were much like the ones Harry included in her paper. Josie did look forward to each new addition of *The Chronicles*, curious who would be the feature story, feeling closer to the person after reading Harriet's words when in reality the person was always someone she'd never heard of and probably would never meet. The power of personal narrative had always made an impact on Josie, and it was one of the qualities she believed made a speech not just good but one for the ages. Harry had a knack for getting a person to open up, and she was able to craft the words so the reader could feel the emotions behind them.

The waitress set down their plates and hurried away.

"Unlike the waitstaff, the kitchen is on top of things." Josie eyed the food. "Shoot. I forgot to tell her to hold the grilled tomato. I hate wasting food."

"Do you like black pudding? I'll trade you." Harry laughed, showing both palms. "Just kidding."

"I can't have your black pudding?" Josie asked.

Harry furrowed her brow. "Do you even like it?"

Josie nodded enthusiastically.

"Do you know what it is?"

"I do, but if you don't mind, I prefer not to think about it. Let's trade." Josie motioned for Harry to take the tomato.

"How can you like the pudding but not the tomato?" Harry shivered.

"It's a texture thing. Tomatoes are too squishy. Can't eat bananas either."

"I'm with you about the bananas, unless it's banana cake."

"Never had it. Is it like banana bread?" Josie took a bite of black pudding.

"I've never had banana bread."

"Tell you what, I'll make you banana bread if you'll make me cake. We can have a Bake-Off of sorts."

Harry laughed. "You're on, but I should warn you, baking is a family skill."

Josie rubbed her hands together. "Looking forward to munching on your cake."

Harry choked on her coffee.

Josie grinned, enjoying how easy it was to be around Harry. Like they'd been friends for ages. "Sorry, I couldn't help it. It's possible I have an odd sense of humor that's a bit sophomoric. I chalk it up to working with white males for the majority of my life."

Harry dabbed her mouth with a napkin. "Now that I've been warned, I'll be on the lookout to avoid choking to death."

"That would be a shame. You're my only friend here."

"I guess I can say the same."

"You're friends with yourself?" Josie cracked.

Harry shook her head. "You weren't kidding."

Josie shrugged. "You coming to the pub tonight?"

"It's possible. I haven't been in a few days while finalizing next week's edition. I tend to hole up when working on a story."

"Sounds like you have a scoop." Josie added more hot water to her tea.

"Not really. But I've been interviewing a man who recently lost his wife of sixty-seven years. It's been a struggle to get all the emotions on the page. The article is his final love letter to her, really, and I want to do it justice."

"From the stories I've read of yours, you'll nail it. You have a skill most would kill for. The first time I read one, it reminded me as to why I became a speechwriter. Wanting to connect with people through the power of words. Basically, even though we think the other is evil in their profession"—Josie winked at Harry—"our career choices are quite similar. I was just thinking about a book I read in college about World War II. It contained snippets of interviews that really brought the war to life: the good, the bad, and the ugly."

"Are you referring to Studs Terkel's *The Good War*?"

Josie snapped her fingers. "That's it. Your stories are just as good, if not better."

Harry squirmed in her chair.

"You can be so very British sometimes. Just a compliment makes you visibly uncomfortable."

"It's one of our traits."

"Have you always been interested in the lives of ordinary people?" Josie held her mug in both hands.

"Oh yes, but in my past jobs, I wasn't able to dabble too much. I love to learn interesting facts that are locked away in someone's head. In any area, locals are the best source to truly get a sense of a place, even if their tales aren't entirely true. They supply flavor that facts and data can't begin to add to the human experience."

"True. I was the same when I wrote speeches. I loved going to a diner in town and shooting the breeze with folks." Josie spooned some beans onto a piece of toast.

"Did you ever want to be the one to give the speeches?"

"You mean run for office?"

Harry nodded.

"Oh, no." Josie leaned back in her chair. "I'm the type who prefers being behind the scenes. Not sure I could handle the stress."

Harry held her cup to her lips and spoke over the brim. "I think you'd be a killer candidate."

The blue in Harry's eyes deepened, causing Josie's heart rate to jump off the charts. "How do I make it a certainty for you to make an appearance in the pub tonight?"

"All you have to do is ask."

"I think I already did."

"Did you?" Harry's smile was teasing. "Then I guess that means I'll be there."

* * *

THE FRIDAY NIGHT crowd in the pub hadn't reached the

manic stage yet, which suited Josie. While she had started in the afternoon to prep for the *show*, Josie still hadn't hit her groove from the days when she tended bar during her college years in the States. Also, she occasionally helped out in the bar her parents had owned in Boston when her dad was still alive.

Harry and a woman roughly ten years younger than Josie's new best friend walked into the pub, looking chummy, albeit not touchy-feely. For some incomprehensible reason, Josie took a sudden dislike to the strange woman, but Josie squashed this emotion and plastered on a fake smile. "You made it after all."

"You asked at breakfast, so here I am." Harry made a ta-da motion.

Josie laughed. "What's going on in the news biz?"

The grin on Harry's face fell, and she sighed, placing one hand on the bar. "Not a lot on the breaking-news front, and the feature story is still giving me trouble."

Harry's companion looked askance at the publisher. "I'm picking up on a teensy-weensy flaw in your venture."

Harry's eyes darted to the low pub ceiling in a *heaven help me* way.

Josie laughed uncomfortably, unsure if she should come to Harry's aid or let Harry put her date into place. Josie reached over the bar, "I'm Josie. You are?"

"Camilla." The posh woman accepted Josie's handshake with a firm grip. The type that said *back off, bitch*.

Josie wanted to laugh in the woman's face but knew that wouldn't go over well with her boss, who was also her mother. Eugenie was behind the bar as well, keeping a close eye on Josie's every move.

Clive sidled up to the woman. "What brings you back to The Golden Fleece? If I'm not mistaken, this is your third visit."

Camilla slowly turned her face to him, as if wanting the action to have a profound effect. "Looking for my ginger George Clooney."

Josie controlled her jaw from dropping.

"You found him. Two Stellas for the lovely ladies." Clive slapped the bar with his palm for emphasis, much to Josie's annoyance, although it was nice to see Clive actually enjoying a woman's presence, unlike the ginger-ad ladies, whom her uncle tolerated, but it was clear to Josie he didn't respect them. "Allow me to lead you to the best seat in the house." He crooked his arm, and Camilla threaded hers through it, the two of them leaving Harry at the bar.

When Josie thought they were out of hearing range, she asked, "Is one of the Stellas for you?" Her voice made it clear Josie was highly doubtful of the beverage choice.

"I'd rather have a gin and tonic."

Just like she'd thought. Josie gave herself a mental high five for knowing Harry better than Clive or Camilla. What a pompous name. "Do you have a preference on the gin?"

"I'll leave it up to you. When did you start working behind the bar?" Harry ran a hand through her short, blonde hair, tousling it just right so it fell sexily over her deep blue eyes.

A pleasing sensation made its way through Josie's insides, making her legs go limp noodle. Josie shook the feeling off to the best of her ability. This wasn't the time to have feelings for anyone. Josie, the disgraced speechwriter, was officially a bartender. What could she offer the likes of Harry? "A few hours ago."

"And already a master knowing my drink preference."

Josie made a silent prayer that the heat rising in her cheeks wouldn't give her away. What was it about Harry that made Josie go all schoolgirl crush? "I used to tend bar in the States, and since I'm plum out of a job, Mum strong-armed me into servitude." Josie laughed nervously, wishing she hadn't pointed out the obvious yet unable to stop herself from continuing. "It'll keep me busy for the most part, not allowing my mind a lot of free time to wallow." Josie selected a local gin for Harry, forcing herself to focus on the task at hand. "I sampled this the other day, and I have to say it's top-notch." Josie kissed her fingertips with a flourish.

Harry read the label. "Ah, I'm a fan of the Yolanda Distillery."

"You have impeccable taste, then. Like me." Josie waggled her brows at Harry. "Does Camilla live in the village?"

"No, thank God. But she tends to visit from London whenever it suits her and doesn't give me the option of saying no to her staying with me. Recently, she came two weekends in a row."

"Are you friends from uni or something?" Josie measured out the gin.

Harry eyed Josie with a peculiar look. "It's funny. You referred to college for your experience, but uni for mine. You really straddle the fence between America and Britain." With two fingers, Harry acted out walking a fine line.

"*C'est Moi!* Now I'm French as well."

Harry laughed, the sound so pleasing to Josie. "I should interview you. I'd love to know more about what it's like."

"Having dual citizenship?" Josie clarified.

Harry nodded.

"Usually I don't give it much thought, but lately I've been feeling like I don't firmly belong in either sphere."

There was sympathy in Harry's eyes. "To answer your earlier question, we're not friends. I mean, Camilla is my cousin."

"Really?" Josie knew her voice sounded much too

relieved by the news, and she tried to tamp down the enthusiasm zinging inside. Camilla would not be interested in Harry, meaning less competition, if Josie—wait a minute, why had Harry made it a point to answer the question? Or was it merely part of Harry's charming manner, always going back to the original topic?

"Yeah. Families." Harry shrugged one shoulder, not seeming to pick up on Josie's internal battle of figuring out why she was drawn to Harry when she should be the last person Josie wanted after the Nora debacle. *Reporters are not my friend.*

"Tell me about it." Josie's eyes sought out Clive. "I'll drop off the beer, and then I'm hoping we can chat."

Harry's eyes shone with curiosity. "I'll be right here." She planted her feet, causing Josie to laugh.

"Two Stellas." Josie set one down for Camilla and then Clive. She sensed her mum's eyes burning into the back of her skull, but from what Josie had witnessed, Clive saw himself more as the charming publican who drank with the patrons and didn't actually work. Josie couldn't remember seeing him pulling that many pints since her arrival.

"Thanks, love." Clive raised his glass to Camilla. "Cheers."

Josie returned behind the bar, which luckily was customer-free aside from Harry, who was all set with a drink. "Now, where were we?"

"You said you had something you wanted to talk about." Harry sipped her drink. "I applaud your gin choice." She held the glass up to the light. "This dances on my tongue, and the slice of pink grapefruit adds just the right balance."

Josie gave a slight curtsy. "I've been thinking about your newspaper." She stopped herself from saying *problem*.

Harry jumped in. "Are you going to ask me to accept all paying ad customers?"

"What? No. I wouldn't interfere in your business. I've been thinking you should compile all of your articles into a book. Shop the idea to publishers."

"Who would buy a book like that?"

"I would, for one."

"That's kind of you to say, really. But I've been mulling over an idea I wanted to talk to you about."

"You wanted to run something by me? The Spin Doctor?" Josie couldn't resist the jab, but she softened it with a smile. "The defective Spin Doctor." Josie tapped her dimple.

Harry gazed deeply into Josie's eyes and then swallowed. "Podcasts. What do you know about them?"

Josie had to laugh over the way Harry shouted the questions, showcasing nerves. What was the root cause, though? Did Harry find Josie attractive? Or did any female attention turn the publisher into knots? "People really like listening to them."

"Including me."

"Okay." Josie wasn't sure where the conversation was going.

"I've been mulling over if it would be worth exploring starting a podcast, but I don't know if—"

"Oh my God! That's perfect and so much better than my idea about a book. Podcasts are all the rage these days. People, like me, still want to be informed, but the information some seek may not be found within traditional news sources. Or, and I don't mean this as a dig against you per se, but trust in journalism is at an all-time low."

"I'm aware. I'm worried, though, that starting one would be a desperate move. It seems everyone is doing it.

I've never been one to jump on the bandwagon." Harry tapped a coaster against the edge of the bar.

"You may be missing the big picture. People are doing them because there's a need." From Harry's increased beer coaster tapping, Josie sensed she needed more convincing. "Listeners like having a choice of thousands of different topics. Podcasts fill a need, hence why everyone and their uncle is starting one." Josie smiled, acknowledging Harriet's *jumping on the bandwagon* worry.

"How would they find mine out of the thousands?" Harry set the coaster down as if she knew it was betraying her inner turmoil.

"Some seek out specific ones and will stumble onto yours, because they're interested in the topic. Such as gardeners who can't get enough gardening tips. Bakers who want to hear about the perfect banana bread, political news junkies, or techies wanting to learn all the latest technology trends. There are probably hundreds of podcasts about topics I've never heard of, and I wouldn't even know how to describe them. That doesn't matter." Josie held onto the bar. "What matters is there isn't a niche that's too small. And, the medium allows people to listen whenever and wherever. During a boring conference call. While doing dishes. Heck, I've even listened to them while in the bathroom."

Harry, openmouthed, remained speechless.

"Sorry. That's the American half of me that overshares."

Harry wore an awkward smile that made her even more adorable in a sexy way.

Josie pressed on, "I know I've only been back for a few weeks, but from the glimpses I've seen, and the articles in your paper, this village and the surrounding ones are full of characters. A real live Lake Woebegone atmosphere."

"Are we allowed to bring up... ya know?" Harry's posh London accent made the hair stand up all over Josie's body.

Doing her best to tamp down the sudden desire to kiss Harry, Josie asked, "Bring up what?"

"Not what. Who."

"The ginger?" Josie scratched the tip of her nose.

Harry waved Josie off. "No. The author of Lake Woebegone. After MeToo."

Josie palm-slapped her forehead. "Oh, that. Now I'm following. I was just using it as an example. I don't think you should follow Garrison Keillor's example exactly. Don't sexually harass people. So not cool."

Harry laughed but stopped abruptly. "Sorry. Not something that should be laughed at."

Josie leaned on her forearms. "I won't tell anyone you did if you don't tell people I cracked a joke about MeToo. Not many would find it all that funny in today's political climate."

"Deal." Harry offered her hand to lock in the pact.

"I really think the podcast idea is a fantastic one. You'd make a great podcaster." For one thing, Harry's voice was sexy as hell. Josie placed one hand on the bar to steady herself.

"I find the idea interesting, but implementing it terrifies me."

"You have passion. Why else would you put out a local paper brimming with charming stories that encapsulates the Cotswolds' village life? That enthusiasm comes across in your writing. How many people have you interviewed since starting this living history project?"

"Around twenty or possibly thirty."

"Perfect. Am I right in thinking you've scored a fair share of charming tales?"

"Oh yes. Many. But, I'm better at writing things down. Not speaking."

"Have you even tried?"

"Well, no."

"That's where I can help!" Josie hopped up and down on her feet.

"I'm not following. Do you mean you'll host the show and I'll write the copy? I can get behind that."

"Not at all. I'm thinking"—Josie formed a trumpet with her hand and made the accompanying *ra ra ra rhaaaa* sound as if about to make an important announcement before the royal court. "Luckily for you, this is my wheelhouse."

CHAPTER TEN

"Wait, you already have a podcast?" Harriet asked. "How did I not hear about this sooner?" She opened a leather iPhone case that was meant to look like a book. "What's the name so I can subscribe?"

"No, I don't have one. But I'm good at coaching people when it comes to speaking." Josie's emerald eyes sparkled.

Harriet snapped her fingers to imply things were finally clicking together in her mind. "That's right! You're involved in politics as a speechwriter. I never considered coaching would be part of that. Sounds foolish to say aloud, but…" Harriet patted the side of her head, knowing she could be a tad slow on the uptake, but once something sunk in, she wasn't likely to forget it.

Josie nodded. "Oh my God. You have no idea. It involves lots and lots of coaching. Sometimes, I felt more like a cheerleader. Or dog trainer, really, saying silly things like, *Who's a good girl*?" Josie said this in a silly voice, clapping her hands together, and laughed. "That's in the past, though. I'm done with politics." Josie slapped her hands together to emphasize the finality of that chapter in her life, but Harriet detected a twinge of regret in Josie's slumped shoulders.

"Does that mean you're staying here, then? Permanently?" Harriet had difficulty believing her good luck. When she'd moved to Upper Chewford, Harriet had believed she'd given up on finding someone like Josie. But six months into her sojourn in the Cotswolds, and here was the perfect woman. Intelligent. Witty. Feisty. Beautiful. Not that Harriet actually ascribed to the notion that anyone could be perfect. There was no such thing. Not even one with the perfect dimple. And the whole spin doctor aspect was a mark against Josie, but Harriet knew her journalism background was a mark against Harriet in Josie's book. Did the two negate each other? No, that made zero sense. Harriet, though, was picking up on a trend when it came to Josie: not much made sense, and that was alluring in an odd way. Josie always made Harriet smile. Could life be that simple? Find someone who makes you smile?

As if she noticed Harriet was lost in her head, Josie waited until Harriet tuned back in before Josie said, "Haven't decided my future fully yet. I'm still assessing the damage so I can move forward." Josie's eyes dropped, while her right hand reached for one of the beer taps as if she needed to hold something solid in her hand.

"Was it that bad?" Harriet asked, concerned.

"Which part?"

"The job?"

"It had its ups and downs, like any career. The end— wait." Josie's hand fell off the tap, and she pointed at Harriet. "Is this off the record? No offense, but I've had rotten luck with media types. One reporter in particular brought my candidate down, and I got fired as a result. It's left me somewhat bitter, and I want to cover my ass."

Harriet showed her palms. "No offense taken. I also

don't have the best opinion of some of my colleagues. That's why I chucked it in and moved here to rebrand a small paper into what I hoped would be more whimsical, pulling in new readers who are tired of boring news. However, I'm finding even villagers in places like Upper Chewford don't want wholesome. Many seem to appreciate the human-interest stories, but what everyone wants more of is scandal."

Josie made a humming sound, showing she agreed.

Harriet continued, "Salaciousness sells, and it's how I've been keeping *The Chronicles* afloat. It's been eye-opening, destroying my belief in the goodness in people." Harriet hefted one shoulder in a helpless fashion, proving she'd really believed outside of the big-city rat race, things would be different. Better. "It's like when you get to know a person on an individual level, you realize people aren't that bad. Most, really, are decent, and we all have something in common. But when I lump people together"—Harriet conjoined her hands—"I just don't like them."

"I understand that. I'm guessing the ginger ads are the salaciousness you're referring to."

Harriet nodded.

A middle-aged man, in what looked like a newly purchased Aran sweater from Ireland and jeans, came to the bar and ordered a pint.

After the transaction, Josie picked up the conversation thread. "I have to admit I was surprised by the ads. I'd assumed things would be simpler in a village in the Cotswolds. Sounds naïve, now, but…" Josie's voice trailed off.

"Yes, even if they are pretty tame. Like I said at breakfast, when the first one was placed, I didn't realize the true meaning of it. It's not unusual to see *missing pet* signs." Harriet stroked her forehead.

Josie's expression became much more sympathetic. "I fell for the first one I read. And the second. Mum had to tell me the true meaning. When did you figure it out?"

Harriet looked away to Winston being fed a slice of steak by a tourist. "It took a few more before I made the connection to your uncle. As Camilla likes to say, I'm a naïve newshound. We have that in common. Not the newshound bit, but being naïve, especially pertaining to our new surroundings."

"That's another thing. We're both restarting our lives in Upper Chewford. Two ticks in the similarity column." Josie made checkmarks in the air. "Oh, we're also considered outsiders. We're on a roll." Josie's smile was kind with a touch of naughtiness.

"I do think the ginger ads have been more playful than anything."

"My mum disagrees." Josie peeked at her mother, who was chatting with William. Actually, Eugenie was talking and William was pointing to the crisps, not looking interested in Eugenie's commentary.

Harriet licked her lips. "She's been clear about her opinions."

Josie's tone was soft. "I've been on the receiving end of many of her dressing downs. She can be... shall we say passionate?"

"An apt description."

"Oh!" Josie palm-slapped her forehead. "I forgot to tell her you've stopped the ads."

"That's okay. I can tell her later." Not wanting to side-track the conversation to something Harriet felt helpless about, she grabbed the bull by the horns. Wasn't that how Americans put it? "Back to the podcast idea. What do you propose?"

"I'm proposing already? Fast work even in the lesbian world." Josie laughed, her hand reaching for the tap again.

"I didn't—"

"I was only teasing, Harry. We haven't even been on a date." Josie arched a playful brow. "If you'd like to chat about podcasting in depth and some of my ideas—I'm not sure this is the best place." Her eyes peeked in Eugenie's direction again, as if worried her mum would disapprove. "I'd be more than happy to meet outside of work hours. We can have lunch. Or dinner. Or meet clandestinely in the woods behind the red barn. Whatever floats your boat."

"That would be great."

"Which scenario?"

"Er… all of them, aside from the red barn, simply because there aren't any in the area. Everything here is constructed with Cotswolds butter-yellow stone. It's one of the things I find so charming about this place. The negative, of course, is the tourism side. Hoards flock to the area to enjoy the charming villages, like stepping back in time."

Josie's eyes looked past Harry to a table of German drinkers. "Our livelihood depends on them, but I do wish they weren't so touristy."

"Exactly!"

"When everything started exploding in my life, the only thought that gave me solace was running to Chewford. It's hard to explain. It's not like I grew up in the village. Occasional visits with my parents and then some quick trips when Mum moved back before she took over this pub. I hadn't stepped foot in the Cotswolds in the past three years, too busy with work. But it was like the very stones in the village whispered to me. That I'd be safe here. I couldn't get back fast enough for that."

"To feel safe?"

"And welcome. Though, I'm still waiting for that part since I'm the American invader."

"I'm a London barbarian. I've been here half a year, and I swear some locals still cross the street when they see me coming."

"Good to know. I'll be sure to avoid being seen with you in public." Josie laughed in her good-natured way. "I still like it here. Just being in this no-drama place is recharging my batteries."

Natalie, the woman who ran her aunt's gin distillery shop in the village, approached the bar. "You're new here. I've seen you in the pub, but I didn't know you worked here."

Josie nodded. "I'm Josie. Eugenie's slave, also known as her daughter."

Natalie, several inches shorter than Harriet, laughed much too hard for Harriet's liking. And, Josie had cracked a joke, much like she had with Harriet. Did Josie do that with everyone, and Harriet was reading too much into things?

Natalie stuck her hand out. "I'm your gin supplier."

"Really? Man, you taste good." Josie's face went up into flames. "Oh my God!" Josie covered her mouth. "I really should think before I speak."

All the muscles in Harriet's body tensed, but why? She had no claim on Josie. Wait, had Harriet just thought that? She absolutely didn't have any claim on any human being. It still stung, though, to learn Josie was this easygoing around everyone. The connection Harriet had been feeling had merely been an illusion.

"No worries. Who doesn't want to hear they're tasty?" Natalie smiled.

"What can I get you?" Josie asked in a voice that seemed flirty.

"Gin and tonic. Gotta stay on brand."

"I love a woman with convictions." Josie fulfilled Natalie's order, while the two of them chatted, seeming chummier with each passing second.

After Natalie retreated to a seat, Harriet wanted to steer Josie back to the matter at hand before all was lost. "As for your question, I'm leaning toward dinner." Seeing confusion on Josie's face, Harriet rushed to add, "So we can discuss the podcast idea."

"Right—"

A woman screamed in delight, "Oh, how cute!"

Harriet wanted to clobber the person for interrupting.

Josie craned her neck to peer around Harriet. "What the—?"

Harriet wheeled about. Two ginger kittens poked their heads out of a cardboard box. With her mouth dangling open, she turned back to Josie, knowing something nefarious was occurring but unable to put the pieces together, even though she knew, deep down, it wasn't that hard.

Josie met her mum's eye, the two of them communicating thoughts Harriet couldn't begin to understand, aside from the fact Eugenie was angry. She glared right at Harriet and then Clive, who was still sitting with Camilla at the table near the door.

Harriet's brain continued to sputter, and she struggled to comprehend why Eugenie was mad about kittens. It wasn't like Harriet had brought them to the pub. If Harriet were honest, she was also upset about the kittens since she was trying to get Josie to commit to dinner so they could discuss the podcast.

Josie rounded the bar and scooped up the box, carrying them back.

Clive sidled up to her, reaching in the box for one of them. "Are they free? Or homeless?"

Josie held a handwritten note. "They're yours or ours, apparently. They have green eyes like us."

"What?" Clive now held both of the kittens in his arms, one of them climbing onto his shoulder like a parrot, making the Ginger Giant laugh. "Can you say, *Polly wants a cracker?*"

Josie held up the note and read, "To the bastard who thinks he's king of the village. These are the only types of gingers any respectable woman should want."

"Let me see that." Eugenie swiped the note from Josie's hand. "Is this a man or woman's handwriting?"

Josie shrugged. "It's printed in block letters. I don't know anyone who writes like that unless filling out a government form."

"I told you something like this would happen," Eugenie hissed at Clive. "What are we going to do with kittens?"

Winston got to his feet and tottered over, curious about the creatures.

"Look at it this way, you wanted me to settle down with two cats. And... voilà!" Josie took one of the kittens in her arms. "They're kinda cute."

"I thought you didn't like cats," her mum growled, not softening one bit.

"Maybe it's time for me to turn over a new leaf."

"The kitten leaf?"

"It's not like we can turn them out." Josie held one at eye level. "I mean look at this face. Who could be cruel to this face?"

Winston growled.

Josie glanced down at the bulldog. "Behave, or no snacks for you."

Winston wandered back to his bed and settled down.

"Clive, since these are technically yours, you better scrounge up supplies."

"Like what?" He tried to feed the kitten on his shoulder a grapefruit slice intended for the fancier gin drinks.

"Litter boxes. Cat food." Josie counted each off with a finger. "I'm not sure kittens like citrus."

"How do you know what cats like?" he asked.

Josie circled a finger in front of her face. "Lesbian. Cats. Directions were included in my Carpet Munching Club welcome packet along with my first flannel shirt."

Eugenie snorted, thawing some.

"All the shops are closed," Clive whined.

"Be creative for the night. Shred some newspapers into a box lid for a makeshift toilet. As for food, surely we have a can of tuna." Josie handed over the second kitten. "Just to be safe, take them upstairs. I'm not sure you're responsible enough to care for them at your place."

"She's bossy." Clive spoke to the kittens in a baby voice parents use when speaking to an infant.

Eugenie rolled her eyes but didn't argue with Josie. Harriet couldn't determine whether or not Eugenie was a cat person.

Looking more like an overgrown child than a man nearing his forties, Clive placed the kittens back in the box, waved Camilla over, and they disappeared behind the bar to the living quarters.

Eugenie made one final grunting sound at Harriet before making her way to the far side of the bar to deal with some patrons.

Josie motioned for Harriet not to mind her mum too much, but that wasn't what upset Harriet at the moment. How could she steer the conversation back to dinner without seeming like she really wanted to have alone time with Josie? Harriet could hear Camilla saying something like, "Desperation isn't a good look for anyone, especially a middle-aged, menopausal woman who needs a good shag."

Josie poured two pints for a couple, while Harriet went back and forth about mentioning dinner again or letting it go.

She stayed at the bar to continue talking with Josie but had finally resigned herself to missing the chance to confirm their dinner plans. It was as if the universe was opposed to Harriet spending quality time with Josie. What would happen next? A plague of locusts? Which part of the Bible was that from? Moses?

Josie snapped her fingers in front of Harriet's face. "You still with me?"

"What? Oh, yes. I'm sorry. I was thinking of locusts and Moses."

"Naturally." Josie slanted her head and grinned. "Before the kitten invasion, we were discussing dinner plans. If you don't mind, I'd rather not eat in a pub. One of the things I missed most when in America was the pub atmosphere. Now that I'm living above one, I'm getting my fill."

Harriet controlled the urge to grin over the fact that Josie had rescued their plans. "I understand. What are your thoughts about home cooking? Not to brag or anything, but I can hold my own in the kitchen. The garden, that's an entirely different matter."

"I'd like that very much."

"What should I make?"

"I'd never deign to tell a chef what to cook." Josie placed her hands on her chest, drawing Harriet's attention to the plunging neckline of Josie's shirt, revealing a glimpse of cleavage.

"I hope I won't disappoint." Harriet laughed nervously.

Josie's cheeks reddened. "What's one of the funny stories you got from your interviews?"

Shoving aside the disappointment of Josie abruptly switching the topic, but relieved dinner was mostly settled,

Harriet answered, "How two tourists scared the bejesus out of Widow Martha."

"What'd they do?"

"They peeked into all of her windows."

Josie crumpled her forehead, rolling back onto her heels, holding onto the bar to stay upright as if she weren't accustomed to standing on her feet for long hours at a time. "Why?"

"They thought her house was a quaint gift shop and couldn't figure out how to get inside. She called the cops."

Josie cocked her head to the side, a delicious smile drawing Harriet's attention to Josie's full, red lips. "Do Brits say *cops*?"

"I just did. Actually, cops is short for coppers, which was originally used in Britain to mean someone who captures. They're also called officers, constables, the police, the fuzz, the filth, and rozzes."

"You seem to know a lot about that. Is this from your London journalism days? Have you had many run-ins with the filth while hiding in bushes trying to get dirt on a politician or celebrity?"

"Ha!" was Harriet's brilliant response.

"What happened to the tourists?"

"They purchased a teapot."

Josie's eyebrows squished together. "I thought you said it was the woman's house, not a gift shop."

"They made her an offer she couldn't refuse. When I interviewed her, she confessed the teapot had belonged to her dead husband's mother, and well... they weren't close."

Josie guffawed. "More proof I should never marry but good to know it worked out for all involved."

"Are you collecting proof against an arranged marriage or proposal?" Harriet joked.

"How did we get back to proposals?"

"I'm not sure, but if it keeps happening, I'll have to ponder the reason. I'm assuming since you didn't answer, it's none of my business."

"It's not like that. Marriage, for some reason, has been on my mind lately."

"Interesting." Harriet wanted to ask why, but didn't think that appropriate. Or was she worried about seeming too interested? Josie clearly didn't want a relationship, given the hints she'd been dropping. Did she suspect Harriet liked her, and Josie was only interested in a friendship?

Theo walked in with a swagger. "There you are, Harry. I didn't see any ginger ads in the latest edition. It seems the women in this village have finally cottoned on about Clive. If they want satisfaction, they should look no further." He thumped his chest.

Josie bristled.

Harriet wanted to say something clever to come to Clive's aid—or did she mean Josie's?—but all words wilted like a rose in the dead of summer. Proof, to Harriet, she didn't have the chops to host a podcast. She wasn't the type to come up with something devastatingly witty days after a confrontation.

"You're new here. I'm Theo." He stuck out his calloused hand for Josie, who didn't shake it.

Instead, she said, "Josie. The ginger's niece."

"This is embarrassing." His face didn't show any shame. "No offence, love. Just good old-fashioned teasing between old chums. Clive and I are Chewford's most sought-out bachelors."

"I'm sure." Josie's tone was neutral, but Harriet picked up on a flicker of anger in the flecks of her eyes.

"How is he your uncle? You two seem to be the same age."

Josie's indifferent shrug made it clear she had no intention of explaining. "What can I get you?"

"A lager, please. You sound American."

Josie gave a slight nod while pouring Theo's pint.

"Can you say fanny pack? Or show me yours?" Theo giggled like a teenage boy.

Harriet's jaw went slack with Theo's crude comment, but she was certain by Josie's stiffened posture she was well aware fanny referred to female genitalia.

"Can you say gobshite?" Josie arched one brow.

"That's Irish slang, not American."

"I'm a collector of useful words for these types of situations."

Theo laughed in the way that implied he wasn't sure if he had been insulted or included in the joke. He turned back to Harriet. "Not much news to report on. Nothing important ever happens in Upper Chewford. Why else would you feature all these interviews with people in their dotage? You must be kicking yourself setting up shop here." He clapped a hand on Harriet's shoulder, laughing like they were best friends.

Once again, Harriet's ability to craft the perfect response, or any, died before forming.

"Here's your lager." Josie set the pint down in front of Theo and accepted payment. When the transaction was over, she leaned on the bar and said, "Back to dinner, Harry. What night suits you?"

Theo took a sip and tried to engage Josie with a meaningful look, but she refused to give him the time of day, turning her head to block him from her sight. He soon gave up and sought out someone else to bother, making his way to a table of two women.

"Sorry about Theo," Harriet whispered.

"You can't be responsible for the village prick."

Harriet laughed. "It'd be a full-time job managing that wanker."

"I believe it." Josie leaned closer, her jasmine scent filling Harriet's nostrils. "How come I haven't met him before?"

"He was up north with one of his cousins, who doesn't like him either from what I've heard, but I suspect Theo's money plays a big role."

"Ah. He's one of those."

"Yep. This area has quite a few in that category." Harriet sipped her drink. "What night suits you for dinner?"

"I happen to have an in with the owner and can make any night work. Since you're cooking, what works for you?"

"Tuesday?"

"Perfect. It'll be slow in the pub, making me feel less guilty."

"Any food allergies I should be aware of?"

"Allergies, no. One or two dislikes." The dimple made another appearance.

"Care to share?"

"I think I can roll the dice. Live on the edge. Unless you were planning on serving me escargot or frog legs."

"No French dishes. Got it." Harriet tapped the side of her head.

Theo had moved on to chatting with William, which resulted in some sharp words, shocking the hell out of Harriet. William wasn't the type to engage.

Eugenie returned from the kitchen, worry creasing her brow.

Josie met her mum's eyes, getting an approving nod. "I think I need to have a talk with Theo."

"May the force be with you," her mum said.

"One thing about my previous job, it taught me how to diplomatically handle the idle rich with a not-so-hidden agenda."

CHAPTER ELEVEN

SUNDAY NIGHT, JOSIE ASKED, "MUM, WOULD IT BE okay for me to take Tuesday night off?" She plucked a glass out of the dishwasher, the steam still billowing out, and proceeded to dry it with a cloth.

Her mum leaned against the bar. "What do I get in return?"

Josie placed the glass on the shelf behind the bar and took another one out of the washer. "A hug."

Her mum crossed her arms, but Josie suspected she'd done so because her lower back ached, not because she was actually cross with Josie. "You usually give me a hug every day."

"What can I say? It's the American in me, and we show affection, unlike you stiff-upper-lip types." Josie put away the glass and reached for another.

"I know. Your father was the same way." Her voice sounded wistful.

Josie set down the half-dried glass and wrapped her arms around her mum. "I miss him, too. He always seemed to know exactly what to say in every situation."

Her mum hugged Josie back. "That he did."

"There are days when I still reach for the phone to call him."

"I want to wake him and tell him about a dream I had."

They clutched each other tighter.

"Am I filling his shoes okay? I know I'm more reserved than he was."

Josie stepped back to make eye contact. "Of course. A girl couldn't ask for a better mum."

Her mum smiled, wiping her nose on a tissue she usually kept stored in the sleeve of her sweater. "Thanks, love. That's good to hear."

"You still rock the bossy category. Dad was never good at that."

"That's because you had him wrapped around your little finger from the day you were born."

"Yeah, he was a good man." Not for the first time, Josie wished she could find a woman who was just as good, but feared no one would ever measure up in the *partner for life* column. "All set for Tuesday, then?" Josie picked up the wet glass again, getting back to work. One of the kittens walked along the bar top. The other slept on the bed with Winston.

"Still haven't heard what I get in return." Her mum's voice was teasing but not completely.

Josie had always enjoyed the banter between them. "Are you saying you want something besides a hug from your loving and devoted daughter?"

"Now what kind of mother would that make me?" Her face intentionally morphed into the definition of innocent, a trick Josie had witnessed and mastered herself.

"Conniving. Manipulative. Honest. Take your pick." Josie held up three fingers.

"I choose the latter."

Josie placed the towel on her shoulder, leaning against the bar. She loved the end of a shift when the pub only had one remaining drinker. The last few nights, she and her mum had engaged in conversations much like this one, bringing them closer after living on opposite sides of the pond. "Okay. Hit me with your demand."

Her mum's eyes sparkled. "Let me set you up on a blind date."

Josie imagined her eyeballs bulging out of their sockets like she'd seen on cartoons.

"Don't act that way."

"Total shock." Josie ran a palm up and down in front of her face to enforce the feeling. "You really need to rein in your expectations for a simple favor."

"Just listen—"

"Nope. Putting my foot down." Josie stomped hers on the floor, ending up looking much more childish than she'd intended.

"Guess you don't want the night off, then." Her mum shrugged.

"Guess you don't want me to continue working in the pub," Josie countered, her temper flaring. One of the not so great traits she'd inherited from her father, meaning no one was perfect.

"Are you saying you'll quit if I don't give you the night off?" Her mum sounded floored, but a smile nibbled at the corners of her mouth.

"I'm saying I won't be forced into dating. Not by my employer."

"I'm also your mum!"

"Who pays me. This is the twenty-first century. Arranged marriages don't happen—well, not legally—in this country. I don't think, at least." Josie consulted her *random facts* file lodged in her brain but came up empty. Harry would probably know the answer.

Her mum blew an angry zerbert with her mouth. "I'm not arranging a marriage—"

Josie put a finger on her mum's lips. "You're not setting me up on a blind date either."

"What if it wasn't a blind date? What if I arranged a dating show or something? We can use the pub for it."

"That sounds like a great idea for the pub," Josie said, meaning it.

Her mum squealed and did a happy jig.

Josie pushed the final nail in. "As long as I'm not involved in any shape or form. I have zero interest in dating. Especially now. I feel like my life is swirling around me, and I need to step back for a bit to regain control."

Her mum stopped dancing. "You drive me insane."

"It's part of my job description as your child. Didn't you read the fine print when you decided to have me?"

"Babies don't come with warnings, or no one would ever have them."

"Yes. That's how getting knocked up by strange Americans blowing through the village, works." Josie placed a hand on her hip.

"I'll have you know your father wasn't a stranger when we conceived you."

Josie stuck her fingers in her ears. "Nope. Still don't want to learn the sordid details involving my conception."

"Why do you need Tuesday night off, anyway?"

Josie was about to spill the beans about going to Harry's for dinner but thought better of it considering her mother's dislike of the newspaper woman, not to mention Josie's own hesitation over trusting Harry completely, even if Harry seemed genuine. Josie had to admit her attraction to Harry grew with each interaction. Half the time, Josie wanted to throw caution to the wind, and the other half, she was reminding herself not to let her guard down. Reporters were the enemy.

"I'm meeting with someone about a potential business deal," she hedged. It wasn't a complete fabrication since they intended to talk about the possibility of Harry starting a podcast. It wasn't a date or anything. Just two lesbians having dinner together at Harry's place to chat about chatting. Totally innocent.

"Really?" Her mum sounded much more enthusiastic about the idea than Josie thought she would be.

"It's just the preliminary stage, so…" Josie finished the statement with a flick of a hand.

"That's great, though. You've always loved to stay busy. You started your first business when you were five, although that involved fleecing your mother."

"Charging you for pulling weeds wasn't a con. In case you don't know, child labor is evil. The least you could do was pay a fair wage."

"A dollar a weed in the eighties was fair?" Her mum shook a finger.

"If I remember correctly, you haggled me down to ten cents a weed."

"I had to!"

"That's what happens when you have a kid with an American. We're extremely capitalistic, and you guys, what with your socialized health care, just don't understand how the economy functions." Josie grinned.

"Yeah, yeah. The NHS system is terrible compared to health care in America. Everything is going so much better in the US."

"Hey. We're making America great again. Just saying." Josie made a *talk to the hand* motion.

Her mum laughed. "Back to your demand. Yes, you can

have the night off. When do I get to hear more about the prospect?"

"If it actually turns into something other than an idea, I'll be happy to share." Josie felt slightly ill for not filling in her mum because there wasn't anything to hide. Business. That was all there was to the dinner.

Then why did the thought give Josie warm, fuzzy feelings that had nothing to do with business?

CHAPTER TWELVE

Monday morning rolled around, and Harriet needed to escape her home after spending most of her weekend researching podcasting, which ended up with her ordering a microphone, downloading Audacity on her laptop, watching YouTube videos, and buying a handful of books on the subject.

She longed for fresh air, but trudging around in muddy fields didn't appeal to her. Not to mention, the wind howled and somehow smacked Harriet in the face no matter what direction she turned. Harriet scuttled her first plan, which was rambling through the woods, and headed to her favorite coffee shop on the square.

Sitting at a table, partially hidden in the corner, Harriet sipped a fancy cup of coffee, because why order a simple one in a shop specializing in different brews? Harriet plumbed her mind to put a finger on what was causing her to feel somewhat off since waking this morning. No, the mood had been plaguing her for days, if not since October. But what was the source?

The paper? The stress of keeping it afloat never seemed

to give her a moment's peace. Would starting a podcast be the best course of action?

On the con side, she noted: possible time waster, her fear of public speaking, and...?

She moved to the pro side: drive more people to *The Chronicles* website, could increase advertising revenue, increase more income funnels, help fill her time, and Josie.

Harriet shook her head. Why did she list Josie in the pro column? Clearly, Harriet needed more caffeine, and she made her way to the counter.

Back at the table, Harriet pondered other causes of her uneasiness. While she was relieved Camilla had left early Saturday morning after being summoned by work, Harriet couldn't shake the feeling of being lonely. Not solitude, which she enjoyed, especially when considering a new project, but loneliness.

She started to jot down possible podcast names but didn't get far. Not being able to think of words was a terrible sign for a journalist and would-be podcaster.

Unable to boot whatever weirdness was crowding her mind, Harriet closed her notebook and reached into her bag for a novel. If she couldn't think of words on her own, she'd bury her head into someone else's, not the things troubling her subconscious. Especially a certain someone with a dimple in the village. Because there was no way that person would consider the middle-aged Harriet as anything but a friend. Harriet was menopausal for Christ's sake. That fact alone, even if she was quite young for this particular stage in life, lumped her forever into the friend zone.

Harriet cracked open a paperback copy of *Pet Sematary* by Stephen King. She'd recently read an interview where the author stated it was his most disturbing book, so when she stumbled on a well-worn edition in a charity shop, she couldn't resist. Surely a novel that King found upsetting would keep her mind off the things she'd rather not focus on. Pointless longing was excruciating. There, she admitted it. Harriet wanted Josie, but she'd never have her. Best to accept that right then and there. Josie could be a friend and nothing more. Now it was time to move on. Pining over something that was never going to happen was useless. Harriet wasn't the type to waste time.

The door opened, and Harriet glanced up to see Eugenie enter, her hand upraised in greeting to a lone older woman sitting at a table near the front window. Harriet reflexively hunched down in her seat, holding the book higher to cover her face, not wanting to be seen, especially by Josie's mother.

Peeking over the top of the book, Harriet studied Eugenie's mate to see if she recognized the woman, but Harriet was still relatively new to Upper Chewford and hadn't been able to put a name to the majority of faces.

Eugenie tossed her arms around the stout woman, who'd lurched to her feet.

"It's so good to see you, Isabel," Eugenie said.

"It's been too long, Genie. Much, much too long. I brought your favorite chocolates."

Eugenie opened a paper bag. "Oh, I haven't had these in I don't know how long. How'd you get your hands on them?"

Harriet couldn't hear the answer, but she took this to mean the woman wasn't local or perhaps had been away awhile. Maybe an American friend or relative stopping for a visit. If that were the case, though, why hadn't the woman met Eugenie at the pub? Surely, she'd know Josie as well. Whatever the case, the two of them talked quietly, causing Harriet to strain a bit to make out the words.

While the two women chatted, catching up as if they were friends going back to infancy, Harriet silently moved her chair to the other side of her table, to keep her back to the women and allow her to hear better.

Why did she bother?

Harriet wasn't the type to eavesdrop on people, not even when on a job. She could never stoop to that level, although Josie seemed to think Harriet had back in London. Now, she was snooping on Josie's mum. Hopefully, Josie would never find out about this, and what exactly did Harriet expect to hear?

Feeling slightly ashamed, Harriet buried her nose in the book, doing her best to blot out their conversation. It wasn't right to listen in. Not in the slightest. If it wouldn't be too obvious, she'd move back to the other side of the table or even farther away. Harriet opted to close her ears to the best of her ability.

She succeeded for the most part, until Harriet heard Josie's name mentioned.

Isabel replied, "I didn't know she was back."

"For now, but I'm not sure for how long. That's the problem I want to talk about. I adore my daughter..." Eugenie didn't finish the sentence.

"But...?" Isabel prodded, relieving Harriet's mind some. Why was Harriet intent on knowing the answer as to whether or not Josie would be staying long term? And, Harriet had to admit, she was dying to know Eugenie's take on things. Could Eugenie be an ally down the road?

"I think my darling daughter thinks she's more suited for America or even London. She sees Upper Chewford as a sleepy village in the middle of nowhere. But I know in my heart of hearts, Josie belongs here. I even got her working in the pub to tie her down some."

"What brought her back?"

"Oh, she claims her life and career are over." Eugenie's voice indicated la-di-da. "You know how the young can be."

"Dramatic, yes. Give her another twenty years, and she'll understand life never works out the way you want it to."

"Tell me about it. I never thought I'd be widowed in my fifties." Eugenie's voice came out hard.

"Do you think she'll get fed up working in the pub and leave everything?"

"So far, she seems to like it, and she has a business meeting tomorrow night. Fingers crossed it pans out and makes her see how much the area has to offer a bright and ambitious woman."

Harriet sensed from the excitement in Eugenie's voice she was crossing her fingers and toes, but hearing the dinner described as business sliced through Harriet.

"Is she dating anyone?" Isabel asked.

"That's the other problem I need your help with. She claims she doesn't want a relationship." Harriet picked up on the exasperation in Eugenie's tone and words. "She's met Natalie and Helen, the two lesbians I know well enough in the area, but Josie hasn't shown any interest. Well, she gets along with Harry, but—"

A man and woman walked into the coffee shop, making a ruckus. Probably American tourists who had never mastered inside voices. The coffee machine fired up, making an obnoxious hissing sound, not allowing Harriet to eavesdrop on the part of the conversation she really wanted to hear.

Probably for the best, given Eugenie's not so secret revulsion toward Harriet. Was it just the ginger ads that hindered Harriet's cause? And, apparently, Josie's disinterest in relationships and Harriet in particular? Surely, that was what the *but* had meant.

The Americans took their coffees and marched back outside, looking as if they wanted to conquer the world.

"What kind of woman would Josie want?" Isabel asked.

"Want or need?" Eugenie asked.

"Uh-oh." There was a rustling sound. "Problems in that department?"

Eugenie let out a sigh only a mum could emit. "My daughter is brilliant, except when it comes to women."

"Surely, she's not that bad."

"She hasn't been able to find a woman who'll stick things out. Tits and ass are hard to resist. Relationships are hard, even good ones. I fear Josie's terrible luck with women has turned her off them for good. I worry what'll become of her when I go."

Harriet glanced down at the front of her shirt, taking in her lacking in one of Josie's must haves if Eugenie was to be believed.

Eugenie continued, "Do you know any eligible lesbians? Or bisexuals leaning toward women? I'm not picky, aside from wanting a woman from around here, not some Londoner. I'm hoping to find a selection to parade before my lovely daughter."

"Let me think."

How many women did Eugenie plan on tossing in Josie's path?

"What about Vera's daughter?" Eugenie sounded excited.

"Married."

Eugenie made a tsking sound. "Oh, that's a shame."

"I hear the woman is difficult, so she may not be permanently out of the running."

"Which one?" Eugenie asked.

"I don't remember."

"Guess it doesn't matter. Both are gay."

"Good point."

The women laughed.

Isabel shrieked, "I know!"

"Tell me more." Harriet could picture Eugenie making a *gimmie gimmie* motion with her fingers.

"My neighbor's sister's cousin is a lesbian!" Isabel slapped a hand on the tabletop.

"And available?"

"I think so. We should set them up on a blind date."

"I've been banned from that."

"Oh dear."

"We'll have to arrange a meeting." There was an evilness to Eugenie's pronunciation of *arrange*.

"How?"

"Family reunion?"

"They're not your family. Or mine."

"True." Eugenie was silent for a moment. "Maybe claim they won a raffle and their entire family won a free meal at The Golden Fleece."

"How do you ensure they bring the cousin?"

"Make it a stipulation one is an eligible lesbian."

The two cackled over this.

Finally, Isabel said, "We'll think of something."

"I have been considering setting up a dating game of sorts and holding it in the pub."

"That's an idea. With a mum like you, Josie won't be single for long. Not if you have your way."

CHAPTER THIRTEEN

JOSIE SPUN IN FRONT OF THE FULL-LENGTH mirror, checking out her outfit one final time before heading out for the night. It'd been the first outfit she'd attempted, ixnayed, and then tossed on again after the fourth, when she'd exclaimed, "Are you out of your mind? You can't wear that to Harry's." While she still wasn't certain about the choice, Josie also didn't have any other options, considering many of her things were still in America. Josie spun again and then sighed. "It's as good as it's going to get."

"Mum! Clive! I'm leaving." Josie did her best impression of a queenly parade wave.

Her uncle whistled.

Josie, feeling somewhat bolstered, asked, "That good?"

"Better than good. Smoking!" He touched her with a finger and then yanked it away as if it'd been singed.

"Thanks, Clive. Are you sure you can manage tonight?"

Clive's eyes panned the two patrons, and then he said in a dramatic voice, "It'll be rough, but I think I'll survive."

"Just checking. I know actual work isn't your thing." Josie waggled her brow.

He belly laughed, not seeming to take offense. "Please. I know you girls prefer doing everything and then saying I don't pitch in enough. We all have a role to play. Mine is punching bag."

"Is that right?" Josie shook her head. "It amazes me. The script you have in your head and how you cater to it." She circled a finger around her temple.

He placed a finger to his lips. "Don't blow it for me, or I'll take away your allowance."

"It's called a paycheck," Josie scoffed.

Her mum came through the front entrance with Winston right on her heels. "Are you wearing that?"

Josie looked down at the casual floral dress that clung to all the right spots. That was if Harry was actually interested in Josie. If she wasn't, the dress was a wasted effort. "What's wrong with it?"

"Nothing if your goal is to get lucky." Her mum's eyes bulged.

Josie mentally ticked the *that's my goal* column but said, "Oh, please. I just tossed this on without a second thought." She gripped the wine bottle in her left hand tighter.

"It's so low cut you don't have to strip to show all the goods. Just lean over." Her mum tsked.

"I'll keep that in mind," Josie said in a playful voice while making note of that nugget in case Harry needed an extra shove to act. All she had to do was accidentally drop something and then lean over to pick it up.

Winston, breathing heavily, plopped down on his bed, not bothering to shake off the rain drops. Josie smiled at the ham. Neither of the kittens were in sight. More than likely the pair were curled up on her mum's bed. British cats seemed to have the same knack as American ones, knowing which family member didn't like them as much and then annoying the shit out of said person.

Her mum crossed her arms. "I thought this was a business opportunity. If it's a date, say so. And, if it is a date, I doubt this is the look a respectable woman would appreciate. Having one Don Juan in the family is too many."

"Who said I wanted respectable?" Josie eased her jacket on, not wanting to wrinkle the dress too much. "Oh, wipe the shock off your face. It's just a business meeting," Josie said with as much conviction as she could summon. Because, really that was all it was, right? If Josie believed that, why was she wearing this outfit? How had Harry gotten her to this point? Not knowing what she truly wanted but also knowing what she wanted. It was fucking confusing.

"Are you interviewing to be an escort? If you hate tending bar that much, just tell me. We can put you in charge of the books or something. Don't stoop to this level." Her mum made erratic motions in the air with a finger.

"Did you just call me a sex worker?" Josie tried to sound as if she were joking, but the comment had struck a nerve. Was the dress too much? Would it turn off Harry, who was a reserved Brit?

Her mum looked Josie up and down, her eyes landing uncomfortably again on Josie's rack. The silence was damning.

Josie did her best to shake it off and kissed her mum's forehead. "Please stop worrying about me. I know what I'm doing." Did she?

"Never going to happen. I'm a mother. There's no expiration on the worrying side of things."

"Do what you need to do." Josie waved bye, not wanting to waste another second, or she'd be late.

Clive hollered from behind the bar, "Have fun!"

Her mum harrumphed but said, "No matter what, I love you."

Did that mean even if Josie were a call girl? The sentiment was nice, but the jab not so much.

Josie opened her umbrella. She shivered slightly, not expecting it to be this chilly, even if it was nearly winter. She crossed the footbridge, the very one where she'd spied Harry on the first night they'd met. Was Josie wrong in thinking they'd shared a moment? Although there had been a fair distance between them, something had happened, hadn't it? As if the world had stopped for the moment and only the two of them mattered.

Josie had to laugh at this thought. When had she turned into this woman? The romantic type that believed in things like fate and soul mates? She'd never much trifled with romance on any level in the past, always too focused on her career. Now that it was dead, was she trying to replace the void with a relationship? Or was there more to it? Was Josie ready to find the one? Oh God, she was sounding like her mum. But…?

Josie followed the path on the far side of the shallow river, past the old stone mill with a red brick chimney, making it stand out from all the yellow stone, and then turned onto Nevern Place.

Her eyes noted each of the attached residences, as she occasionally glanced down to follow Harry's written directions to a T, the paper getting damp. She was supposed to go by a house with a bright blue door and rose garden. Then a cottage covered with vines. When Josie approached Harry's address, she stopped to compare it to the rest on the street. It stood out for one particular reason. The lack of living plants. Every other abode had colorful gardens, the bushes bursting with autumn colors. Harry had a collection of various bushes in different stages, from yellowing to beyond dead. Josie brushed a hand to one of them, all the leaves snapping from the branches. How was it possible when the English weather did most of the work, raining the majority of the time?

Josie had to smile, though, since it seemed to fit Harry's personality. Passionate but also somewhat ignorant of details. What Harry needed was a woman like Josie who excelled in the little details most ignored, while Harry continued her quest to conquer the world, telling one human story at a time.

Holy moly.

Josie placed a hand to her forehead. Where in the fuck did that come from? Like she wanted to be a lesbian house-wife from the 1950s, even if that really wasn't a thing. At least, not openly.

Josie shook her head as if wanting to dislodge the idea from her mind. Checking her dress one last time and using the camera on her phone to ensure the rain hadn't caused her mascara to run, she finally knocked on Harriet's crimson door.

Seconds later, Harry opened it, her jaw momentarily dropping, before she said, "Hi, Josie."

Harry's shyness was so loveable. Josie wanted to take the woman into her arms and hold her close. Josie sensed Harry was the type who'd love with her whole heart. Treat Josie like a woman. An equal. Companion. Not as a neces-sary piece to complete some preconceived notion of what happiness consisted of according to "expert" opinions. Those had been the types Josie had encountered. Nothing killed romance more than expectations. Harry's eyes conveyed she understood everything running through Josie's mind, and she agreed.

Fuck it. Josie wanted the *fifties housewife* life with Harry. For Christ's sake, they hadn't even kissed yet. How could Josie feel this strongly about the woman standing in front of her? It hit Josie. How much she had given up chasing success in her career, only to be tossed out over something that wasn't her fault and had been entirely out of her control. Josie was almost forty and hadn't experienced a moment like this. Being completely in tune with another human being. Maybe her mum was right. It was time for Josie to settle down, and the way Harry stared deeply into Josie's eyes—they belonged to each other. Now, how to convince the aloof Harry of that?

CHAPTER FOURTEEN

"Hi, Harry." Josie's broad smile made Harriet's heart take flight like she'd just dived off a platform heading straight for the deepest part of the ocean, without so much as a life vest. It exhilarated and terrified her all at once. Every other part of Harriet's body shut down, including her brain and legs.

"You going to let me in?" Josie pointed to Harriet, who was literally blocking the entrance.

Harriet's senses slowly returned. "Oh, sorry." She stepped out of the way, overcorrecting, allowing Josie way more room than was necessary, as if Josie had some contagious disease and Harriet didn't want to even breathe the same air. It was a feat, given the cramped feeling of Harriet's two-bedroom cottage built centuries before humans reached present-day height and weight. By the time Harriet grasped her second mistake in under a minute, she wasn't sure how to correct course without drawing even more attention to her blunders.

Josie placed her umbrella in the stand right inside the door of the cottage, and then seemed at a loss for what to do or say next. Harriet dropped her gaze out of fear. If she looked into Josie's emerald eyes right then, she might do something impulsive. Like kiss Josie. Or let out a wolf whistle, which was the first time in four decades Harriet had ever felt that impulse. Then she said something incredibly stupid. "Did you know in France a man can be fined for wolf whistling at a woman?"

"No, I didn't. How much is the fine?"

"If I remember correctly, more than seven hundred euros."

Josie let out a whistle. "Are you going to fine me?"

"I'll let this one slide."

"Too bad, sometimes punishment can be nice."

Harriet cleared her throat.

"I'm curious. Why'd you bring up that factoid right now?" Josie causally glanced down at her dress as if she knew exactly why Harriet had wolf whistles on the mind.

"I was just reading about it." Harriet stared at the jackets on the door behind Josie's head.

"I brought a bottle of red. I hope that's okay." Josie held up the bottle.

"Red works."

Josie laughed, looking at the bottle like it had cracked a joke. "Good. I really hate uncooperative wines."

Harriet joined in on the laughter. "Sorry. That was a stupid thing to say. Kinda like saying it was stupid to say that. No need to point it out. I'm on a roll." Luckily, Harriet stopped herself from saying the truth as to why she mentioned the French fine.

"Not stupid at all. I love a woman who speaks her mind, no matter what. And, usually you excel with using as few words as possible. Brevity is a speechwriter's best friend. I can't tell you how many times I wanted to strangle my politician for going off script." Josie acted out wringing someone's neck.

"I thought you gave it up."

"Good point. But it's a useful tool to carry on through life." Josie offered an ambiguous smile. "It smells wonderful. I'm assuming that's dinner cooking."

Confused by the sudden switch of topics, Harry clarified, "Yes. I'm making a chicken dish from one of Nigella's books. I can't remember which one, now."

"The dish or book?"

"Book."

"That's a relief. I'd be worried if you didn't remember much about prepping the meal."

They still stood in the front area of Harriet's cottage, which was actually the living room. "Let me help you with your jacket."

Josie turned around, allowing Harriet to remove the article. Harriet wanted to place a delicate kiss on the back of Josie's neck, opting instead to clear her throat, yet again, as a preemptive measure. Hanging the coat on one of the kitschy birdhouse hooks on the back of the door, Harriet placed her arms behind her back, looking subservient, but how else to stop herself from reaching for Josie? What was wrong with Harriet this evening? Josie was only there to talk about podcasts, not for Harriet to grope her.

Josie's eyes swept over the space. "Wow. It feels like I'm stepping back in time." She continued taking everything in, nodding with each observation. The oak-beamed ceiling, plaid couch, two modest bookshelves flanking the exposed Cotswold stone around the free-standing black fireplace, which Harriet had lit to add to the quaint atmosphere.

"I had hoped for a pleasant evening so we could have drinks outside in the garden. Yesterday was lovely. Only needed a lightweight jumper. Today not so much. Typical unpredictable English weather. Some days you can experience all four seasons in twenty-four hours." Why couldn't Harriet stop babbling about the weather?

"The garden would have been lovely, but there's something special about a roaring fire. Also, I'm trying to resist the urge to smoke. I promised my mum." Josie edged farther into the room. "Oh, wow, I haven't read her comic strip in ages." She picked up *The Essential Dykes to Watch Out For* by Alison Bechdel.

"Camilla gave me that for my birthday."

"When is it?"

"October twenty-seventh."

"That was the day I arrived here."

"That's right. I remember Clive mentioning you that night in the pub."

"I'm sad I missed my chance to buy you a birthday drink."

Harriet was about to say there was always next year, but that seemed to put too much pressure on a new acquaintance. Her eyes once again took in Josie's dress, which, in the full light of the room, showed how revealing it was, delightfully so. Harriet cleared her throat again. Shit. Would Josie think Harry had a cold, wrecking any chance for a good night kiss? "Would you like a glass of wine?"

"I would. Before that, though, is it possible for a tour? I love cottages like this and dream of someday living in one of my own."

If that were true, why was Eugenie so concerned about Josie leaving the village? Or was Josie simply being polite? Perhaps Josie wanted one in the States. Did they have cottages like this there? "Of course." Harriet motioned for Josie to enter the kitchen.

"I adore the pale-yellow walls," Josie exclaimed. "Oh, you've already set the table. The plates have polka dots."

She picked one up, running a hand over them. "So cute." Josie replaced the plate and then gave Harriet's arm a quick squeeze, reigniting the frisson Harriet experienced the first night on the bridge when she'd spied Josie outside the pub talking to Clive.

"The office slash guest room is right over there." Harriet pointed to a room off to the side. "And the bedroom is upstairs..." Harriet's voice trailed off, unsure if she should actually take Josie there.

"The bedroom is the most important room of the house."

"I thought the kitchen was."

"That's where people congregate during dinner parties. At least, that's how it works in the US. But the bedroom shows a person's true personality." Josie's voice connected with Harriet in a way it shouldn't. Harriet couldn't dislodge the idea that Josie, the American, was simply being overly friendly. Like when Josie had flirted with Natalie in the pub. There was absolutely no way someone as beautiful as Josie was interested in Harriet. The idea was preposterous. Beautiful redheads simply didn't come on to Harriet, and Josie had stated unequivocally that she was not in the market for a wife or what have you.

"Is that right?" Harriet asked, unable to come up with a clever response.

"Unless, of course, you don't want me to see the goods?" Josie winked.

"Wouldn't deny you that." Harriet's stomach plummeted. Would Josie think that too much?

"Good to know."

Much relieved, Harriet smiled, but her top lip caught on her bone-dry teeth. Did it look more like a *back off* snarl? "Shall we?" She motioned to the stairs.

Josie took the lead, while Harriet brought up the rear.

God, Josie's dress hugged all the right spots from this angle as well. Harriet did her best to dial back the heat level surging through her.

"Love the robin's-egg blue walls." Josie stood in the middle of Harriet's bedroom, surveying the quilted bed, chest of drawers, and black-and-white photos of the area.

"Do you?" Harriet placed a finger on her chin. "I can't tell if I like the color or not."

"Oh, it's a like. A strong like." Josie stared deeply into Harriet's eyes. "Not what I was expecting at all."

"I can't take the credit. This is my uncle's place. He needed a caretaker, and I needed a place to live after the divorce."

"Good." Josie smiled shyly. "I mean, you won't paint them. I could get used to spending time here."

Harriet laughed nervously. What did Josie mean by that? Harriet did what she usually did during these situations. She rambled. "I'd love to buy a place. Have more control. Bigger. I'd like an extra room. Maybe two. As it is, Camilla's always bunking in my office every other weekend, or so it seems." So much for brevity.

"Or sleeping with my uncle."

"Yes, there's that." Harriet shifted on her feet, unsure how to handle Josie's American bluntness when it came to certain subjects. "Wine. You ready? We should go down. To the kitchen. Not…" Harriet's voice died as the heat intensified in her cheeks. And other places. Damn. It should be illegal for women like Josie to wear dresses like this unless the intention was to get into Harriet's bed. Which surely that wasn't Josie's goal. Josie was so out of Harriet's league it was laughable to even think Josie put on the dress for any reason other than she needed an outfit to wear.

CHAPTER FIFTEEN

"YES, WINE SOUNDS GOOD." JOSIE BEGAN THE trek back downstairs, or to earth rather. She struggled getting a read on Harry. There were flashes in Harry's eyes that clearly indicated Harry was chomping at the bit. Okay, maybe that wasn't the best way to put it, but the hot and cold were doing Josie's head in. One minute, Harry seemed beyond interested. The next it morphed into indifference as if Josie wasn't even in the room.

Did Harriet follow a weird mantra like *Keep Calm and Don't Fornicate*? Was that why she secreted herself in Upper Chewford? To avoid temptations of the female variety? If that were the case, how was Josie to penetrate Harry's *stiff upper lip* reserve? And damn, Harry's lips were so very tempting: pink and plump. As if waiting for Josie to press hers against them.

Josie spied a notebook on the kitchen counter and glanced at Harry's writing. "Chain stitches and Anne Frank's house. That's a curious pairing."

"Now who's the nosy one? After all your cracks about

journalists, here you are in my home, snooping." Harry wore the most beautiful smile.

"I wasn't exactly prying. It's right here out in the open." Josie knew that was a weak defense. "Can I ask how the two are related?"

"I was brainstorming ideas for the podcast. Do you know about chain stitches?"

"Not at all."

"It's a type of stitch that loops together, making it somewhat stronger, but if you pull a thread, it comes apart quickly. They use it on certain bags to close them, but also to make it easy for people to open." Harry made a ripping motion with her hand.

"Like pet food bags."

"Exactly. Whenever I think of how humans are connected, I think of chain stitches. We can feel connected, but when someone pulls a thread, like fomenting racism, we easily break apart." Harry shrugged bashfully. "I was considering using that as the title of the podcast, but I'm not sure it would work."

"And the connection to Anne Frank's house?" Josie had to admit she was curious where Harry would take this.

"Don't fear. I'm not considering that as a title. I was thinking of times when recordings and videos truly moved me. A few years ago, I was in Amsterdam and made myself go to the house. I'd avoided it in the past because, usually, I was there on holiday, and it's not the most cheerful place.

"But I'm glad I went. It's one of those experiences that impacts your very being. What really hit me, though, wasn't the house itself, but the museum portion. There were videos with testimonials, and some of them were hard to watch. I was there with Alice, who wasn't the most compassionate, so I slipped into the bathroom for a quiet moment. In the stall, I heard others sniffling and blowing their noses. If only everyone could visit and be moved by Anne Frank's story, I think humanity would be slightly better off. Momentarily, at least."

"Is that your goal?"

"Saving humanity?" Harry laughed. "I'm not that ambitious or insane, but I do think it's possible to get some people to see eye to eye. It's worth a try."

"I know you're on the fence about the podcast, but if you speak like that, you will move some people." Josie placed her hand on Harry's shoulder.

"You think so?"

"You moved me."

"Yes, but you're receptive to my ideas."

What exactly did that mean? The usually inquisitive Josie clammed up at the worst possible time, and her hand fell from Harry.

Harry stepped away and poured the wine she'd decanted. "I'll serve yours with dinner. I promise."

Josie took the glass, wanting to get the playfulness back into the night. "Trying to get me drunk?"

The color drained from Harry's face, to the point Josie started to wonder if it were possible to kill a proper British woman with inappropriate American comments.

"Hey. I was kidding. I promise."

"I..." Harriet looked to Josie's bottle sitting on the kitchen counter. "I should have thought of that. You bringing a bottle."

"Please, Harry. Don't give it a second thought. The worse thing that can happen is we wait for a nice evening for us to enjoy my bottle together." Josie held her wineglass strategically between her breasts, delighting in Harry taking notice, before Josie finished the thought, "Outside."

"You'd have to put up with me again."

"Much worse things can happen in life. I can probably

rattle off five that had already occurred in my life without much thought."

"Such as? As you know, I like to collect stories." Harry seemed genuinely interested.

"Let's see. In grad school, I was stung by a bee on the back of my right hand." Josie tapped the spot on her hand, in the middle of the fingers and wrist. "As it turned out, I'm allergic to bees. Not the best way to find out. After going to the health center on campus, where they placed a fizzy tablet on my tongue to immediately get into my bloodstream, they sent me home with the advice to get some rest.

"Unfortunately, that weekend, I couldn't take time off because I was in grad school." Josie shrugged as if saying, *American*. "The pain was excruciating, so I kept an ice pack on it for the weekend, while I crammed for a test in one of my classes." Josie pondered a second, studying the ceiling. "I can't remember which class, which goes to show how important it was in the long run. Anyway, on Sunday morning, I decided not to use the ice bag because I was tired of the ice melting, getting my notes all wet." Josie picked up on a flicker in Harry's eyes at the mention of wet and had to wonder why. Surely, Harry's mind hadn't gone that route, imagining Josie turned on. "Good thing I did, because I noticed two red streaks moving up my arm."

Josie set her glass down on the table, held out her arm, palm up, and traced where the streaks had been. "Moving up from my wrist and, at the time, they were almost halfway to my elbow. I called my doctor, who instructed me to get to the hospital right away, before the streaks reached my lymph nodes, which if I remember correctly, would kick the infection into high gear, spreading rapidly throughout my body, requiring what could turn out to be a rather long hospital stay to get it under control."

"Wow. What happened?" Harry shifted on her feet. "I mean, I know you didn't die"—she pointed to Josie—"but were you quite ill?"

"For a few days, but I didn't have to stay overnight in the hospital at all. I haven't gotten to the bad part yet, though."

"What's worse than having to rush to hospital?"

"I love how you guys say *to hospital*, not to *the* hospital. Another one of those brevity things." Josie glanced downward and then slowly raised her gaze to meet Harry's. "On the way there, my girlfriend at the time had been staying at my apartment to take care of me." Josie rolled her eyes. "However, when I really needed her to act, she didn't drive directly to the hospital, instead stopping at Burger King since she was starving and assumed there'd be a long wait at the hospital."

Harriet's eyes grew three times as large. "You're joking."

"Nope. I started yelling at her as I watched the redness move, or so I imagined. We ended up having a screaming match in her car. She got so worked up, she four-wheeled over the curb out of the drive-through line, skidded to a stop at the entrance of the ER, and then drove off in a huff once I got out of the vehicle."

"I can't believe that. Who does that?"

"Andrea."

"Andrea doesn't rank high in my book."

"Nor mine. She did come back hours later to pick me up."

"Hours after you were treated?"

"Oh, no. It took that long in the ER. She'd been right about that part."

"Still doesn't make it right. Did she offer an apology?"

Harry's expression continued to harden, making it clear what she truly thought of Andrea.

"Yes. She was really great at apologies. It's part of the reason why we lasted as long as we did."

"Which was how long, exactly?" Harry narrowed her eyes.

"Two years."

Harry's eyes bugged out yet again and not in a good way. Not like they did when Josie had shown off her ta-tas. This was more out of disgust. But was it contempt for Andrea or Josie? For both?

"It's kinda known by my friends and family that I have terrible luck in the female department," Josie explained in a tiny voice, realizing her mistake. This was the type of story not to be shared, especially not with the likes of Harry, because Josie didn't come across that well. Andrea had treated her abominably, and Josie had put up with it for too long. And to the best of Josie's recollection, she hadn't shared this one with anybody.

"I see," Harriet said in an uncomprehending tone.

Josie wanted to give herself a swift kick in the ass, but failed when trying to think of a way to repair the damage. Another thought struck Josie. Did Harriet think Josie had already dumped her into the bad luck category? Or that Josie wasn't interested and that was why she'd shared this story, because Josie wasn't trying to impress Harry?

"We should eat," Harry turned her back to attend to the stove.

CHAPTER SIXTEEN

"WOULD IT BE OKAY FOR ME TO POWDER MY nose?" Josie asked.

Harriet nodded. "The bathroom is to the right of my office. Just through the hallway."

Josie's footfalls grew fainter, and the door closed.

Harriet heaved a sigh, focusing on getting dinner on the plates. It was difficult to banish Eugenie's words, echoed by Josie just now, that Josie had terrible taste in women. If Josie had been flirting with Harriet earlier, what opinion did Josie actually have of Harriet? If Josie thought Harriet had a bad-girl streak buried deep within, what would happen when Josie discovered she was so very wrong?

Also, what did Josie's taste in women say about her? That she allowed herself to be treated in such a way? Albeit, the bee sting incident occurred presumably when Josie was in her early twenties. Before the frontal lobe was fully developed. Yet, her grandfather's words about people not changing, but becoming more like themselves over the years rang through her ears.

There was also the possibility that Josie hadn't been

flirting with Harriet at all and shared the story because they were becoming mates and nothing more.

How was it possible the Josie Harriet knew, the one who exuded strength and determination, had such a blind spot about women in her life? Harriet wanted to take Josie into her arms and tell her everything would be okay. It was okay to be vulnerable and to need a decent person by her side. Was it presumptuous to think Harriet could be the woman to bring Josie fully into her own? To give her the nudge to want it all? Because Harriet knew Josie was the one who could help Harriet reach happiness. Together they could have it all. Deep down, Harriet believed that.

Harriet slipped on two extra-thick oven mitts. The chicken thighs were crisp on top, and the veg medley looked mouthwateringly good. "Perfect." Harriet started to ease the tray out—

"What can I help with?"

Not expecting Josie back so soon, Harriet fumbled the dish.

Josie reached out to save the meal from crashing to the floor. "Fuck, that's hot!"

Harriet dropped the tray, which somehow flipped over, upsetting the contents, some peas rolling here and there. "Are you okay?"

Josie's eyes were glued to the ruined dinner splattered on the braided-straw rug in the middle of the kitchen. "I'm fine. Dinner, not so much." She pointed to the destruction.

"Let me see your hand." Harriet reached for Josie's hand.

"Really, Harry, it's fine. I'm so sorry about your meal."

"It's just food. You're more important to me."

"But I ruined all of your hard work." Josie's voice quivered some.

"Josie, please. Let me look at your hand," Harriet spoke softly.

Josie cradled it close to her stomach.

Harriet tried to put Josie at ease by saying, "I'm not Andrea."

"What?" Josie scrunched her face.

"Do you need a doctor? Shall I get my car?"

Josie finally held out her hand. "I don't think so. It burns, but I'm pretty sure it's not hospital worthy."

Harriet inspected Josie's singed fingertips. "Let me run cold water—no, I remember reading cool water is best." Harriet's brain stumbled as she tried to figure out what qualified as cold and cool.

"But your beautiful dinner is all over the floor." Josie's gaze cast back to the disaster at their feet. "I ruined everything."

"No, you didn't." Harriet flipped on the water, testing it on herself. That didn't seem too cold. "I don't give a damn about the dinner. If you're experiencing any pain or discomfort, let me take care of you. Please."

Josie allowed Harriet to guide her hand under the stream of water. "Oh, that does feel better. Why do burns have to—?"

"Burn?" Harriet stared into Josie's eyes.

"Yes. That." Josie stared back.

"They're annoying like that. Living up to their potential." Now, why had Harriet said the last part? Wanting to avoid Josie's penetrating gaze, Harriet consulted a webpage on her phone. "It says here to run cool water on it for twenty minutes."

"Twenty!"

Harriet nodded, setting a timer on her phone. "Yes. Then we should wash it with mild soap and water." Harriet glanced up. "What constitutes mild soap?"

Josie shrugged.

Harriet googled it. "Oh. My face wash falls into the category. I'll be right back. Or do you want me to stay?" Harriet appraised the fingers again.

Josie laughed. "I think I'll survive."

"Are you sure?"

Josie gave Harriet an odd expression that could be interpreted fifty different ways, causing Harriet's brain to sputter with indecision.

After a second too long, Harriet finally said, "As long as you're sure."

Josie nodded, her expression deepening but not becoming clearer.

Without another word, Harriet dashed to the bathroom in search of soap, antibiotic ointment, and a sterile bandage. All of which she had on hand.

She was back in the kitchen within moments, only to discover Josie trying to clean up the mess. "What are you doing?"

"Cleaning." Josie had a chicken thigh skewered on a fork.

"No, you don't." Harriet took the fork from Josie and flipped the water back on. "I insist you let me take care of you."

"Are you always this nice?"

Harriet cringed. One of Alice's parting statements had been Harriet was too nice, and it had taken Alice years to realize nice girls lacked the passion needed to sustain a long-term relationship. Shoving this aside, Harriet replaced Josie's hand under the water.

Josie rested her head on Harriet's shoulder. "Will you at least let me order something for dinner?"

"That's not necessary. I may have something in the freezer that'll do."

"But—"

"Josie, really. It's not a big deal." Harriet hadn't meant to snap, but she couldn't comprehend why Josie was fighting her about taking care of the burn.

Josie pressed her lips together.

Harriet wanted to bang her head against the wall.

It wasn't only the dinner that had been destroyed but everything.

CHAPTER SEVENTEEN

"HAS IT BEEN TWENTY MINUTES YET?" JOSIE asked. Surprisingly, holding her hand under the water was becoming quite exhausting.

"Not even five." Harry tapped her phone and showed Josie the screen: 16:14. And counting down in mind-numbing slowness.

"Seriously, my fingers are fine. Also, isn't this wasteful." Josie watched the water circle the drain.

"You still have fifteen minutes, and right now, you're my concern, not my environmental footprint." Harry's smile was sweet and sexy.

Suppressing an *I want you to jump my bones* growl, Josie tried to focus her mind on something else. But, thoughts of the woman standing intoxicatingly close to her made it impossible. How could Harry come across as both sweet and sexy? Josie had always believed in an either/or world. Was it possible to have it all? Or would Harry's true colors come to the fore at a trickle? Should Josie worry that she told the bee sting story to a journalist? She wanted to believe Harry wasn't the type to betray her. Was she being too trusting? At the moment, with Harry standing so close, Josie could feel Harry's body heat. "This is nice."

"What? Burning your fingers?"

"Not that part. You taking care of me. It's just nice." Josie shrugged, because her inner thoughts were hard to explain to herself let alone to Harry.

"Of course, I care. You're a guest in my home, and I burned you."

"For the record, the pan burned me. Not you." The words *guest in my home* ping-ponged in Josie's head. Was that the sole reason for Harry's TLC? Was she simply concerned about getting sued? Were Brits as litigious as Americans? Josie remembered breaking her arm when she fell out of her best friend's tree. Her friend's mom had called Josie's mum asking if they planned on suing. Eugenie had been floored and assured the woman she had no intention of doing that, saying, "Kids will be kids."

Harry pressed, "I was the idiot who dropped the pan."

"Because I startled you." Now, Josie tried to determine if Harry was just being British. Helping because that was what a proper Brit would do. Meaning, Harry didn't feel a connection with Josie, because why would she? Especially after the Andrea story. Josie wanted to bonk her head, but she kept her hand under the water.

Harry stood closer to Josie. "Are you really okay?" Her voice was caring and compassionate, confusing the heck out of Josie.

Josie swallowed a lump in her throat. "Yeah."

"Let me get you something for the pain." Harriet disappeared before Josie could say a word.

Josie wasn't in much pain, or any at all, now. Lust. Pure animal need. What would Harry do if Josie shoved her against the pale-yellow wall and kissed Harry? Hard. Maybe slow to start, but deepening it.

Harry returned. "Do you have any allergies, aside from bees that is?"

"Nope." Josie licked her lips, eyeing Harry's mouth, catching a glimpse of her pink tongue.

"You're being very brave," Harry said.

"Not really." Considering Josie was terrified to make the first move or to even say, *Hey, do you feel this connection between us, or am I imagining things?* Josie was nowhere in the brave zone. Coward. That was more like it, because if she made a move and Harry shot her down, it would crush Josie.

Harry placed two white tablets in Josie's good hand, followed by a glass of water after Josie popped the pills into her mouth.

After drinking the water, Josie blurted, "Chinese!"

Harry looked over her shoulder. "Where?"

Josie laughed. "For dinner. Let's order Chinese."

"Oh. That makes much more sense." Harry's cheeks tinged pink.

"You really are adorable. You know that?" Josie's face inched closer to Harry's.

Harry locked her eyes onto Josie's.

Neither of them moved or said anything.

Josie's stomach grumbled.

Harry smiled. "I'll order from my favorite place, or do you have a preference?"

"I trust you, Harry," Josie said with meaning.

Harry didn't break eye contact for several ticks according to the noisy, but adorable sheep pendulum clock, which had a tail that moved side to side, on the kitchen wall.

To Josie, so much more had been conveyed during those silent moments than all evening. For one thing, Josie was sure, beyond a doubt, that Harry did feel the connection between them. Also, like Josie, Harry was scared to make a move. The latter may have been discouraging, aside from the feeling Josie suspected Harry was the type to figure things out and wouldn't let a little thing like fear keep them apart. Not in the long term. They were both in it to win it. Josie wanted to do a happy dance, but she contained herself. First, she needed to survive the rest of the evening without inflicting more damage. Then, she needed to kiss Harry. Oh God, she really wanted to kiss the serious but sweet and fucking sexy woman.

CHAPTER EIGHTEEN

Two Friday nights after having Josie over, Harriet, with Camilla in tow, arrived at The Golden Fleece a little after eight. Work had kept Harriet from the pub the past week, and before that, when she stopped by, Josie had been too busy to say more than hi. Constantly thinking about Josie was probably why Harriet had to work late hours to get everything done. Too much daydreaming about emerald eyes and a dimple.

Clive drifted over to them before they could reach the bar. "What can I get you lovely ladies?"

"My usual." Camilla linked her arm through Clive's, and Harriet was in the path of Beatrice's menacing glare at Cam.

Harriet took a tiny step to the right to be out of the line of fire.

"Of course, love." He gently patted Camilla's hand. "Harry?"

Harriet looked at Josie, who was deep in conversation with a stunning and much younger woman Harriet didn't recognize, but she remembered Eugenie's mission of parading all available women for Josie to take her pick. "Tell you what? I'm not sure what I want yet. Why don't I get this round?"

The two accepted the offer faster than Harriet anticipated, ditching her in the middle of the pub.

When Josie met her eye, Harriet thought she detected an ounce of happiness in Josie's expression, but she returned her attention to the woman.

When Harriet reached the bar, Eugenie pounced. "What can I get you, Harry?"

"Uh." She looked to Josie.

"We've made the first batch of mulled wine," Eugenie offered in a tone that said, *Take that or nothing at all.*

"Sure. And two Stellas." Again, Harriet tried to engage Josie's eye.

"Go have a seat with Clive and your cousin. I'll bring the drinks out in two shakes." Eugenie's expression was even bossier than her tone.

Harriet, shoulders slumped, made her way past Beatrice whose stink eye intensity had been significantly upped, making the hair on Harriet's forearms stand on end, and Harriet heard the *Psycho* soundtrack play in her mind. She sat at the table with Clive and Camilla, but the two had their heads huddled together, not taking much notice of Harriet. She pulled out her phone and started reading a *Guardian* article about the Brexit mess, but her mind wandered. She casually glanced in Josie's direction to see Josie's head tilted back, laughing. The pretty woman's shoulders also bucked up and down as she laughed along with Josie, grating on Harriet's nerves. Could she somehow focus Beatrice's laser-like stare from hell to intimidate the other woman?

"Here you go, Harry." Eugenie placed a mulled wine and a mince pie on a small chipped white plate in front of Harriet.

"My feet are killing me tonight." Eugenie sat down across from Harriet, blocking her view of Josie. "I've been thinking. You haven't interviewed Agnes about her safaris in Africa for your paper. She's here tonight. You should ask her to tell you everything."

Before Harriet could explain this wasn't the right atmosphere for an interview, Eugenie was waving Agnes over. Surprised Eugenie beckoned Agnes like a servant, Harriet didn't know what to do. She jumped to her feet, but she was too late.

"Harry wants to interview you. Isn't that nice?" Eugenie's sickly-sweet, but victorious, smile was like a punch to Harriet's chin.

Josie's mum didn't want Harriet to interact with Josie. Period. Harriet had put a permanent stop to the ginger ads, making her wonder if Eugenie's dislike originated from a different source. Or was Eugenie the type to hold a grudge for decades? This wasn't good news. Not one bit.

"Really?" Agnes beamed.

"Yes." Harriet still stood. "When would be a good time for us to meet? We'd need a chunk of time and some quiet." Harriet hoped the last part wasn't overly obvious. She was already on Eugenie's naughty list and didn't want to incur even more wrath.

"It's not too loud in here tonight," Eugenie countered, but as luck would have it, a group of tourists started singing a bawdy rendition of "Santa Claus is Coming to Town," waving their pints in the air, *German beer-hall* style.

It may have been the first time Harriet was grateful for drunk and obnoxious American tourists.

Agnes tutted, but her face was still aglow with the interview prospect. "Would Monday at my cottage work?"

"Monday is perfect!" Harriet wanted to kiss Agnes.

Eugenie's deep inhalation and tight smile made *Psycho* music play once again in Harriet's head.

"I should get back to work." Eugenie lumbered to her feet.

"Thanks for your help. Agnes will be the perfect subject for a concept I'm working on," Harriet said in hopes to ease some of Eugenie's dislike, but the comment seemed to put Eugenie even more on edge.

Agnes retook her seat, picking up a copy of *Sense and Sensibility*.

Josie still chatted with the mysterious woman, but Josie went out of her way to wave at Harriet. There was that dimple again. Harriet could sit for hours to catch glimpses of the adorable depression in Josie's cheek.

Harriet gulped the mulled wine, and when Eugenie was ambushed by the singing Americans for another round, Harriet made her move.

"I was wondering if you were going to say hi." Josie smiled.

Harriet's insides went gooey.

The woman checked her phone. "Oh, I gotta run. I'll see you on Sunday, Josie."

Josie waved bye. "Do you need another mulled wine?"

"Gin and tonic please." Harriet sat on the stool the woman had vacated, with no intention of budging from the spot the rest of the evening just in case other beautiful women had their sights on making plans with Josie. "Your mum helped me set up an interview with Agnes."

"Did she?" Josie prepped Harriet's drink, adding extra gin.

"How's the vibe been here since the ginger kitties arrived?"

Josie's eyes panned the pub. "It's been a bit more tense. And the women involved have taken their suggestive wardrobe choices to a whole new level."

Harriet's gaze landed on Celia, who had a Christmas jumper on with Mrs. Claus doing a pole-dance routine. "I see that." However, Celia was talking with two men in their fifties and not paying Clive any attention.

Josie served Harriet her drink and then leaned on the bar. "Clive seems to have taken a fancy to your cousin. She's the only woman he actually talks to like he enjoys her company. Does she like Clive?"

Harriet scouted over her shoulder and saw Camilla's hand tenderly placed on Clive's arm. "I think so. She doesn't like to discuss feelings, but she keeps coming back, and I know for certain it's not to see me."

"They're kinda cute together. Clive, the simple village guy. Your cousin, the snooty Londoner. It's like watching a real life sappy *against the odds* Hallmark Christmas movie."

"You think so?" Harriet asked, wondering if Josie thought Harriet a snooty Londoner like Cam.

"Josie? Can you help me?" Eugenie waved her daughter over.

Josie straightened. "Be right back."

That turned out not to be the case. Every time there was a chance for Josie to break free, either someone approached the bar, or Eugenie sent Josie off on an errand, although Josie made eye contact with Harriet as much as possible. And there was a lot of smiling, forcing Harriet to cross her legs. How could a simple dimple have that kind of effect on her?

Around ten-thirty, Harriet noticed Clive and Camilla

were nowhere to be found. The Americans had left. Agnes tucked her book into her handbag, her eyes lingering on the snoozing William for several moments before she left. Winston raised his head momentarily before he settled back down.

"Whatcha thinking?" Josie leaned on her forearms, giving Harriet a peek down her shirt.

"Why Winston is named Winston."

Josie cocked her head. "What should he be named?"

"Jason."

Josie looked at the slumbering bulldog and laughed. "He doesn't look anything like a Jason. Have you ever met a dog named that?"

"No, but it goes with the name of the pub."

Josie started to speak, but Eugenie called her back over. "I'm getting the feeling she doesn't want us to talk."

Harriet was certain that was the case but didn't confirm or deny. "I should head back to my place."

"So soon?"

Harriet laughed. "It's well after this old lady's bedtime." Her words sunk in, and Harriet was convinced some evil force had made her utter them.

Josie laughed. "You are many things, but you are not an old lady. Hopefully, I'll see you tomorrow. Maybe I'll bump into you when I'm running or at the café gorging on your fave: black pudding." She left.

Harriet made the trek home, the low-hanging clouds seeming to press down on Harriet's shoulders. When she reached the middle of the bridge, the moon made a brief appearance, and Harriet gazed at the man's image, silently asking if she was being silly or if there was something between her and Josie. A crack of wind slapped Harriet across the face, and the moon slid behind more clouds. Harriet decided it was a sign. Tomorrow morning, she'd go to the pub and ask Josie to join her for a walk. It was time to put herself out there more to find out if it were possible for the two of them to be more than friends. Harriet glanced upward again, and the moon was in full view once more. The universe, so it seemed, approved of the plan.

CHAPTER NINETEEN

EARLY ON SATURDAY MORNING, JOSIE AND HER mum sat at one of the tables in the pub, both drinking heavily from their tea mugs.

Josie set hers down with a little too much force, slopping some of the tea over the side. "So, what's your deal with Harry?"

"Harry Powell?" her mum clarified as if there were more than one Harry who regularly came to the pub. She avoided Josie's gaze, adding jam to her scone.

"Yes. Her."

"Why do you ask?" Her mum took a bite, some crumbs falling onto the table. She wiped them into her hand and discarded them onto a napkin.

Josie wanted to take this conversation slowly, sensing her mum's not-so-veiled aversion to Harry. She started off with, "She seems interesting."

"She's a know-it-all. Do you know the first time she met me, she asked why I was named Eugenie, saying it hadn't become popular until Fergie and Prince Andrew named their daughter that in 1990. The next time she talked to me, she proceeded to list the Eugenies she researched, including the daughter in *Gone with the Wind*— the one who died in a horse-riding accident, and Empress Eugenie who married Napoleon III. They lived in exile in the UK." Her mum harrumphed. "The nerve of the woman but pretty typical for a wanker from London. The type who comes here thinking they're superior to us yokels."

Harry's curiosity had evidently needled Josie's mum, but Josie found Harry's thirst for knowledge about everything under the sun charming.

"Did you tell Harry it was your grandmother's name?"

"No. Why should I?" her mum snapped.

"Because she was trying to bond with you in her Harry way."

"She was being haughty! She also wondered why we named the pub The Golden Fleece but didn't have it decorated appropriately."

"What would be appropriate?" Josie jacked up one eyebrow, pulling one leg up onto the seat of the chair, as she checked out the leather books on the shelves and black-and-white photos of the area from a bygone era.

"She said something about a Greek myth and Jason and the Argonauts." Her mum made a *whoop-de-do* flick of the hand.

That was why Harry had questioned Winston's name last night. "I'm not familiar with that one." Josie brought up the Wikipedia page on her phone. "Oh, Jason searches for the Golden Fleece. Did you know that when you chose the name?"

"Of course, I knew that!" Eugenie said in an indignant tone that made it clear to Josie she hadn't. "But we named it after the sheep in the area. The wool industry used to be the backbone of the Cotswolds."

Josie conceded the fact with a nod. "You know, Empress

Eugenie was quite fashionable in her day, and there's a hat named after her. Greta Garbo wore a Eugenie hat in the 1930's film *Romance*. It was all the rage. We should get you one. You'd look adorbs."

"You sound just like the patronizing Harry." Her mum's cheeks reddened.

Josie stopped her eyes from rolling, not wanting to agitate her mum further. "She's just curious about things. There's nothing wrong with that." Luckily, Harry had only questioned Josie's mum about her name and didn't accidentally call Eugenie defective. Josie replayed that moment a lot in her head, and each time, she thought it so very Harry. Adorable in a special kind of way. Josie understood not everyone would appreciate Harry's ways, but that only endeared her more to Josie. Josie got Harry. Most of the time. More importantly, Harry understood Josie.

"What do you think of Natalie?" Her mum's eyes lit up. "She's your age, and she grew up in a nearby village."

"Meaning?" Josie had a good idea where this was heading.

"She's one of us." Her mum placed a hand over her chest. "Everyone in the village thinks the world of her. She had a brief fling with a Londoner, but it didn't last. Nothing ever does with those types."

Josie attempted to sound neutral. "She seems nice."

"Nice is a good start." Her mum fluttered her eyelashes.

"Oh no. Don't go there." Josie scraped her chair back.

"Go where?" Her mum's expression was blank, a clear warning sign that the hamster wheel inside in her head was kicking into manic gear.

"Thinking things." Josie rapped her forehead.

"What things might those be?"

"The *Natalie is nice, and my daughter isn't dating anyone*

tract. You know I don't want you to interfere in my love life."

"I wasn't aware you had a love life, and I hadn't thought about Natalie in that way at all." Her mum took a dainty bite of scone, getting jelly on her upper lip. After wiping her mouth with a napkin, she said, "But now that you mention it…" Her mum tapped her fingertips together, in mad plotter fashion.

"Stop." Josie held up a palm. "Just stop."

"Stop what?"

"Whatever plot is going on in your head. I'm not interested in a relationship. And, definitely not with Natalie. She's too… short." Josie, the speechwriter, cringed thinking that was the best she could come up with, considering how lame it sounded, but her mum could be a force that would only complicate the thoughts in Josie's head about Harry and the fact that Josie didn't have a career at the moment. This really didn't seem like the ideal time to be having any thoughts about any woman. Logically, she got that. Her heart was an entirely different matter. Josie raised her hand to her cheek, running a thumb over the hidden dimple.

The kittens skittered into the room, their backs arched, doing their sidewinder attacks on each other before dashing back toward the arch on the other side of the pub.

Josie needed to pivot. "If you must play matchmaker, fix up William and Agnes. They need your help. Night after night, they both dress up, come here, and sit on opposite sides of the pub, stealing looks at the other."

"But they have one foot in the grave. You're full of life and at the age when you should settle down. Have I mentioned that before? You're still young, but not for much longer."

Josie chose to ignore the settling down comment and dig at her age. "All people deserve love, Mum."

"Are you including yourself in that box?"

Josie groaned. "All people who want love should be able to find it, no matter their age. I'm not one of those people. Not one who's looking."

"So you keep saying." Her mum popped the last bite into her mouth, licking her fingers. "Not even contemplating the endearing Natalie."

Josie couldn't determine if the sentence was a statement or question, but decided to put the matter to rest. "Natalie is the last woman I would date."

Her mum nodded, seeming to agree with Josie's assessment. "What about Helen Swift? She's a professor. Has a fancy house. She'd be able to take care of you."

Take care of me!

Did her mum think Josie was a total wreck who needed someone to show her the way? If that was the case, no wonder her mum was pushing Josie to settle down. Her own mum thought Josie was a disaster who needed a caretaker. Did everyone in the village think that way?

Did Harry?

Josie knew her life was turned upside down at the moment, but it wasn't like she was destitute or anything. She was simply taking the time to figure out her next move. Was there something wrong with that?

Josie didn't want to open Pandora's box by pressing Eugenie. Time for another pivot. "William and Agnes would be cute together. Like Christmas ornaments that hang on the tree, side by side, but don't talk."

"You have a very strange way of imagining relationships."

"The man has only said a handful of words to me. The

most memorable being *Doom Bar* and *crisps*. Granted, he's old and probably reserving his energy… for other things."

With a curious expression, her mum asked, "Like what?"

Josie fumbled for something that didn't have to deal with sex or relationships. "Fox hunting."

"It's illegal in this country."

"Is it? I could have sworn I saw a painting in one of the antique shops on the square."

"It goes back centuries, and it was in an antique shop." Her mum waved a hand, implying that answered it completely.

"The murder of beautiful animals should still be celebrated?" Josie could barely believe she was charging down this path, considering how flimsy it was. But her mum always took the bait when Josie utilized the obnoxious American role.

"It's not just the UK that hunted foxes, darling daughter. They did so in America as well."

"Not sure how that's helping your argument. Americans and violence go hand in hand."

"Oh, this sounds like a light and frothy conversation to start off the day with." Clive sat with a steaming mug of tea.

"It's either this conversation or dating." Josie's shrug implied she'd rather talk about murder.

"I'm curious why those are the only two conversation topics today or ever." Clive raised his brow.

"Don't pay her any attention. Josie's being dramatic because she doesn't want me to know she likes Natalie."

"Natalie. I had my money on Harry." Clive ran his hand over his short ginger hair, yawning.

"That's because you're an impractical man!" Her mum's face turned beet red.

"That might be the case, but Camilla mentioned Harry needed a good shag. Knock the cobwebs loose, so to speak."

Josie's jaw dropped.

"She does seem a bit uptight," her mum conceded.

"I am not having this discussion. Not with my mum and playboy uncle who receives threats via kittens. It's weird. So very, very, very, very weird. Times a million."

"Would that be four million, then, since you said *very* four times?" her mum asked in all seriousness.

"Doesn't matter. As long as you get the point that we aren't discussing me shagging Harry to make her less uptight as some type of Good Samaritan thing."

Her mum looked past Josie, a wicked smile on her lips. "Good morning, Harry."

"Very funny." Josie sipped her tea angrily.

"Should I come back?" It was Harry's voice.

Josie's heart briefly stopped before it went into hyperdrive, thudding to the point Josie felt it in her toes. She spun around in her chair. "Oh, fuck. You really are here."

"There won't be any chance of shagging any time soon now," her mum whispered much too loudly to Clive, wickedness in Eugenie's eyes.

If it were possible to stop her heart, Josie would have done so.

Harry looked just as mortified but seemed frozen, unable to think or say anything to extract herself from the situation.

"What brings you by?" Clive asked as if Harry were there for business.

"Uh, I really can't remember. I did have a purpose, but…" Harry visibly swallowed.

"Josie, didn't you mention something about going for a

walk? It looks like a lovely morning." Her uncle looked forcefully at Josie as if trying to use Jedi powers to get her to act.

Her mum tried to speak, but Clive made a *keep your trap shut* motion.

"It is nice out," Harry said, still shell-shocked, but some color slowly returned to her cheeks.

"That settles it," Clive said. "You two are going for a walk." His tone sounded so much like a relative trying to rid himself of bored children during a school break. "Get going."

Josie rose to her feet. "Would you like to?"

Harry nodded. "I'm pretty sure that's why I stopped by."

Josie was touched Harry had thought of her, but the conspiratorial look on her uncle's face worried her. Had Camilla asked him to help Harry get laid? While Josie enjoyed Harry's company and wanted to get to know the woman more, Josie didn't want to deal with anyone's matchmaking tendencies. Even if Clive didn't mean any harm by it. Josie hated being managed by family and friends.

"I just need to pop upstairs to change." Josie raised a finger as if saying she would be quick about it.

Harry nodded, visibly not enthused about being left alone for any amount of time with Josie's mum.

Josie sprinted upstairs, located a wool sweater, shoes, and beanie, and assembled herself in record time, dashing back downstairs to rescue Harry from her mum's withering stare and Clive's goofy grin.

"Shall we?" Harry waved for Josie to go ahead.

"You two have a lovely walk. Take a long one. Your mum and I can set up everything." Clive shooed them out, all the while digging his phone out of his pocket. Did he plan to text Camilla that step one of their machinations had been accomplished?

CHAPTER TWENTY

IN SILENCE, THEY WALKED OUT OF THE PUB, making Harriet even more uncomfortable than normal. Harriet now knew for certain Josie was not interested in her in any fashion aside from being friends. That had been made perfectly clear in humiliating fashion, and in front of Eugenie and Clive. Her brain floundered for an acceptable excuse to allow her to make a clean getaway.

"Uh, I think I left my kettle on. I should go... turn it off." Harriet hiked a thumb over her shoulder in the opposite direction of her cottage.

"Don't you have an electric one that shuts off?"

"Oh, right. I forgot that part." Harriet nodded absently, upset she'd botched the excuse and was coming across even more pathetic now than two minutes ago. Harriet really didn't think that was possible. Never underestimate a fool's ability to make an arse out of themselves.

"Do you have a preference on the route?" Josie asked, stopping in her tracks to bend to the right and then left, limbering up for the stroll.

Harriet searched the countryside. "It rained yesterday. Are you opposed to mud?"

"Depends. I don't mind trudging through mud when I have on wellies, but I'm wearing sneakers." Josie pointed to her Nikes and made a motion with her hand that suggested *So, what do you think?*

"Right." Harriet wore wellies. "If we head to the square, take a left and then right, we'll reach one of my favorite treks. It takes us past a manor, cricket field, a charming row of cottages…" She let her voice trail off, aware she was rambling.

Josie motioned for Harriet to lead the way, the two of them walking in increasingly uncomfortable silence. After they crossed a couple of streets and made it to a metal gate, they started out on a footpath that led to a bridge taking them over a larger river than the one in Upper Chewford, reaching another path on the left. Through the trees on the right, Harriet could make out a cricket field.

Josie stopped and took in the view of the Mansfield House in the distance.

Harriet struggled to think of something clever to break the awkwardness, but the unfortunate kettle comment had her rattled. "I've always had a knack for showing up at the wrong time." She opted to joke about what had just happened, thinking it might help crack through the tension like a pick separating an ice chunk. They'd have a good laugh. Deepening their friendship.

"As a journalist, though, isn't that kinda a good thing?" Josie kept her eyes on the grand house in the distance that could be used as a location for a Jane Austen film.

"You'd think so, but my knack only seems to involve personally humiliating scenarios. Like when I walked in on my wife taking a shower with her best friend."

Josie looked at Harriet. "Ouch!"

Harriet nodded.

"Wait. I thought you said your ex claimed you two had grown apart or something. You never mentioned the shower bit."

"It's not something one mentions so early to a new acquaintance or ever, but she did say that as an excuse as to why… she… you know."

"Earlier, then, only ticked one or two notches on the embarrassment factor." Josie laughed nervously.

"My timing was truly awful." Harriet couldn't mask the mortification in her tone.

"May I ask exactly what you heard?"

Harriet released an anguished sigh. "I'm not sure I remember it exactly. I kinda froze, but it was something about us…" She couldn't bring herself to complete the thought.

"Shagging," Josie supplied. "I'm sorry. It seems my family is intent on me hooking up with anyone."

"I see," Harriet said with even more mortification evident in her sagging shoulders.

"I didn't mean for that to sound like—that." Josie laid her hand on Harriet's shoulder, and Harriet couldn't help to think that was the only touch she'd ever receive from Josie. A sympathetic gesture.

"I understand." It was Harriet's turn to keep her eyes forward, imagining Mr. Darcy or another Austen bloke charging over the grass on horseback or whatever. Perhaps if luck was on her side, the imaginary rider would knock Harriet to the ground, blotting out all memories of the morning thus far.

Josie squeezed Harriet's shoulder before letting her hand slide off. "Please. I really didn't mean it that way. I think my brain and tongue are on different wavelengths. That always spells trouble for me." Josie's tongue lolled

out of her mouth, as if she really needed Harriet to understand Josie wasn't in control of what she said or did.

However, it was difficult for Harriet to believe that
completely. Josie was a speechwriter, meaning she had a
way with words. Maybe she hadn't anticipated how the
statement would impact Harriet and was doing damage
control out of guilt. How exactly did it impact Harriet? If
Harriet was honest with herself, it hit hard. Much harder
than she expected it to.

How to respond, though? Harriet settled with honesty
and a pinch of humor. "Says the speechwriter." Harriet
forced a lighthearted laugh as a way of saying, *Isn't this such
a ridiculous situation?*

"I'm much better at telling others what to do or putting
words into their mouths."

"Is that right?"

"Yes. That's one part of the job I'll actually miss."

"Maybe you need to find a career choice that'll allow
you to channel your bossy ways into your new life path,
whatever that may be."

"Bossy ways, huh?" Josie seemed to brush that aside
with a smile. "Not sure the pub is the best place for my
skills. I have toyed with starting an online management
course. Learn more about the business side: accounting,
ordering supplies, and all that jazz. Not sure it'll offer
much advice about how to control a philandering uncle and
meddling mother. At least Clive isn't sleeping with anyone
on the kitchen staff."

"Oh, I imagine his comeuppance will arrive in spectac-
ular fashion. Not in the form of cute kittens." Harriet
didn't trust herself to crack a joke or even comment about
Eugenie's meddling ways without too much honesty
spilling out. Insulting Josie's mum didn't seem like the
best course of action.

Josie's smile fell from her face. "I think you're right. It won't be pretty, and I fear Mum will end up in the crosshairs. Meaning the business and her financial well-being will take a hit. And mine now."

"He seems to have settled some. Are you worried it won't last?"

"He's a Johnson. From what Mum tells me, stupidity goes back generations. According to her, though, it's only those with XY chromosomes."

"That makes some sense."

"She doesn't like to point fingers at all the males in the family, but she totally does, although I think she secretly chucks me into the mix because of the whole *girl chasing* thing. Maybe the connection isn't the XY but chasing girls."

"Has there been a lot of that?" Harriet had to admit she was more than slightly curious. Was Josie the type to love them and leave them? The tits and ass comment she'd overheard that day in the coffee shop gave that impression.

"Girl chasing?" Josie arched one eyebrow in what Harriet determined was her playful way. Was it also flirty? Why did it matter, though? Josie wasn't interested in Harriet for anything. Not even a fling.

Harriet nodded, once again determining it was best not to speak and give away too much.

"I wouldn't say that, exactly. Not in Clive fashion. But I have been known to go gaga over one or two."

Perhaps the pressure of knowing they were simply buds, emboldened Harriet to prod, "Do tell."

Josie laughed, looking much more comfortable as they continued along the path. "Can this be a quid pro quo thing?"

"Do you want it to be?"

"I absolutely do. I'm not going to dish the dirt if there

isn't a payoff." Josie joggled Harriet's shoulder with her own.

Harriet laughed. "I fear the payoff you'll receive will be a disappointment."

"I sincerely doubt that." Josie sounded genuine and spoke with a whiff of sadness. "You remind me so much of a girl who got away."

"Me?" Harriet placed a hand on her chest, her heart thundering deep inside, but tempered it with the thought that it was the reason Josie liked her. To be reminded of what might have been.

"She was a lot like you. Intellectual. Shy in groups but more confident in a one-on-one situation. She could be bossy when she needed to be. She even wore similar sexy black-framed glasses. Just so you know, the last two qualities are an extreme turn-on for me."

Harriet stared straight ahead, trying to parse that one out. Did Josie say that to give Harriet some hope? Or was it simply informational?

Josie, not picking up on Harriet's thoughts, continued, "The woman in question barely knew I existed."

"Was it a celebrity crush? One of your candidates, perhaps?"

"Not a celebrity or a candidate. They do nothing for me. We worked on the same campaign, but this was way back in the day when I was only a volunteer. I was very low on the totem pole." Josie held her hand down below the knee. "If I even was on the totem pole. She wasn't the type to appreciate the masses."

"Interesting. And, you wanted to date her?"

"I know. She sounds terrible. When you're all of twenty, you have no idea what people can really be like behind closed doors. I probably assumed she'd be different if there were more between us. Like somehow I could dent her hard exterior."

"Do you regret not asking her out?" They were on pavement now, with some cottages on their left.

Josie took a moment to think over her answer. "Yes and no. She ended up marrying a woman she met on a different campaign, and surprise, surprise; from what I've heard, she's exactly like she is in the working world. Demanding. Expecting her wife to cater to her career ambitions and rigid schedule. Dodged a bullet there, I think." Josie laughed. "But I regret not getting over my fear of rejection. In many situations, I have no fear. When it comes to intimate relationships, I…"

"Even now?"

"To a certain extent. I've asked out some women after that to prove to myself I can, but it's still a part of me I have to push myself on."

"I never would have guessed that." Did Josie's confession cement their friendship since Harriet couldn't factor out why anyone would confess this to a potential love interest?

"Why's that?"

"You have that American confidence." After passing the cottages, Harriet pointed out another footpath leading through the trees.

"Like I said, I do in most categories."

"But not the girl-chasing one?" Harriet cringed over her desire to hear from Josie loud and clear that Harry had no chance whatsoever.

"Let's just say I don't take after Clive."

Harriet laughed. "That's probably for the best."

"A small part of me does envy him some. I have to wonder how much of it is due to the fact that he's a man. The whole genetic predisposition to spreading his seed. I've noticed over the years that men have extremely inflated egos. The thought that they'd get shot down doesn't seem to dawn on them. I'm not saying all guys are like that. Those like Clive are. It's odd seeing him dealing with all the women in this village, knowing I'm related to him and struggling with my own confidence." Josie tucked her chin to her chest. "Losing my job hasn't boosted my self-esteem any. I mean, what can I offer a woman right now?" She pitched two hands in the air. "And Mum seems intent on marrying me off, like I'm some type of burden. Do you know what she said earlier? She thinks I should chase after Helen because the professor could take care of me. All these thoughts"—Josie circled a finger around her temple—"it's kinda doing a mind-fuck, ya know?"

Harriet nodded, understanding why Josie was confused, but not seeing Eugenie's reasoning. Josie seemed quite capable of taking care of herself. While Josie was in the process of rebooting her life, Harriet had no doubt Josie would come out on the other side in impressive fashion.

"I wouldn't take your mum's comments to heart. You have a chance to examine your life and decide which direction you want to go. Not everyone gets a shot at that, too busy living day to day, making ends meet. Give yourself the time you need to become the person you want to be. I have every confidence what you decide will be the right decision."

"Thanks, Harry. I really needed to hear that." Josie inhaled deeply before letting the air out of her lungs. "I love mornings like this. Crisp and clear."

Harriet looked into the endless blue sky.

"Your turn," Josie said.

Slowly, Harriet lowered her gaze. "For?"

"I shared about my girl-chasing past. Now I'm dying to hear about yours."

Harriet stopped on the path, took off her glasses, and wiped the lenses with the hem of her jumper. Replacing them, she said, "I'm not sure where to begin."

"By all means, start with the juicy bits." Josie's smile contained a hint of naughtiness.

Incredulous laughter bubbled out of Harriet. "How do I follow that?"

Josie waved to a bench overlooking the rolling hills to the west. "Shall we sit for this portion?" Not waiting for an answer, Josie took a seat. "Just to let you know, I'm old enough for the X-rated version."

Harriet, still standing, said, "You see. This is why I'm shocked you didn't ask out that woman. Does she have a name?" It was also further proof Harriet shouldn't take Josie's flirty statements too seriously. This was only part of Josie's American personality, not a sign of mutual attraction.

"She does. It's a thing we do in America. Supply names to everyone once they're born. It got confusing to remember everyone's assigned numbers." Josie cupped her mouth and shouted, "Hey, Number One Billion and Seven."

Harriet pointed at Josie. "You're hedging. Does that mean you don't want me to know her name? I promise I'm not working you for a juicy story." Harriet took a seat next to Josie and squeezed her thigh, surprised by the firmness.

"I should hope not, but that's a good reminder you're on the enemy's side." Josie laughed. "She does have a name, but she's very well-known in the political sphere. I'm not sure if you watch many American political shows with pundits, but if you do, odds are you've seen her. She makes the rounds more frequently than a case of herpes on prom night." Josie shook her head as if puzzling out if that made sense or not but plowed on. "Let's just call her The Ballbuster."

"Okay. How is it you never worked up the courage to ask out Madame Ballbuster?"

"Ooooh, I like Madame Ballbuster. Nice job." Josie elbowed Harriet's side.

Harriet waited, unsure why she really needed to hear the answer given what she'd overheard earlier. Josie didn't want to shag Harriet. Period.

Josie tugged on her earlobe. "I don't know. I just didn't. It's not something I'm proud of. The crippling fear around beautiful women."

"I didn't mean to upset you. Forgive me for pushing the subject." Yet another sign Harriet was alone in her wanting. It was hard not to glance at her own chest, remembering Eugenie's comment Josie chased tits and ass.

"You didn't upset me, although you did push a bit." Josie held up a finger and thumb without much space in between. "It's hard to explain. Why I can be confident in some areas and not others. I mean, I feel completely comfortable around you."

"That's because you don't want to shag me," Harriet said with too much honesty.

Josie turned her head to look Harriet full-on. "For the record, I never said that. Not once."

"Still, it was made clear earlier—"

"I'm not sure it was. Maybe you're projecting."

"What does that mean?" Harriet sounded as baffled as she felt.

"You don't want to sleep with me, so you're trying to plant the seed in my head I don't want to have sex with you." Josie spoke in a tone that conveyed what she was saying made perfect sense.

But it didn't to Harriet. "That's preposterous. Who in their right mind wouldn't want to have sex with you?"

"You, apparently." Josie crossed her arms. "Not once did you try to make a move when I was at your place. I practically threw myself at you."

"I don't remember that part of the evening, and if you really think I don't want to, you're as mad as a hatter."

"Does that mean you do want to fuck me?"

Harriet's attempted retort morphed into incomprehensible sputtering.

Josie sprung to her feet, forging ahead in the direction they'd been heading before stopping.

Harriet gave chase. "Where are you going?"

"I'm walking. That's why you stopped by, so we can walk together. As best buds. That's all." With a hand to her forehead, Josie muttered more to herself, "I've been such a fool."

Harriet shook her hands in the air, before saying, "Josie, please stop."

Josie did, but she didn't turn around.

Harriet asked, "Can you tell me why you're mad at me?"

"I'm not." It sounded as if Josie spoke with clenched teeth.

"You are. Please tell me. I can't make it better unless I know what I need to fix."

Josie flipped around. "Do I need to draw you a map so you can figure out where this went wrong?"

"It would be helpful."

"I feel like an ass. That's all. When I feel this way, I go into attack mode. It's one of my many flaws."

"Why do you feel that way?" Harriet knew she was missing the obvious, but what was it?

"Jesus!" Josie spat out. "Do you need an ego boost or something?"

"What are you talking about?" Harriet didn't even attempt to mask her exasperation. "All I know is we were having an enjoyable stroll together, and now you're staring at me like you want to pluck out all my eyelashes, one by one."

"I would never do that."

"Are you sure?" Harriet circled a finger in the air. "That's the vibe I'm picking up on."

"You have lovely eyelashes. Thick and long. They draw attention to your stunning deep-blue eyes."

Harriet's mouth opened and then closed.

"Are you getting the picture yet, Harry?"

"I..."

"Don't worry. I know you don't find me attractive." Josie started to march away again.

"I've already told you only an insane person wouldn't find you attractive."

Josie flipped around. "I don't care about anyone else."

"Who do you care about?"

"Oh. My. God." Josie shook her hands in the air. "How am I having this circular debate with you? It's maddening."

"What do you want me to say?"

"You don't have to say anything. We should finish our walk, say goodbye, and continue our days as if nothing ever happened. Yet another example of how putting oneself out there doesn't pay off when it comes to women." Josie wheeled about.

Harriet reached for Josie's hand, but she couldn't think of the right words, let alone utter them aloud to convince Josie she was wrong. So very wrong. Harriet did the only thing she could think of. She kissed Josie full on the mouth.

CHAPTER TWENTY-ONE

Shocked, Josie instinctively pulled back, but luckily her senses returned quickly, and Josie placed her hand on the back of Harry's head, pulling her lips back to Josie's and deepening the kiss. Josie didn't want to waste any more precious time dancing around her attraction to Harry, even if she was Harry the Scandalmonger. That didn't matter right then or there. All that did was Harry.

Harry's hungry tongue pressed farther into Josie's mouth, causing Josie to moan in ecstasy, spurring Harry to push the kiss past the hot level to a knee-buckling, *I hope this never stops* stage.

In between, Josie panted, "Why didn't we do that earlier?"

Harry kissed her before responding, "I didn't know you liked me."

Josie pressed her forehead to Harry's. "I really thought I was being obvious about it. I mean, I wore my *I want you* dress to dinner. Even my mum said I looked like I was trying to get lucky."

"Can you wear it again?"

"Did you like it?"

"You have no idea." Harry nodded excitedly as if she needed to be understood completely. "It took everything I had not to, how would an American say this, jump your bones?"

"Proper Brits don't say that?" Josie teased.

"Oh, it was used in a British song, but the meaning meant to literally stomp on someone. I think the first time it was used to mean sexual intercourse was in an *Esquire* magazine article sometime in the mid-sixties. According to something I stumbled upon on the internet, so who knows if it's true or not."

Josie chuckled, her smile widening. This moment was just so Harry. "And you remember the details?"

"Well, I thought of the phrase recently and decided to research it." Harry ran her thumb over Josie's bottom lip.

"You were thinking of the phrase just 'cause…?" Josie left the rest unsaid but then corrected herself by adding, "Or were you thinking of wanting to jump my bones? Given our miscommunication since day one, apparently, I want to avoid it as much as possible from now on."

Harry laughed. "When thinking of you after you left my cottage, I couldn't sleep, and the phrase popped into my head. Being the nerd that I am, I dug a little deeper."

Josie kissed Harry on the mouth, sweetly. "It's one of the things I like about you." *My mum not so much*, but Josie kept that thought to herself. It wasn't like Josie could tell Harry not to be Harry-like around her mum. It'd probably make Harry even more uncomfortable around her mum, and Josie couldn't imagine how that would play out.

"Is it now?"

"What can I say? Nerds get me hot."

Harry really laughed. "So, I've been put on notice that

all nerds will benefit from sharing odd factoids during intimate moments?"

"Not all. I don't know how to say this, but ever since that first night, when I saw you on the footbridge, I felt a connection to you. I know it sounds ridiculous, and I'm not really the type to believe in bullshit like that, but it happened. I've been trying to process it ever since." Josie waved a hand in front of her face as if saying it was driving her mad.

"What have you come to?"

"I don't know. How's that for an answer?"

"It's honest. And you aren't alone."

"What do you mean?"

"I felt something, too. That night."

Josie had to laugh, considering Harry had said the bare minimum, while Josie had shared a tad more. "Ah, your brevity also gets me hot."

"I've never been known for being verbose. Unless incredibly nervous."

"You aren't now?"

Harry shook her head. "This feels right."

Josie threaded her fingers through the hair on the back of Harry's head, pulling them into another kiss. One that started sweetly but passionately. Slowly, the heat factor edged up. And up. Harry's hand snaked underneath Josie's shirt, the cold fingers making their presence known on Josie's bare skin. Harry's other hand worked its way under the shirt as well. The woman may be short with words, but her actions were doing wonders for Josie.

"Why are we nowhere near a bed?" Josie asked.

"Only seems fitting given everything."

"I'm done with the universe being against us. It's time we wrestle our fate back into our control." Josie acted this out.

Harry grinned. "Spoken like a speechwriter."

Josie laughed. "It may have been slightly over the top. That's why speeches are reworked and reworked usually right until the words are finally spoken."

Harry's hands gripped Josie's sides. "What do you propose?"

"You really like the idea of me proposing, don't you?"

Harry sputtered, "I-I... it's just a word."

"Says the woman who crafts crossword puzzles. I loved yesterday's clue for flirt."

"I needed a word that started with a V." Harry shrugged.

"Does that mean the vixen answer had nothing to do with me?"

"Are you working tonight?"

"I guess the abrupt change of subject means that's a yes. And to answer your question, I am working tonight. Why?"

"We still haven't had your wine in the garden. It'll be chilly, but the night will be clear."

"That's right. God, that Tuesday night was a total disaster." Josie rested her forehead against Harry's.

"Not completely. It gave me a great clue for the puzzle."

"I knew it!" Josie pulled away to gaze into Harry's amazing eyes.

"How are your fingers?" Harry boosted Josie's hand to her lips and kissed the tips.

"Are you asking out of politeness or for another reason?" Josie winked.

"I... Oh..." Harry's face went up in flames.

"I'm sorry, Harry. I didn't mean to shock you. Not in that way. Please excuse my American crudeness."

"Only if you excuse my prim and properness."

"I couldn't figure out the simmering clue," Josie said. "In the crossword."

"Yearning."

"Really?" Josie's voice cracked with enthusiasm.

Harry nodded.

"I'm off tomorrow night."

"Care to come over? I promise not to burn you this time." Harry looked to the blue sky overhead. "If I remember correctly, the weather will be slightly warmer. Not much considering it's December, but one glass in the garden won't be too painful."

"Will there be more kissing involved? I know we've only just entered that phase, but I can't lie. I'm hooked." To emphasize this, Josie kissed Harry.

"Yes. Lots and lots of kissing." Harry kissed Josie.

"Sounds promising."

They sealed it with another kiss. A long, lingering kiss that neither of them seemed interested in ending.

CHAPTER TWENTY-TWO

AFTER ESCORTING JOSIE BACK TO THE PUB, Harriet walked into her cottage, feeling as if she could conquer the world. Or at least next week's crossword, because doing anything that required more brain power would take her thoughts off Josie, who truly was the Sultana of Seduction. Oh, that should be a clue!

She made a cup of tea and cracked into some of her special shortbread she'd purchased in Edinburgh last summer. Harriet had been saving it for the right occasion, and this seemed like the perfect moment.

Sitting at her desk in her office, she got to work on the puzzle, wanting to drop more clues for Josie to demonstrate how smitten Harriet truly was.

Not too long after, there was a Skype call.

"What's a good clue for bones?" she asked Camilla.

"Hi to you, too."

"Oh, hi."

"Are you referring to human bones?"

Harriet dipped shortbread into her tea. "Yeah, I think so."

"What are you eating?"

Harriet mumbled around a bite, "Shortbread."

"I want some."

Harriet lowered her hand as if making sure Camilla couldn't reach through the screen and snatch it.

"Oh! Stephen King wrote a novel called *Bag of Bones*."

"Not sure that's the image I want."

"You're a huge King fan. I thought you'd get a kick out of that one." Camilla scrunched her face. "Wait. You want a bone image for what?"

"Oh, nothing." Harriet dipped a shortbread into her tea out of view of the camera, replaying the jumping-bones conversation with Josie. Realizing she'd been silent for too long, she asked, "What's new with you?"

"I'm thinking of coming up tomorrow."

Harriet dropped the shortbread into her tea. "You can't!"

"Why not?" Camilla tilted her head to the side, like a confused puppy.

"Uh, I'm having the room painted."

"Why? It's our uncle's place, not yours. No reason to improve a place that isn't yours. If you want to throw out money, just give it to me." Camilla stretched out her hand.

"Regis is paying for it."

"And it has to be done tomorrow?"

"Yes," Harriet lied, adding, "it has to be tomorrow. He was very clear about that." Harriet remembered feeling Josie's lips on hers and their plans for more tomorrow night. Having Camilla in the guest bedroom simply wasn't feasible.

"That seems out of the blue."

"X-ray!" Harriet snapped her fingers.

"You're getting weirder and weirder the longer you stay there. You know that? I'm actually worried about you."

"It's for the puzzle."

"Oh, for bones. Yes, that's a good one. Back to the matter at hand, I don't think you understand. I need to come up this weekend."

"Need to? As in it's life or death?" Harriet could practically taste the sarcasm in her mouth.

"Yes. Exactly like that."

Harriet sat up straighter in her chair. "What's going on?"

"I can't talk about it now. I need to be there, though."

"Now I'm worried about you. Can't you give me something to go on?"

Camilla shook her head, pressing her lips tightly. But she always had thinning lips whenever Harriet wanted her to spill a secret.

"Can you stay...?" Harriet was about to say *with Clive* but corrected to, "At the inn on my street? I don't want you getting ill from the paint fumes." She nearly choked rushing this lie out of her cotton mouth.

"Is this really how you treat your cousin? If need be, I can share the bed with you."

How could Harriet tell Camilla the truth? That Harriet hoped Josie would be staying the night? Even if they had only kissed earlier today, the kissing made Harriet hope for more. So much more. But her cousin was right, of course. "Okay, okay. I'll make it work."

"Thanks, Harry. I really need you."

Harriet wanted to kick something but said with as much conviction as possible, "I'm always here for you, Cam."

"You hardly ever call me Cam."

"It felt like the appropriate time to."

Camilla smiled. "I knew I could count on you."

Josie probably won't feel the same way.

"See you tomorrow." Harriet waved, feeling rather foolish.

The call ended, and Harriet steepled her fingers, trying to decide what to do. Call Josie right then and there and explain the situation? Go to the pub and do it in person?

Was it too early for a gin and tonic?

* * *

JOSIE GLANCED up from the pint she was pouring and smiled at Harriet as she entered the pub, causing the stab of guilt to work its way further into Harriet's side, as if a knife was trying to pluck out a rib.

William shuffled to his favorite chair with his pint.

"You're here early." Josie leaned over the bar and whispered, "Are you hoping for another kiss so soon?"

Harriet giggled like a schoolgirl.

"You okay?"

Harriet nodded.

"Do you want a drink to loosen up your tongue some?"

"Please." Harriet tugged on the neckline of her jumper.

"What's wrong? You've gone a bit green around the gills."

"Camilla."

"Is she okay?" Josie measured out the gin for a double. After taking a peek at Harriet, Josie shook out a bit more.

"I don't know. She insisted on coming up tomorrow because she has to talk."

"Gosh, I hope everything's okay."

"But... *tomorrow*." Harriet stared into Josie's sparkling green eyes to impress the importance of the date.

"At least you won't have to wait long to find out what's going on."

"True. But we had *plans* for tomorrow," Harriet whispered.

Josie's smile lifted the cloud. "It's okay, Harry. I totally understand." She twisted the cap off the tonic bottle and set it next to Harry's glass. "Just for you, two slices of grapefruit."

"That's sweet. Don't get in trouble with the boss lady. She's not my biggest fan." More like bitter enemy.

"She's not here at the moment."

"Does she have a favorite treat I can bribe her with?"

Josie's smile broadened, really bringing that dimple to life. "Chocolate."

"Any chocolate or a certain type?"

Josie blew out a breath. "She really liked this chocolate place in Boston. It was in the Back Bay, if I remember correctly. Are you planning on dashing over to get some?"

"Would it help?"

"You really are sweet. She may warm to you if she found out about earlier. The woman would marry me off to the highest bidder if that meant keeping me here."

"I'm not sure how to take that." Harriet knew Eugenie wasn't her biggest fan, but the way Josie said *may warm to you* made it seem like Eugenie would never take to Harriet.

"If it makes you feel better, we're in the same boat. I'm not sure how to handle my mum these days. I'm sure you don't have anything to worry about. Dowries aren't a thing anymore, are they?" Josie rubbed her head. "Wait, I have that backward. Mum would have to pay a dowry. Or would you? How does it work in lesbian marriages?"

"Are you proposing again?" Harriet laughed, realizing Josie was doing her best winding Harriet up, but it didn't grate on her. In fact, she found it charming.

"It's my thing these days." Josie rested on her fore-arms. "Be honest; were you nervous to tell me about postponing tomorrow? Was that the guilt I picked up on?"

"Was it that obvious?"

"Yes. Really, Harry, it's not a big deal aside from the fact I have to keep my hands off you longer than I'd planned on."

Harriet's mouth watered. "Is it wrong of me to wish Camilla's life could fall apart at a different time?"

"Wouldn't that be nice?"

"She can be infuriating sometimes."

"Who knows? She may still end up with Clive for the night, although ever since you stopped running the ginger ads, more women seem intent on coming here looking like ladies of the night hoping to snare his attention." Josie leaned over the bar. "I think he's getting tired of it. The only woman he talks about is your cousin, so fingers crossed they end up shagging." Josie crossed her fingers with both hands.

"That'd be lovely."

"I like this side of you." Josie gave Harriet's hand a pat.

"Desperate?"

"Desperation can be good in some departments. Makes me know you want more time with me. That's a very good thing. Considering all the misunderstandings, the look of wanting in your eyes is crystal clear."

Josie had no idea how much Harriet wanted it. Wanted her.

A group of tourists charged in, laughing, two of the guys in the group slapping each other on the back as if coming in from an epic adventure. Josie held up a finger, implying she'd be right back.

Harriet walked to the far end of the bar, sitting on one of the available barstools. While Josie poured pints, Harriet was able to check out Josie from the side. Her tight jeans hugged Josie's ass in such a way... Harriet swallowed a healthy portion of her G&T, trying to temper the desire raging inside. What was becoming of Harriet? She wasn't the type to objectify anyone, but some switch in her brain had been tripped, and all she could think about was Josie. Not just having sex with Josie. Listening to her talk. Wanting her advice. Feeling her body against Harriet's.

Harriet took another long tug of her drink, draining it.

"Easy, tiger. The next one is only going to be a single." Josie took the empty glass, dumping the ice before putting it in the dishwasher. "Still upset about tomorrow night?"

"I like your jeans," Harriet blurted.

Josie glanced over her shoulder at her backside. "I was hoping you'd come in tonight. It's not my dress, but..." Josie arched her eyebrows. "Now, don't suck this one down like a frat boy, because I may have a solution to our problem."

"What's that?"

"Getting off work tonight around nine."

"I like the sound of getting off—" Harriet couldn't complete the sentence once she registered the words she'd just spoken.

"On second thought, maybe you should down the gin and tonic. It's really loosening your tongue."

Another patron stood at the bar, and Josie left Harriet once again, but Josie gave Harriet another chance to check out her ass.

"The best view in the village," Harriet said to herself, but Josie turned her head and gave Harriet a *you're a saucy minx* grin.

Harriet raised her glass in Josie's honor and took a drink.

CHAPTER TWENTY-THREE

"Mum?"

Eugenie groaned. "I hate when you say *Mum* in that tone."

"What tone?" Josie did her best to sound innocent.

"The *I want something* tone." Her mum wore her playful *let's do battle* face.

"You have a very low opinion of me."

"Does that mean you're not going to ask for a favor?"

"Oh, no, I am, but I would prefer if you pretended this isn't my usual song and dance." Josie attempted her cutest smile, the one she'd perfected when she was a toddler and wasn't ashamed to resort to when something really mattered, although she had no desire to fill in her mum about everything for the favor. They were close, but not that close.

"Try it again." Her mum crossed her arms.

"Mum?"

Her arms fell, and she shook her head. "Nope. Can't ignore the tone."

"Fine." Josie groaned. "Can I leave at nine tonight?"

"For what? A business meeting?" her mum scoffed. "If you think I'm falling for that again…" she said in a disapproving manner, which was somewhat confusing since Josie was convinced her mum wanted her daughter to be in a relationship. But she was so against Harry. Eugenie continued, "Or a late-night walk, perhaps, so you can sneak more cigarettes?"

No. I plan on shagging Harry. There was no way in hell Josie would admit that now considering her mother's hardening expression. Why did Harry have to question the name of the pub and décor? It was such a little thing, but something like that needled her mum more than Eugenie would admit considering she gave up the chance to go to college because of Josie. "Now, I don't like your tone. Or the expression on your face that implies I'm either a hooker or sneaking cigarettes behind your back."

"Are you? About either?"

Josie took a step back. "I can't believe you actually asked me that. The hooker part."

"It was meant to be a joke." Her mum sighed.

"Didn't sound like it."

"I know. I could feel it when it came out. But I can't get over the feeling that you're hiding something from me, and I don't like it. Not one bit."

"Oh, please. It's not like you tell me everything going on in your life."

"When you say things like that, it really makes me think you're keeping something from me."

"Mum," Josie muttered. "I'm thirty-eight, not eight. Of course, I don't tell you everything."

Her mum stared at her.

"Please, can I scram at nine? Clive said he'd stay, and one of the girls in the kitchen can pitch in if it gets super busy."

"You told Clive about your plans but not me?" Her mum rested a hurtful hand on her chest as if Josie had said, "I hate you!"

"No, I didn't tell him about my plans. He didn't ask. Clive treats me like I'm an adult."

"No, he doesn't. Clive treats you like you're one of his mates. Ask no questions; tell no lies. For all I know, we'll be receiving more kittens on your behalf as some type of threat."

"I'm lying now? Jesus. All I wanted was a few hours to myself tonight. I didn't know that warranted the fucking Spanish Inquisition. It's not like everything in my life has been smooth sailing. In case you missed the memo, my life fucking fell apart. I don't have a career. I'm in a country I don't know. Everyone corrects me when I say sweater instead of jumper, like they can't help pointing out I'm a stranger." Josie waved a hand in front of her face in an attempt to stop the tears and to get control of her quivering voice. "Everything I've worked for went up in smoke. You'd think my own mother would give me the time and space I need to get my shit together. Not fucking ride my ass." Josie tossed the towel she'd clenched in her hands onto the bar counter. "I quit!"

Her mum hollered, "You can't quit family!"

As she charged out of the pub, her back to her mum, Josie screamed, "There's a first for everything!"

Outside the pub was a group of French tourists at a table, drinking red wine and smoking. They must have overheard the commotion because not one said a word, staring with their mouths open at Josie the American Barbarian, who'd just yelled at her mum in front of a roomful of strangers and some of the villagers.

Josie sniffed and tried to smile as if saying *nothing to see here folks*, but in all probability, it turned into a grimace.

She turned toward the river, needing to walk off the feelings.

She didn't get far when she heard Harry call out her name.

Josie slowly turned, fully aware she was crying, but she forced out a *hi* that came out garbled, and then Josie burst into full-on waterworks.

"Hey, it's okay." Harry pulled Josie into her arms.

"I don't even know why I'm upset. Or why I just yelled at my mum in front of the entire pub." Josie mumbled the words into Harry's shoulder, unsure if Harry was able to understand her. "I should go apologize." Josie straightened.

"Do you think you two need time apart to let the dust settle?"

"I don't know. We don't really fight. This is a whole new world. Everything in my life is so new." Josie held onto Harry tighter.

"I'm sure it's all overwhelming. You've had some major life changes, and it might all be hitting you right now." Harry placed a hand on Josie's shoulder.

"Exactly. It's like it's really sinking in. My career is gone. What am I going to do? I feel like a boxer in the tenth round." With frantic hand motions, Josie mimed getting hit from all angles.

Harry slanted her head, giving Josie her full attention. "Do you want to come back to my place so we can talk?"

Josie nodded. "Yes, but I'll meet you there. I want to say sorry to my mum. I can't leave it like that. We don't act that way, ever. Not even when I was a teen."

"Do you want me to go with you?"

"I won't turn down your company."

They walked silently, side by side, back into the pub.

Josie's mum, her eyes puffy, talked to Clive behind the bar. Upon seeing Josie and Harry, Clive jerked his head so

Josie's mum would take notice. Without words, her mum came out from behind the bar and wrapped Josie into her arms.

"I'm sorry, Mum. I don't know what's going on with me."

"Me neither. I mean with me."

"I'm going over to Harry's to talk and unwind. If that's okay with you."

"Of course, honey. Clive and Olivia are taking over for the night, so I'm going to take a hot bath. Maybe he's not as useless as I thought."

They said goodbye, and Harry held the door open for Josie.

Josie sucked in a deep breath, feeling much better.

Walking along the river toward Harry's cottage, Josie said, "You know, Mum didn't even give it a second thought that I was heading to your place."

"Oh, I doubt she thinks you'd be attracted to me."

Josie flinched as if someone had tossed cold water in her face. "Why would you say such a thing?"

"I have it on good authority."

"Meaning?"

"It's possible I overheard your mum and one of her friends talking about fixing you up on a date, and your mum categorically declared her daughter wouldn't date someone from London or a woman with small tits."

"She actually said small tits."

"Not in those exact words. At least not the word small."

"And you overheard this?"

"Yes. In the coffee shop on the square."

"That explains some of your hesitancy around me. Just to clarify, I have no idea why she thinks I focus on breasts."

Harry shrugged.

"She's told me the same. About dating someone from

London. I don't know how to tell her out of all the women I've ever been interested in, you're by far the best of the bunch."

Harry smiled.

"I'm not sure that came out exactly how I meant it." Josie's gaze fell to the pavement. "I think you got a sense the night I ruined dinner that my taste in women up until this point has been abysmal. I was horrified after I shared the bee sting story."

"Why?"

"I don't want you to think poorly of me."

"I don't, Josie. Not at all."

"It was like I couldn't stop myself from sharing the story. For some reason, I want you to see the real me. Not the Josie I show the world. I need you to know me. Really know me. And it scares me."

"I understand." Harry threaded her fingers through Josie's. "My ex-wife once told me I was too nice and didn't have any passion. Not just for her, but for life. I'll admit hearing her say that did a number on me. It's not until I met you that I started to realize just how much I had absorbed those words and started to live according to her beliefs. Soon after she said it, I moved here, cutting myself off from everyone and life."

"I'm glad. Not about what she said or how it made you feel, but I can't lie about being happy to have met you. Out of everything going on in my life, you're the one shining light. There's something about you, Harry Powell."

CHAPTER TWENTY-FOUR

Harriet wanted to sweep Josie into her arms, but given Josie's emotional state, and Harriet's shyness seeping back into her core, or lack of faith in herself, if she were being honest, she had a hard time believing the words completely. Clarification. That was what she needed as much as that made her feel idiotic. "And what's that?"

"I don't know how to describe it. There just is. And I'm pretty sure I haven't even scratched the surface of how wonderful you are." Josie squeezed Harriet's fingers tighter.

"What if you scratch the surface and discover what Alice found out?"

"No offence, and I know I haven't met her, so this assessment is completely biased, but I think your ex-wife is a bitch. Or should I say the c-word since I'm in Britain?"

"It's a divisive word."

"I'm in a divisive mood." Josie ground a fist into her left hand.

They entered Harriet's cottage. "We can't have that.

Not after your evening. Tell you what, why don't you go out into the garden? I'll pour us some wine, and we can sit back and bash our exes to our hearts' content."

Josie laughed. "That sounds delightful. The wine in the garden bit. Not sure I need to bash my exes, though. I'd rather get to know you better."

"I have it on good authority—"

Josie silenced Harry with a kiss. Quick and sweet. "Wine, please. I'm going to freshen up. And this time, when I come back into the kitchen, I promise to be as quiet as a mouse so you don't drop the wine. The chicken incident was a travesty. Ruining an entire bottle of wine would be the end of the world."

"Truly." Harriet wanted to sweep some hair off Josie's face, but refrained. Her need to touch Josie grew with each breath.

When Josie left Harriet in the kitchen, Harriet rubbed the top of her head, trying to get her nerves under control. It'd been a long time since she'd been this interested in, not to mention attracted to, someone. Actually, her wanting may not have ever reached this level. It was as if Harriet couldn't survive being away from Josie.

"Geez, which one of us is more dramatic this evening?" Harriet glanced over her shoulder to ensure she was indeed alone.

She uncorked the wine and started to pour. While pouring the second glass, Josie reentered the kitchen.

"Nice job with being quiet. It must be hard to control your Americanness."

"Ha! Even my own mum bad-mouths Americans, and she married one and has a daughter who's half American. It's a black mark against me as soon as I step into a different country."

"Well, as you know, most here think of me as the

London snob."

"Are you?" Josie's smile was teasing.

"Most definitely. You ready for the garden?" Harriet swept both glasses into her hands.

"More than ready."

They made their way to the small garden, where there were two wicker seats and a tiny table on a flagstone patio.

"This is perfect. If I had a place like this, I'd spend all my time out here no matter the season."

"I'd love that. Too bad the British weather is so British-y."

"Not tonight, though. Just look at the clear sky." Josie peered up. "And I love how it gets so purplish at the end of the day. It's like nature is saving up the best color for the last gasp of daylight."

Harriet handed Josie a glass and took a seat. "Does that mean purple is your favorite color?"

"It is. What's yours?"

"Yellow."

"Really?" Josie squinted at the sky.

"Yeah. Why?"

"I've never known someone who's favorite color is yellow. It's usually blue, red, or purple."

Harriet pulled out her phone. "Let's see." She entered the question into the search bar and then started laughing. "According to the first result that popped up, the most popular color is blue. Followed by red, green, and purple. Then black, orange, yellow, and gold. Aren't the last two the same? And"—Harriet counted—"black comes in fifth. It's the absence of color, so I object to it being higher than yellow."

Josie laughed.

"You see, more proof you shouldn't scratch below the surface. You'll keep finding out things like this. My favorite color is one of the last. Surely that says something about me."

"That you aren't afraid to be yourself. If you ask me, that's a good thing. I admire people who are themselves, no matter what. Not ones trying to please others. Maybe that's what actually upset Alice and why she said what she said. An attempt to tear you down. So many are terrified of people who know who they are."

Harriet mulled that over. "Okay. Going on that, wouldn't that mean I'd be the worst person to get involved with since I don't try to please others?"

"Maybe I wasn't lumping myself into the *others* category."

"Is that right?" Harriet held her wineglass in both hands. Staring into the glass, she asked, "What category do you *lump* yourself into?"

"Not sure there's a definition yet, but I have a good feeling about it."

Harriet met Josie's eyes. "You may be changing my mind about my color preference."

"How am I doing that?"

"You have the most stunning emerald eyes."

Josie smiled, not saying anything for several seconds. "I know I said I didn't want to bash exes, but I really do have to question Alice's mental state. How did she not realize how wonderful you are?"

"Don't get ahead of yourself. I only said you have beautiful eyes."

"I know, but it's also how you said it and how it made me feel."

"How'd I say it?"

"Like you meant it." Josie leaned over in her chair to rest her hand briefly on Harriet's cheek.

"I do."

"I know. I can see it in your stunning blue eyes."

Harriet wanted Josie's hand back on her skin, her cheek feeling the absence of Josie's heat. "How did it make you feel?"

"So very good. I'm sure there's a better way to put that, but words are failing me right now."

"Says the speechwriter."

"You love that line." Josie sipped her wine, her eyes sparkling more by the minute. "I like the way I feel when I'm around you."

"That's good to hear. I like being around you."

"To a brilliant beginning." Josie raised her glass.

Harriet hoisted hers before taking a teensy sip. "What's your favorite movie?"

"Will you judge me if I say *Notting Hill?*"

"Is that the truth?"

"It is." Josie dipped her head with the admission.

"No, I won't judge you."

"What's yours?"

"Will you judge me if I say *Citizen Kane?*"

Josie's smile widened. "I should have guessed that. It's so you."

"Is that a good or bad thing?"

"Good. I wasn't lying earlier when I said I like you because you are you."

"You'll have to give me some time to get used to that."

Josie relaxed into her seat, resting her head against the chair. "It's getting dark."

Harriet looked up into the darkness. "It is. Are you cold?"

"Nope. I can sit here for a bit more."

"I have no objection to that."

Their eyes met, and each took a lustful sip of their wine.

CHAPTER TWENTY-FIVE

"OF COURSE, THESE CHAIRS DON'T ALLOW FOR snuggling." Josie took another sip of wine, wondering how obvious she would have to be to crash completely through Harry's reserve. While this evening was different from the previous time Josie was at Harry's, Josie wasn't going to kid herself. Harry was still reserved and polite to an almost annoying degree.

"They do limit us on that front." Harry's eyes were on her wineglass, not Josie.

"Is this a limitation we're wanting to live with at the moment?"

"Depends." Harry's chin lifted to meet Josie's gaze.

Josie laughed. "Does that mean you'd rather not be the one to say it?"

"Say what?" Harry's smile was an indication she was being playful, which Josie had to admit was a turn-on.

"I'll have another glass of wine." Josie decided to give Harry a taste of her own medicine.

Harry rose. "By all means. I'm not one to deny a beautiful woman."

"Ha! Nicely played."

Harry clutched the front of her shirt. "What game are you accusing me of playing?"

"None whatsoever." Josie handed off her empty wineglass.

Harry finished her wine. "I'll fill both of these and be right back."

"No rush, Harry. The stars will keep me company."

Harry looked toward the heavens. "I've always been a fan of Ursa Minor, also known as Little Bear."

"I never studied astronomy," Josie confessed.

"Let me fill these, and I'll give you your first lesson."

Josie liked the sound of *first lesson*, implying there'd be more opportunities to stargaze with the stunning blonde. "Looking forward to it."

While Harry was inside, Josie rested her head on the chair, glancing into the blackness, trying to make rhyme or reason of the dots of light slowly coming to life.

"Here you go." Harry returned Josie's glass.

"I'm ready for my lesson."

"I'll do my best. There are some wonderful hills in the area that offer superb views, given the low light pollution in the Cotswolds. Even here, on a clear night like this evening, you can make out some of the constellations."

"Do you stargaze often?"

"Not as often as I should," Harry said with regret.

Curious by Harry's slumped shoulders, Josie pressed, "What do you mean?"

"Like most, I take them for granted."

What other laments did Harry have? "Unless on the road, I've always lived in cities. The night lights I'm used to seeing consist of skyscrapers. Which are beautiful in a different way."

"True." Harry set her glass down on the table. "Okay, what do you know about Ursa Minor?"

"Nothing, although I'm guessing there's an Ursa Major."

"Good guess. Ursa Minor, as I said earlier is also known as Little Bear. Has been for eons. Ptolemy, in the second century, listed forty-eight constellations, including Ursa Minor."

"How many do we know about today?" Josie looked at the heavens again.

"Eighty-eight."

She met Harry's gaze. "Not bad for Ptolemy. He got more than half."

Harry glanced up, pointing. "You see that star? It's the brightest one in the constellation. You probably know it. Polaris, or the North Star. Mariners have been using it for navigation over the centuries."

Josie got to her feet, standing close to Harry. "Which one?"

Harry repositioned behind Josie. Taking Josie's right hand into hers, Harry guided them to the star in the north. "Follow our arms with your eyes to find it."

Josie's heartbeat sped, while her breathing slowed. Harry pressed against Josie's backside. After a glance over her shoulder at the concentration on Harry's face, Josie allowed her eyes to follow their conjoined arms and fingers to the bright yellow star. "I see it."

"If you ever lose your way, you can locate the star and know where north is." Harry's breath tickled the back of Josie's neck, causing her to close her eyes momentarily to focus on the sensation of her skin.

"Have you ever needed it?" Josie asked, opening her eyes.

"Can't say that I have, but I know it's there if I do."

They both still had their arms in the air as if afraid to break apart.

Harry moved them a bit. "The North Star is the tip of the bear's tail. The constellation is sometimes called the Little Dipper, since the stars make up a smaller version of the Big Dipper." Harry traced the pattern of the stars.

"Is the Big Dipper part of Ursa Major?"

"It is." Harry's voice indicated she was impressed by Josie's deduction.

"It's ringing a faint bell."

Their arms lowered, but Harry still stood behind Josie.

"Here's another part of the story. Ursa Minor is named after Ida. She was one of Zeus's nurses when he was a baby on Crete."

Josie wheeled about, her arms now on each of Harry's shoulders. "Why is she a bear?"

With her arms around Josie's waist, Harry pulled them closer together. "Unfortunately, that bit is unclear."

"I guess only so much of the past can be known."

"That's very true."

"I'm kinda glad we stayed out here, even if you were playing a mind game."

"I would never." Harry's *aw shucks* smile and delivery made it clear she knew she was busted. "Okay, fine, but why are you glad?"

"Because I want Little Bear to witness this."

"What?"

Josie leaned in to kiss Harry, who met her halfway.

"Why did you want Ida to see that?"

"In case I lose my way, she'll lead me back to you."

Their lips met again, neither willing to break apart.

CHAPTER TWENTY-SIX

HARRIET STARED AT THE PATIO LIGHT flickering in Josie's green eyes, making them more emerald-like and intoxicating. "You have the most amazing eyes. I can stare into them for hours."

"Aw. Is that a line you use on all the redheads?"

"I've never dated a redhead."

"Are you prejudiced against them?" Josie's smile was teasing.

"You know what they say."

"No. What?"

"I have no idea, but I did buy a book about the history of redheads."

Josie tilted her head back, laughing. "That seems so like something you'd do." She tapped her chin with a finger. "Wait, when did you purchase this book?"

"Not that long ago."

Josie motioned she needed more details. "Out with it."

"The book hasn't arrived yet."

"That recently, huh? May I ask what prompted the sudden interest in redheads?"

"A clue I was working on for the crossword, led to some googling, which led to the acquisition."

"What was the clue?"

"I wanted someone who was a redhead that many might not know about, and I discovered Oliver Cromwell, in all likelihood, was a ginger. Does that word offend you?"

Josie shook her head. "Nope. I remember getting onto a subway in New York last year, and this man gave me a pound while he said, *Keep it real, sister ginger*."

"Why'd he give you a quid?"

Josie's confused expression slowly dissipated. "Oh, not a pound as in British money. A fist bump." Josie made a fist for Harriet to bump. "Don't leave a girl hanging."

"Oh, right." Harriet lightly tapped her fist against Josie's.

"You're a gentle pounder."

Harriet felt heat prickle her cheeks.

Josie cupped the side of Harriet's face. "I'm sorry. I didn't mean to embarrass you. That one wasn't intentional."

"Have the others been?"

"In all likelihood, yes."

"Just to let you know, any type of innuendo makes me turn three shades of red." Harriet felt the heat inside intensify, but it wasn't solely due to Josie's comment.

"Does an outright dirty joke take you to the fourth dimension?"

"Time will tell."

Josie burst into laughter. "Nicely played."

"I think that's the only thing I remember from physics, that the fourth dimension is time."

Josie scrunched her nose. "I only remember: more time, less force."

"Yes, it's why dashboards are padded. To reduce the impact in car accidents."

Josie's hand snaked to the back of Harriet's head, pulling her closer.

Before their lips met, Harriet asked, "I never knew physics could be hot."

"The hottest." Josie kissed Harriet again.

Harriet stroked Josie's cheek with a fingertip and hopscotched from one tiny freckle to the next, leading down Josie's face, past her neck, to the top of her shirt. Harriet's fingers slowly undid the second button from the top, allowing Harriet to place a soft kiss on the hollow of her throat.

Josie's chest hitched slightly. "I need to order more books on the fourth dimension if this is how it'll keep playing out."

Harriet traced Josie's collarbone with a thumb. "Any type of random facts really gets me going. I'm determined to win pub quiz night at least once before I die."

"I'll see if I can plant some redhead questions for you."

"Will Helen let you suggest questions? She seems to like being in control."

"A woman after my own heart." Josie's tongue was back inside Harriet's mouth. Warm and inviting. Josie attempted to lift Harriet's shirt but was stopped.

"I think we should move inside."

Josie nodded and let Harriet lead her by the hand upstairs to the bedroom. Standing at the foot of the bed, Josie once again tried to undress Harriet but was rebuffed.

"All good things come to those who wait." Harriet's breathing increased as she undid another one of Josie's buttons.

"Is it weird how turned on I am about you undressing me?"

Harriet eyed the way Josie's breasts heaved up and down as the level of excitement jacked up. "It's working for both of us."

Another button was popped open, revealing a hint of pink lace. "I have to admit I wasn't expecting pink."

"It's my second favorite color."

"Is that a thing? Second color choice?" Harriet kissed the swell of Josie's right breast.

"It is for me," Josie panted.

"You can have all the colors, as long as you leave me green."

"I thought yellow was your fave."

"Like I said, your eyes are swaying me."

"Not my ginger hair?"

"Excellent point. I'm claiming red and green."

"Christmas colors. Bold choice."

"It's the best time of year." Harriet freed another button to discover tiny black polka dots on the cups of the silky bra. "Now, this is you."

"What?"

"The dots. Very playful." Harriet placed a finger on Josie's lips.

Josie sucked the finger into her mouth, causing Harriet to close her eyes for several ticks, before she continued her exploration. Josie studied Harriet as she scrupulously exposed Josie's body. Harriet's heart raced, and the warmth below intensified.

Taking in a fortifying breath, the next button bared the top of Josie's taut stomach. And the following one, Josie's tiny belly button. At last, Harriet cracked open the remaining one and eased the left side of the shirt over Josie's shoulder. Harriet placed a kiss on the fully exposed collarbone. Then she eased the rest of the shirt off Josie's torso, letting the shirt flutter to the floor. Goose bumps sprang to life on Josie's skin.

"Are you cold?" Harriet asked, skimming a finger across the waistline of Josie's jeans.

"No," Josie whispered in the tiniest voice as if not wanting to destroy the moment with sound. She beckoned Harriet with a crooked finger, demanding Harriet kiss her. Harriet inched closer, savoring Josie's breath on her lips. Even though they'd kissed before this moment, it still seemed like the stakes had raised for Harriet, as if the next few seconds would make or break the moment. Not that Harriet was big on pressure. Who was she kidding? Harriet lived and died by high pressure moments. It was like she couldn't succeed unless pushing herself to the brink.

"What are you waiting for?" Josie asked.

"I'm slightly nervous," Harriet confessed.

"Does it help you to know I am, too?"

"It does. Like I'm not alone."

"You aren't, Harry. Not by a long shot."

The space between their mouths was less than an inch. Harriet smiled, which Josie reciprocated. The amount of promise in the air between them practically sizzled.

"Still nervous?" Josie whispered.

"I think I've been searching for you all my life."

Josie cupped each side of Harriet's face. "What took you so long?"

Harriet laughed. "I guess I wasn't ready."

"Are you now?"

"Yes."

Their mouths found each other, skipping the soft phase and sliding right into the *wanting to fuck* stage. Harriet deepened the kiss even more, eliciting an ecstatic moan from Josie. Harriet gently shoved Josie onto the bed before climbing on top of her. Josie tugged on Harriet's shirt, indicating it had to go. Harriet obliged, and when their bodies pressed together, a jolt of electricity pinged every single nerve ending in Harriet's body.

Harriet's fingers found their way under Josie and unhooked her bra. Josie's ample breasts were punctuated by delicate pink nipples. Harriet's thumb circled one nipple, hardening it as they kissed again.

Harriet moved down to tease the other nipple with her tongue. Josie clamped her hand to the back of Harriet's head, running her fingers through Harriet's short hair. Josie's attention to Harriet's head was a huge turn-on. Harriet bit down harder on Josie's nipple. Josie's back bowed, while Harriet's hand traveled down toward Josie's stomach.

Josie hoisted her lower body and attempted to remove her jeans, but Harriet prevented Josie from following through.

"Please, let me finish undressing you."

Josie grinned. "By all means, have your way with me."

"I plan to." Harriet undid the top of Josie's jeans, lowering the zipper ever so slowly, not wanting to rush but also waiting with bated breath to see if Josie's knickers matched the bra. "I wondered if it was a set or not," Harriet said, as the black polka dots appeared on the silk knickers.

"It's important to always match."

"Always?" Harriet's hitched breath showed her excitement. Harriet's fingers walked over the silk, soaking in Josie's warmth. Harriet eased the jeans off, leaving the knickers for a moment.

Josie quirked one eyebrow as if asking why.

"They're sexy as hell; it's almost a shame to take them off, although…" Harriet pressed a finger to inspect how wet Josie was. "I think you're more than ready for me."

"I am. So, so, so ready."

Harriet eased the silky fabric down Josie's legs, taking note of the shimmer on her inner thighs. "I can't wait to taste you."

"Nothing's stopping you now."

"Very true. However..." Harriet arched one eyebrow. "Not sure it's time to dive in. Is that how an American would phrase it?"

"You want a language lesson now? You're killing me." Josie's grin testified she wasn't too put out.

Harriet kissed her way down the inside of Josie's left leg, boosted her foot, and nibbled on each toe. Then Harriet's hand ran up and down Josie's other leg, the calf muscle tight.

"Your legs are so smooth."

"Don't forget the other toes," Josie practically begged.

"I would never play favorites." Harriet sucked on the remaining ones.

"Oh, God, that feels amazing."

Harriet's mouth began the trek up Josie's right leg, stopping before reaching Josie's Holy Grail. Her musky smell filled Harriet's senses, making Harriet take several deep breaths, unable to get her fill.

Josie's hips moved as if doing their best to guide Harriet to where she should be. Where Harriet longed to be as close as possible to Josie.

Harriet couldn't stop the grin from forming on her face as her fingers separated Josie's lips, allowing Harriet to insert a finger inside. Slowly, giving Josie time to welcome Harriet with a don't stop exhalation.

Harriet added a finger as she repositioned to kiss Josie again. Josie's insides constricted around Harriet's fingers. Easing the fingers in and out, the two of them kissed, Josie's fingers digging into Harriet's back.

"I want you," Josie whispered.

Harriet knew exactly what she meant. She gave Josie one final kiss on the lips, and then her tongue made its way southward, while Harriet's fingers still eased in and out of Josie.

Harriet bypassed Josie's nipples this time, knowing Josie's urgency was growing by the second. Not to mention Harriet was dying for that first taste.

Past the belly button.

Her teeth raked Josie's pubic hair.

Harriet plunged in deep at the same moment her tongue lightly flicked Josie's clit, releasing an *oh God* moan, her mouth needed more of Josie.

"You feel so good," Josie purred, fisting Harriet's hair.

Harriet increased the speed of diving in and out of Josie, unable to keep things going slow. Not after delaying the undressing and full-body exploration. Harriet needed to fuck Josie. Right then and there. Harriet's tongue concentrated on Josie's nerves, enjoying the increase in Josie's frantic gyrations and moans. Not to mention Josie was getting wetter with each flick of the tongue and the movement of Harriet's hand. Josie's lower half jounced about, making it difficult for Harriet to keep her mouth where it needed to be, although Harriet wasn't complaining. No amount of work would stop her from getting Josie to that point where everything went black before the orgasmic meteor shower.

Josie made a whimpering sound and writhed on the bed. God, Harriet loved the way Josie moved. Her sounds. All of it was quickly becoming addictive.

Josie's heavy breathing accelerated, and Harriet guessed Josie was close to reaching climax, which was confirmed when Josie's upper body bolted off the bed and she clasped her hands around Harriet's head, as if saying, *Whatever you do, don't stop.*

Harriet's fingers hammered in deep, curling upward. Josie's nails scored Harriet's scalp.

Josie's legs started to tremble, the quake moving into a full-body spasm. Harriet held her fingers in the spot she assumed was triggering the spasm, and her tongue circled Josie's clit with determination. Soon, Josie's body vibrated, as the orgasm progressed to mind-blowing levels, causing Josie to utter, "Jesus fucking Christ, this feels amazing!" Josie had such a grip on Harriet's head, and for a few moments, Harriet couldn't breathe at all.

Another wave seemed to burst through Josie's body, forcing her to tense every muscle, until she collapsed onto the bed. Harriet repositioned on top of Josie, both breathing heavily as they recovered together, neither woman moving for quite a spell.

"Tell me again why you took so long to find me," Josie said.

"I'm a fool." Harriet spoke into the crook of Josie's neck.

"You don't fuck like a fool."

Harriet laughed. "I really don't know how to respond to that."

Josie pulled Harriet's face to hers.

In one swift motion, Josie rolled Harriet onto her back, hovering over her. "You have way too many articles of clothing on." Without another word, Josie stripped Harriet of her jeans and knickers.

Harriet beckoned Josie for another kiss. "I could kiss you for an eternity."

Josie responded with fervor, suggesting she was in the same boat.

Harriet tensed briefly as Josie's fingers parted the lips below and worked their way inside.

"Pretty sure I won't ever get my fill of fucking you." Josie worked her fingers in deeper. "Or should I say shagging?"

Harriet whispered, "Choose whichever word you like, but please don't stop."

"I never want to let you down." Josie's tongue teased Harriet's earlobe, getting an excited moan from Harriet. Josie seemed to take notice and licked the inside of Harriet's ear, causing even more excitement. Even Harriet's toes curled.

Josie's tongue moved down Harriet's body, seeming to find spots that had never been brought to life, each lick and nip bringing forth a flood of emotions.

When Josie arrived at Harriet's bud, sucking it into her mouth, Harriet nearly launched off the bed up to the ceiling, catlike. As Josie circled the clit, Harriet edged closer to bliss, unable to sense how deep Josie's fingers were, but wanting her to go even deeper.

Josie did.

"This feels so fucking fantastic."

Josie's gaze landed on Harriet's, the sparkle in the green flecks coming more alive as she gorged on Harriet. Unable to keep her eyes open, Harriet shut them to fully experience the stars exploding in her mind.

When the lights faded and Harriet's breathing returned to somewhat normal speed, she pulled Josie into her arms.

"I'm thinking never having a redheaded girlfriend has been a big oversight," Harriet joked.

Josie pinched her side. "I know you have sex brain, but that's not something any woman wants to hear."

"All women? Or just redheads?"

"You're cruising for a bruising. But just to clarify, no

woman wants to hear how the woman they just made love to wishes they'd slept with lots more people."

"Not just any people. Redheads."

Josie hovered over Harriet. "What's about to happen is all your fault."

Harriet slanted her head. "Your smile isn't all that terrifying. Maybe you should work on your threatening technique."

"Maybe my plan is to lull you into a false sense of security."

"Now you have my full attention."

"It only took a threat to get it. Who says women are difficult creatures?"

"Every person on the planet who has met one."

Josie's hip rubbed against Harriet's pussy.

"Is this the torture part?"

"You have another comment you want to voice?" Josie tried to appear stern.

"Say it ain't so, because this is terrible. Absolutely horrendous. I may not survive."

"Something tells me you're being sarcastic. I didn't think Brits did sarcasm."

"Are you kidding? We invented it. You Americans have so much to learn in the snide area."

"Is that right?"

Josie tweaked Harriet's left nipple. "Am I a fast learner?"

"I don't know. Are you?" Harriet goaded Josie.

Josie ground her hip even more into Harriet.

"It's amazing you guys won the Revolutionary War given—"

Josie sucked Harriet's nipple completely into her mouth. She released. "You were saying?"

"Don't stop. Like it… much."

"Given your inability to speak in full sentences, I seemed to have found your weakness. One of them at least." Josie worked on the nipple more, practically bringing Harriet to the brink. "Oh my, you really love nipple play."

"Doesn't everyone?"

"Some have sensitive ones that don't allow for too much."

Harriet quirked her brow.

Josie hurried to say, "So I've heard. Before today, I was as pure as the driven snow. Even had a chastity belt."

"I don't remember taking that off earlier."

"I broke free all on my own before coming over."

"I love a woman with a mind of her own."

Josie grinned. "That's good news for me. I don't like being told what to think. If you really want to start a fight, tell me what I'm thinking. Or interpret my thoughts and feelings. That goes over so well. Not."

Harriet tapped the side of her head. "Taking notes."

"Do I need to write it down for you? You are getting up there in years."

"Did you really just—?" Harriet didn't complete the thought but flipped Josie onto her back. "Let me show you how much energy I have left."

"That was much easier than I thought."

"Shut up, and let me fuck you."

CHAPTER TWENTY-SEVEN

A STREAK OF SUNLIGHT LANDED ON JOSIE'S FACE, and a warm body pressed up against her. Josie wiggled farther into Harry's body, loving how she felt in this moment. It wasn't solely the results of making love the previous night. Josie enjoyed the comfort of having Harry next to her, knowing she wanted more than sex. She craved so much more. Human touch. Snuggling on the couch, watching television. Reading the Sunday paper in bed. Going for long walks. Cooking dinners together. Growing old together. How was this happening now? When nothing else in Josie's life made sense?

Josie rolled onto her side carefully so as not to disturb the slumbering blonde. She stared into Harry's peaceful face and took in all the different directions of Harry's hair. So fucking adorable.

Wait, what did Josie's look like? She ran a hand over her head to assess the damage.

"Did I wake you?" Harry asked in a sleep-filled voice.

"I'll never complain about waking next to you. Besides,

I think I'm the one who woke you." Josie pulled Harry's hand up to her lips for a kiss.

"I'm glad we got past the *never say what's on my mind* phase."

"Me too. Is this the time to say I love tea in bed?"

Harry started to lift the bedcovers.

Josie laughed. "I was kidding. Mostly. I don't want you to leave the bed quite yet."

"Oh, really?" The tiredness gave way to excitement.

"You can't possibly have energy for that, can you?"

"Is this the time I confess I'm a morning person?"

Josie buried her face into the plush pillow. "How am I in bed with a morning person?"

"You seduced me last night."

Josie rolled over and faced Harry. "Wait? I seduced you?"

"Absolutely."

"Says the woman who was pointing out the North Star and talking about how not to lose one's way."

"That was my seduction plan?" Harry asked in a confused voice. "I don't think any woman has ever said my nerdy side worked that way. Usually, they stare at me as if wishing I'd just shut up."

"It was romantic!"

Harry beamed. "It was?"

"Very much so." Josie planted her hand on Harry's cheek.

"If I remember correctly, I pointed out the North Star. You were the one who said you wanted Ida to witness our kiss in case you needed her help to find your way back to me. That was romantic." Harry pressed the tip of Josie's nose.

Josie propped up her head, staring at Harry. "Can we agree that we're romantic together?"

"It's a difficult concept for me to understand."

Josie draped an arm over Harry's stomach, needing skin-on-skin contact, which was somewhat confusing since Josie wasn't the cuddling type. Or hadn't been until this moment. "Why?"

"I don't think anyone has ever said I was romantic or contributed to romantic notions." Harry gave a half shrug.

"We've already established I'm not a fan of your ex-wife, but are all of your exes like her?"

"In what sense?"

"Negative Nellies."

"How does their calling out my behavior classify them that way?" Harry questioned without contempt in her tone or body language.

"Does that mean you agree with their assessment that you're not romantic?"

"I wasn't with others. I'm realizing that." Harry patted Josie's hand.

"No ifs, ands, or buts?"

Harry shook her head. "I'm a practical person."

"And romance, or love for that matter, isn't practical?"

Harry squinted one eye, seeming to mull over the question or a tactful way of answering. "I… I may need time to figure out an answer."

"Take as much time as you need."

"What do you think?"

"If love is practical?" Josie laughed. "Not by a long shot. People seem to lose their fucking minds when love enters the equation."

"You're smiling about that."

"It's the best kind of mental derangement. Everything seems possible. Colors are more vibrant. Annoying people don't seem too annoying. Food tastes better, but you hardly ever notice you're hungry. Things that usually make your temper flair just make you laugh. Even family isn't so annoying."

"Are you saying when I don't find Camilla obnoxious, it means I've fallen head over heels?"

Josie regarded Harry. "Have you not been in love before?"

"I haven't experienced any of the signs you listed."

"And you got married?" Josie attempted to sound nonjudgmental, but she couldn't understand why anyone would marry unless they thought the person was the one. Like what her parents had. What Josie wanted but feared she'd never fully achieve.

"Yes."

"Why?" Josie's voice came out much too high-pitched, making her sound overly screechy. So much for not judging.

Nonplussed, Harry explained in her calm Harry way, "We'd been living together for a few years when marriage became legal in the UK. It seemed like the right thing to do."

Josie waited a few ticks for the words to sink in. "Wow. That's the exact opposite of romance. Who asked whom?"

Harry slitted her left eye again. "It just kinda happened. We were having dinner. Alice mentioned something about what we should do, and one thing led to another. The next thing I knew, we were getting married."

"That's insane."

"But not the right kind of insane according to your pinched face." Harry methodically rotated a finger in front of Josie's face.

Josie attempted to relax her facial muscles. "It's not the way I'd go about getting married. Is this common in the UK?"

"Common-law marriage doesn't exist in the UK."

"No, I didn't mean that. Are marriages entered into without a lot of... how do I say this... feelings?"

"Was that the gentlest way you could think of?" Harry's smile eased Josie some.

"Yes. How should I have phrased it?"

"I feel like we're getting away from how we felt moments ago." Harry bit down on her lower lip.

"How was that?"

"Happy," Harry stated simply but conveyed so much more with her piercing blue eyes.

Josie smiled. "I was and still am, but if I'm making you uncomfortable, I can stop grilling you."

"I didn't say you were doing that. It's just... I don't want you to think I'm always so logical."

"What's the last illogical thing you've done?"

"I placed the milk in the cupboard, not the fridge."

"That's being absentminded," Josie scoffed, but had to laugh over the image of Harry realizing the error.

"Is there a difference?"

"Most definitely." Josie punctuated the sentence with an exuberant up and down head motion.

"Give me an example of something illogical you've done."

"You mean besides giving up my career? I know I was fired, but my mentor urged me not to flee the country, saying she could get me on to another campaign within twenty-four hours. I just couldn't face it anymore."

"I understand. I did the same when my paper sacked me. Can we count that?" Harry looked genuinely hopeful.

"I don't think so."

"But you just counted it for you."

"I set the rules, so I can disqualify what I want."

Harry grinned. "You're not playing fair."

Josie hiked a thumb at her chest. "Woman." After a

chuckle, she explained. "You picked up your career by taking over *The Cotswolds Chronicles*. I'm working in my mum's pub. There's a big difference." Josie held one hand high above Harry for emphasis.

Harry eased Josie's hand back down. "Nothing wrong with work."

"True," Josie said, not really believing it. The more she thought about working in the pub, the more she realized how much she missed using her brain and the thrill of having an exciting job. Or was it the stigma she placed on having a service job?

"Since we're not counting careers, tell me something illogical you've done because of love." Harry's question snagged Josie's attention.

"From which angle? When falling for someone or when it's *ending*?" Josie couldn't help herself from stressing the last word.

Harry's eyes started to bulge slightly. "I'm almost afraid to ask but can't seem to stop myself. What's something you've done at the end? From the look on your face, I have a feeling it was on the extreme side?"

"Are you sure you want me to answer? Once you hear things, you can't unhear them."

"It's like driving by a car crash. I can't look away."

"Okay. The first thing that popped into my head was when I woke up earlier than normal to surprise a woman I'd been dating somewhat casually, but I had thought there could be more. I picked up her favorite coffee from Starbucks and drove to her house before six in the morning. I'd planned to slip into bed with her, and I knew her garage door code. But her ex's car was in the driveway, and there was no way her ex popped by at that time of day."

"What'd you do?"

"I went back to my place, gathered up all the things

she'd left in my apartment from the nights she'd stayed over, drove back to her house, and tossed them all onto her front lawn. I texted her saying she'd better get her stuff. Oh, I hung one of her bras, she was a double D and had a thing for lacy underthings, from the antenna of her ex's car." Josie ran through a mental check sheet to ensure she got the highlights.

"Did the ex see it?"

"Not sure. They ended up moving back in together for a hot second before things spiraled out of control again. The bitch had the gall to seek me out when it blew up in her face, wanting to get back with me."

"Did you?"

"We had sex again. She was good in bed." Josie shrugged.

Harry laughed.

"That didn't bother you?"

"Should it have?"

"Not sure. A lot of women don't really like to hear the woman they just slept with for the first time talking about how they treated a woman in a breakup. Maybe it's another difference between Americans and Brits."

"Hard to know. Should we do some research at the pub? Set up a table for people to sit down and rate how they would react in certain situations."

"That could be entertaining. Mum's been talking about setting up some type of dating game to pull in more villagers. Not just the women sleeping with Clive." A thought struck Josie. "Maybe it *is* a British thing. God knows how many Clive has slept with, and from what I've seen, the women seem to think it's all in good fun."

"Should that be our target pool? How do I phrase it? *Excuse me. Have you slept with Clive Johnson? Do you know he has* been with almost every woman in this pub? On a scale of one to ten, how does that make you feel?"

"Is one not angry and ten is?"

"Haven't put much thought into it. Can this be counted in my illogical column?" Harry's expression was hopeful.

"Um, no."

"That hardly seems fair." Harry pouted.

Josie rolled on top of her. "Are you trying to act illogical now to get points in some imaginary column?"

"Would that count?"

Josie rubbed the tip of her nose against Harry's. "Nope."

"You're cheating."

"Are you objecting to my methods?"

"Again, this is a highly unscrupulous method. I mean, you want me to argue against you being on top of me naked, while I'm also unclothed?"

"Unclothed? Is that a word you say often?"

"I have no idea. It seemed to fit the situation."

Josie stared into Harry's eyes. "Is it weird that I find your British reserve so fucking adorable?"

"Again, is this a trick question?"

Josie kissed Harry's forehead. Above her right eye. Then the left. Working her way down Harry's astonishingly straight nose, which seemed to fit Harry's personality to a T. Josie's lips landed on Harry's, their kiss starting off sweet, as if both were still getting accustomed to the other's preference.

Soon, though, Harry amped up the passion, biting down on Josie's lower lip, eliciting an excited moan from Josie, before Harry took full possession of Josie's mouth. Josie's knee separated Harry's legs. Their bodies fully awake now, acting as if they had minds of their own and each part wanted to participate in what was clearly morphing from morning talk to full-on sex.

Josie's mouth traveled down Harry's neck, as she nipped and licked the warm flesh, leaving a trail of desire. Josie landed on Harry's left nipple, the soft nub taking its time coming alive with each flick of Josie's tongue. Josie had all the time in the world to breathe life into it, not to mention into Harry, who desperately needed a woman like Josie. Passionate. Loving. Kind. Josie sensed Harry had the same bad luck with women, even if Harry hadn't come to that realization on her own. Perhaps because Harry didn't allow much time for introspection. If that was the case, Harry was in for a rude awakening living in the Cotswolds. The sleepiness of the village would offer lots and lots of time for thinking. Living in a place like London kept a person on her toes. Not so much with Upper Chewford.

Not that it was the time for Josie to calmly explain this theory to Harry. The left nipple hardened, and Josie sucked it deeply into her mouth, giving it one last hard bite before moving to the right one, which was much more eager at first touch.

Josie laughed.

"What?" Harry asked.

"Your nipples are like a warring couple."

Harry stared at Josie, the most wonderful, curious expression on Harry's face. Josie wanted to freeze the moment because Harry had never looked so sweet, vulnerable, and fuckable. Yes, so much so.

"Your left nipple isn't all that accommodating and takes much more coaxing, while your right one is jumping at the bit to get into the action." Josie licked it.

"Aw, yes, my left one has always been stubborn."

"You're aware of this tendency, then." Josie quirked an eyebrow.

"It's been noted before."

"Is that right? What to do with this information?" Josie bit down hard on Harry's right nipple.

"I wasn't aware this would lead to some type of action." Harry moaned when Josie sucked the nipple into her mouth.

"It's important to get to know all aspects of your body so I can make every part of you happy."

"You're well on your way to succeeding." Harry dug her head into the pillow, her back arching some in reaction to Josie's hip rubbing between Harry's legs. "Oh…"

Josie's mouth was back on Harry's, kissing the woman hard. One of Harry's hands held the back of Josie's head as if not wanting them to ever break free, while Harry's other hand trailed up and down Josie's back.

Josie moaned into Harry's mouth.

Their bodies danced in unison, each woman becoming more and more enflamed with desire.

Josie's lips broke free, and she began working her way down Harry's torso, leaving a path of kisses, keeping their connection alive and well. When she reached right above Harry's pubic hair, Josie took in a deep breath. Harry may be reserved, but the aroma drifting from Harry's hot zone made it perfectly clear when it came to this aspect, Harry was full of life. And wanting. There was nothing more erotic than a woman who wanted to be fucked.

Josie raked her fingers through Harry's coarse hair, while Josie's mouth continued the trek past Harry's surging bud to the fleshy part of Harry's leg. Each lick, kiss, and nip got a rise out of Harry in the most delightful way. While Harry didn't utter a peep, not any verbal utterances that could be interpreted, the way her body moved and the moans escaping from the usually controlled woman were getting Josie so bloody hot.

Moving on to Harry's other thigh, closer to the knee, Josie worked her way north, Harry's thrashing reaching the point of no return. If Josie didn't provide a release soon, Josie wondered if Harry would start to address the urgency on her own. While it would be hotter than hot to witness Harry pleasure herself, Josie didn't want to be a witness. Not this morning. She made a mental note to get Harry riled to this point again to test the theory. While Josie loved to be in the right, she also didn't enjoy being denied.

Her tongue separated Harry's swollen lips, releasing the loudest moan so far from Harry. Josie was determined to hear an even louder one from Harry before she was done this morning. Maybe that could be an ongoing goal. To get Harry to the toe-curling, *screaming at the top of her lungs* stage each and every time Josie made love to her. Because right at this moment, Josie knew this wouldn't be the last time she woke Harry up in this manner. Josie had already learned, from the previous experience, Harry wasn't just a taker, but the most wonderful giver. Warmth pooled between Josie's legs.

CHAPTER TWENTY-EIGHT

Harriet kissed Josie goodbye and rested her head on the back of the door after it shut, wishing they could have stayed in bed all day. Sighing, Harriet headed to the shower. Before she could flip on the water, there was a loud pounding on the front door.

She slipped her robe back on.

The knocking intensified.

"Coming," Harriet said, annoyed the person was being so impatient. It was after nine in the morning, but still.

Harriet swung the door open to reveal a distraught Camilla. "I wasn't expecting you until later this afternoon. What's wrong?"

"Everything!"

Harriet put an arm around Camilla's shoulders. "Come in. Let's have some tea."

"I don't know if I can drink tea," Camilla said in a dramatic fashion and placed her head on Harriet's shoulder.

"Are you ill?" Harriet deposited her cousin on the sofa.

"Worse."

Harriet perched on the edge of the coffee table. "What's worse than being ill?"

"I don't know if I can say it." Camilla wheezed, as if she were trying to breathe through a clogged snorkel tube.

"Say what?"

Camilla flung herself against the back of the sofa and pulled a throw pillow to her face. "Oh, Harriet. What am I going to do?" The words came out garbled.

"I have no idea, considering I don't know what's wrong. If you tell me, I can try to help."

Camilla tossed the pillow to the side, took in a deep breath, her fingers fidgeting with the drawstrings of her cranberry jumper. "It's hitting me hard. I mean, when I saw… it… I didn't believe it. So, I did eleven more. They all turned out the same."

"Okay. Whatever it is, then it's… happening. What exactly is that?" Harriet tried to ask in a calm voice.

"It doesn't have to, but I just don't know. I think it has to. You know what I mean?" Camilla's watery eyes stared into Harriet's.

Harriet chomped down on her bottom lip to prevent herself from screaming *just bloody tell me*!

"Are you sure you don't want tea?" Harriet popped off the table. "I'm going to make a cup."

"Herbal, please." She added, "Rooibos if you have it."

"One rooibos coming up."

In the kitchen, Harriet filled the electric kettle and flipped it on, smiling over the thought of her weak attempt yesterday to ditch Josie on the walk. Oh my, things really worked, and Harriet thanked Josie for calling her out on her bullshit excuse. The thought of Josie made Harriet miss her, and she texted: *Camilla is here acting stranger than usual.*

Josie responded: *Just because?*

Harriet punched out: *No idea. Something happened, but she*

can't face telling me. Something tells me it's going to be big. But Camilla can be a drama queen, so maybe she has a pimple on her right tit.

Josie shot back: *LOL. I really hope that's what it is. Good luck.*

While waiting for the kettle, Harriet researched rooibos on her phone, quickly learning it wasn't a true tea. The African plant, after picked and dried, could be brewed into what the tea industry dubbed red bush tea. It didn't become commercial until the 1930s. Harriet wanted to call Josie to share this info, but the kettle was done, so she prepped herself an Earl Grey with a splash of milk and then Camilla's drink.

When she returned, Camilla was curled up in the fetal position on the sofa.

"Cam, please tell me what's going on."

Camilla sat up, sniffling. "I'm pregnant."

Harriet almost dropped both tea mugs onto the floor. "What?"

"Pregnant."

Harriet blinked.

Camilla made a *rock a bye baby* motion to hammer home the news.

Harriet set the mugs down on the coffee table. "I... not... I... wow."

"Exactly," Camilla said as if she was thinking the same thing.

"Do you know the father?"

"Of course, I know the father!" Camilla's expression showed her betrayal for Harriet asking such a question. "In fact, so do you."

Harriet narrowed her eyes. "Is it your ex-husband? I didn't know him well."

"It's not John!"

"Matt?"

"No! I wouldn't have a child with either of them."

"What was the name of the bloke you broke things off with recently? It started with an N, I think." Harry tapped her fingertips against her chin.

"Neil."

"Yes, Neil," Harriet said, feeling comforted by latching on to a simple fact. "Is he the father?"

"Nope."

"Who, then?"

"Clive."

"Clive?" Harriet parroted, not truly believing she'd heard Camilla correctly. Or, perhaps, Harriet was dreaming and she'd wake laughing about the ridiculousness of the situation.

"Yes, Clive." It was as if Camilla had to keep saying it for the news to truly sink in.

"How is this possible?"

Camilla's eyebrows shot upward, seeming to land in a different galaxy. "Surely, I don't need to explain how a man impregnates a woman."

"I'm versed in the subject, but Clive? How did you let this happen?"

"Me let it happen?" she protested.

Harriet splayed her fingers on her chest. "*I* didn't let it."

"I knew you'd act this way."

"If that's true, why'd you come here and tell me?"

"Because I have no one else to tell."

Harriet picked up her tea mug, holding it in both hands, needing the warmth and a moment to gather her thoughts. "Have you told Clive?"

"No!"

"Are you going to?"

"Do I have to?" Camilla seized her mug. "What good would it do to tell him? He's not the settling down type."

Funny. Harriet thought the same about Camilla. "He's going to be a father. It seems like something he should know."

"I just... How do I break the news to him?"

"That's a good question. He's nearing forty and has never been married."

"Does he have any children?" Camilla sipped her tea.

"How would I know?"

"You live in the village."

"I haven't done DNA tests on everyone." Harriet chewed on her bottom lip, nearly drawing blood.

"You make it sound like he sleeps with everyone."

"He does!" Harriet regretted saying it so bluntly. "You've seen the ginger ads yourself. You thought they were funny."

Camilla closed her eyes. "Why is this happening?"

"Do I need to explain to you how it happened? Are you in such shock you can't remember the steps to getting pregnant?"

Camilla's head drooped as if all the muscles in her neck suddenly disintegrated. "I don't know what to do, Harry. What should I do? What would you do?"

"Can I think about it some? I mean, this is big. The biggest. And, I only just learned of it. This isn't something to make a snap decision about." Harriet gripped the back of her neck, kneading the tightening muscles.

"Whatever you do, don't tell Clive I'm in town."

"Uh..."

"Uh, what?"

"Josie knows you're in town," Harriet confessed, her eyes dropping to her folded hands in her lap.

"How? I just arrived."

"I texted her while making tea," Harriet explained, realizing it sounded pretty lame.

"You texted Josie to say I was here?" Camilla's expression inquired how Harriet could betray her like that.

"I had no idea what was going on. At the time, it seemed so innocent. You being pregnant never entered my mind."

"Text her not to mention me to Clive."

"Won't that raise unnecessary questions?"

"I don't care. She means nothing to me." Camilla's hand motion made it clear she'd lumped Josie into the annoying local-yokel category. No wonder Eugenie didn't like Harriet, if this was how most of the city people treated the publican.

Harriet didn't know how to convey how much Josie meant to her. "It's not that simple."

"Just text, *Don't tell Clive about Camilla.*"

"She'll ask why, though. Josie's always asking why." It was one of the things Harriet found so charming.

"Tell her to mind her own beeswax. Honestly, do you like her more than me?"

How to answer? "Maybe I should call her. Make it clear it's imperative."

"Do what you need to do. The last thing I need this weekend is for Clive to find out I'm in Upper Chewford. I need time to figure out what to do. There has to be a simple solution."

Harriet didn't know how to break it to Camilla there weren't any simple solutions to this situation. Instead, she asked, "Do you know how far along you are?"

"Seven weeks."

"Seven!" Again, Harriet regretted the accusatory tone. "How'd you not notice earlier? Or were you ignoring it in the hope it would resolve itself?"

"Work has been stressful. And, the idea never entered my mind. Well, not until yesterday. One of my coworkers said she thought she was pregnant until the doctor told her she was perimenopausal. She's your age. And, I was like, *wouldn't that be great if I could stop buying tampons* and wished I would enter that stage soon. Then I started to think about the last time I had a period and couldn't remember. I couldn't get a doctor's appointment right away, so I took a test to rule it out and then..." She waved for Harriet to fill in the blank.

"Eleven more makes it hard to ignore."

"I really thought I'd lucked out like you. You're already menopausal and never have to worry about this." Camilla motioned helplessly to her stomach. "I mean, you never had to worry about getting pregnant, but you don't have to pack tampons for holidays or keep them on hand at the office. I really wanted that to be the case. Now..." Camilla stood. "I'm going to take a nap. This has worn me out." Without another word, Camilla retreated to the guest bedroom with her tea.

Harriet slipped out into the garden to make the call to avoid Camilla overhearing it.

"Hey there," Josie's voice was sultry, nearly making Harriet forget the reason for her call.

"Are you working?"

"I'm helping Mum get the pub ready. You need a gin and tonic already?" Josie joked.

"I just may." Harriet glanced down at her outfit, wondering if it would be okay to head to the pub in a robe and slippers.

"What's wrong?" Josie sounded alarmed.

"Did you mention to anyone Camilla is here?"

"No. Why?"

"Please don't. I'll explain more... at some point."

"That was vague. Are you okay?"

Harriet ran a hand through her hair. "Of course."

"Are you coming to the pub tonight? Maybe we can chat."

"I'll try my best."

"I gotta run, Harry. I'm sending positive thoughts."

"Thanks. I might need an army of positivity."

CHAPTER TWENTY-NINE

Josie tucked her phone into the back pocket of her jeans, concerned about Harry's call, but truth be told, she didn't want to draw her mum's attention to her chatting on the phone. That would invite questions Josie wasn't ready to face.

"I'm not paying you to talk on the phone," her mum teased.

Shit. Best to go on attack, to deflect. "You know, as a boss, you aren't really easygoing."

"As an employee, you're kinda surly."

Josie laughed. "I'm not as your daughter?"

"Oh, you are. I was hoping you could tame that side more while working." Her mum's expression softened. "Everything okay? You seem stressed."

"Yeah. Just a friend checking in to see how I'm adjusting to sleepy village life."

"Are you?" Again, her mum spoke with compassion.

"I seem to be managing." Josie gave her best stiff upper lip expression. After spending the night with Harry, conflicting thoughts and emotions roiled deep inside.

Worried what it all meant and if Josie had been a complete fool trusting a journalist.

"You don't miss city life? London is one of the most exciting cities in Europe, you know."

Josie crossed her arms, unsure what her mum was hinting at. "Are you trying to get rid of me?"

"No!" her mum protested. "After last night, I got to thinking about you and know you're used to different things in life. I grew up here. I'm used to nothing ever happening—"

"I wouldn't say nothing happens here." Josie's mind drifted to Harry the previous night and then the phone call minutes earlier. It seemed a lot was happening all of a sudden. But what?

Her mum didn't seem to notice Josie's mind drifting. "Am I being selfish? After your father died, I moved here, and I dreamed of you moving here as well. And then you showed up out of the blue, and it felt like my hope was coming true. But does my wanting you to stay here stop you from chasing your dream?"

"What dream would that be?"

An odd expression crossed her mum's face. A mixture of pain and understanding. "Are you sure you're done with politics? I remember when you were ten and begged us to take you to the National Democratic Convention. It's not like you can willingly shut that side off." She mimicked flipping a switch.

"I... I better finish setting up for the mad dash." Josie wheeled about before her mum could do her motherly thing—an inquisition to pry details out of Josie. Instead, she started to slice oranges for the inevitable mulled wines given the festive atmosphere.

Clive burst into the pub with a stack of papers in his hand. "Where's that scoundrel Harry!"

Winston jumped off his bed, growling, and one of the kittens scattered out from under Josie's feet.

"How would I know?" Josie deflected.

"Didn't you stay at her place last night?" Clive demanded.

"Is that true?" her mum asked in a confrontational tone, that she seemed to try to control, but couldn't.

Josie couldn't understand how her mum's attitude had veered so quickly considering moments earlier Eugenie had been more understanding than she'd been since Josie's return. And now there was fire in her mum's eyes simply because Josie stayed at Harry's. Or was Josie missing something? Reading into things too much?

"I thought you liked Harry. Why are you mad at her?" Josie asked Clive.

"Because of these." He held up the papers. "I thought she was done with the humiliating ginger ads."

It was the first time Clive expressed exasperation over the ads. Things were starting to click into place in Josie's brain. Clive had a place of his own, but more often than not, he stayed in one of the available rooms upstairs, making it difficult to have women over considering his sister and niece shared common bedroom walls. When one of his *suitors* was in the pub, he was polite but kept a distance. Josie had thought he was acting like a calculating, modern-day Lothario, but had she read Clive all wrong? How did the ads factor in? And, what was in the paper that had riled Clive?

Her eyes scanned the black ink, but her brain couldn't comprehend the meaning.

Many moments passed before her mum started to screech, although nothing comprehensible came out of her mouth except two words: *Kill Harry*.

Josie's brain finally registered the headline: *The Ginger*

George Blotter, which from a cursory glance was formatted like a police blotter, listing sightings of Ginger George leaving certain homes at all times of the night.

"Ginger George?" Josie sputtered. "That nickname rings a bell?"

"Camilla calls me that because she thinks I look like George Clooney," he confessed.

Yes. Josie remembered that now. It was a stretch, but hey, he was her uncle, so Josie might not be able to see how anyone was attracted to him, let alone think he looked like the actor.

"How could Harry print such rubbish?" Her mum's face shot right past angry red to apoplectic purple.

"Uh…" was Josie's brilliant reply.

Clive's stare dug into Josie.

"But, it's not in Harry's paper. I don't know what this is." Josie held it between two fingers as if it were a stinky piece of wet garbage. "It looks like someone printed it at home."

"Harry runs her operation from her cottage." Her mum rolled her copy and beat it against her leg.

"But she doesn't actually print it at home on some cheap paper like this." Josie couldn't believe the woman she'd slept with last night could do such a thing. Or had Josie been fooled yet again? Why had Josie trusted Harry? It wasn't like either had professed their love or anything. Sexual attraction warped minds. This was why Josie had sworn off women.

"Maybe she did it like this to throw us off the scent. It's no secret her paper is struggling."

Josie scanned the single printed page again, trying to make sense of everything, and having her mum glaring at her wasn't helping Josie's spinning mind. "But how would she make money from this? There aren't any ads. No one is paying for it. None of this makes sense. None of it." Josie stressed the last sentence.

While her mum paced from the pub entrance to the bar, Josie texted Harry with the words: *My mum wants your head on a platter*.

Harry's reply only contained a question mark.

Josie snapped a photo of the Ginger George Blotter and sent it.

Within a few seconds, Harry returned with *What is that?*

"Get Harry over here now," her mum demanded of Josie.

"Why me?"

"You're *friends* with her."

"We're not... super close," Josie stumbled over the words.

"Kidnap her for all I care." Her mum tossed her hands up in the air and fled to the kitchen, presumably to toss some pots and pans about. That had been a thing when Josie was a teen.

Clive jacked his eyebrows up at Josie. "I didn't think she'd take it out on you."

Rather me than Harry.

"Clive?" How to ask if he'd actually slept with the women who placed the ads? "Um, did you ever play a role in the ginger ads?"

"How do you mean? I never paid for one if that's what you're asking." He seemed genuinely perplexed.

"No. Not that. Is any of this accurate?" Josie pointed to the blotter.

He still wasn't following her questioning.

"Are you, or have you actually had... relations with any of the women who've placed an ad?"

Clive shrugged helplessly, his gaze dropping to the stone floor, his shoulders collapsing into his body. He started to speak, resorted to answering with a shake of his head, and exited the pub with his hands tucked into his pockets.

"Oh, Clive. Why didn't you tell me earlier?"

"Tell you what?"

"Jesus!" Josie turned around to her mum. "You scared the shit out of me."

"Is Harry coming here?" Her mum barked as if Josie was in control of Harry, forgetting her prior question.

"Harry didn't do this." Josie held the paper in the air, desperately wanting that to be the truth. Or was Josie grasping at straws because she didn't want to admit she'd trusted a person she shouldn't have?

"What proof do you have?"

"I know her. She stopped running the ginger ads even though she needed the money." That was a check in the *Harry was a good person* column.

"That only proves she did this."

A growl ripped through Josie, but she wasn't sure if it was directed at her mum or herself. "No, it doesn't. There's no way for anyone to make money from this. The only reason behind this is to get even with Clive or the women involved. Use that brain of yours."

"Are you calling me stupid?"

Was Josie? Or was she thinking herself stupid and lashing out? Josie took several shallow breaths to calm down. "Not at all. I'm telling you not to let your dislike of Harry interfere with your ability to see what's going on."

"What do you think is going on?"

"I just told you. Revenge. It's been simmering in the village for several weeks. Harry stopped the ads. Then the kittens showed up. The women involved have been trip-ping over themselves to garner Clive's attention, but he only spends time with Camilla. All of this has to add up to—"

"Just because you slept with Harry doesn't make her innocent. We both know your track record with women has been atrocious. *You* need to wake up! Not me!" Her mum stormed back into the kitchen.

Josie stood in the empty pub wanting to be anywhere else in the world.

Her phone rang.

"Hello?" She tried to sound as normal as possible.

"Josie?"

"Yes." Josie didn't recognize the voice at all.

"This is Blythe Tanner. I'm calling on behalf of Melissa Mitchell to see what we have to do to get you to work for us. I understand you're in the UK at the moment. Would a first-class ticket home tempt you, along with doubling whatever Nora was paying you?"

* * *

HARRY APPEARED NOT TOO MUCH LATER, glancing about the pub like a skittish rabbit who sniffed a fox nearby.

"She's in the kitchen," Josie said, hiking her thumb over her shoulder.

"She still mad?"

"She thinks you're responsible for the blotter and I can't see the truth because we're fucking." Might as well give it to Harry straight, without filling Harry in about Josie's conflicted thoughts trampling through her mind like a herd of lemmings running toward the nearest cliff.

Harry shook her head as if Josie had hit her with an uppercut, and Harry was seeing stars. When she recovered some, Harry asked in a meek voice, "Do you think I printed it?"

"I don't see how you'd benefit from it." Aside from being a scandal-chasing journalist. Although, from everything Josie had seen and read, Harry was more like Studs Terkel, not a *National Enquirer* type. "But I have no idea how to convince Mum of that."

"That's a relief." Harry sighed. "But, it's not as simple as that."

"I know!" Josie raked a hand through her hair.

"No, I mean there's more to the story."

Josie's insides went cold. "Shit. Is she right? Were you involved somehow?" She sniffed. "I'm not sure I can handle this right now." Josie started to walk away.

"Josie, please. Hear me out. It's not what you think."

Before Josie could listen to Harry's explanation, her mum charged past Josie, looking like a hunter out for blood. She shook a finger at Harry. "Explain yourself!"

CHAPTER THIRTY

HARRIET TOOK A SEAT ON ONE OF THE BARSTOOLS, resting her left cheek on the counter, unable to think of any words even though the fact was simple. Harriet had nothing to do with the blotter, but the thought of standing up to Eugenie made Harriet's resolve wither. How could she tell Josie's mum to go to hell?

"Oh, don't you sit there, acting like the injured party." Eugenie whacked the bar with a palm.

Harriet's head snapped up from the cold surface. "Eugenie—"

"Don't start. I want you to listen. This madness needs to stop. Right here. Right now." She pressed her finger onto the wood, whitening the tip.

So much for Eugenie wanting an explanation. All the woman cared about was being right in spite of her being so very wrong.

Eugenie had no idea just how insane all of this was about to get. It was only a matter of time before Camilla found out about the blotter, and Harriet had no idea how that would play out with her pregnant cousin. Camilla hadn't been too upset about Clive's philandering ways. That had been before she got pregnant. Or at least before she'd found out about the baby. Harriet couldn't believe Camilla had been unlucky enough to get pregnant the first time she'd gone to bed with Clive. Wasn't he the type to know how to prevent that from happening? Or were half the women in the village carrying his child? Was this his comeuppance?

And now Harriet and Josie were in the midst of this family drama, when everything was beyond their control.

"What do you want me to do?" Harriet asked, resigned to Eugenie never believing her.

"Get them back."

"Get what back?"

"All the papers!"

"Where did they even come from?"

"Don't play stupid." Eugenie shook one of the sheets in the air. "I know you're not from here, but publishing trash like this is... is... so inappropriate. No one in Upper Chewford likes you or your paper."

"Mum!" Josie gasped.

Harriet stared at Eugenie, processing the words, but not able to grasp the meaning entirely. The people in the village had seemed to enjoy the *missing ginger* ads, and many of the locals had carved out time to sit down for interviews, several of them speaking candidly with Harriet, as if grateful someone took an interest in their lives. But, overall, did everyone in Upper Chewford wish she'd leave? Was Eugenie's assessment correct?

How was it possible Harriet had woken up with a sexy woman in her arms, and within hours, her cousin had shown up announcing she was pregnant and Josie's mum had told Harriet she wasn't wanted in the village?

It was like the universe was adamantly opposed to Harriet experiencing any type of lasting joy.

Finally, she said in a dejected voice, "I'll do what I can about the papers."

Theo burst through the front door, holding one up in the air. *"The Ginger George Blotter!"*

Harriet couldn't determine if Theo was upset or thought it brilliant. The only part she could focus on was Theo, who was worse than any of the gossipers in Chewford, had already read the blotter. It was only a matter of time before he spread the contents far and wide.

Eugenie met Harriet's gaze, the publican's eyes burning a hole into Harriet's soul. If all wasn't lost, Harriet couldn't see a way out of the conundrum. What was a good crossword puzzle clue for *tits up*? Titanic? The Hindenburg? San Francisco Earthquake? The Irish Famine? Black Plague? The Blitz?

Was it a bad sign that every example that came to Harriet's mind involved hundreds of deaths and vast human suffering?

"Hi, Harry," Clive said as he entered the pub, his head not held as high as usual.

"Clive." Harriet seemed to pronounce every letter in his name as a way of an apology. "I'm—"

Clive waved for her not to say another word. "I'm sure Eugenie has abused you enough."

That she did, but Harriet attempted to shrug it off. "I'm sorry you're caught up in whatever this is." She wanted to state unequivocally she had nothing to do with it, but the words wouldn't come. "I better go."

Josie walked with her to the door. "You coming in tonight?" She wrung her hands.

Harriet wasn't sure if Josie was strangling her hands out of frustration about the blotter or if she wanted to strangle Harriet still thinking she was somehow involved. Also, there was the Eugenie problem. Even before today, Eugenie hadn't been a fan of Harriet. Even less so now.

Harriet finally said, "I don't think that's a good idea."

"Can we talk?" Josie glanced around. "Not here."

"Where?"

Josie sighed. "I'll text you. Something's come up that we should discuss."

Harriet didn't like the sound of her voice or the look of defeat in Josie's eyes. "I can't kick the feeling that everything under the sun is out to get me."

Josie started to speak, stopped, and then finally choked out. "Please tell me you had nothing to do with this."

Harriet stared, gobsmacked. "I don't even know what to say to that. Even you think I'm involved." Harriet let out a tortured breath. "Perhaps this isn't the place for me after all."

* * *

WHEN HARRIET WALKED through her front door and saw her cousin, she knew she was in for more trouble. Camilla sat on the sofa with *The Cotswolds Chronicles* spread out in her lap. This was highly unusual and a great indicator that her cousin was one step away from losing her mind. Harriet needed to exude calmness so Cam didn't pick up on the shitstorm swirling throughout the village. And what good would it do to unburden herself on her cousin, who was dealing with so much more than Harriet? So what if Josie didn't believe in Harriet? Camilla was pregnant. Her life would never be the same. How did that compare?

Harriet, though, wanted to curl up in bed and have a good cry.

Not quite yet.

Camilla's puffy eyes tore at Harriet's heartstrings and stiffened her resolve to stay strong.

"What's another word for guillotine?" Camilla asked.

"Behead." Harriet watched Camilla fill in the letters in the crossword. "How are you feeling?"

Camilla sniffled, but her eyes lit up as she filled in another answer. "I thought the puzzle would take my mind off things, and I'd already solved the sudoku."

"I thought you hated puzzles."

"I do. Maybe it's a pregnancy thing." Camilla shrugged.

"Are you hungry? Should I make something?"

"What do you have?"

"Admittedly, not much. But we can get fish and chips. There's a great place on the square. It's called The Plaice to Be. Get it? Plaice?" Harriet gave it more consideration. "Can pregnant women eat fish and chips?" *That's right, Harry. Focus on these elements to get you through everything.*

Camilla shrugged again. "How in the world would I know?"

"You're pregnant." Harriet couldn't stop herself from pointing out the obvious.

"I've only known for a hot minute."

Harriet looked it up on her phone. "Okay, according to the internet, cod, plaice, and haddock are acceptable. Does that sound good to you?"

"You just said I could."

"I meant do you want fish and chips? Or, are you experiencing morning sickness? That's more prevalent in the first trimester."

"Not really. And greasy food always appeases me when stressed, as you know. Can you bring it here? I don't want to be seen in the village."

"If you want some fresh air, you can wear a floppy hat."

Harriet tried to picture Camilla wearing an ugly gardening hat. Should Harriet don one now that she knew no one wanted her in the village?

"I just had my hair done."

"Right. How foolish of me."

Camilla returned to the crossword. "What's the answer to five across?"

Harriet responded with honesty, "I can't even remember my brother's name at the moment."

"That's dramatic of you. My life is falling apart. Not yours."

Yet it seemed like everything around Harriet was crashing down.

CHAPTER THIRTY-ONE

THE VIBE IN THE PUB WAS DIFFICULT FOR JOSIE to get a feel about. One group in the front debated who had penned or contributed to the blotter. Another group claimed there could be more useful blotters, like a tourist watch or who was cheating for the December to Remember decorating contest. So far, Josie hadn't detected too many angry women who'd been named and shamed. That was the part Josie couldn't wrap her head around. If her name had appeared in it, she'd want reparations, or she wouldn't leave her house again. Or both.

Granted, most of the women mentioned in the blotter were older. Did being implicated in a sex scandal at their age in the likes of Upper Chewford count as something to brag about? Was this the difference between life in the political eye, like the politicians she worked for, and a village? Josie, though, had fled the US to put a sex scandal in the rearview mirror, and she had no desire to wade through another quicksand that sucked everyone in, including her uncle and Harry.

When people thought of the area, they probably

pictured charming cottages, rolling green hills, and adorable sheep standing on stone walls waiting for a tourist to snap their photo. That was the wildest it was supposed to get in Upper Chewford. What Josie was experiencing was more like a reality TV show designed to shock and awe the masses. "The Ginger George Blotter," Josie muttered under her breath as she wiped the bar with a wet rag.

"Doom Bar."

Josie looked up at William in his usual mismatched outfit and scarlet tie that seemed more outrageous than it should. "Sorry, William. I didn't see you there."

"Doom Bar," he repeated, pointing at the tap as if Josie hadn't poured him a pint before.

At least, William was the same, making Josie feel somewhat better about the world. "Take a seat, and I'll bring it out to you."

He retreated to his leather chair, the fire crackling, Winston on his bed.

Josie grabbed a bag of cheese and onion crisps for the man and delivered both with a slight dip of the head, receiving one in return. These were the interactions Josie wanted from now on. Nonverbal. She almost had to laugh given her previous career as a speechwriter. Life was hilarious in a devastatingly ironic way.

The job offer tumbled around her mind, knocking into every hidden corner. Should she accept? Decline? Catch the next flight to hear them out?

"Whoever is keeping tabs on Clive, I suggest you tail me instead." Theo stood in the middle of the pub with his chest puffed out. "I see more than one woman a night."

There were some murmurings throughout the pub. Most unbelieving, but Josie detected several older women taking note as if they wanted to book some time with the pompous prick. Is that what became of people after divorce or the death of a partner? Going from one sexual conquest to the next? Wouldn't they prefer to find someone steady in their life? But how many lucked out like her parents, finding the person who truly got them?

Or was Josie's image of her parents all wrong? Had she simply forgotten all the fights? Had they hidden it from her? Earlier, Josie saw a side of her mum that shocked Josie into near inaction. Had her father seen that on a regular basis? Was it ever possible to know what happened in anyone's relationship?

Agnes, in her usual pub attire, which was probably what many would consider church clothes, made an appearance, her eyes flitting to William and then to her usual table, which was taken by tourists.

"Hello, Agnes. Gin and tonic?"

The older woman nodded.

"We should put a plaque on your table saying it's always reserved for you." Josie reached for the gin bottle. "The leather chair across from William is free. Take a seat, and I'll bring you the drink."

Agnes remained frozen.

"Go on. We're expecting a tour group soon, and there won't be a free seat."

With a submissive expression, Agnes followed Josie's prodding.

Maybe this was the true purpose of Josie coming to the village. To help two old people find love and companionship, not find true love herself. If Josie couldn't be happy in love, then she could help others find their soul mates. Should that be her motto? *I can't find it for myself, but I can for you. Trust me.*

Harry edged into the pub as if worried she'd be shot on the spot. Her eyes landed on Josie, who gave her a helpless stare back. Why had Harry chosen this moment to appear? Was it a sign? What did it mean? Josie noticed her mum, sitting with some of the regulars, tossing Harry a sickening stink eye.

Harry, to her credit, didn't completely melt into the floor despite Eugenie's intensifying glare. She made her way for Josie. "Hi."

"I wasn't expecting you tonight," Josie said as if that was the only acceptable statement considering the past twenty-four hours. Then she added in a softer tone, "What can I get you?"

"Gin and tonic."

"What type of gin?" It was as if Josie couldn't remember simple things, even Harry's gin preference, which usually would be a no-brainer.

"Uh, you choose." Harry made a flick of her fingers as if saying all simple questions were unanswerable. They were on the same page in this matter.

"Okay."

"Any chance we can slip out for a private word? I really need to talk to you." Harry's eyes implored Josie.

Josie glanced at her mum. "It's pretty busy right now."

Harry took in the crowd. "So it seems. I'm sorry... it can wait."

Josie sighed. "I don't know..."

"You're working. I get it." Harry showed placating palms.

Josie couldn't reconcile the Harry sitting before her with the type to print the blotter, especially after she'd stopped running the ginger ads. Josie should at least hear Harry out. "I should get a break in an hour or so."

Harry consulted her watch. "Eightish, then?"

"Or thereabouts." Josie was kicking herself for delaying the inevitable. Learning if Harry was involved or not.

"Would you like to sit at the bar? Keep me company. I can give you my copy of the paper to work on the crossword. Wait. That was stupid. You—"

"That's okay. I already helped Camilla with it."

"Is Camilla here?" Clive seemed to pop up from the floor, like Harry had stepped on the end of a rake.

"Sadly, no," Harry said, her gaze on Josie's face.

"Shame. She's the only person I want to see tonight." Clive sat next to Harry.

This seemed to snag Harry's full attention. "Really?"

"Yeah. She's the only one who gets me."

"Again, Clive, I'm so sorry this is happening. I tried to find the source of the blotter, but I don't even know where to start." Harry's hand was on his shoulder, but her attention was on Josie.

Clive stared deeply into Harry's eyes.

Harry clutched the front of her shirt. "I promise you. I had nothing to do with it."

This appeased her uncle, and truth be known, Josie believed her, too. Harry was many things, but not a convincing liar.

"Thanks for trying to find out who was behind it." Clive blew out a breath. "Who knew the *missing ginger* jokes would lead... to this?"

Josie appraised Clive's drooping shoulders and sallow complexion, making him look so unlike the Ginger George described in the blotter. Whoever devised the concept had finally found Clive's kryptonite. Perhaps, in the long run, this would be the best way to end the madness. Josie, though, wasn't sure her mother would see it that way. Not at the moment, with the buzz in the pub surrounding the blotter, although unlike her mum's fears, the pub was much busier than usual. Another sad fact about scandal. It did sell.

An even worse thought infiltrated Josie's mind. When her mum attacked Harry, Josie didn't rush to Harry's aid. No, Josie stood there, dumbfounded. How could Harry respect Josie now? To add insult to injury, Josie asked if Harry had been involved. The image of Harry's agonized look flashed in her mind.

But how to apologize? No words besides I'm sorry came to mind. How could a speechwriter completely fail in the apology department? Maybe she should call her ex Andrea, the apology queen, for tips.

"Clive, can you hop back here so I can sneak a cigarette with Harry? I've been trying to resist the urge, but I'm losing the battle." Josie knew how pathetic that sounded. It was hard enough knowing Harry knew Josie's weakness; she didn't want her uncle to know Josie's fears about journalists and women were rearing their ugly heads, toppling her shot at happiness.

"Of course. Don't let your mum catch you," he warned, adding, "although, it might help me if she did find out."

"My own uncle!" Josie laughed. God, it felt good to laugh. Surely, all was not lost if laughter still existed in the world.

"You know I'd never throw you under the bus." He fluttered his eyelashes, doing his best impression of innocent but failing miserably.

"I have no doubt you would. Luckily for me, I'm a grown woman, and if I want to smoke, I can."

"Yeah, I keep telling myself that, as well. Your mum, though, has a way of making me feel like I'm a naughty kid who can't do anything right."

"I feel ya, which is why Harry and I are slipping out back." Josie beckoned Harry to join her in the kitchen.

They exited through the delivery door.

Josie lit up almost immediately. "Thank God all the

tourists are ordering the fish and chips. It might mask the smell."

"I had some for lunch. Not here. The place on the square." Harry shuffled her feet, tucking her hands into her sleeves to stay warm.

Josie nodded, unable to think of something to add to that.

Harry glanced about. "Is there a way we can move farther afield? I need to tell you something, and I really don't want to risk anyone overhearing."

Josie took another drag. "Why am I getting the feeling I'm not going to like what you have to say?"

"Because it's that kind of day."

They crossed the river, past a block of houses, and ended up on a strip of grass in the middle of the square. Given the busy holiday season, people had spilled out of the two pubs on the square, but they huddled close to the entrances, nowhere close enough to hear whatever Harry had to say.

When it became clear the woman needed some prodding, Josie said, "I'm so sorry for what I asked earlier. I should have known you wouldn't have anything to do with—"

"I've given it a lot of thought."

Josie braced for the inevitable.

"And I understand why you had to ask, given how your career went up in smoke because of an unscrupulous journalist. If I were in your shoes, I'd ask, too."

Josie waited for the final word that even though Harry understood, she couldn't be with someone who didn't trust her. But Harry just stared into her eyes.

"Are we okay, then?" Josie asked.

"I think so." Harry looked relieved for a brief moment. Then her eyes clouded over again. "There's still the issue that your mum hates me. I'm not welcome in the village—"

"Don't believe the village part. Mum tends to think she knows a lot more than she does. I know, for a fact, many here like you. Me, most importantly."

Harry smiled a sad smile. "Things are about to get slightly more complicated on all fronts."

"How?" Josie asked, wishing she hadn't.

"Before I tell you, I need to know what I'm about to say will stay between us. You see, I found out something earlier, before… and it makes the blotter even worse than you know."

"How is that possible?" Josie sucked on her cigarette.

"It just does. Do you promise?"

"You have my word."

"It's about Camilla."

"Jesus. I forgot about her. Is she going ape shit over the blotter? Her name wasn't on it, was it?" A thought infiltrated Josie's mind. "Oh, fuck. She isn't the one responsible, is she? Clive mentioned she was the one who gave him the Ginger George nickname. Is that why she doesn't want Clive to know she's here? She clandestinely arrived in the village just in time to watch the fallout of her dirty deed?"

"I know it's upsetting, but I don't think Cam—"

"Don't you see. It makes sense. Camilla never seemed too upset about the *missing ginger* ads. I've always wondered about that. Maybe she was upset. Not at first, but after hooking up with Clive she thought he would nip them in the bud. When he didn't, she took matters into her own hands."

"Things have changed. Drastically. But not in the way you're conjecturing."

Josie tapped ash onto the frozen lawn. "Do you plan on enlightening me about what you think is going on?"

Harry started to speak but stopped.

Josie used her lit cigarette to light another, as if needing the comfort of having a second ready to go. "Well?" Josie swore under her breath. "I'm sorry, I'm not trying to be bitchy. It's just I'm worried about what you're about to say. After everything."

"I'm not exactly sure how to break the news to you."

"I've found in these situations it's best to get it over with using the least amount of words." Josie mimed ripping a bandage off.

"Pregnant."

"Who? Not you, because I don't think women get pregnant that quickly. It takes time to fertilize the egg." Josie felt like a moron and tapped her forehead. "There's also the fact we used the *no sperm* method."

"It's not possible for me to get pregnant anyway."

"Ever?"

Harry shook her head.

"I didn't know. Did you want to have kids?"

"Uh… it's not important right now."

"Are you sure? You seem…" Josie peered into Harry's eyes. "Distant."

"My cousin."

"Your cousin what? Distant cousin?"

Harry took in a deep breath, seeming to hold it in her lungs for as long as she could and then expelled the breath. "Cam is pregnant."

"Camilla is pregnant?" Josie said in a not-so-loud voice, but Harry still motioned for her to be quiet. "Since when?"

"She told me this morning."

"This is why I can't tell Clive she's in the village, because she's off the market or whatever?" Josie flicked ash onto the ground.

"I'm not sure she's off Clive."

"I don't understand." Josie stubbed out the spent cigarette and inhaled on the newer one. "Wouldn't the father object to Camilla seeing Clive?"

"Clive is the father."

Josie's vision went fuzzy. If this were a movie, her character would wake up and all this would be a terrible dream that she and Harry could laugh about.

Sadly, this was Josie's life.

CHAPTER THIRTY-TWO

Harriet placed a hand on each of Josie's shoulders. "Do you need to sit down?"

"Why is this happening?"

"Which part?"

"Every single part. The end of my career. Getting mixed up in a family sex scandal that doesn't involve much sex. Working for my mum, who is intent on fixing me up on dates with any lesbian within a hundred-mile radius, except you. To top it all off, the day after I sleep with you, I find out about Camilla—Jesus, will we be related now?" Josie was nearing hysteria, and she waved a hand in front of her face, the red tip of the cigarette moving up and down in the darkness.

"How do you figure that?"

"My uncle has knocked up your cousin!" Josie forced out through semiclenched teeth.

"That doesn't alter history by making us blood relations."

Josie tossed the cigarette onto the ground and rubbed her arms. "It's weird. Even you have to admit it's weird."

Harriet slipped off her jacket. "Here. Put this on."

Josie did, dipping her head in what Harriet interpreted as thanks.

"What did you mean when you said *even you*?" Harriet pressed. The way Josie had said the words bounced around in Harriet's skull.

"You're so logical and don't react to things. But...?"

"But what? It still doesn't make us blood relations. It just brings our families closer, but it's not like—" Harriet stopped herself from saying more.

"My brain gets that, but it still has an icky factor."

Harriet didn't know how to alleviate Josie's mind at the moment. "And the other comment about the sex scandal that doesn't involve much sex?"

Josie moved closer to Harriet and whispered into her ear. "Clive isn't a playboy. The only person he has slept with, at least recently, is Camilla."

"But the ads."

"Were made up. I think he was too embarrassed to admit that."

"Clive's a victim of sexual harassment?" Harriet stared into the darkness.

"Yes."

"Wow. I never would have guessed that. He never let on or asked me to put a stop to the ads." Harriet ran a hand up and down the back of her head.

"Men are weird but not surprising. Back in high school, usually the guys who bragged about their sexual conquests weren't having sex. I can't believe I missed it this entire time."

"That makes the blotter even curiouser."

"It does. It also explains why the women didn't get too riled up about the ads. Do you think all of them were in on it together?"

"For what purpose, though?"

"A bit of fun. Excitement. Who knows?" Josie's attention focused on a group leaving the nearby pub. "I should get back."

"We need to talk—"

"I know, but I'm on the clock, and I left Clive behind the bar."

"Josie, please let's not leave things this way. Not after... No, not just because of last night. Ever since I first laid eyes on you, I've been pulled into your orbit. I know that makes zero sense, and it may shock you given your assessment that I'm the logical and unfeeling one."

"I never said unfeeling."

"Not with words, no."

Josie closed her eyes briefly. "I'm sorry. I never meant to hurt your feelings. Last night was so lovely. It's just that I'm feeling like the world is against us, and I don't know if I have the energy to fight it. The Clive and Camilla news— it's upsetting." Josie massaged her forehead. "I'm so tired."

"I have the energy to fight for us." Harriet stood straight. "Lean on me, Josie."

"How can you say that? After...?"

"It's been a confusing day, with some ups and a lot of downs. It doesn't change how I feel about you."

"But, my mum treated you horribly, and I didn't say anything. I just stood there."

"She's a force to be reckoned with, and I don't think anything you said would have helped."

"I could have stood up for you."

"I could have stood up for myself, but she scares me." Harriet stroked Josie's cheek. "I never gave that part a second thought. Really."

"You really can be sweet. Logical, yes, but also so very sweet. I love the combination..." Josie's voice drifted off.

"I'm not going to ask what the *but* is."

"I'm sure you can guess." Josie avoided looking at Harriet.

A few things crowded Harriet's mind, but were they the same things? "I'd rather not put words or thoughts into your head. After work, can we talk?"

"Not tonight, Harry." Josie tapped the side of her head. "I need to process everything."

Harriet suppressed a bitter comment about Josie thinking Harriet was too analytical. Who was the thinker now? "Tomorrow, then? Breakfast at the café?"

For a fleeting moment, the stress and worry dissipated from Josie's face, replaced with a hopeful expression. It didn't last long, but Josie said, "Does nine work?"

"Yes."

"Have a good night."

Harry watched Josie disappear down the side street, heading for the bridge to take her over the river, a swirling sensation in the pit of Harriet's stomach that she couldn't quite put her finger on. Given the situation, on the surface it would seem the cause was unease. But Harriet couldn't banish the thought that everything would work out and the swirling was a good sign. Did this count as something illogical? But how to share it with Josie without freaking her out even more?

* * *

"Is he at the pub?" Camilla pounced as soon as Harriet returned to the cottage.

"He is."

"Did you say anything to him?"

"You asked me not to."

"Good." Camilla mangled her left hand with her right.

"Did you want me to say anything to him?"

"Of course not! Clive cannot know he's the father."

"Not ever?" Harriet didn't understand this, nor did she entirely believe Cam. Why else rush to the village where the father-to-be lived? True, Harriet was Camilla's sole confidant, but the expression of longing and wistful sighs made Harriet think Camilla was battling herself to figure out the right thing to do. Which was understandable.

Camilla stared blankly.

"Have you ever wanted to be a mum?" Harriet asked.

Camilla collapsed onto the sofa. "I never really thought about it. It's no secret I'm selfish."

Harriet decided to sidestep this bullet. "What's the first thought that pops into your head when I say baby?"

"Food."

"Your baby?"

"Food."

"Pregnancy?"

"Food."

"Winston Churchill?"

"Food."

Harriet chuckled. "Something tells me you're hungry."

"Famished. Can you get fish and chips again?"

"Sure."

"And orange juice. I really want some."

"Fish and chips and OJ." Harriet held two fingers in the air. "Anything else?"

"Peanut butter and cucumber."

The requests roiled Harriet's stomach, but she refrained from saying anything. It seemed fitting Camilla would have strange cravings. Even as a kid, she loved soy sauce on her vanilla ice cream, although Harriet wasn't sure the cravings were pregnancy related since Camilla was still in her first trimester. Harriet had been doing some sleuthing about what to expect ever since hearing the news, knowing she would be by Cam's side every step of the way. That was what cousins were for.

Heading back to the village square, a place she couldn't escape today, Harriet spied Eugenie alone on a bench near the World War II memorial. The way her shoulders stooped worried Harriet. Should she tuck her head into the collar of her jacket and walk by, so not to provoke Josie's mum? Harriet wasn't the type to walk away when someone seemed to need a shoulder to cry on. And, if she wanted things to work with Josie, she'd need Eugenie's dislike to thaw some. Was this the right time, though? Another glance hinted the woman had been sobbing, or were her shoulders still juddering up and down?

"Everything okay, Eugenie?"

She sniffled and dabbed her eyes with a tissue. "Too okay."

Harriet wasn't quite following. "What does that mean?"

"Ever since the blotter appeared today, the pub has been hopping."

"That's good, right? It hasn't hurt your business."

"I don't understand it. Don't the women in this town have any decency? Clive is the one acting downcast. The women are cackling over it."

"Why do you think that is?" While Harriet knew the truth, she didn't know how much Eugenie knew, and she didn't want to betray Josie's confidence.

"I thought I understood this place, but maybe I was gone too long and I'm as much of a stranger as you are. Or perhaps this means I'm just old. I don't feel old—oh, I have aches and pains." Her wave implied *who didn't?* "But I don't feel like a woman who's reached her dotage stage and is completely out of touch with the way things are."

Harriet took a seat next to Eugenie. "You're nowhere

near that stage. As for the women in the village, it just seems to be good fun. I doubt we'll know half of what's really going on."

Eugenie whipped her head around.

"I don't mean there's more to it." Harriet did her best to block out the Camilla situation so she could sound sincere. "I wouldn't be surprised if it's all just a joke."

"Sex isn't a joke. It drastically changed my life."

Harriet rested her hand on the back of the bench, as she pivoted to face Eugenie. "What do you mean?"

"I got pregnant with Josie when I was so young. I loved her father, but sometimes I wonder what would have happened if I'd waited until I was Josie's age to settle down. Now, I'm back in the village I grew up in, working in a pub, and I'm a widow."

Harriet attempted to find the bright spot, once again shoving down the knowledge that Clive's life was about to drastically change because of sex. That was if Camilla told him. "You own the pub, though."

"Doesn't change the fact it's a pub. Now Josie's here, following in my footsteps. I worry so much about her. I want her to stay, but I also want her to live up to her potential."

"I'm sure you do."

"When I seriously think about it, what does this village have to offer her?"

Me. "Do you think she's unhappy here?"

"I don't think Josie knows what's good for her. Why did you move here, Harry?" Eugenie seemed genuinely interested.

"I wanted a peaceful life."

"Alone?"

"I was alone when I moved, yes," Harriet hedged.

"Are you happy?"

No. "It's hard to answer that question."

"You should get a cat. Trust me when I tell you letting people into your life only complicates it to kingdom come. I wanted to get closer to Clive after living in America for so long. Look how that turned out."

Eugenie may not have spoken truer words, but Harriet didn't want to untangle herself from the complications in her life. If the only way to have Josie in her life was to embrace the complications, she'd do it. The thought of not having Josie was too painful.

"I think you're selling Josie short. She's intelligent and will figure things out in due course. Pushing her in either direction won't help."

Eugenie's head once again rounded on Harriet like a momma bear on the attack. "I'm a pushy mum, am I? You have no idea what it's like to be a mother." With that, Eugenie rose to her feet and left Harriet on the bench.

"Well, that worked out well," Harriet muttered to herself.

CHAPTER THIRTY-THREE

Josie wiped down the final table, marking the end of another shift. Her yawn, a mile wide, wasn't an accurate measure of how exhausted she truly felt. If she didn't think she'd wake up sore as shit, she'd curl up on Winston's bed and drop off to sleep right then and there.

"Josie, love, care for a cup of tea?" Her mum already had two steaming mugs in hand. "Join me in the kitchen."

That was the last thing Josie wanted, but how could she tell her mother, who was nineteen years her senior, she was too knackered? Josie also feared they'd get into a verbal brawl, and Josie was still processing everything. "I really hope it's herbal."

"It's bedtime tea."

They sat on barstools around the butcher-block table. Josie sipped the tea, feeling soothed. Or maybe just the suggestion the tea should be soothing calmed her. "Ah, I needed this."

"Your mum always knows what's best for you."

Josie laughed. "So she thinks."

"You don't?" Her mum held her mug at chin level with both hands.

"Oh boy. Is this one of our motherly chats that involves me staying quiet while you tell me what I should do with my life because I'm so young and stupid?"

"You are young."

"Do you also think I'm stupid?"

"I've never called you stupid." Her mum set her mug down.

"Yes, you have, when I stole your car when I was fourteen."

"The act was stupid, not you."

"If I remember correctly, you called me a *stupid twat* in front of the cops who brought me home."

"I was worked up, and you, young lady, were lucky those cops were friends of your father's," her mum scolded, adding the finger shake Josie had seen on numerous occasions. "Your life would have been much different if you'd ended up in juvie."

"I'm well aware. I didn't say you were wrong to say that. I'm just clarifying that you have called me that."

"You love being right."

"I'm a woman." Josie sipped her tea.

Her mum ran a finger along the brim of her mug. "Where do you see yourself in the next year?"

Josie leaned on her forearms, gearing up for whatever battle was brewing. "I have no idea, Mum."

"That's a problem."

"For whom?"

"You."

Josie shook her head. "I disagree. I'm rather liking not having the next twelve months plotted out. I feel like every aspect of my life has been planned out until this point, and look where that got me." Maybe if Josie repeated these types of thoughts one hundred times every day, she'd start to believe them.

"Is this the part where you blame me?"

Josie squeezed her mum's hand. "I don't blame anyone. I'm just telling you how I feel."

"I'm listening. I mean really listening to whatever you want to say. This hasn't been the best day, and I regret some of the things I said."

"Only some?"

"Maybe all. I'm not sure I remember everything. Anger has a way of doing that to me. I'm worried about you."

"What about Clive?"

"Yes, I'm concerned about his situation. You're my daughter, though. You'll always come first."

Josie sat up, crossing her arms. "I'm waiting for the *but*."

"No buts."

"Since when?"

"Since now."

Josie took a healthy slug of the tea. "In that case, I'm off to bed. I'm having breakfast with Harry tomorrow."

"Why?"

"Don't start. I like Harry."

"But—"

"I knew there'd be one before the night was over." Josie shook a finger at her mum.

"That's not fair. You haven't even heard me out."

"Life isn't fair. Didn't your mum teach you that? Mine did." Josie heaved a sigh. "Please, stop taking everything out on Harry. She's a good person. Harry had absolutely nothing to do with the blotter." Josie kissed her mum's cheek. "Good night. You can continue plotting against me without me sitting here."

"I'm not plotting against you." Her mum made harrumphing sounds.

"Sure, you aren't."

"You make me so mad sometimes."

"I can say the same about you, but I won't."

"You just did."

"You're right. See, I don't always have to be right." Josie left her mum sputtering, not wanting to enter a useless debate that wasn't winnable. She'd learned long ago her mum was as stubborn as a mule and tangoing with her could leave Josie metaphorically battered and bruised.

In bed, Josie's mind decided to kick into hyperdrive in a maddening way. Every time she closed her eyes, Josie pictured Harry from the previous night. Or standing on the bridge that first night. Stumbling upon her in the café. The woman even had Josie looking forward to each week's crossword puzzle to discover another adorable way Harry flirted with her. Harry, Harry, Harry. How had she gotten inside Josie's head and heart? The last thing Josie needed was a woman to cause ripples. Josie craved calm. Like a summer day with the slightest breeze. She could practically feel the sunshine on her skin. Hear the birds chirping, squirrels foraging in the leaves, kids laughing.

Oh, shit. Josie lurched up in bed. She'd totally blocked out that Camilla was preggers.

Josie's life would be perfect if she were the only person on the planet.

Then she'd get the calm she craved.

Josie rolled onto her side and pulled the pillow over her head to blot everything out.

CHAPTER THIRTY-FOUR

Harriet rose earlier than usual, unable to sleep past five. Camilla had been up a few times during the night, watching the telly. At one point, Harriet thought she'd overheard Camilla on the phone, but she wasn't positive. So far, a knocked-up Camilla was proving even more taxing than teenage Cam. Yet, Harriet really didn't mind. What caused her more distress was not being able to fix the problem for Camilla. When they were younger, Harriet had always bailed Cam out of whatever trouble she got herself into. This was one situation that Harriet couldn't solve for Camilla. It made her feel helpless.

Adding the Josie situation on top of that drove the logical Harriet insane. Why couldn't Josie see how good they were together? Or trust that no matter what, they could work things out? While it was early days in the relationship, Harriet was convinced they were meant to be together. How she knew, Harriet had no idea, but she believed it wholeheartedly.

She had to laugh, because that was illogical.

Harriet slipped on a blue pair of wellies, needing to

stretch her legs and clear her mind. For the first time in days, when she left the cottage, it was raining outside. Harriet pulled her warm hood up over her head and headed for her favorite walking path. Given it was early on a rainy Saturday days before Christmas, Harriet had the path to herself, much to her relief. After dealing with Camilla, Clive, and Eugenie, Harriet needed time and space. She'd always been the type to crave alone time to sort out her thoughts. Some of her former colleagues could write in busy cafés. Not Harriet. She'd always been drawn to peace and quiet.

On her way back, the rain eased, allowing Harriet to remove her hood, her body now warm from the exercise.

She rounded a corner and nearly crashed into someone.

"My apologies. I wasn't expecting—" Harriet stopped when she realized Josie stood right in front of her. Harriet finished, "Anyone to be out this early."

"Me neither." Josie, in leggings and a running top, hugged her chest. "I'm just starting out and haven't warmed up yet."

Harriet took off her jacket. "You're freezing."

"Won't you get cold?" Josie balked.

"I'm warm enough from walking." Harriet shoved the jacket into Josie's hands.

Josie gratefully slipped it on. "You always seem to be rescuing me."

Harriet shifted on her feet. "I don't mind."

Josie elevated an eyebrow, but Harriet thought she detected a slight grin. "Says the understated woman."

Harriet rolled her eyes.

"An eye roll. I didn't know you had it in you." Josie jabbed her elbow into Harriet's side as if saying no hard feelings.

"I'm sure I'm capable of much more than that if given the chance."

"Is that a challenge? You want me to press your buttons to see what I can bring you to?" Josie pressed a finger into Harriet's arm.

Harriet didn't know how to respond, so she reacted instead, pulling Josie into her arms and kissing her. Much to Harriet's surprise, Josie didn't push her away, but deepened the kiss.

A snap of a tree branch reminded them they were visible on the path to all weekend ramblers. Harriet's eyes panned the area, seeking out the widest tree, that also happened to have a cluster of bushes offering some privacy. She took Josie's hand, leading her to the secluded spot.

"What do you have in mind?" Josie asked, her eyes wide with bewilderment.

"This." Harriet kissed Josie again.

Josie hesitated at first but succumbed to the moment. "Are you sure no one can see us?"

"Not entirely. In all probability, the sound we heard was an animal, although I have to admit I don't care right now. All I care about is this." Harriet kissed Josie again, and Josie's cold hand slipped under Harriet's jumper.

Josie's other hand sought Harriet's warm flesh, her fingers digging into Harriet's back as their tongues participated in a sensual dance, causing the two of them to ramp up their need to touch the other person. Harriet buried her nose into the crook of Josie's neck, smelling her natural musk. Harriet's tongue tasted the saltiness of Josie's skin before she nibbled Josie's earlobe.

"Harry, if we don't stop now, I'm not sure I will be able to. And we can't go to your place because of Camilla. The pub is off-limits. No way we can check into an inn without spurring the gossips. I rather stay out of that mess in this place. I swear no one here has enough to do, ensuring all they talk about is who's doing who. Or who they think is doing who."

"What's wrong with here?"

Josie looked around at the dirt and detritus underneath them. "Here?" Her falsetto voice displayed her complete shock.

"You asked when I'd been illogical. This seems like a good opportunity."

"Oh, I see. You're just trying to prove me wrong," Josie teased. "Such a woman."

Harriet kissed Josie, her tongue forcefully claiming space in Josie's mouth. "It's not that. I need you, Josie. If I can't be inside you soon, I may explode."

"Harry, I've never done this before. Not out in the open."

"Neither have I, but I'm game."

Josie stared at Harriet, the desire in her emerald eyes burning bright. "This is crazy."

"You drive me crazy. So much so, and I love it." Harriet slipped her hand under Josie's shirt, cupping Josie's breast. Harriet pinched Josie's nipple through the sports bra, causing Josie to moan. "If you want me to stop, you need to tell me."

"I don't."

Harriet's knee separated Josie's legs as she lightly pressed Josie against the tree. Harriet's eyes queried Josie's face to see if she was uncomfortable, but Josie responded by capturing Harriet's lips as if she could never get enough of kissing. Not that Harriet was complaining, because she could never get her fill of Josie.

Harriet's hand slipped under the band of Josie's shorts, heading downward. Josie was warm and inviting. Harriet cupped Josie's pussy, not ready to take the next step. She wasn't far from reaching it, though, considering the surroundings. It was only a matter of time before visitors tumbled out of their rooms to experience the great outdoors, the weather be damned.

Josie slipped her hand under Harriet's bra, pinching a nipple between two fingers. Harriet reciprocated in kind with Josie's nipple. Josie sunk her teeth into Harriet's neck, biting just hard enough to really get Harriet's engine revved. Her fingers eased under Josie's knickers, finding Josie slick with wanting.

Harriet moaned into Josie's shoulder. "I love that I turn you on this much."

Josie separated her legs farther, allowing Harriet's fingers full access. "Don't stop now."

Harriet plunged two fingers deep inside Josie. "I don't plan on it."

Their mouths found each other, and with each thrust inside Josie, they reciprocated the passion with the kiss. Both of their chests heaving with the exertion. Moments before, Josie had been shivering, but Harriet could feel the heat coming off her. Josie pulled her mouth away, burying her head into Harriet, holding on tighter. Harriet positioned her legs to give Josie the support she needed, while not letting up on her finger thrusts.

"Oh, Harry," Josie moaned. "Oh, God."

Harriet went in deeper, her other hand stimulated Josie's nipple under the sports bra that had been shoved up nearly to Josie's throat.

Josie, her body quivering, held on even tighter to Harriet.

Harriet's wrist throbbed from the awkward angle, but she pushed through the pain, sensing Josie was edging ever closer to where Harriet wanted to take her.

Josie shuddered, her fingers gouging Harriet's back.

Fuck, it felt good. To get a woman as fantastic, exciting, and sexy as Josie to come—was there a better experience? Harriet couldn't think of one.

Josie's grip on Harriet ratcheted up to the point Harriet struggled to breathe, but she didn't relent with her fingers. One final finger thrust brought Josie to bliss. Harriet curled her fingers upward, and Josie let out a satisfied growl. Fitting, considering they were in the open and Josie sounded more animal-like. Perhaps if there were people nearby they'd stay away, thinking Josie was some feral beast that would shred them.

Josie went limp in Harriet's arms, making her seem so much less dangerous. Not that passersby would know that.

"Wow," Josie said.

"Yes. Wow." Harriet held Josie close to her.

"I should challenge you more if this is the outcome."

"Challenge away." Harriet's hand was still inside Josie's knickers, her wrist throbbing now. Slowly, she eased it out.

Josie took Harriet's hand, massaging it, the wrist making popping sounds. "Poor you."

"It's nothing."

"Such a Brit." Josie kissed Harriet's cheek. "I'm freezing."

"We should get you home and in a hot shower."

"I wish you could shower with me."

"Would it be that terrible if Camilla knew we showered together?"

"Given all the drama, I think it's best not to add to it."

"Fine," Harriet grumbled. "Can I still take you to breakfast?"

"Oh, a quickie in the woods doesn't get you out of that obligation, dear. I still haven't forgotten about Clive and Camilla and us being in need of an action plan."

"Wouldn't dream of shirking my duties. As you like to keep pointing out, I'm very British in that regard."

"I had no idea a Brit would seduce me in the outdoors."

"I'm learning it's best not to have expectations. Just let things be."

"Oh really?" Josie squeaked. "When did you adopt this mantra?"

"About ten minutes ago."

Josie tilted her head back, laughing.

It was the best sound on the planet. Well, second best. Harriet could still hear Josie's gasp when Harriet had entered her moments ago. That was the most amazing thing she'd heard.

Josie looped her arm through Harriet's, resting her head on Harriet's shoulder. "You're so warm."

"You're absolutely beautiful, Josie Adams."

Josie stopped in her tracks and gazed into Harriet's eyes. "What are we going to do?"

Harriet brushed her lips against Josie's. "I may not have the answer at my fingertips, but I know everything will eventually work out if we want it to."

"I want to believe you. I really do."

Harriet held Josie close, but another snap of a twig wrenched them apart.

"I should jog back," Josie said, not going into more detail, but Harriet suspected Josie wanted to return on her own to keep people from discovering their secret. Given everything that had happened in the past twenty-four hours and that they'd just shagged in the woods, Harriet couldn't fault Josie.

"I understand. I'll see you soon."

Josie kissed Harriet's cheek.

CHAPTER THIRTY-FIVE

JOSIE SLIPPED THROUGH THE BACK OF THE PUB, taking the narrow and winding stairs to the living quarters two steps at a time, hoping to return undetected. Why, she didn't know. It wasn't unusual for her to go for a run early in the morning.

"There you are!" Her mum stood in Josie's bedroom.

"What are you doing up so early?" Josie asked, her eyes glancing about as if trying to determine if there was any incriminating evidence, as if she were a teenager.

"Is that a new jacket?"

Shit. She'd forgotten to return it to Harry. "Uh, yeah."

"It looks expensive. Where'd you get it?"

"What did you need, Mum?"

"I wanted to chat about the dating show we discussed."

"What dating show?" Josie shrugged out of the jacket and casually hung it on the hook on the back of her bedroom door.

"For the pub. We'll have bachelors and bachelorettes with three contestants vying for a date. I've decided to go all in after the ginger ads and now the blotter."

"But you despise both." Josie shook her head. "I'm not following."

"What I've learned from yesterday is this village loves relationship drama. Instead of fighting it, why not embrace it."

"To make a buck." Josie didn't like the sound of this idea or the look of greed in her mum's eyes.

"What can I say? Living in America rubbed off on me."

"Okay, but this is the type of thing I left behind in America."

Her mum plowed on, not seeming like she'd heard Josie. "I was watching this show last night about two people who were getting married the first time they met. It's addictive."

"You want to marry people off in the pub?" Josie's voice nearly reached hysterical screeching level.

"Oh, I don't think we can take that on," her mum said in all seriousness, with a resigned sigh.

Josie was aghast her mum was actually disappointed by this.

Eugenie pressed on. "I mean, the liability would be too much. But we can host dating nights. The more I think about it, the more I think it'd be a hoot."

"A hoot?" Josie could only see bad things coming from this.

"I think it's important for us to include lesbians." Her mum avoided looking directly at Josie.

"You want to include lesbians in this sham?"

"Yes. You're close with Harry. Maybe she could be our first bachelorette. Do you think you can convince her?"

No! "Let me get this straight. You woke at seven on a Saturday and rushed in here to tell me about this dating game and enlist me to get Harry, who you know I like, on board as the test lesbian in your dating show gambit to capitalize on all the drama you've been against since day one? This is your solution? If you can't beat them, join them?"

"Yes."

Josie placed a hand on her mum's forehead. "Are you ill?"

"Don't be stroppy."

"Stroppy. You haven't used that word since I was a surly teenager."

"Who stole my car."

"It was very stroppy of me."

"The word doesn't work that way."

"I know. I was being belligerent using it that way. You aren't the only word lover in the family."

Her mum groaned. "Harry? Will you talk to her?"

Oh, Josie wanted to do more than talk to Harry, which was a confusing idea for an entirely different reason. "I don't know, Mum. It doesn't seem like her thing."

"Exactly. That's why it's so perfect."

Josie crossed her arms. "What do you mean?"

"She's such a bumbling priss. It'll be comic gold." Her mum pressed her hands together.

"You want Harry involved so everyone will laugh at her."

Her mum bobbed her head.

"That's mean. I know you don't like her, and you keep ignoring the part that I do, but putting that aside for now"—Josie made a motion of sticking a pin into her hand —"which I can't believe I have to, it's just wrong. How do you not see that?"

"It'll just be for fun."

"It doesn't seem like it."

"What if we gave some of the money to charity? Would

that persuade your do-gooder heart?" Her mum flashed her best persuasive smile.

"Because that'll make humiliating Harry okay?"

"Listen"—her mum made placating motions with her hands—"I discussed this idea with the girls last night, and everyone agreed it'd be great. We should record it and put it online."

"You want to humiliate Harry for all the world to see?"

"Not just Harry. People will do anything for their fifteen minutes of fame. I'm sure we'll get people pleading with us to be next on the show." Her mum could barely contain her excitement. "The pub already has a certain reputation thanks to Clive. We might as well capitalize on it."

"I need to hop in the shower." Josie barged past her mum to grab her things to change into.

"You still having breakfast with Harry?"

"Yes."

"Will you ask her?"

"Mum." Josie searched for the right words without telling her to simply go to hell. "If I do ask her, I'll have to tell her why you've chosen her."

"Because it'll be funny."

"Because you'll be laughing at her."

"*With* her. Stress that." Her mum tapped a finger against an open palm.

"She's going to think this is your way of getting revenge for the Clive business."

"She may, but she's arrogant, so she may think she can outsmart me."

Josie sputtered, "She's not arrogant. She's one of the sweetest people I've met. Why can't you see that?" Josie shook exasperated hands in the air.

Her mum blinked until a smile returned to her face. "That's good. Tell her that malarkey. She'll fall for it, hook, line, and sinker." Her mum pretended pulling in a whopper of a fish. "Thanks, Josie. I've tapped you to be the emcee of the show. You're witty with the right amount of American snark. Viewers will love it."

"You do know it's not actually a TV show. We don't have producers, a TV crew, set, or any of the other components."

"I'm working on it." Her mum left Josie in the room.

"She's lost her mind." Josie grabbed her robe.

* * *

HARRY WAS WAITING in the café when Josie arrived.

"I forgot to return your jacket." Josie held it in her arms. "Where'd you get it?"

"You like it?"

"Yes, but I got myself in a jam earlier when my mum saw me in it. I told her I recently purchased it, and she doesn't forget details like that. It's like she's always trying to trip me up on the lies I tell her. I'd blocked that out when I decided to move home." Josie stared down at Harry, her eyes taking in the swell of Harry's cleavage. Could she stand over the woman for the entire breakfast?

Harry peered up into Josie's eyes, seeming not to notice Josie's ogling. "Do you often lie to your mum?"

"Uh, she brings it out in me." Josie waved it away.

Harry seemed taken aback. "Why?"

"Because she's always in my business." Josie finally took a seat, denying her the pleasant view down Harry's shirt.

Harry nodded as if she understood, but her forehead was still creased. "Tell you what, keep the jacket. I got it years ago, and I don't even know if you can find one like it anymore."

"I can't steal your jacket." Josie tried to hand it off again.

Harry pushed Josie's hand away. "You aren't. I'm giving it to you."

Torn over the jacket and the guilt of knowing her mum was doing everything to humiliate Harry, Josie opted not to fight about the least trifling matter at hand. For the moment at least. "Okay. But I insist on paying for breakfast."

"You're a master negotiator."

"I feel like a swindler. I'm positive the jacket cost way more than a full English breakfast."

"A decade ago. The value has dropped significantly, I may be ripping you off." Harry's smile was sincere.

"Good. Rip me off." It might assuage the guilt roiling through Josie.

The beginnings of a blush prickled Harry's cheeks.

Remembering what they'd done hours earlier caused heat to form inside Josie.

The two of them stared at each other, seeming to communicate things no one else on the planet would comprehend. It was such an incredible feeling for Josie. In a terrifying way. Compound that with the feeling of culpability of not standing up to her mum... was it possible Josie was just as bad as her mum?

A waitress in jeans and a white T-shirt held a notepad. "Can I start you two off with tea or coffee?"

"Coffee for me," Harry said.

"Tea please," Josie piped up. "I think we're ready to order. Two English breakfasts, please."

When alone, Josie joked, "It's hard to believe you're the Brit and I'm the American."

"I don't understand how you don't drink coffee in the morning. I can't get my brain going without it."

"It tastes like barf."

Harry laughed. "Don't hold back."

"I thought you liked that about me. You weren't complaining earlier."

Excitement flittered in Harry's eyes. "Only an idiot would complain about that."

"Are you referring to my not holding back or"—Josie leaned over the table—"the way you wanted to be thanked in the woods for lending me the jacket?" Josie's playful tone hopefully conveyed she wasn't serious.

"Is that what it was?"

"Yeah. Isn't that the custom here?"

"I was unaware of it until now, but it seems I need to buy a lot more jackets."

Josie crossed her arms. "To hand them out to all the girls you stumble upon?"

"Perhaps just one in particular."

"Sounds promising. Is the jacket incident causing the glint in your eyes?" Josie circled a finger in the air.

"You could say that."

"I want to be absolutely clear about things from now on. What are you thinking about?"

"Where does Robin Hood run around?"

"Nottingham?" Josie didn't sound confident at all. "I think I remember seeing his statue near the castle when I went with my mum years ago."

"Be less specific."

It hit Josie. "Oh, that's your nerdy way of saying the woods. What about the woods do you like, Harry?" Josie fluttered her lashes and leaned on her forearms, drawing attention to her girls.

"Here you go." The waitress placed a teapot down for Josie with an empty cup on a saucer and then Harry's coffee. "Your food will be out soon."

"Thank you," Harry said, briefly looking at the woman, but her eyes returned to Josie's assets.

"I'd love to know what you're thinking right now."

"You're going to have to use your imagination." Harry sipped her coffee.

"I am." Josie held up her hand, indicating hold on a second.

Harry laughed. "Why don't you tell me what you're thinking?"

"I'm not sure you want to hear it," Josie said, sounding graver than she had intended.

"Uh-oh. What's wrong?"

"Two things. One is annoying."

"And the other?"

"Something we need to talk about."

"Does it involve the two Cs in our lives?"

Josie shook her head.

"Okay, hit me up with the annoying one first. Ease me into things."

"My mum wants to set you up on a date in front of the entire village."

CHAPTER THIRTY-SIX

"C-CAN YOU RUN THAT BY ME AGAIN?"

Josie shook her head. "I'd rather not. I feel slimy enough saying it once."

"Why in the world would your mum want to set me up on a date? And how does the village factor in?" Harriet tried her best to see the logic, but it was as if her brain spluttered like an outdated car unable to keep up with the newer models on the motorway.

Josie heaved a sigh, the one she released whenever her mum factored into the conversation. "Mum has it in her head that it would be a great idea to film a dating show in the pub, and she wants to be inclusive and feature lesbians."

Harriet placed a hand on her chest. "I'm the lesbian?"

"So it seems."

"But I would be the last lesbian—no, person—in Upper Chewford to sign up for something like this."

"I think that's her point." Josie sipped her tea.

"How does something so absurd seem to make sense to

her?" Harriet's voice was too loud, and she shifted in her seat. "I'm sorry. I know she's your mum."

Josie grinned. "Don't be. I like it when you get hot and bothered."

Harriet started to drop the Eugenie thread but didn't. "Nice try. Does your mum think I'll agree to this absurdity as a way of penance? That's it, isn't it?"

"Partly. She also thinks I can convince you and you're too smug to turn down the opportunity to show her up."

"Basically, she has the worst opinion of me on all fronts." Eugenie hadn't even found out about Camilla and Clive yet. Harriet feared the woman would twist things to lay all the blame at Harriet's feet, like she'd done with the blotter.

Josie shrunk into herself, retreating back in her seat as the waitress placed her plate down.

"Need anything else?" the woman asked.

They shook their heads.

As soon as the woman turned her back, Josie forked Harriet's black pudding, while Harriet stabbed Josie's grilled tomato.

"We're like an old married couple." Josie shivered.

"Not a happy thought for you?" Harriet sliced into one of the grilled sausages.

"It's not that."

"What is it?"

"I've seen couples who knew each other so well they stopped communicating completely, not needing to speak."

"Are you afraid we would reach that stage too soon if we became more than… whatever we are?" Harriet made a sorry gesture for the awkward phrasing.

"I don't know. I'm not one hundred percent certain about the thoughts going through my head."

"Is that one of the reasons you don't want anyone in

the village to know we're more than full English breakfast buddies?"

"Maybe. I know it's not fair to you. You probably think it silly."

"It confuses me. I think you're fantastic, and I have no issues if anyone knows we're… What are we?"

"Fr-friends?" Josie stumbled as if she knew the word would hurt.

Harriet swallowed some coffee. "I see."

"I really hate it when you say that."

"Why?"

"Because it makes me feel terrible, knowing something I said hurt you."

Harriet didn't waste the energy saying it didn't hurt. She could see in Josie's eyes she was well aware of how the butchered word had landed. "Are you asking me to agree to this dating show for your sake?"

"I don't want you to do it. Not at all."

"Why?" Harriet buttered her toast, doing everything she could to focus on the task.

"Because it's not your thing."

"Dating?"

"Being made a spectacle of. That's how it would turn out. It's the whole point of the show. To humiliate those involved for cheap laughs and publicity for the pub."

"I see."

Josie closed her eyes and held her head up with her palm. "I'm not handling this right."

"What's the second thing?"

Josie uncovered her eyes. "Maybe this isn't the right moment."

"That's been the theme lately, hasn't it? Might as well get it over with."

Josie's gaze momentarily fell to her plate, but with what

seemed like monumental resolve, she looked Harriet in the eyes. "I've received a job opportunity back in the States."

Harriet steadied her breathing. "What's the offer?"

"Speechwriter for a Georgia politician."

"I thought the election was over."

"There's always an election in the US. This is a special election for senator after the current one resigned due to a sex scandal. Another theme we can't escape."

Harriet ignored the last comment, laser focused on the question she was terrified of asking. "Are you interested?"

"Yes."

No hesitation on that one. "When is the election?"

"Early spring."

This relieved Harriet some. "You wouldn't be gone that long, then."

"It depends. If the candidate wins, there's a strong possibility she'd be a contender for the Oval Office in eight years. She's the *It* girl these days."

"What does that mean?"

"It would be another shot at me working for a future president of the United States."

From the glimmer in Josie's eyes, this was something she wanted. "It sounds like a wonderful opportunity."

"You think I should take it?"

"I think you want to take it, but I can't tell you what to do." Harriet squeezed her hands under the table, cutting off the circulation in all her fingers.

"But if you had a say, what would you tell me to do?" Josie's eyes brimmed.

"To be true to what you want."

"What if I want two different things?"

"Life has a funny way of doing that." Harriet did her best not to display any emotion, not wanting to sway Josie in either direction.

Josie flicked a tear off her cheek.

"If you turned down the job, would you regret it?" Harriet asked.

"I-I don't know."

"I think you would, otherwise you wouldn't be struggling with the decision."

"Why aren't you trying to convince me to stay?" Josie asked with anguish in her voice.

"Because it would be wrong of me to do so." Harriet spooned some baked beans onto her toast and placed it in her mouth, reminding herself to chew before swallowing. Just act normal. Completely unfazed by the situation. To make it easier for Josie. Harriet could break down later. Josie needed her to be strong.

"But—"

Harriet squeezed Josie's hand. "When do you have to leave?"

"There's a flight later tonight they want me to catch."

The thought their last time together would end up being a quick shag in the woods nearly crushed Harriet's heart. There was no denying she was falling to pieces inside. "Do you need a ride to the airport?"

CHAPTER THIRTY-SEVEN

JOSIE, WITH HANDS SHOVED DEEP INTO HER JEANS pockets, walked across the village square with her head down, her mood plummeting further with each step.

"Hey, Josie."

Josie looked up. "Theo."

"Have you seen Harry? I have an idea for a new column in *The Chronicles*."

"Sorry. Haven't seen her."

"Your mum said you were having breakfast with her," he protested in a whiny voice.

"Oh, right. I meant, she left before I did, and I have no idea where she was going."

"Don't you want to hear my idea for the column?"

Josie absolutely did not, but she also didn't want to get into a debate. It seemed best to let him talk while she tuned him out. "Sure. Hit me with it."

"A day in the life of a stud."

"Sounds good."

"You really think so?" He looked eager. "How should I pitch it?"

Josie searched her brain for any recall of what he said. Stud. That was the word that stuck out. "Farming. Go with farming."

Theo placed a meaty hand on Josie's shoulder, laughing. "Farming. Yeah, yeah, that's good. I'll tell Harry that to get it past her. Thanks for the suggestion." He tipped his hat and marched toward Harry's street.

Josie didn't bother shouting after him that Harry would be smart enough to avoid Theo like he was Typhoid Mary. "What's wrong with the people in this village? Sex, sex, sex, that's all they care about." And not one, apparently, believed in love. Not even the woman she was in love with. Josie sucked in a deep breath and released it slowly, doing her best to staunch the threatening tears.

While she stopped those, she couldn't block out the voice in her head stating, "Said the woman who shagged in the woods."

It wasn't just sex, though. Not with Harry. Even the quickie that pretty much came out of nowhere had been special. Too special. To Josie at least.

Why had Harry acted so cold after learning the news? Of course, Harry had gotten married to Alice without having deep feelings, so what did Josie really expect from the reserved woman?

Back at the pub, her mum greeted her with, "Well?"

"Well, what?"

"Did Harry say yes?"

"I didn't ask her to marry me."

"Very funny. She's about as loving as a cactus." Her mum blew a raspberry. "Did she agree to do the show?"

Had her mum been right about Harry from the start? No matter. Josie was leaving for the airport in a matter of hours, and Harry would become a distant memory.

"We need to talk about something else," Josie said.

Taken aback, her mum said, "Why do you look like you lost your best friend."

"Not at all," Josie said as breezily as possible, not able to get over the thought she'd lost her shot at love. Josie had been right to focus on her career all those years, and it was best to throw herself back into it. Coming to the village had been a mistake, and it was time to correct it. "I'm leaving tonight."

"To go where?"

"Home."

Josie's mum didn't speak.

"I got a job offer." Josie couldn't say more to ease the pain on her mum's face, which didn't bode well for her reentrance to the speechwriter role.

"And you have to leave so soon?"

"They wanted me to come back before now, but I've been stalling. If I don't leave today, I won't." Josie sniffled.

"What about Harry?"

Josie massaged her forehead. "Now you want me to think about Harry?"

"You like her, don't you?"

I'm in love with her. "Yes, I do."

"Doesn't she want you to stay?"

"She thinks I should take the job if that's what I want."

"How very noble of her.

"It's very British. Stiff upper lip. You said it best. She's like a cactus."

Her mum shrugged this off. "She keeps letting me down."

Join the club. "I need to pack."

Clive and Winston came into the pub. After looking at his sister and then niece, he asked, "Who died?"

"Josie's going back to America, and Christmas is only a few days away," her mum stated, her teeth piercing her bottom lip, probably in hopes of stopping it from quivering.

Winston waddled over to Josie, and slammed his body into her legs.

Josie hunched down, "I'm going to miss you too, big guy. So, so, so much." She burst into tears, holding Winnie close to her.

CHAPTER THIRTY-EIGHT

"Harry!" Clive motioned for her to come over to the entrance of the pub.

Harriet, standing on the bridge, the very one where she'd first seen Josie, detoured toward Clive. "How are you?"

"Can you believe this weather? It's the end of February, and I'm drying my sheets outside." There were no sheets in sight, but Harriet took his word for it. She determined the dark circles under his eyes were the reason why he avoided her question.

"Me too." About the sheets and being heartbroken.

He glanced at the blue sky overhead, and asked without much emotion, "How's Camilla?"

Harriet wasn't buying his *cool as a cucumber* vibe. She'd also been sworn to secrecy. "Uh, I haven't seen her lately."

"Me neither."

Harriet didn't know what to say, so she asked something she already knew the answer to. "She's still not responding to your overtures?" She didn't like the word choice, but other options failed to come to mind.

"Not a one. What'd I do wrong?" His bravado ebbed.

She placed a hand on his shoulder. "Not a thing. Cam can be this way."

"Can you put in a good word for me? At least tell her I miss her?" His shoulders sagged.

"Of course. How's Josie?"

Clive blew out a breath. "She doesn't call much. A text here and there to her mum. She's back to her old ways."

"Going Mach speed?"

"Yep. Eugenie is worried about her."

So was Harriet, but what could she do? "Why?"

"She says it seems different this time."

"In what way?"

Clive hefted one shoulder. "Dunno. Just different. The amount of work hours or whatever."

Harriet had feared Josie would do that to herself, remembering her words that she tended to work until she broke. "Well, if you do talk to her, say hi for me."

"Are you two not talking at all?" he asked, concern evident in his expression.

"Not really."

"Why is love so painful?" The wounded look in his eyes communicated much more than his words.

Harriet searched his face, surprised by his question. Was Clive really in love with Camilla? What to do with this knowledge? "I don't know, but it is."

"Your podcast, though. *A Shot at Love*. It's all about people beating the odds and finding the one. Doesn't it give you hope? Hearing all the stories from the people you interview?"

Not at all, since Harriet's shot had been so fleeting, yet the lingering pain seemed to be never-ending. "Of course. I better get home. I have a crossword puzzle to finalize."

"Don't be a stranger. I miss talking to you. I know it

must be difficult to come to the pub and not see Josie. We can always meet away from here, if you need a friend."

How was Clive such a sweetheart given everything? More importantly, how could Harriet convince Camilla he'd make a great father? "Now that the weather is improving, I promise to visit more. I tend to be a hermit during the dark days of winter." Also, when nursing a broken heart.

They said their goodbyes, and Harriet headed home. When she opened her front door and walked in, Harriet found Camilla standing in the middle of the room, completely naked.

"Harry! What are you doing here?" She attempted to cover her bits, but ended up looking like an uncoordinated contortionist, her body still mostly on full display.

"I live here. What are you doing? Why are you naked in the front room? The shutters are open." Harriet didn't know where to look, so she stared at the floor.

"People can't see in," she said in a dismissive tone.

"Yes, they can. Tourists are constantly peeking inside."

"Why didn't you tell me that?" she screeched.

"Didn't know I had to explain how windows work. Are you going to tell me what you're doing?" Harriet closed the wood shutters, keeping her back to Camilla.

"Yoga."

"Every woman on the planet owns at least one pair of yoga leggings."

"I don't."

"Apparently."

"Do you not own a T-shirt?" Harriet pressed.

"Of course, I own a shirt."

"Why aren't you wearing one?"

"I get hot. It should be illegal to be pregnant when it's this hot. You can turn around; I put on a robe."

Harriet slowly pivoted to face her cousin. "It's still

winter. Some women are fully pregnant in the summer."
She held out her hands to stress how pregnant Camilla
would become.

"Not the smart ones."

Harriet swallowed the comment that Camilla got
knocked up by a man she barely knew, which wasn't
entirely fair since Harriet had just left the man who was
torn up about Cam not being in touch.

"Can you go for a walk or something?" Camilla made a
shooing motion with her hand.

"I just got back from a walk, and now you're asking me
to leave again so you can continue to do naked yoga?"
Since learning she was pregnant, Camilla had been coming
to the village every weekend to be close to Harriet. Or so
she said.

Camilla nodded, not seeming to comprehend the imper-
tinence of her request.

There was a knock on the door.

"Who's that?" Camilla hissed.

Harriet shrugged. "Like you, I don't have X-ray vision."

"Harry! You in there?" It was Clive's voice.

Camilla thwacked the back of Harriet's head.

Harriet rubbed her head and whispered, "What was
that for?"

"For bringing Clive here."

"I didn't. Stop talking, or he'll know you're here."

"You aren't going to answer, are you?"

Harriet tapped a finger to her lips, not moving toward
the door.

"Harry!" Clive called out louder.

Camilla clung onto Harriet's arm.

Harriet winced in pain. "Nails, Cam. Nails."

Not understanding, Camilla dug them deeper into
Harriet's skin.

Withdrawing footfalls suggested Clive had given up.

Harriet pried her cousin's fingers off her arm.

"Close call."

"Do you think of that before you come here every weekend? The possibility of running into the one person you don't want to see?"

"Yes, but where else can I go? I don't want to be alone." Camilla cradled her belly.

Harriet regretted her harsh tone. "I'm sorry. You know you're always welcome here, although we need to discuss the clothing-optional plan, as in that's not allowed."

"You're such a prude. You know what you need, cousin dear?"

"To get you yoga outfits."

"No, to get laid."

Oh, how wrong you are, Camilla. Sleeping with Josie had opened up Harriet in a way that threatened to do more damage than good. Now, Harriet realized she'd been waiting all her life for a woman like Josie, and her chance at love was as useless as attempting to build a time machine so she could go back in time and tell Josie not to take the job offer.

CHAPTER THIRTY-NINE

JOSIE SAT IN A CHEAP HOTEL DESK CHAIR BY THE open window, vaping. There was a knock on her door. Her eyes sought out the green digits of the chintzy alarm clock on the nightstand. 10:58 at night.

She rose to her feet, her body resisting the sudden movement after sitting in the chair for the past hour.

Swinging the door open, Carol held up a bottle of Cooter Brown Ale, by Jekyll Brewing, in each hand. "I come in peace."

"How could I possibly turn down a woman offering me a free Cooter?"

"I knew this would be my way in." Carol, a stout gray-haired woman in pajamas, robe, and slippers, sidestepped Josie. "Not many can turn me down."

"How does your husband feel about your ways?" Josie retook her seat by the open window.

"He loves my cooter," the older woman purred in the way that made it perfectly clear she had a healthy sex life when she wasn't on the campaign trail.

Josie groaned. "I walked right into that one. Have a

seat." Josie motioned for Carol to choose between the free chair or bed.

Carol popped the tops of the bottles with the opener on her keychain, handed one to Josie, and then settled on top of the bedspread, her back against the headboard. "When this is all over, I'll miss these." She raised the bottle. "Cheers."

Josie took a deep swallow. "Why'd you only bring one each?"

"Because I happen to know you have some in your mini fridge."

"Fresh out."

"Luckily, my room is right next door." Carol took another glug. "How are you doing?"

Josie shrugged. "Not bad. Today was slightly brutal."

"It was only a matter of time."

Josie sighed. "Every campaign has to bat away some type of smear tactics. You'd think they'd get more creative instead of shouting about an affair that isn't happening."

"But it works so well. Monogamy is so rare."

"Have something you want to confess?" Josie took a hit on her vaporizer, causing a plume of smoke, which Josie batted toward the window.

"I thought you quit smoking."

"This is vaping."

"God, I love speechwriter types. The way you make things sound so innocent."

"Vaping is innocent." Josie spoke with what she hoped was a confident tone.

"I doubt your mother would think so."

"What she doesn't know won't hurt her." Josie looked out the window.

"And what would your father think?"

"He's dead." Josie spoke more to the dark sky than Carol.

"I know. I went to his funeral."

"We've worked on a lot of campaigns together." Josie's gaze panned the hotel parking lot. "Did you always want this life?"

"Living in one cheap hotel after another?"

"Yeah." Josie's chest heaved up and slowly down.

"Yes and no. There are parts of the job I'm addicted to. It's like going to the races and laying down a bet on a winner. Except it takes a lot longer to find out if you won or lost. Wouldn't it be great if we knew in under five minutes whether or not we were on the right side? That would probably ruin the fun, though."

"How do you define the right side?" Josie drank heavily from the bottle.

Carol chuckled, sounding more evil than happy. "There isn't an easy answer to that. The pols we work for are so very human. We have to know everything about our candidate. Even things their loved ones don't necessarily know or want to know. And then we have to work our butts off to get them elected even with the knowledge we have."

Josie nodded thoughtfully.

Carol sighed.

"What don't you like?" Josie asked.

"Being away from home so much. Mike and I never had kids because I went all in for the job. I was lucky to have a husband who supported that decision." Carol tilted her beer bottle so she could stare into it. "Now that I'm nearing sixty, I wonder if I made a mistake."

"About not having kids?"

"Y-yeah," she stuttered. "But too late. Everything is shriveled up now." She laughed, circling a hand over her female parts. "And the hot flashes have subsided mostly."

Josie remained quiet.

Carol pointed her bottle at Josie. "You were brilliant earlier."

"I'm not all the time?" Josie joked.

"Oh, you are, which is why I insisted the campaign hire you. But today was especially clever. The way you mocked the press for tarnishing a good woman like she was a woman of the night simply because she's young and beautiful. I can't remember everything you came up with on the spot, but the way you spun it to get them on the backs of their heels. It was a brilliant stroke, considering."

Josie's grin was hollow, as she remembered Harry's opinion of political spin doctors.

Carol took another long tug of her drink.

"What do you mean *considering*?" Josie braced for the answer she suspected was true but didn't really want to know. There had been a time when she pried a lot more about her candidates, but this time around, she just wanted to do her job without getting her hands dirty.

"Considering our sainted candidate is having an affair."

Josie's mouth went completely dry, and her shoulders slumped forward.

Carol lowered the bottle from her lips. "You didn't know."

Josie shook her head in slow motion. "I wasn't one hundred percent positive. A sliver of me held out hope."

"Gawd, I wish I was your age again and still believed in people."

Josie didn't really, but wasn't it possible for one person to be honorable? Just one? "I wish I was your age and had stopped believing."

"Are you okay? Your face has gone completely white like you're about to puke."

Josie wanted to do just that to get all the shit out. Deep

down, she knew it wouldn't really help. It might feel good for a minute, but it didn't change the facts. Harry had let her go. Josie was back in the States doing a job she'd lost passion for. And she didn't know what to do. "I'm fine. Why didn't you tell me sooner? I should know everything so I can craft appropriate responses." Might as well do her best to sound professional, because that was all she had left.

"I really thought you knew. Or maybe a part of me wanted to protect you this time around. You know better than most that finding out the truth about anyone is a dangerous business if you want to be able to respect any human being walking this miserable earth."

"Do you respect anyone?"

"Besides you?"

Josie's eyes darted heavenward, and she let out a bark of laughter. "You're such a con artist."

"It's my job."

Josie nodded in agreement. "Did you ever believe there was more to this? Like we were taking part in bettering peoples' lives?"

"In the beginning. Or probably before I ever worked on a campaign. It doesn't take long to get jaded in politics."

"I think it took longer for me." Josie's shrug confessed she was a chump.

"That's because you're a believer. It's what makes you so good at your job. It's also what will destroy you."

"Why'd you bring me back into it?" Josie asked with sincerity.

"The campaign needs you to win. If she does, in eight years, she's going to be sitting at the Resolute desk in the Oval Office. I thought you'd want to play a role." Carol set the bottle on the nightstand. "I know the news she isn't perfect is hitting you hard, but given that knowledge, she's still the politician I believe in. No one is perfect. No one is close to perfection. But, at the end of the day, I'm glad to be on her side fighting for this job. I think she can make a difference. Or at least not screw up things as much as the other side."

"It's funny. The word lie is right in the middle of believe. As if the word gods never wanted us to truly believe in anything."

"Please tell me the news didn't break you. Not only do we need you, but I don't want to participate in wrecking you beyond repair. If I had a daughter, I'd want her to fall head over heels in love with you."

"Like love exists!" Josie scoffed. She pointed her beer bottle around the room. "This is life. Everything is temporary."

Carol took in a deep breath. "Are you ever going to tell me what or who you ran away from?"

"What gives you that idea?" Josie hardened her voice to make it as convincing as possible.

"I saw it in your face when you arrived here. I've known you since you were wet behind the ears."

Josie took another hit, not bothering to sweep away the smoke this time.

"You must be in pain if you can't even put it into words."

Josie didn't take the bait.

"I've been addicted to this new podcast called *A Shot at Love*. This woman interviews someone who has lost the love of their life, either from death or a breakup, and she's able to get the person to really open up. Most of the time, I'm bawling, thinking love is so beautiful but knowing not everyone on the planet is brave enough to let themselves fall completely. So many are too scared. Or too busy chasing things that are illusionary."

"Like what?"

"Having a career complete you."

"Did you grab onto your shot with Mike, or was there someone else?" "I grabbed on. It's the best thing I ever did. It makes this"—she waved to the cheap furnishings in the room—"bearable."

Josie's eyes traveled through the room, taking in the oil painting knockoffs, battered dresser that listed to the side, and finally landing on the carpet that Josie was afraid to walk on barefoot, thinking she'd contract a life-threatening disease. "So, it's possible to hold on."

"I'm living proof. After this, why don't you come spend a few days with me and Mike. We'll help you see the way."

"To where?"

"The person keeping you up night after night in that chair as you vape and knock back Cooters. I'm in the room next door. I know how often you sit there, smoking."

"It's vaping."

"It's pining. You aren't the only word specialist on the team."

"Do you like crossword puzzles?"

"That's a weird evasion."

It's not. "Sorry. It just popped into my head. Probably too many Cooters."

Carol sucked her lips into her mouth.

"It's okay. Get it out of your system." Josie waved for her to say whatever lame joke had popped into her head.

"You've always had cooters on the brain. I'm sorry. I couldn't hold that in."

"Don't ever stop being you."

"Don't ever stop believing in love. You, Josie dear, deserve it."

CHAPTER FORTY

On an early March evening, Harriet sat on the couch with Camilla as they watched an episode of the crime drama *Vera*.

"Can you massage my feet?" Camilla asked.

Harriet shuddered some. "Will you keep your socks on?"

"Seriously? We're cousins."

"You won't ever let me forget that part. Socks or no massage."

Camilla repositioned on the sofa, placing her feet in Harriet's lap. "Who needs a man when I have you?"

Harriet dug into the bottom of Cam's right foot. "Clive would probably get some fancy foot lotion and really spoil you."

"Yeah right. The only thing that man cares about is himself."

"What makes you think that?"

"He hasn't tracked me down," Camilla stated as if that was the only proof she needed.

Harriet stilled her hands. "I know for a fact he's been trying to contact you."

"All he texts is hi and asks how I'm doing." Camilla wiggled her foot for Harriet to get back to work.

Harriet complied. "What do you want him to do?"

"I don't know. More."

"If you want him to do more, give the poor man something to go on. Or do you not care that he's in love with you?"

"He's what?"

Harriet winced.

"Harry, do you know something I don't know?"

"I've had a few conversations with him." Harriet continued rubbing Camilla's foot.

"And you talked about me?"

"He's mentioned you, yes," Harriet conceded.

"Did he say he was in love with me?"

"Not specifically."

"What did he say, specifically?" Camilla's eyes narrowed.

"He asked why love was painful."

"Is he still the village's playboy?"

"I don't think he ever was."

"What does that mean?"

"As it turns out, the ginger ads were a hoax. Around Christmas, Theo printed a *Ginger George Blotter* as a way of getting even with Clive for garnering all female attention in the village, but it eventually came out that the first ad was meant as a joke. The other women placed theirs to toss their hats in the ring for Clive's attention. None of it really makes much sense to me, but the entire time, Clive was innocent."

"He didn't sleep with any of the women?" Camilla's lips thinned.

"Doesn't seem so."

Camilla lurched forward, her feet digging into Harriet's stomach. "Why didn't you tell me that sooner?"

"You didn't want to hear anything about Clive. You made me promise not to say a word about him." Harriet tossed up a helpless hand.

"That was because I thought he was living the high life while I'm growing this." She rubbed the swell of her belly.

"If he was such a playboy, why do you think he tried to get in touch? He gave me the impression he's reached out on many occasions."

"I thought he liked the game. Or the chase."

"Would you want more with him if he did with you?" Harriet closed one eye, determining if that made sense or not.

Camilla was dead silent. This wasn't her typical stalling method, so Harriet had no idea what it could mean.

After several moments, Harriet asked, "Are you okay?"

"Do you think it's possible?"

"What?"

"That I could find happiness with Clive?"

"I don't know the answer, but I do know if you don't give him a chance, you won't ever find out."

"But if I give him a chance and it doesn't work out, how does this little one fit in?" Camilla's arms protectively cradled the baby bump.

"I hate to break it to you, but Clive is already involved with the little one. He has been since day one."

"I'm scared, Harry. About all of it." Tears streamed down her face.

Harriet motioned for Cam to move to allow Harriet to wrap her arms around Cam. "I know. Whatever you choose, I'll be with you no matter what."

"How do I tell Clive without him thinking I'm trying to trap him?"

"Is that your concern?" Harriet had never considered this possibility.

"I can't escape the responsibility. It's different with men."

"It shouldn't be."

"It is, though. No matter how hard we push for equal rights. Men can walk away. I literally can't."

"A good man wouldn't, though."

"Is Clive a good man?"

"I can't say definitively."

"If you had to guess."

"Oh, Camilla. How can I make a guess about this?"

"Please, Harry. I trust you."

Harriet pictured the pain in Clive's eyes. "I think he's a good guy." Did that mean he'd make a good father? Harriet had no idea. But did anyone know that about anyone?

"What should I tell him? Or how?" Camilla rested her head on Harriet's shoulder.

"We could have him come over."

"Here?" Camilla glanced around. "We can't have him over here."

"Why not?"

"I... I don't know. It just seems wrong."

"Okay. Did you want to go to the pub?"

"I can't drink."

"You can't drink alcohol. You can have orange juice or something. But, it's not like you have to order anything. It's not part of the process. It's not like you say, *I'll have OJ, and I'm carrying your child.*"

Camilla started to laugh uncontrollably, until she started to hyperventilate.

Harriet rocked Cam in her arms. "It's going to be okay."

* * *

CAMILLA HUNG on to Harriet's arm as they entered The Golden Fleece.

Eugenie and Olivia were behind the bar. Much to Harriet's surprise, Eugenie cheerfully waved them inside. Did Eugenie have some devastating news to share, and she couldn't contain herself? Like Josie had gotten married or something along those lines?

"Hello, you two. Harry, I know you'd like a gin and tonic, and Camilla, Stella for you?" Eugenie reached for a pint glass.

"Just an orange juice for me."

"Are you up the duff?" Eugenie laughed.

Camilla pressed into Harriet for support.

"Camilla!" Clive shouted from the other side of the pub and rushed toward her like a bull charging a matador.

Harriet stepped in his path, providing cover for Camilla. With her hands up she said, "Easy."

He pulled up, peering around Harriet. "Are you injured or something?"

"No," Camilla replied in a whisper.

"Sick?" he whispered back. "Is that why you haven't been in?"

"Kinda," she said.

Harriet still stood between them, not that either of them seemed to take too much notice of her.

Eugenie watched the back and forth like it was a tennis match, her eyes showing she was catching on much quicker than her brother.

"Are you feeling better?" Clive asked, concern written in his furrowed brow.

"It's an ongoing thing," Camilla explained in a strained voice.

"Is it...?" Clive swallowed, his Adam's apple bobbling up and down.

"What?" Camilla asked.

Harriet wanted to end the misery for both but remained quiet.

He mouthed *deadly*, or so Harriet thought.

"I can't read lips," Camilla said.

Good grief. Harriet shifted a little to the right, giving Clive and Eugenie a look at Cam's slight baby bump. The baggy shirt did a decent job concealing it, but Camilla's habit of cradling her belly made it more noticeable.

Eugenie's eyes popped open, and Harriet wondered if Eugenie would ever be able to close them again.

Clive still didn't seem to get it.

Camilla smoothed her top over the bump to make it more prominent.

"Stomach bug?" he asked.

Harriet massaged her forehead.

Eugenie whacked him with a towel she had on her shoulder. "She's pregnant."

Clive had his eyes on Eugenie as if he needed to know the definition of the word. Slowly, he turned his head to Camilla, who had a frightened expression on her face. In slow motion, Clive pointed to her belly and then aimed his thumb at his own chest.

Camilla nodded.

Clive remained frozen.

Harriet wished she'd never encouraged Cam to tell him.

Eugenie's expression was blank. Was she having a stroke? Harriet inspected her face to see if one side drooped.

"We're going to have a baby?" Clive whispered in a barely audible voice.

Camilla nodded again.

The Ginger Giant jumped in the air, tapping his feet. "We're going to have a baby!"

Camilla burst into laughter.

Clive took her hands in his. "When did this happen?"

"The night we met."

"Winner right out of the gate," Clive shouted, slapping one hand onto the bar. "Drinks all around!"

Eugenie started to balk but said, "Why not?"

The pub wasn't overly crowded.

"Am I your uncle now?" Clive picked Harriet up and spun her in the air.

Harriet laughed over his antics, but it made her think of Josie and her reaction when she had found out. "I don't think it works that way."

"Josie. I need to call Josie." Clive fished out his phone from his pocket. He held the phone to his ear. "Josie... is that you?" He pointed to the phone as if confirming it was indeed his niece. "I'm going to be a daddy... Camilla... Here, Harry can explain everything."

Before Harriet knew what was happening, she had Clive's phone to her ear. Not knowing what to say, she said, "Hi."

"Hi."

"Did you hear the news? Wait, he just told you." Not to mention Harriet had already told Josie. "Sorry, everything is a bit confusing here. Clive thinks he's my uncle now."

Josie laughed. "How are the parents-to-be?"

"I think they're happy in that *holy fuck, we're having a kid* way. Or so I imagine."

"Did you just say holy fuck?"

"Did I?"

"Yes. You did." There was a pause. "How are you, Harry?"

Harriet straightened. "Good. I'm good. You?"

"Busy."

"I should let you go."

"That's not what I meant. I just meant the job is keeping me on my toes. I haven't been on a run since my plane landed. Hold on. Let me step outside." There was a rustling sound. "Okay, I have a few minutes to chat."

All words fell out of Harriet's head as she stepped outside of the pub since Clive kept shouting he was going to be a father. She reached for the first thing that came to her mind. "The moon is full."

"Can you see the North Star?" Josie asked.

Harriet nodded. "Yes, I can. Can you?"

"It's not dark yet."

"Right. Sometimes I forget you're in a different country." Harriet closed her eyes to stop them from watering.

"I'm in the South. It feels so foreign to me."

There was silence.

"If I can, I'll step outside tonight and see if I can find Little Bear."

"Call me if you need help. I'll do my best to navigate you from here."

There was laughter. "It'll be super late there."

"It doesn't matter. I like stargazing with you."

"I'd like that." There were some muffled sounds. "Harry, I have to run. It was good hearing your voice."

"Same here," Harriet said, only to realize Josie had already ended the call. "Same here," she said to Little Bear.

Eugenie stepped outside. "This has been a shocking night."

Harriet smacked her lips. "The first of many for those two, I think."

"How have you been?"

"Good." Harriet imagined the stars realigning in the sky to spell out liar in all caps.

"I've been listening to your podcast. It's good."

"Thanks. That means a lot coming from you."

"Harry," Eugenie said with sweetness seeming to ooze out of her eyeballs. "Can I interest you in testing something?"

Harriet took in a mouthful of air but couldn't stop herself from saying, "In what way?"

"Since you're Upper Chewford's new love guru, I want your assistance in planning some events for the pub to help drum up business. Since the blotter, business has been somewhat slow."

Harriet's eyes clamped onto the Northern Star briefly, before she said, "Are you talking about the dating show Josie mentioned before she left?"

"Yes," Eugenie said, giving her best angelic expression. "I'm calling it Blind Date. I have the first one planned, but I'd like to include lesbians in the second."

Harriet took another swallow of fresh air. "Sure. Why not?"

CHAPTER FORTY-ONE

"Do you ever sleep?" Carol whispered in Josie's ear as they rifled into the conference room for their 7:00 a.m. briefing.

"About as much as you," Josie whispered back.

"Don't try that. You look worse than usual. The black circles under your eyes have circles of their own."

"Geez, thanks."

Everyone quieted when the campaign manager swept into the room looking like he was ready to murder someone. "I don't know whose fault this is, but we have some work ahead of ourselves to save this campaign." He tossed blurry photos of their candidate in what seemed like an intimate moment with a female, not her husband.

Carol stared at Josie.

Josie mouthed, *What?*

"Josie, have something to say?" Brad, the manager, barked.

Josie ignored the disgust inside and went into action mode. "The photo looks like nothingburger to me. Women are naturally more cuddling with other women. I bet if we polled women, the majority would agree."

Brad snapped his fingers. "Start with that. Get polls going. Fucking get a thousand women to lie if you have to. We have less than a week until election day, and until this morning, we were fourteen points ahead. I will not let us lose now. Get this done, people." He clapped his hands and made *rah rah* sounds like a high school football coach when rallying his team in the fourth quarter.

Josie and Carol headed back to their windowless office. "Thanks for tossing me under the bus," Josie said.

"I didn't, really. It was just unfortunate timing."

Josie parked her butt on the edge of her desk. "You know the photo looks bad."

"Real bad. I cuddle with friends but not like that." Carol sipped her Starbucks latte. "Quick thinking, though."

"But it's a lie."

"The way I see it, it's payback."

"How do you figure that?"

"Think of all the male politicians who've cheated on their spouses, only to have their wife stand by. Now, our candidate gets to force her husband to stand by her side. It's almost beautiful revenge."

"Just once I would like to work for someone who didn't end up breaking my heart."

Carol studied Josie's face. "That's your problem. You think work will be able to fill you with joy. Work is work. You need someone to go home to at the end of the day."

"You don't go home to Mike every night."

"We talk on the phone and say good night. Who do you have?"

"Little Bear."

"Little who?"

Josie waved a hand. "Nothing. I'm just tired. We should get to work."

* * *

AROUND SEVEN THAT NIGHT, her mum rang, but Josie wasn't able to answer the phone. Her mum messaged: *Watch this video*. The attachment just included today's date, no other clues.

Josie scrunched her face, but tucked her phone into her pocket when Melissa Mitchell came into the prep area wanting to clarify a line in the speech that was scheduled to start in five minutes. Carol walked her through it, while Josie's mind wandered.

Carol snapped her fingers in front of Josie's face. "Josie? You with us?"

No. "Yes, sorry." Josie scanned the line Carol had highlighted on her tablet. "How do you want to change it?"

Both of them talked at once, each raising their voice to overpower the other. The crowd was growing restless. Josie picked up enough snippets and said, "Hold on." She retooled the sentence and then showed the two of them.

"Perfect. You're fucking good at this shit." Melissa allowed her assistant to straighten her shirt and blazer. Another person did a last-minute makeup touchup. Done, she walked onto the stage, waving her hand, then placing both hands over her heart and moving her hands away, conveying to the crowd she loved them. Yeah, right.

Bile rose in Josie's throat. "Excuse me."

"You okay?" Carol asked.

"Dinner didn't agree with me."

"Go back to your room. I'll handle the spin after everything."

Josie placed a hand on Carol's shoulder. "Thank you."

"You got it, kiddo. I'll get even tomorrow."

"I know you will," Josie said in a teasing voice, but she meant it. She was literally falling apart, but no one seemed to notice. Or maybe everyone was so jaded they stopped caring. All that mattered was winning. Not being on the right side.

In her hotel room, Josie slipped out of her heels, pencil skirt, and blouse. She cranked the shower water onto scalding and finished removing her underthings. Standing under the water, she tried to let the filth of her job wash off. Josie placed her hands on the shower wall and allowed the water to pummel her face. Flipping around, she had the water beat down between her shoulder blades and didn't move until the water started to cool.

After toweling off, she slipped into a pair of sweats and a hoodie to go have her nightly chat with Little Bear, but she remembered her mum's message. Cold now, she climbed under the bedcovers and hit play on the video.

The image was wobbly at first, making Josie squint to make out what she was supposed to see. Four women sat on bar stools in the middle of the pub. Natalie was on the far left, a Japanese-style white paper screen blocking her view of the three other women.

Her mum had finally gotten the dating show off the ground. Good for her.

The video cut out for a second and then zoomed in on Harry.

Harry?

Josie held her phone closer to her face. "Why is Harry on my mum's dating show?"

Natalie asked, "What's the hardest thing you've ever had to do?"

Harry took the handheld mic from the woman on her

right. "Um, the first thing that pops into my mind is letting someone go."

There was a voice, either Natalie's or someone else's in the audience.

Harry looked uncomfortable, clearly not wanting to elaborate. "Um... a woman I cared deeply for had an opportunity of a lifetime in a different country, and as much as it killed me, I encouraged her to take it. I wanted to plead with her not to go. But I didn't, knowing if she didn't take the job, she'd always regret it."

There was another voice that was hard to make out.

"Do I regret it?" Harry placed a hand on her chest. "No. Sometimes you have to do what's right, even if you know it'll hurt. And it does. I feel her absence every second of the day. But she's chasing her dream. I'm proud of her." Harry seemed to look right into the camera. "I'll always want what's best for her."

Natalie seemed to say *wow* and then asked another question. Harry passed the mic to the woman on her left, the poor woman seeming shell-shocked by Harry's vulnerability.

Since Josie had left, Clive had been sending her copies of Harry's newspaper, each with a note saying *I know you enjoy the crosswords*. Until that moment, Josie had only stored them, but never had the heart to solve them. She pulled them out and arranged them chronologically. With trepidation, she started to solve each puzzle, looking for clues. The first she found was *agony* for *heartbreak*. In a different puzzle, she solved: *torch songs* for *tunes about unrequited love*. Each crossword had more hints about Harry's heartbroken state. When Josie figured out the answer to Casablanca as the saddest movie ever, Josie knew she'd made a dreadful mistake.

An ad about a podcast caught Josie's eye. *A Shot at Love*.

Wasn't that the one Carol had mentioned that night a few weeks ago? Josie searched for it on her phone and hit play on the most recent episode. Harry's posh voice filled Josie's ears. After listening to Agnes and William talking about how they finally realized they were meant to be together, tears streamed down Josie's face.

She looked up at the ceiling and expelled a breath. "I wish I could tell you how terribly sad and alone I am, but I don't know how."

* * *

FIVE DAYS LATER, Josie's candidate stood in front of her fans, giving an acceptance speech, the crowd bursting into cheers at every opportunity. Balloons and confetti streamed down on everyone.

Carol dug her hands into Josie's shoulders. "We fucking did it!"

Josie leaned against Carol, wiped out from the final push.

"In eight years, you'll be writing an inauguration speech, kiddo. We're in the big leagues now!"

Eight more years of this shit. That sounded like hell.

Josie peered over her shoulder and stared into Carol's face. The older woman seemed to know what Josie wanted to say. Carol nodded and spun Josie around to face her. Josie sucked her lips into her mouth so she wouldn't cry.

Carol said loud enough to be heard, "Go home, Josie. Chase your heart or Little whatever. All I want is for you to be happy."

"You won't hate me for leaving?"

"I'll be jealous as hell picturing you living in a quaint village away from all this, but I could never hate you. I want you to be happy."

Josie hugged Carol. "Promise you'll visit me."

"In Upper Chewford? I wonder if I can meet that podcaster."

Josie grinned. "I hope so. I plan on marrying her."

"Little whatever is the podcaster?"

Josie nodded.

"Get the fuck out!"

Josie continued nodding.

"What fucking took you so long? Better yet, why'd you leave in the first place?"

"I had to know if I was truly done with politics." Josie scanned the pandemonium of the crowd as well as Melissa and her husband, their conjoined hands raised victoriously in the air. "I'm so done with this."

CHAPTER FORTY-TWO

IT WAS THE NINETEENTH OF APRIL. THE SUN WAS shining. Birds chirped sweet melodies. The sound of a child laughing floated in the air. It was the picture-perfect spring morning in the Cotswolds. Harriet even spied a precious lamb frolicking in a field, happy to be alive.

It was as if the universe was screaming for Harriet to appreciate the beauty surrounding her. Yet, Harriet tucked her head down into the collar of her jacket, blotting out all the fucking signs of happiness and life marching on.

She was miserable and didn't think she'd ever snap out of it.

Harriet stopped in her tracks on the footbridge, remembering the night she had stood there, laying her eyes on Josie for the first time. Slowly, she scanned the morning dew on the grass, up to the horizon, where the deep-blue sky met the brilliant green landscape, and finally landing on the spot where Josie had stood when it seemed the world had stopped for the two of them to see each other. Making a connection.

On this beautiful spring morning, no one was there.

Harriet turned around and made her way back to her cottage.

Before she could put her key into the lock, someone shouted, "Harry, there you are!"

She turned to see Theo.

Before she could greet him, he said, "I have another idea for the paper. Hear me out." He planted his feet wide apart, with his arms out as if ready to stop Harriet from fleeing.

Harriet effectively closed her ears but managed to nod her head occasionally to give the impression she was taking his concept to heart. Even with the ginger ads fiasco finally put to bed, Theo was determined for everyone in the village to believe he was the true Romeo of Upper Chewford and kept concocting bizarre ways to solidify the image. The success of her podcast compounded the issue, and everyone was under the misconception Harriet believed in love. Ha! In her experience, love only left one broken and scattered, like a scarecrow pecked away by the birds.

Why did she keep doing the podcast, then? Was she just a glutton for punishment? Or a sucker for holding out for a glimmer of hope?

How was it possible that the end of her marriage with Alice hadn't left Harriet with the pain of Josie's absence? She'd only met Josie last October, less than a year ago. And her life would never be the same.

"What do you think?" Theo stared at her with wide eyes.

"I'll give it some thought."

"Great!" He had no idea Harriet hadn't heard a word.

"I have an interview, so I better get going."

"Of course. Love stops for no one." He waved for her to get to her important work.

Harriet wanted to punch the man in the nose. Instead,

she offered a thin-lipped smile and left him next to the river.

Inside her cottage, she sighed when she spied the empty space. She missed seeing Camilla sitting on the couch. Hell, she even missed walking in on her cousin doing naked yoga. No, that wasn't right. She just missed having Cam's company.

There was a knock on the door, but Harriet didn't have time to answer. She had to prepare for her Skype interview. Whoever it was would just have to come back.

The interview was with a woman who had emailed Harriet saying she had to be on *A Shot at Love*. She didn't elaborate much, but it had been a blessing to Harriet since the one she had lined up for this week had to cancel at the last moment for a family emergency. Whoever wanted to be interviewed had saved Harriet from missing a weekly episode.

Harriet filled her thirty-ounce Yetti mug with enough tea to power her through the next couple of hours. Settling into her desk chair, Harriet opened Audacity on her laptop and then plugged in her microphone, tilting it upward.

She tapped it with a finger and then said, "Testing. One, two, three. Testing."

She hit play and heard her words.

After taking a sip of tea, she cleared her throat. "Now or never."

She entered the person's details. There was the distinct Skype ring. Another. After the fourth, the screen was filled with light. Harriet could see her own image in the upper right-hand corner, but not the person on the other line.

"Hello? Can you hear me?"

"Yes, I can."

Harriet shook her head as if she were hearing things.

Josie's image appeared. "Hi, Harry."

"Josie... I-I... wasn't expecting you."

"That was the point."

Harriet's stomach roiled. Josie had a love story that had to be shared. How would Harriet get through this without breaking down?

"O-okay," Harriet stuttered.

"Are you all right?" Josie asked. "We have a weak connection, and the image froze momentarily."

"Fine. I'm fine." She spoke quickly. "Do you need to talk some before we start recording, or are you ready to dive in?"

"I'm ready." Josie didn't seem all that nervous, unlike most of Harriet's interviewees.

"Great." Harriet wanted to disappear. What happened to the speechwriter who preferred putting words into someone else's mouth? "Let's begin."

"Let's." Josie sounded so happy and relaxed.

This was going to be worse than hellish. What was the word for it? Diabolical? Infernal? Vicious?

"Okay. We're recording." Harriet did her intro to the best of her ability, which wasn't great. She could barely get out the word episode and then butchered the podcast title. But she pressed on, not wanting to stop for a redo. She just wanted the experience done with.

After introducing Josie, Harriet said, "Before diving into the juicy bits..." Bile rose in Harriet's throat as she said one of her typical lines. "Why don't you tell the listeners a bit about yourself?"

Josie obliged, seeming more and more comfortable the longer she spoke.

Harriet mangled her stress ball out of sight of the camera.

When Josie started to talk about the latest election, she

became even more animated. "I started getting an idea of what I had to do the closer the election got."

"What you had to do?" Harriet repeated.

"I think I knew all along, but it wasn't until I saw this video that everything became clear. Well, also after I solved all the puzzles and then listened to this podcast, actually."

"My podcast?" Harriet placed a hand on her chest.

"Yes. As soon as I heard your voice, I knew what I had to do."

"Which was?"

"Well, I had my mum email you and set up an interview."

"Your mum?" Harriet squeezed the ball until it was nearly flat.

"Yes. Then I had her cancel at the last minute."

"Why?" Nothing was making sense.

"So when I emailed, you'd be desperate for an interview and not ask too many questions." Josie's smile was wide.

"But… why put me through this? It's… mean."

Josie's smile fell. "Oh, Harry. Don't you see?"

"That you've fallen in love and want to rub my nose in it?"

"You're only half right." Josie put a hand up. "Just listen."

Harriet stared into the shining light on her laptop.

"I am in love. So very much in love. With you."

Harriet continued staring at the white light.

"Harry? Did you hear me?"

"Say it again."

Josie smiled. "I love you, Harriet Powell."

"Where are you?"

"At the pub."

"What pub?" Harriet barked, looking at the image

behind Josie, but she only saw windows. She counted. Nine panes.

As Harriet was putting the pieces together, Josie answered, "The Golden Fleece. Where we met."

Harriet jumped to her feet.

CHAPTER FORTY-THREE

"Harry? Harry, are you there?"

Josie looked at her mum and then Clive.

"Where is she?" her mum asked.

"Gone."

Her mum walked behind Josie to look for herself. "Where'd she go?"

"Maybe she fainted. Should I go check on her?" Clive also looked at the screen.

"Maybe she doesn't feel the same," Josie said.

Clive shook his head. "She loves you, or I'm a monkey's uncle. Isn't that what you Americans say?"

Josie stared at Clive, unable to utter a word. She raked her hands through her hair, staring at the pub's ceiling, her eyes brimming with tears. Josie hadn't considered Harry would react that way. To just bolt. Harry wasn't the bolting type. The woman had to think everything through. Action wasn't a word Josie ever associated with Harry.

Until now.

"Just when I was starting to warm up to her." Her mum blew out a helpless breath. "Would you like some tea?"

The pub's door burst open.

Harry stood there, struggling to breathe.

Josie rose and rushed to her. "Are you okay?"

"Ran… here." Harry bent over, trying to catch her breath.

Josie laughed. "I thought you were the type to walk and smell the flowers."

Harry straightened. "Maybe I never had something to run to before now."

Josie tossed her arms around Harry's neck and kissed the out-of-breath woman. On her forehead. Her cheeks. She smothered every inch of Harry's face with tender pecks.

Harry finally captured Josie's mouth and kissed her deeply.

Clive hooted.

Her mum clapped.

Winston barked.

The cats left the room with their tails upright, making it clear they had zero interest in human happiness.

Everything was perfect.

* * *

"HAVE YOU RECOVERED?" Josie asked.

Harry held Josie in her arms. "From what?"

Josie bopped Harry on the head. "You can be terrible when you want to be."

"Says the woman who left me and then had her mum help set me up with a fake interview."

"I was trying to be romantic."

Harry stared into Josie's eyes. "You should leave the romance to me."

Josie laughed.

Harry climbed on top of Josie.

They hadn't left Harry's bed in hours.

"What exactly were you referring to? Have I recovered from all the sex? From running to you? From thinking you'd fallen in love with someone else?"

Taken aback, Josie asked, "How could you think I'd fallen for someone else?"

"It was the only thing that made sense to me in the moment."

Josie's eyes misted. "Oh, Harry, I could never love anyone like I adore you. Wait. Do you actually think I'd pull a trick like that to rub your face in it?"

Harry kissed Josie.

"Nice recovery." Josie laughed.

"I'm learning to act on my feet or—" Harry eyed their naked status. "Or whatever."

"Yes. Clearly."

Harry kissed Josie again.

"I love having you on top of me." Josie ran her hand up and down Harry's back.

"It's becoming my favorite place in the world."

"Does that mean we can't shag in the woods ever again?"

Harry smiled. "We'll see, but I am glad that wasn't our final time together, although you made me wait months for this."

"You're the one who told me to take the job," Josie corrected her.

"No. I told you to do what you wanted to do. You took the job."

"Because I thought you didn't want me to stay."

"Why would you ever think that?"

"You offered to drive me to the airport."

Harry sighed. "You were the one who complained about

working in the pub. I really thought you wanted to be a speechwriter again, and I refused to be the person to hold you back."

"I think part of me wanted to find out if I was done with politics for good. It didn't take me that long to realize how much I hated it. And I missed everything here. You. Mum. Clive. Even pulling pints for silent William."

"He's not so silent now. He and Agnes sit for hours in the pub, talking."

Josie shook her head. "It's funny. William's now a chatterbox, and it took us months to figure things out. For two people who love words, we fucking suck at communication."

Harry glanced down at their midsections. "We're kinda good at nonverbal communication."

"Are we? It's been so long since we communicated that way."

"Is that right? We should correct that as soon as possible." Harry leaned down to kiss Josie. "Do we ever have to leave this bed?"

"Never."

EPILOGUE

HARRIET STOOD TO THE SIDE AS JOSIE frantically waved her arms and spoke at rapid-fire speed, directing a team of workers in the pub. The crew nodded, possibly afraid to say a word to Josie, who was six months pregnant and even more determined than ever. Being a bossy but gorgeous American was probably in Josie's favor. Who didn't love an American accent?

Eugenie met Harriet's eye with a look that said, "Can't you control your wife?" before Eugenie sought refuge in the pub's kitchen, her favorite hiding place.

The simple answer was no. And why would Harriet want to. She trusted Josie and her vision.

At first when Josie proposed the idea of Harriet recording her weekly episode at The Golden Fleece, Harriet responded by laughing. But Josie had come prepared with a presentation. Photos of radio programs that broadcasted from public spaces, like a coffee shop in Boston. How some podcasts were recorded among the so-called masses, like *Fortunately... with Fi and Jane.*

Josie had argued a pub wouldn't be that different.

It was Josie's point that they'd met at the pub, via the bridge, which didn't allow for Harriet's laptop and microphone, that had sealed the deal for Harriet right when the words had left Josie's mouth. Where else would Harriet record a podcast about love beating the odds? She and Josie were as much a part of the story as all of Harriet's guests over the past couple of years.

Besides, if Harriet was honest with herself, she'd practically do anything her wife asked of her. The usually no-nonsense Harriet was that much in love with Josie, even more so since they'd married the previous year.

"How do you put up with her?" Clive asked, his massive hand gripping his son's tiny hand.

"Love." Harriet hunched down. "How are you, Oliver?"

"Hungee." His wide green eyes implored Harriet to fix the problem right then and there.

Harriet rubbed the top of his ginger head. "I'm hungry as well. Let's get some lunch." She waved for Josie to come over. "Oliver is insisting on lunch. You're joining us."

"You and Oliver are very bossy." Josie grinned.

"Yes, we're the bossy ones," Harriet said in her dry way that made Josie smile more broadly.

The four of them trooped into the pub's kitchen, where Eugenie was already in the process of prepping lunch. "Is Camilla joining us?" she asked Clive.

"Not today. The missus had to head to London for a meeting." Clive placed Oliver on his lap at the table in the corner, where the family ate an early meal together most days before the pub became flooded with the lunch crowd.

Josie took a seat, one hand on her belly. She took Harriet's hand and placed it on the baby bump. "She's kicking."

"She's taking after her American mother for sure." Harriet smiled at Josie.

"Will she be bossier, then?" Clive asked with honesty.

"I hope so. Only seems fair." Eugenie set the large ploughman's platter in the center of the table for everyone to fix whatever they wanted and then grabbed Josie's meal.

"I'm getting the feeling I'm not appreciated." Josie tucked into the chicken and spinach salad.

"Not true. I'd be lost without you," Harriet said, boosting Josie's hand to her lips.

"I can vouch for that. She was when you ran off to America." Clive handed Oliver a slice of cheese.

"What about me?" Eugenie compiled ham and Stilton onto a chunk of crusty bread. "You left days before Christmas."

"You're never going to forget that." Josie speared a piece of chicken.

"Oh, no. It's too good to pass up." Eugenie wore a conniving smile. "I can't wait to teach your little one all the ways guilt works on you. It's the best revenge of any mum."

"Careful. Or I'll dock your pay." Josie pointed her fork at Eugenie.

"You're the manager. I own the place," Eugenie countered.

"Are you sure about that? I'm in charge of all the accounts and paperwork. How do you know I haven't done anything nefarious and taken your name off things?"

"Because you take after your father: honorable to the core." Eugenie spoke like a woman who knew she was correct.

"Whatever." Josie ground her teeth.

"Don't worry. I know you can be dirty in some situations," Harriet whispered into Josie's ear, much to Josie's delight if the sparkle in those emerald eyes was any indication.

"Winnn." Oliver jabbed his chubby fingers at the bull-dog, who was giving his best begging face.

Eugenie slipped Winston some ham.

"You're getting soft in your old age," Josie said.

"I'm just happy." Eugenie looked around the table.

Harriet squeezed Josie's thigh.

Josie stared into Harriet's eyes.

Alfred, the roly-poly ginger cat, chased his scrawny brother, but gave up after a few seconds.

"It's always chaos here," Clive remarked, not seeming put out by everything.

"That's what happens when you run a thriving pub and podcast with family." Josie motioned to the food. "Speaking of. Eat up and get back to work. Time's wasting."

"You know I went into business with Clive so I could whack him without worrying about being sued. Now, you're bossing me around." Eugenie crossed her arms playfully.

"You can keep whacking Clive if it makes you more productive."

Clive ducked. "Watch out for my boy."

"I'd never hit an innocent child," Eugenie protested.

"Is this how families operate in America?" Harriet asked, her mouth slightly agape.

"It's how ours does, and I wouldn't trade any of it for anything." Josie kissed Harriet on the cheek.

The front of the pub got louder.

The pub is officially open for lunch." Josie rose. "Let's get to it, folks. Back to work."

"I prefer it when you say *I love you*."

"That is how I say *I love you*," Josie joked. She leaned in and whispered, "I'll show you how much later tonight and every night."

"Then let's get to work so I can get my reward." Harriet popped up off the bench.

Josie laughed.

AUTHOR'S NOTE

Thank you for reading *A Shot at Love*. If you enjoyed the novel, please consider leaving a review on Goodreads or Amazon. No matter how long or short, I would very much appreciate your feedback. You can follow me, T. B. Markinson, on Twitter at @IHeartLesfic or email me at tbm@tb-markinson.com. I would love to know your thoughts.

ABOUT THE AUTHOR

TB Markinson is an American who's recently returned to the US after a seven-year stint in the UK and Ireland. When she isn't writing, she's traveling the world, watching sports on the telly, visiting pubs in New England, or reading. Not necessarily in that order.

Her novels have hit Amazon bestseller lists for lesbian fiction and lesbian romance.

Feel free to visit TB's website (lesbianromancesbytbm.com) to say hello. On the *Lesbians Who Write* weekly podcast, she and Clare Lydon dish about the good, the bad, and the ugly of writing. TB also runs I Heart Lesfic, a place for authors and fans of lesfic to come together to celebrate and chat about lesbian fiction.

Want to learn more about TB. Hop over to her *About* page on her website for the juicy bits. Okay, it won't be all that titillating, but you'll find out more.

Made in United States
Troutdale, OR
08/06/2023